Destiny's End
The Last of the Cross

WRITTEN BY

Kol Sterlin Meckley

Destiny's End
The Last of the Cross

ILLUSTRATED BY

Kol Sterlin Meckley

&

Natasha M. Meckley

To my patient and loving parents.

For my wonderful wife, and our life together.

By my faith, and the blessings God has given.

To focus,

To follow one course until successful...

Acknowledgments:

No story comes to pass without a price. It has taken the events of a lifetime to reflect into the manifestation that is, but this tale is only the beginning. I cannot express the amount of gratitude necessary to accommodate for the love, patience, and guidance I have received from those closest to me. There are the nameless ones whom I will not mention, but you know who you are. If you were a part of my life then you have undoubtedly helped to inspire. To name a few,

Margaret Meckley, for giving me this life against all odds, and for persevering through unworldly hardship to make everything that I have done possible.

John Meckley, who made me his son, and made the best man he could with what he was given to work with.

Natasha, for your love, patience, and for your beautiful works of art that have helped breathe life into my story.

Tony Nuttall, for being my best friend all these years, and for all your help making this possible.

Heather Hommowun, for working out the kinks and helping to fine tune this story into what it is.

To Danube and Karie, I wish you the greatest of happiness and love in your life.

To Albright, I pray that you find yourself again my brother, and that God guides you to be the man you were meant to be.

Table of Contents

Prologue:

The Disgrace of the Cross

I

The sweet perfume of spring blossoms filled the air amidst the forests of Trengar as the men of the Cross led the soldiers of Lindell to war. Not one of them agreed with the war, but despite their true feelings they were forced to follow the decree of their superior lords. The men found it strange that politics had turned to hostilities and betrayal so quickly given the lands long history of peace. For centuries the regions have remained, but their borders have changed through minor skirmishes, trade, and commercial establishment. But never in all of recollected time had two regions of Selador waged war upon one another in the scale in which these men now marched.

Certainly the land had its share of greedy land barons, bandits, revolutionaries, and otherwise unseemly groups who existed on a plane of skewed morals, and certainly the people of each region had forged means of defending themselves against such. Means that could in turn be used for war, but no one had ever dared defy the kingdom of Jerum in such a manner nor that which was law set in stone by the ancients passed down from the creator himself.

The men of the Cross were not meant to be the pawns played at the hands of bureaucrats and council clergy for war and tyranny, no, these men were cut from a much greater stalk. Descended from the bloodline of the ancients themselves the Cross became the knights of Lindell, its sovereign protectors. Trained from the age of seven the young men and women of Cross blood grew to become the only true guardians of the Great Sword of Lindell, a mysterious and powerful weapon that had been safeguarded since the time of the immortal. This legendary weapon was one of seven.

In the time of the birth of man, the last immortal forged seven weapons from the power of the heavens, and divided the land of Selador into seven regions. The kingdom of Jerum resides to the north, guardians of the Bow, and the throne to the kings of Selador. To the west of Jerum lay the mountains of Zwentor, guardians of the Axe, masters and lore keepers of the earth magicks. And to the south of Jerum are the wastes of Gell.

Gell had once been the heart of Selador; its massive volcanic mountains had been the birthplace of the land. Where there were no volcanoes, no unbearable sulfur and ash, there were deadly swamps and barren wastes. It was as though the world had been wounded in the creation of Selador, wounded by the very immortal who created it, and out of that wound had poured the very blood of the land, the birth of a world. That wound however, had never truly healed and became the wastes of Gell. They remain as guardians of the Katana, and protectors of vast archives of ancient lore.

To the west of the wastes of Gell, ten leagues across the ocean of Belle, is the Island of Laotia. Half of this island is covered in lush tropical life with trees of fruit that are always plentiful. Its inhabitants are an honorable race of islanders bound by their code and lore, devoted solely to the preservation of guardianship over the Spear. The other half of the island, however, is a lost and uninhabitable desert. Its dunes forbidden, no one dared to linger into its unwelcoming sands, and henceforth it became the origin of many outlandish tales of the unknown.

To the southeast of the wastes of Gell, across the river Theed are the Plains of Reum, a region of undaunted beauty. Rolling plains, and almost mystical fields, it was a place of utter serenity. Once, a place of valiant warriors driven by honor and resolve, but over time the Lords of Reum have grown corrupt, and moved to ensnare their people in a grip that not even the kingdom of Jerum has been able to hold any jurisdiction over. The plains have been slowly choked of their beauty with the tightening grip of this corruption. Yet despite their dark hearts, they retain their responsibility as guardians of the legendary Scythe.

West of Reum reside the forests of Trengar, the richest, densest forests in all of Selador. Every tree imaginable makes up these lush woods. There the people live high amongst the trees, growing and building their lives within the protection of the dense wood. This is the home to the protectors of the legendary Staff.

This is where Lindell's high Lords have decided to invade. To drive the forest dwellers from the land surrounding the out-skirting region, and to claim it as their own by force. To harvest its resources and consume it into the ever growing metropolis that is the massed collection of cities that make up the region of Lindell. The men of the Cross know that it is selfish greed that drives their lords, but they are helpless to deny them their plunder without causing a civil uprising within their home. However it is not for that reason alone, nor is it simply for their honor which binds them. The men of the Cross have gone to war to protect those of which their hearts love most.

2

One week prior, this most solemn of nights, the men of the Cross had taken to meeting as they always do thrice per season. Gathered together amidst their keep, within the stonewall sanctum of the Cross, they held their palaver. Whilst they discussed what action to take against the rumors of war, their absence from home proved to be their undoing. For upon their return home that night they found their families taken. Only a scroll remained; it decreed that no harm would come to the families if only they retained their allegiance to the council and followed orders with no public outcry or attempt at any civil unrest. Any attempt to try and discover the location of their whereabouts or to free any of their loved ones by any one man would result in the death of all captives.

They had no trails to follow, no clues as to who was really behind this treachery, and no evidence to accuse those of the council they did suspect. Their hands were tied, and not one dared to risk the lives of the entire clan, and so they awaited further instruction. The wait was short lived, for upon the dawning day, the council summoned a massed attendance. War was declared upon Trengar and the men of the Cross were given their orders to march.

Now, the men of the Cross gather again after taking rest upon a long day of pillaging the outer laying villages and towns that resided amidst the sage. Though they had all slept, none had rested easy. They took leave from the rest of the forces to palaver amidst the privacy of the moonlit woods. As they trekked through darkness they discussed that which they all had sensed amidst their slumber. For they had shared the waking dream on that most peculiar of evenings, and been given a brief but brilliant glimmer of the horrors to come. They spoke full and true of each of their experiences, but before any conclusions could be drawn as to the nature of this dream they found themselves at the foot of an ancient temple.

It was here, amidst the sage, in this humblest clearing of pillars and ruins that the men of the Cross were visited by a specter of fate itself, a diligent servant of darkness whose very presence meant that the time of this world was short. He was dressed all in black, his large brimmed hat hiding the stone like features of his face as he greeted them. "Hail ye men of the Cross! Come one, come all, for I have been expecting you!"

Lord Samuel Cross, the eldest of the Cross line, was the first to speak as they approached the mysterious stranger. "What is it that you want with us silver-tongue?" He asked the dark salesman. "Only a moment of your time, that is all. For I believe I know the real reason that you are here. I know that it is not for Lindell that you fight or for the further development of commercial opportunities…it is because someone has taken something from you?"

The men of the Cross had encircled around the man in black and now looked to him with an alarming eagerness upon the mention of their families. This could be the lead they were looking for, this could be the chance to save their families and stop this senseless war.

"Go on…" Samuel spoke again.

"I know that a deep seeded anger quells within you all like a storm ready to be unleashed. You want them back…you not only want them back, you want those responsible to pay for what they have done…be it death or the cut of your commission. The *Cross* - as you call it - bore upon their faces

---

like a scar for all to see their treachery and sin no doubt?" The man paused to let this hook sink deep in their hearts.

He was right, the men did yearn to pay back those who had wronged them, and many did crave to carve the *Cross* upon the faces of the true enemy. It was this symbol, this scarlet letter that had been used since the time of their ancestors to punish the guilty. It meant disgrace and dishonor rather than merely death for those that had committed crimes against the people and the land. Those that a Cross descendant decided were better to live the remainder of their life in shame rather than have the peace that death brings were to wear this symbol upon their face, and it had thus become their namesake.

"You speak true, but it is not simply justice we seek, or our family's safe return...we wish to end this blasphemous war before any more innocent blood can be shed." Samuel spoke direct. He hoped for their sake this man was an angel in disguise, come to deliver them and to set things right, but a fear crept close next to the anger in his belly.

"This I can do...for a price." The man said as he removed a small item from his long black coat and placed it gingerly upon the smooth granite surface of the alter before him.

"What are the terms?" Samuel spoke for everyone present.

"Like I said, all I want is a moment of your time...three days to be exact. Three days under my power and I will end this war, you will see those responsible punished, and your loved ones will be returned to live out the remainder of your lives with them in peace."

"What is it you would have us do during that time?" Another man of the Cross spoke up eager to be once more in the arms of his young wife.

"That is for me to know and you to find out. As I said, three days

—

under my power is what I ask in return for my three favors, and it is a fair enough bargain for any mortal. Take it or leave it, it is for you to decide." He spoke with the carelessness of any who had sold a good line before. After several minutes of discussion, Samuel and the other men of Cross turned and held the gaze of the dealmaker. Samuel's mind drifted to thoughts of his pregnant wife, and the child within her womb, *'Anything for them...even my soul.'*

Samuel took a single step forward; eyes locked with the specter, and spoke for everyone present, "We will take your deal sorcerer, but know this...if you betray us...then you shall be cursed, and your life will be spilled by that of our blood."

With that his shadowed face grimaced slightly only to quickly form a sinister smile. "Very well then..." The sorcerer said as he unfolded the black silk cloth of the item before him. The air grew cold as the wind in the treetops of the forest began to rustle wildly against the millions of leaves like the waves of the ocean. Beneath its silken shroud, now exposed to the moonlight lay a crystal skull "...behold, men of the Cross...gaze upon a power even greater than your own." As he spoke, the skull began to emanate a faint red hue of light that grew stronger with each word.

The men of the Cross gazed into the eyes of the crystal skull as it glowed with crimson light. The sorcerer whispered inaudibly to the enchanted relic in tongues not dripped from lips in centuries. The temple ruins were bathed in the light of the skull, and cast strange shadows upon the men before it. Even if they had wanted to look away they could not, for they were transfixed by its power. In a flash, red lightening shot forth from the eyes of the skull and into the men of the Cross. Their screams tore through the scene, and the maniacal laughter from the specter in black

---

echoed coldly into the night air of the sage.

3

With the twilight of the following day, the forces of Trengar had finally caught up with the army of Lindell. The battle had already begun with no sign of the Cross, and it would seem without the guiding orders of their leaders they were going to lose. The warriors of the forest assaulted them with a vengeance. They paid back the pillaging and pain these men had caused, and punished them wave after wave. They fought valiantly in protection of their home, but then the men of the Cross appeared. Emerging from the tree line of the battlefield like specters of the spirit world they stood, and all as one cried out in a wail of madness.

The massacre of the Cross lasted three days. On the third day, the white horses of the riders of Jerum broke through the forests of Trengar and ended the Terreign war. Those of the Cross bloodline and the soldiers of Lindell were arrested in the name of the High king. The riders of Jerum were appalled to see the atrocities done to the soldiers of Trengar, every one of them, wounded, dead, and dying, bore the symbol of the *Cross* upon their face. The riders took the Cross and any other soldiers into custody and took them to Jerum where they would face trial.

The accounts of the war were told mostly by the men led by the men of the Cross and those surviving soldiers of Trengar. They told of the atrocities they had seen committed, the brutal nature in which they fought, the frenzied, uncontrollable bloodlust that seemed unquenchable. The men of the Cross, however, held barely any recollection of the events that had transpired and felt as though they had been possessed. Not one of them was able to speak of their encounter within the ancient ruins, and thus they were unable to explain their actions.

Jerum quickly implemented an internal investigation into the council of Lindell, and the real criminals were brought to swift justice. The treasonous actions against the Cross families were found out, and those responsible were executed by the hand of the king himself with the legendary bow of Jerum. The remaining council members of Lindell were impeached from their positions, along with various particular punishments enacted upon those more involved of the members. A new council was formed and new Lords and Ladies were elected by the people under supervision of the council of Jerum. Trengar was returned the lands that were seized, a treaty was signed, and compensation measured and paid.

As for the Cross, the king was conflicted in his decision. The atrocities they committed were inexcusable, the fury they carried on in their blood could not be accepted, but their presence was necessary. They were the only ones capable of ever wielding the legendary great sword of Lindell. If that need arose, the presence of a Cross would be dire. The king knew that he could never inflict any more punishment on the Cross that could be greater than the shame and disgrace they now felt, but something had to be done. Something was *expected* to be done.

The decision was made that the Cross and all their family would be exiled from the known lands of Selador, sent away on massive ships across the ocean to an unknown land, though it remains *unknown* that there is such an uncharted landmass residing within the world. All but one would go. One son of the Cross, the first born after the conclusion of the Terreign war, would remain in the land of Selador.

Prior to their departure, the king of Jerum stood before them upon the coast. In the Audience of representatives of all the regions of Selador, holding the son of Lord Samuel Cross in his arms, the king led the Cross in an oath. It was an oath that the Cross would never use their symbol of hatred again, to never again carve the *Cross*. As they departed the king placed the child in the hands of the lords of Lindell to be raised with the law of the land and the lore of the legends, and to be trained as the men of the Cross had been trained for centuries.

It has been two and a half decades since this time, and Michael Cross had long since been forced to recite his own oath when he had come of age. It was this oath that he had shattered in his moment of furious passion. It was this oath he had broken as he carved his own hatred into the face of his now mortal enemy Lord Raymark Lafey.

Part I:

The Cross of Hate

I

A thousand heartbeats from the nearest human soul sat a young but weary man solemnly collecting his thoughts on the recent events of his life. Though he had not yet reached his twenty-fifth year, his expression held the weight of time. His furrowed brow set aloft clear grey eyes which stared calmly and unfocused as though in a trance. Collected, steady in mind, but far away from the perceptions of the body.

Against an old tree, Michael Cross sat on the overhang of a hill. A brook was slowly trickling past with a shimmering cascade of light and reflection cast by the warm afternoon sun. The gates to Lindell were to his back, several miles or so down an old road that wound past outcroppings of trees and fields. A road not often used by the people of the cities. Michael found this place peaceful. It was far from the confines and noise of the metropolis, and free from the scorn of those who knew of his dishonor, of his alleged fall from grace.

Michael's eyes suddenly focused with a dull intensity, but not on any image directly before him. Not the bubbling brook or the leaves drifting from the treetops slowly making their descent to the forest floor. Not any image or perception of this world, but of his mind. His thoughts rapidly drew to a fine line of images that flashed the events of his memory. In a single night his whole life had changed.

Darkness had swept the great cities with the storm that began to call its rage in the sky overhead. He had followed his wife, stalking her like a shadow amidst the dark shapes and silhouettes of the alleyways and amongst crowds of faces lingering about in the night air. Everyone hastened to finish their tasks before finding shelter against the storm. Yet it was not shelter that his wife sought. No, he knew that much, she sought something far more precarious. It was something primal, that she wanted, and had delved upon on more than one occasion.

He calmly lingered just beyond, watching...waiting. Each step took him closer and closer to the sickeningly painful satisfaction of his suspicions. Until he had at last found her at the sight of her intended destination. It was the home of the esteemed Lord Raymark, a man who stood in line to be the next High Lord of Lindell.

Standing in the alley across the muddied street, sheltered from the heavy rain by the overhang of a building's guttering, he waited in silence. He watched as his wife entered the lavish estate of Lord Raymark under the shroud of darkness. She had worn a thick hooded cloak, but as he watched her enter into the house locks of her golden hair fell innocently from her shroud and draped across her form. It was those same golden locks that had fueled his initial attraction to this woman he had taken as his wife. Wonderful memories slithered into his thoughts as he watched her from his shadowed place from across the street. The memories, however, were rolled in the disdaining poison of the present circumstance and spoiled quickly.

It was raining hard for this late in summer, but Michael didn't care about the pelting rain. He waited cautiously for a brief moment that felt like a lifetime before crossing the street.

Speed was the last thing on his mind. It was not the prevention of the act that was his objective, only the final confirmation. A trembling sickness

———

was welling up within him, and it took all of his strength not to cry out against the storm overhead. He stood silently before the front door of the home of his once friend and countryman, and looked up. The house loomed over him like a monolithic tomb that was mocking him, daring him to press on. To go farther and to see what needed to be seen. He had entered the threshold a thousand times with gratitude and hospitality, but only shame and ruin grasped Michael's heart in these moments. His eyes held an eager resolve as he gazed up at this monarch of structures. He held the same fear in his heart that he had for several nights such as this, always lacking the courage to continue the plight of following his wife into the house itself, falling short at this door. Unable to find it within him to confront his darkest fear, he would simply stand in this place until his knees grew weak. He would crumble in spirit, and would at last stagger to the nearest tavern to drink himself away broken and defeated. "Why couldn't I face it before?" Michael whispered to himself.

It was time for Michael to begin opening the doors in his life, and it would prove that this door would be the first, the beginning, the seal of the destiny laid out for him. Michael Cross entered the house of Lord Raymark with determination as the thunder rolled heavily in the clouds overhead. His movements were so brisk, that even the brushing of his wet clothing against his body went unheard over the power of the storm.

Michael made his way up the winding staircase leading to the sleeping quarters. The staircase was a wide tower decorated with intricate stained glass windows flashing their tales with each burst of lightening. It seemed the storm was picking up in its fury. Michael could hear the scraping of branches against windows, and the unfastened shutters relentlessly tapping with each gust of wind. He cautiously followed the

---

stairs, which were covered in a fine red carpet. The carpet that wound up with the stairs branched off and led down the hallway of the second floor. Michael moved quietly down the corridor, ignoring the many rooms to his left and right. His eyes were drawn to a single door at the very end of the hall. The edges of this door illuminated with the flicker of candlelight from within its chamber.

He approached the door slowly. Emotion welled up within him, threatening to wrench his soul in two. His heart ached with every step as he drew closer, and began to find the truth in his doubt. From the massive wooden door looming several meters in front of him escaped the muffled pleasing cries of his wife.

He stood poised at the outside of the chamber door listening to the betrayal being sung out to him. His eyes could no longer bear to hold back the emotion he had allowed to build within. Michael Cross wept. His sorrow ran deep within his flesh as he shuddered with the raw pain, and his body began to weaken. His knees buckled and his legs, with one final cramping pain gave out beneath him. He let himself crumble to the red carpet upon the stone floor. He tried to find some security in the solidity of the rock itself. His world seemed to be falling to pieces around him, and it was all he could do to keep himself from making a sound.

'Is this my fault? Did I push her away?' he thought, but knew that he had done everything to try and keep her close to him.

'Would things have been different if we hadn't lost the baby?' his thoughts pried deeper, fueling the raging turmoil within him. The stones upon the floor in which he clung to were the only thing that seemed real. His life, his love, his honor were all blowing away from his mind like the sands of the desert. But even still the stone floor held.

Its cold solidity was real; its existence was unshaken by the emotional afflictions and conflicts of life or the world. It proved the truth of the matter at hand; it proved to Michael he wasn't dreaming, and from this foundation Michael drew his strength.

He rose, struggling to regain his bearings as he wiped the tears from his cloudy grey eyes. The world was distorted, shrouded by raw emotion and fatigue. It was his third night without any real sleep. He'd spent each night drowning himself with his suspicions and pain, until he had at last found the resolve to do what he felt was necessary. As he reached for the brass knob upon the door he heard his wife cry out again in ecstasy, and the sound made his weakness return sharply. Yet he refused to lose his gall again. Taking the brass knob in hand he silently tested it, and found it to be locked.

Michael leaned against the doorframe in a brief moment of silent frustration; his cheeks were streaked with tears, his hair ragged, and his face unshaven. He looked pale, his head hung low, his face contorted with utter grief, his eyes dilated with defeat, and yet something lurked deeply in those incandescent pupils; something that grew with every second. It was something he had never felt before.

It seemed to flow in unison with the beating of his heart, and pounding deeply in his ears, as it coursed through his veins. As though he were ablaze within himself, a strange power consumed him. Michael had never had any affinity in the arts of magick, and he wondered if perchance this was what such mystical influences felt like. But before he could actively pursue these thoughts, a far more assertive process of thinking had already consumed the conscious mind of Michael Cross. At the peak of his emotional standing, Michael turned and kicked open the door in one swift

—

solid movement.

The luxurious room was lit by four torches, and garnished with any imaginable nature of lordly extravagance. Michael's wife, Helin, lay naked on the massive ornate bed her lavish breasts still swaying from the arduous thrusts of Raymark Lafey. She quickly struggled to cover herself in the silky throws and covers. *'Nothing I haven't seen before…'* Cross thought derisively. Shame and guilt burned in her eyes with the horror of her exposed sin.

Michael's gaze, however, quickly drew itself upon Lord Raymark, who was stumbling in his efforts to dawn his breeches. As he fumbled to button his trousers, he stammered an apology, excuse, or whatever one would say in such a position as he. Michael however, heard nothing, not even the screaming of his wife, as he grabbed the half naked lord by the throat and cast him to the rug covered stone floor.

For a moment, Michael's perception of the world fell away and he was deaf to all but his mind's vacuous space. Just as sudden, he began to hear a faint noise somewhere within him as it grew slowly in intensity. He was overcome with the deep pounding resonating within his mind. His whole body, even his heartbeat seemed to be pounding in unison with the rhythm of the beating. This rhythm, this feeling within him, was crying out as if it commanded action,-some deed or act to relieve the pressure that was building in his blood. Consciously he knew not what action to take, but his body, what flowed through his heart, acted regardless.

As the redheaded Lord Raymark stood pleading like a dog before him, Michael Cross unsheathed his dagger. In two swift strokes, both burning with the heat of his cursing rage, he broke the oath of the Cross, and damned Lord Raymark to bear the *Cross* upon his face in shame

---

forever. Yet before the blood could spray from the open wounds upon the lord's face, Raymark's guards were already in the room, called by Helin's screams. Michael left with no incident. He simply dropped his blade, and walked silently from the room.

2

The memories echoed in Michael's thoughts like a nightmare come to pass. *'Who am I?'* Cross thought to himself, as he brushed aside the strands of dark brown hair that blew rebelliously into his face. *'The last of the Cross family…the only one left.'* He knew the answer before he even processed the thought. He knew the history of the Cross legacy, and felt contempt for being bestowed such responsibility with no consent on his part. Regardless, after the painful recollection, he couldn't keep his mind from the fact that he had fulfilled his bloodline's destiny and changed his life forever on that fateful night. He began to recall the legacy of his forefathers.

As Michael began to remember the history of his family, he stood, making his way closer to the brook which flowed beneath him. He reached down and removed a stone from beside the creek, wedged in the sandy mud on the bank of the stream. He studied it with empathy, rolling it back and forth between his index finger and thumb, watching the mud and sand collecting on his fingertips. His weight shifted as he let his strong shoulders sag with his painful memories. The legacy was his pride, and his undoing.

The Cross had once been the guardians, the heroes of Lindell. They defended honor and punished the guilty. Anyone who defiled justice met the fate of their commission. The cut of Cross, as it was, held a power of punishment without death. A symbol of ones sin forever carved diagonally

—

across the whole of a persons face. It was cut deep, to the bone at times, from one side of the forehead to the opposite cheek, and again in reverse contrary to the first cut. The eyes, however, were never touched. Only the face, mere flesh, was scarred with the curse of their sin. This punishment to those of misdeeds was the call sign, the insignia, the source of the name of Cross. They were the most prestigious and revered family of Lindell, but oh how they had fallen. Now more than ever Michael felt truly at one with his namesake. For with time the stories of the rage of the Cross had grown to that of demonic summoning and evil powers. The once legendary heroes and become the villains despite what had been done to them to place them in that position of war in the first place. Their memory had been tainted with dishonor and he now held a mouthful of that familiar taste.

Michael lobbed the smooth stone he was holding into the creek, it bounced twice across the glassy water, struck a protruding rock, and dropped to the bottom of the creek. The ripples cast by the stone quickly vanished with the current of the stream. Michael watched the vanishing ripples intently, returning from the echoing thoughts of his mind. He loved this place deep amidst the wood. He only wished he could see the forests of Trengar. *'How marvelous they must be,'* he thought. But he was forbidden, as part of his oath, never to enter the Forests of Trengar. For the whole of his life he had lived with such punishment of a sin he never committed. With such restrictions, he was forced to only visit the small patches of forest that bordered between Lindell and the mountains of Zwentor. Nevertheless, he enjoyed his time away from the cities.

The sound of the flowing water brushing against stone seemed to call to him. He undid his black leather boots, and rolled the legs of his loosely fitted trousers up to his knees, and waded into the stream. The water was cool and refreshing, just slightly warmed by the rays of the sun. He waded into the stream until the water touched his knees, roughly four feet from the bank. His hands were at his sides and held parallel with the surface of the water. For the first time, he felt the rippling flow of the energy within the stream.

He remembered the ancient lore, the forgotten magick that he could never yield. Despite rigorous training, and grueling study, Michael could not use even the slightest bit of magick. His teachers had suspected at first that Michael held only a specific magick, but despite all their efforts and all the different types of magick tested, Michael showed no sign of even the slightest evidence of the world's elemental powers. Despite his failure, Michael never stopped trying.

As he stood in the shallow water, he attempted to use several techniques of standard water magick, but it was to no avail. He could clearly feel the energy around him, as well as a strange power within, but no incantation or kata would draw the power out. Frustrated, he stared intently at the flowing water beneath him, the individual ripples, and reflections of the glassy surface. Closing his eyelids slowly, he focused deep within his mind, trying to find himself within. Once he truly felt the inner walls of his mind, he drew from the strange "power" that seemed hidden within, just beneath the surface. He gathered this sensation of power at his center, his aura, and let it flow throughout his body. He then focused this power into his fingertips. He could feel the pulse of his blood beating out the rhythm he had felt that fateful night. Somewhere within the depths of his heart, he found a trickle of that which he had seemingly awakened before. Slowly, steadily, he began to feel the strange power within as if it were beating with his very blood.

Michael drew from it, and the water around his form began to ripple. He tried to keep his focus on the rhythm, letting the power flow through him freely. He had never successfully channeled any elemental energy by will, but this was different. This was no power of lore, but of the very soul within him that cried out for release.

Ever since that fateful day when his honor was lost he had felt the strange pulsing within his heart and his strength had never depleted. He was weak of heart, broken inside, but he somehow felt like he was getting stronger. He felt a connection to something deeper and far greater than that of anything he had never known. He knew not if this power was some form of magick, or something else.

With this new found strength channeling into the water around his body, he began to swirl his hands in a large counter clockwise circle. The water barely rippled from the movement, but it seemed to be growing warmer. The water gradually began to swirl like a miniature whirlpool, gently gaining, just barely taking form.

'This…this is impossible. I can't use an elemental technique, I have no power!' As though the doubt within his mind had summoned the interruption, suddenly a messenger shouted gaily from atop the hill next to the tree Cross had been leaning on previously.

"Pardon my intrusion of your meditations, but are you Lord, uh I mean…" The hesitant pause after the ill-placed former title of Lord stung harshly. "…are you Michael Cross?" The messenger managed to stammer out the last of his words with a humbled admiration and fear.

"Yes, I am he. What message do you bring?"
"Only that you are to immediately report to the high council." The haste in his voice and the mention of the council brought a shudder to Michael's

—

heart. As the expression upon Michael's face seemed to hint at a subtle lingering fear, the messenger continued, "You need not worry my liege. It is not any personal matter that requires your presence. All of the lords have been summoned, for word has arrived from a great distance across the land of Selador from the region of the plains of Reum. Something stirs in the land." Michael felt a sense of relief that it was not about him, but of this message. He returned to the shore, awed by the feeling of power that seemed to be resonating within his fingertips still. They tingled with the numbing prickle of a thousand needles, as though the blood was slowly returning to his hands, but his circulation had not been ceased. In fact, it was as though he was beginning to feel the circulation of something more than his blood for the first time. He dried his feet with the edge of his coat before draping it comfortably over his shoulders. He donned his boots and unrolled the cuffs of his pants. He continued to kneel, ensuring everything was in place, his composure, and items. Facing the messenger, he stood. "What do you know of this ill-word we receive from across the land?"

The gaily dressed man frowned with his long drooping mouth. "I know nothing of that which has transpired. Only that I have never seen such strain upon the faces of those in which I serve."

"I trust your judgment." Michael solemnly said, and climbed the hill to stand before the messenger. As he approached, Michael could see the man clearly now for the first time. He was slightly aged, in his mid forties, with a quiet gaze that always seemed to be looking three inches below their intended observation. His face beheld a silky black handlebar moustache, which he stroked with his fingers religiously.
"Shall we go my liege?" He muttered with one hand still stroking his moustache.

"Yes, I will follow you there."

"But sir, it is not proper for a messenger such as…"

Michael cut him short with a glare. "Do I look like the type of *man*," he said the word with disdain, "…who cares about proper etiquette? I choose to follow you, and I will do so. Besides, I do not know the quickest route from here." He finished with a smirk, but his fierce eyes still held their commanding gaze.

"Understood my liege, I will lead you there." He humbly replied as he swiftly turned toward the path leading back to the gates of the city.

As the messenger turned, Michael let his gaze fall as he thought, *The ground is the only suitable place for my eyes. This man has no reason to lower his gaze simply because of his position before a Lord, or former Lord far that matter. Only one thing should lower the gaze of a man, shame in his dishonor.*

Michael followed him through the forest along the old dirt path. He tried desperately not to think of anything. He longed only for the warmth of the sun and the noise of the forest. He listened silently to the fanatic buzzing, chirping, and screeching of the creatures who inhabited the wood. He could still hear the faint trickle of the stream as it flowed past the stones of the brook. The forest was not very dense, with only a tree every eight or nine yards. The forest floor was practically barren of all grass and underbrush, and was clean except for the random array of leaves that littered the scene. The trail was very difficult to judge, the packed dirt path blended with the strikingly clean forest floor, but Michael's familiarity with its twists and turns, allowed him to find his way effortlessly. They continued on this winding trail downhill for time, until they approached a clearing of open land that stretched the remaining distance to the city walls. Thirteen acres of open ground, kept low for the defense of the walls. The

—

plain always gave the guards enough time to send word of an arrival, or an alarm of an attack. The same plains were often used as fields for crops when famine threatened the people of the cities, though only in grave times were they used for these purposes. Otherwise, they served as the first defense of the region of Lindell. Michael stood for a moment with the messenger at the base of the hill. The messenger turned to Michael and reassured him of the little distance they had left to travel. They marched steadily the six mile distance to the walls of Lindell.

It took them a little under an hour and a half to breach the distance, at which point the walls of Lindell towered over them like mountains. At their three story peaks were the guard posts, which were always manned. A small group of the city's policing guards stood in front of the massive iron gates of the wall. Two massive gates of iron that could be swung open on either side, but at this time they remained sealed. Instead, a small gateway was opened near the bottom of the gate on the right side. At the entrance to this door were two guards who checked those entering and leaving the city. Just inside was a group of inspectors who would intercept foreign travelers for questioning. The city was well guarded, or so it seemed.

They passed through the gates without question; the guards didn't even rise from their lounged positions in their seats. *'Well guarded indeed...'* Michael thought to himself. One only nodded as he dragged off a lengthy pipe, which trickled a spiced blue smoke. The man's face was angular and stern, but it held respect and acknowledgement in his nod. The other man averted his eyes; aware, but refusing any absence from his study of the book he held on his knee. They then moved briskly past the tables and guards within the gates. They were busy inspecting the goods of a small group of traders who appeared to have come from the mountains of Zwentor to the north. Their dark brown and black tunics were drawn closely about their stocky bodies, which appeared to be muscled to the density of stone. A few of them had full beards, while the others sported intricate braids and dark matted dreads. They seemed each to be unique and defined; only their body structure and dark hair were similar. They were grumbling about the search through the goods. They all seemed to find it rather unnerving. They glared at Michael and the messenger as they strolled past, but remained silent.

Michael hated the feelings of being watched. He cursed in his mind the following eyes of the foreign men. He could feel them looking through his soul, burning out the evils within him and exposing them to the world. He wondered if they knew of his crime, of his dishonor.

He knew his thoughts foolish, but he held to them nonetheless. He found that he felt shame in everyone's eyes. Not because they were shameful of him, but because of his inner shame. Their gaze seemed to reflect back in him the feelings he felt within himself. Cross calmly pondered his fate, if such shame were to continue for much longer. His lowly thoughts continued as he walked briskly through the entrance to the cities of Lindell.

3

The sun was high in the sky as its searing rays beamed down upon the cobblestone streets of the cities of Lindell. People moved about their duties briskly, not paying any mind to the passing of Cross. He noted the varying structures of the houses, keeps, inns, and shops. Most were only two or three stories high, but the houses of those who could afford it

---

reached to as high as ten stories. Some were made of stone and mortar, others made of wood. Along the cobblestone streets of the city were wooden sidewalks, fastened in place to lessen the traffic in the street for the passing horses and carts.

Michael followed mechanically behind the messenger. He ignored the stares of those who noticed his presence, and tried to focus only on the rhythmic clicking of his gait. After walking for several blocks, turning at random places, down old streets and new, Michael finally found a grasp on which path the messenger had led him.

As they turned the corner, Michael was stung with the raw familiarity of the place. It had been exactly one week- seven days and seven nights, since the last time he had stood in this spot, looking up at the house before him. Michael stopped for a moment, just looking at the small mansion that overtook the scene. He let the image waver in his mind as though it were a ghost of something past.

The home of Lord Raymark stood as a testament, a tombstone marking his place of dishonor. Cross felt the pain anew, and struggled to avert his gaze to the path ahead, but he could not help the flow of memories which came.

When he had been escorted from the scene, upon that dark and stormy night, taken without incident to one of the city's more *secured* jailhouses, he sat quietly in the cell he was given, contemplating the consequences his own self-destruction would hold. For three days the council discussed the matter. For three days Cross contemplated his suicide, his penitence for dishonor. Yet he waited, and as the grueling discussions proceeded, Michael was brought before the council itself to receive his sentencing.

"We have decided, that you, Lord Michael Cross, have committed a grave act of vengeance, but we cannot judge your current intentions, nor the true gravity of your crime due to the circumstances involved. We have decided that you will be freed from your cell. However, you may not return home, and you will be stricken of your lordly title and duties …… as well as your marital. Your wealth and estate will hereby be liquidated into your wife's possession, who under the circumstance has requested the grounds of your marriage to hereby be annulled. Only one duty we require you to keep at this time. It is the most basic duty of all residents of Lindell itself. You must always protect the Sword of Lindell, as you swore even before you became a lord. With this sole duty, if the need arises you may have the chance to regain your title of Lordship, but from this moment on, you are to be known only as Michael Cross. You may go freely as you wish until we can receive the appropriate instruction from the kingdom of Jerum regarding any further punishment for your crime. You are restricted from disturbing the Lady Helin or Lord Raymark Lafey under any circumstances. Until the time of your sentencing do as you will, but you must remain within the borders of Lindell." With that, the council dismissed the dishonored Michael Cross.

Lost in his despair, Michael strained to remain active. Instead of letting his thoughts consume him, he began to study intently, trying to understand the new feelings within him. He would wake every morning before the city had fully risen to its blustering hustle, and walk to the same late hour shop, pay for a day's provision, and some form of manuscript, book, or scroll in which he found interesting. He would place it all in his pack and walk solemnly to the city walls. From there, he would venture north amidst the borders of the mountains of Zwentor. After exploring the

—

trails and rivers of the area, he would head east. In one days' time he could walk to the river Varian. He would stand triumphantly at the edge of the swift river; stare out over the water at the dark region known as the wastes of Gell and shudder.

Gell was a region feared by many. Its barren plains, swamplands, fiery mountains, and blackened ash-filled sky was not a welcoming region, despite its residents renowned hospitality. The people who live in this place were known to be practitioners of dark magicks, but they were also known for their kindness and aid to travelers. Despite its people, the region was still a dark, barren, and menacing place. In spite of his awareness of the good people of this land, the scene always seemed to spark deep thoughts of pain and a dark suffering within his soul, as if feeling something yet to pass.

The only borders Michael was wary of were those of the Forests of Trengar, to the south. Due to the remaining victims of his forefathers, those that were scarred with the *cross* during the Terreign war, he did not linger near the borders for fear of being recognized. Something deep within Michael made him feel as though at this time, he would be far more welcomed by his forefathers' enemies than his own people, who now shunned him at each passing.

Cross found it more and more difficult to ignore the glares and the comments cast from hate filled eyes and uttered amidst malice-toned whispers. Even now as he stood staring up at the house of Lord Raymark, he could hear the familiar murmuring amidst the people making their way down the cobblestone streets. He ignored their scorn and turned to continue following the messenger. It wasn't long before Michael and the messenger had found their way to the estate in which the council was held.

It was also Michael's current home.

After his suspended trial and release from jail, the Lords had seen to the preparations of a room for the fallen lord. He was allowed to come and go as he pleased. The colossal estate stretched the length of several acres. Its massiveness towered above the other buildings surrounding it. The estate was surrounded by a thirty foot wall on all sides, with the walls of the east and west sides meeting at the house. Facing north, the walls extended several acres before adjoining as a third wall holding the front gate. This created a large and ornate courtyard decorated with all sorts of plants, beautiful fountains, mesmerizing waterfalls, tiny bridges spaning over pools of glowing fish, and elegant statues depicting legends of long ago.

To the back of the house, the south facing side possessed equal amount of space that formed a second courtyard. This one, however, was the serving purposes of the state and region. It held the stables, barracks, armory, and training grounds. This single house, this estate of government, housed over a hundred people; most of whom worked on the grounds. This place was the capital of Lindell.

During the day, the building was open to the public. Trials, appeals, council meetings, schooling, and historical documentation were only a handful of the government duties the estate gave home to. However, only one task was truly significant.

That was the guardianship over the legendary great sword. Protected in this place for over a thousand years, it remained under the safeguard of the cities impenetrability. It was guarded constantly in one of the four, seven story towers that loomed overhead at each corner of the rectangular house. The towers themselves were astonishing, but even they were dwarfed by the immense twelve story dome which consumed the center of the roof on the seventh floor. It was the outside of the mural ceiling that loomed above the massive observation chamber where the council held discussions. The great dome was coated in a polished silver metal that reflected the light of the blazing sun. Upon its peak was a golden pier supporting a large red orb that seemed to be emitting some sort of aura of light unlike any Michael had ever laid eyes on.

"What's that?" Michael asked the messenger as he pointed at the glowing orb.

"It is the reason this meeting has been called, my lord, but I know nothing of its meaning." The messenger said with emotionless exuberance. He looked at him as though Cross really knew what the red orb meant, but that perhaps he was only testing him. After a moment of searching Michael's confused expression, the messenger seemed satisfied with the certainty that Cross really was clueless to this new anomaly requiring the summoning of all the lords. With his curiosity fulfilled, he turned around and continued briskly toward the main gates of the estate.

Despite Michael's knowledge of the land, magicks, history, and other secrets, he knew nothing of this. The lords, ladies, barons, and other officials all received a fairly high level of education throughout their lives. Michael however, was prone to the study of many crafts, few of which he perfected, let alone mastered, but he was fairly able in most aspects of different trades and positions. This orb was not something that Michael, nor would any ordinary lord would have any knowledge of. Only the high lords of the council itself would possess such knowledge.

Michael walked beside the messenger for a moment as they passed through the gates. Michael thanked the man for showing him the route and

---

immediately tried to forget it due to its untimely passing of lord Raymark's house. He gave the man a coin from his purse and they parted.

Michael walked alone, past fountains and beautiful pools without the slightest sign of acknowledgement. His head was low and his hair hung loosely over his face. One arm held the strap of the pack slung over his arm as it drooped lazily across his back over one shoulder. He entered the estate without anyone paying any mind to him. His brisk movements went entirely unnoticed by the fellow lords and officials. They were too busy themselves, anxiously trying to get to the council meeting. Michael simply followed the flow of people, quickly herding along like cattle. Michael found the animalistic qualities in people to be appalling at times, and generally tried to stay away from mass quantities of people. In this instance, however, Michael seemed overwhelmed with an intrigue that could not be resisted.

His curiosity piqued, Michael made his way with the crowd that poured through the hallways and corridors to the stairways and entrances to the observation room. As he followed a crowd of lords and ladies up the stairs, Michael realized just how few government bodies were present in this meeting. It really did consist of only the high lords and the next three lower classes. Even with all the people, they still only filled the first level of seats surronding the huge center ring overlooking the table of council. Michael looked down at the empty ring of seats and pedestals upon the stage. He knew from recent experience that the high lords only entered when all were seated.

As Michael waited patiently in his seat amongst the other lords and ladies, he noticed how truly enormous the room really was. Its dome reached the twelve story mark, while the observation levels climbed to the seventh floor. The dome itself was made of a strange metal; the outside mirrored and reflected most of the sun's rays, and transformed the rest into a colorful dim lighting within. The strange texture of the dome could be changed from the mirrored exterior to a clear one; this changed the lighting and potential view above. The dome transfixed Michael; its inside was currently depicting a mural of the seven regions of Selador, and the seven weapons they hold guardianship over. Something, however, caught his eye. Looming above his head, engraved within the mural, was the scythe of Reum, glowing vividly with the same strange red glow of the orb that hovered upon the pier of the dome. Michael stared at this image intently, quickly he studied the other images upon the ceiling, but only the scythe was emitting the aura of colors.

So entwined with the mysticism of his discovery, Michael didn't notice that the high lords had entered the room and taken their seats. The Chief High Lord addressed the assembly with a booming voice that reverberated throughout the observation room. Everyone bearing witness to this address remained absolutely silent to ensure clarity of the information they were about to hear. It was as though the entire assembly was holding their breath as the High Lord spoke.

"My Lords and Ladies, I apologize for the sudden haste of this calling of assembly, but I fear that something grave has happened. Something, I believe all of you should be made aware. As I am sure by now that some of you have taken notice to the red spectral orb which ascends above this very observatory, as well as the illumination of the legendary scythe above you." Those that had not previously noticed the illuminating image of the scythe above them now looked up at once.

"What you are looking at is a magick ward constructed by the very ancients who first safeguarded the legendary weapons. This observatory is in itself a relic of a time long passed. The ward serves as a beacon that is connected in each of the seven regions of Selador. Each region has an observatory similar to this one within their main estate. The purpose of this ward is in direct correlation with the wellbeing of the seven weapons. If one of the weapons is removed from its place within their immortal shrine, upon the alter in which it sits without the words spoken to break the seal of magick that surrounds the weapon, the alarm of the magick ward is triggered, Every region would know of its disappearance in this form of warning that you see above you. As you can see, the Scythe of Vengeance, the legendary weapon guarded by the region of the Plains of Reum, glows red like the orb hovering above this dome. This means the legendary scythe has been taken, and has no doubt fallen into the wrong hands." A sudden dread rushed over the crowd.

Nothing like this had ever happened before. Sure there have been wars, and great glorious battles in the time of the ancients, but they seemed almost myth and legend involving the weapons themselves. Never has anyone dared to try and steal one! Michael thought.

"We will not be paralyzed by the foreboding that this signal brings, but instead we must be fortified in our oath by the warning that comes with it. We will send riders to Jerum to receive any orders which may come our way. As of the moment, we are safe from harm. The alarm was only triggered three hours ago, and not even the fastest horses can make the journey of the plains in less than three days' time. We must rest easy on this night, for it may be the last evening we will have that chance. We have already doubled the guard, and will continue to increase our defenses and wait to hear direction from the King."

Michael listened curiously to this news, but to him it was only a means of distracting his thoughts from his inner frustrations. It was not that he wasn't interested, only that his inner turmoil threatened to take hold. He was, however, deeply pondering the possibilities of what might have happened to trigger such a magick ward of that caliber. His thoughts drifted creatively through his mind, *'Who might have taken the scythe? What kind of person would have the guts to attempt such a thing? Hell, what **army** would?'* His conspiracy theories and daydreams all twisted within his mind as the council continued the address.

After the assembly was dismissed and he had vacated the inside of the observatory and stepped into the courtyard, it was dusk; the sun had nearly vanished over the horizon casting dark shadows of the tall towers and buildings of the city onto the streets below. It was still too early to return to his quarters, so he wandered the streets of Lindell as the hazy dusk transformed to night until he came upon a less than respectable area of the city.

As he wandered amongst the slums he came to a familiar tavern. 'The Shed', the simple wooden sign read. The letters, engraved deeply into the wood with a black stain finish, were cut with the surprisingly ornate precision of a steady knife. The wooden sign hung from two black chains, one on either side, which were attached to an iron pole protruding from the stone and mortar building. Michael moved in front of the massive wooden door. He could see that the door had a wide slot which slid open from the inside in order to see the visitor before admittance was granted. As Michael observed this he was suddenly shocked with the unexpected presence of a shaky, cold grip upon his arm and a deep voice echoing in his ears from behind him.

Part 2:

A Slave Girls Dream

I

Across flourishing forests and flowing plains, deep in the capital city of Reum a place where corruption has seeded itself deeply in the hearts of men. Within the stone walls of the largest house, amongst the paper and wood framed rooms, several men have gathered to eat at a large round table that sat only a few feet off the ground. The men were gluttonously devouring the meal before them, large and fattened from complete lack of any personal labor.

Amongst the five feasting lords two young girls served, both covered in dirt, and weak from malnutrition. They wore rags about them, and seemed absent of all pride. This, however, was only true for one of them.

Kaire Ra still had hope. She felt it every time she fell asleep, but when she awoke this feeling was replaced with fear. As she reached to remove an empty dish from the table, she brushed the strands of her long curly black hair aside. This allowed her emerald green eyes to flare and glitter like embers in the candlelight radiating from the paper lamp that hovered several feet above the table with no form of suspension. It was instead held in place by the power of a ward. These lamps always mesmerized Kaire. It was compelling to see such magick creations. The flickering flame within the hovering lamp reflected in Kaire's eyes as she let her gaze linger on it while removing the dishes. As she moved for another empty glass, she suddenly felt a firm grasp upon her wrist. Pain rippled through her arm as she felt the drunken lord who grabbed her tighten his grasp and twist her arm behind her in a terrible contortion.

The lord was standing over her now, and as he slammed her onto the table she let out a whimper. She thought she caught the eyes of the other girl across the table, but just as she'd met her gaze, the girl lowered her eyes and continued to pour the wine for the other lords, the spectators. Kaire felt her rags tear effortlessly from her body, and shuddered at the thoughts of the coming onslaught of pain this contemptible man would provide her. She held to the hopes of her sleep, the dreams that awakened her to her true self. As the man forced himself on her she let herself slip quietly into the depths of her mind, unwilling to bear witness.

After each lord had his share of the girls, the two were each taken to the slave quarters on the lower floor and placed in the bathhouse. It was a collection of steaming, bubbling pools of foamy water, and cool springs that ran up from deep underground. The room and all the walls seemed to glow with a cloudy blue light reflecting in the water with a stunning luminance. After the girls had cleansed themselves uninterrupted, they were taken to separate cells carved deep in the foundation of the house. There, Kaire curled herself in the loose rags of her makeshift bed upon the dirt floor, and she let herself shake with the pain. Hot tears streamed down her face. Hot like the blazing anger within her heart.

"I've learned so much... You've taught me so much....but you won't let me use it!!!" She cried out loud.

"Why did you teach me such things, why did you come to me in my dreams, if I am never to use what I've been given?" Her vision blurred with her frustration and tears. "Why do you say you love me...if you allow this to go on....?" The words fell somewhat short as her eyes finally fluttered shut from the exhaustion. Immediately she was swallowed up by the

—

subconscious of her mind and carried gently to her state of peace, her place of hope.

There, in the eternal depths of her mind, she saw the shadowy silhouette of the man who appeared to her in her dreams. His dark form empowered her thoughts, and consumed her. Taking control of her heart and aiding in her escape. His thoughts seeped into hers as they had done several times, she found it truly compelling, and did not decline. She listened fiercely to the instructions he gave her. She knew in her heart that it meant her escape from her hell, her slavery. Understanding this one absolute conclusion, she found peace with the bombarding instruction, and found exceptional comfort in a singular thought, *'it is time'*.

2

Kaire Ra awoke to the bleak cold of her dark chamber, deep in the basement of the estate of Reum's capital city. Her dreams had ripped her from one reality into the next. Her head spun with the confusion of what had taken place within her slumber. She desperately tried to focus her eyes on the reality of her life of slavery in the dark confines of her cell.

She stood, her long legs aching with the stiffness of her hard sleep upon her pile of straw and rags which served as her only comfort from the dirt floor it sat upon. She stretched her lean, burdened muscles intensely for several moments, striving to regain proper circulation in parts still numb from the hard sleep. As she regained her feeling she recollected the events, the direction, within her dream.

A hard knocking came at the door in three quick thumps. They've come early this morning, Kaire thought. She could hear the old key grating within the lock, the hard twist as the teeth turned, and the shifting of the

---

50

finite gears. The latch turned, and with a heavy groan the door opened. Two guards stood outside her room, one working the door, the other smiling as though venom were upon his teeth. "Rise and shine young woman! Your humble Lord Bardi has requested your service. Let us not disappoint, my lady. It is rare for a specific girl to be requested for the morning foul, but it would seem you have caught the eye of lecherous Bardi."

Kaire said nothing, only stood and made her way from the room. As she passed the young guard who was working the door, she realized the shame he was bearing. He strayed from her gaze. His head was bent low, dripping in shame and unable to let his eyes focus upon his actions. He was only doing his job, just following orders like a machine. But at least his heart felt shame for the time, and he remained not as corrupt as the other men in her world.

While brushing past him, she placed a gentle hand of reassurance upon his arm. The man's gaze rose, and connected with the eyes of Kaire Ra. 'I'm sorry,' they seemed to say. The sinister guard put his hand up slightly as she continued past the younger guard, and loomed over Kaire, "You can't fuck him just yet sweetheart, maybe after this morning's foul, but not yet. Just wait though; you'll get a piece..." The younger guard slammed the door behind them, and they both jumped. "Shut the hell up Jet!" The young guard said, "She done sufferin' enough anyways."

"What'd you say to me?!" Jet suddenly turned on the young guard. "I said..." was all the young man managed to say before Jet's fist collided with his jaw, making a hollow thud. The young guard hit the floor with a clatter of flesh and steel; out cold. "Stupid fuck knows better than to talk back to me. Now, where was I ...?"

———

51

The guard had intended on warming the body of Kaire that morning, but with the thought of the consequences, he withdrew his exploring hands and led the slave girl down the passages and up stairwells until they came to the room in which her *service* had been requested. She grimaced at the thought of what lie ahead.

As the guard led her into the room she felt a sudden twinge of memory, images she had already seen. The images she had seen in the dream were *really* happening right before her eyes. She instantly knew what she was to do. As she entered further she noted the cathedral ceiling, the paintings, sculptures, tables, and of course the Alter for the fouling which sat before the shrine of Reum. The shrine of Reum was a massive stone pillar scribed with an ancient tongue and hovering above it was the Scythe of Vengeance, bathed in a brilliant pillar of light.

Kaire walked emotionlessly into the room. Her eyes traced the faces of the six lords seated at the long ornate serving table; she looked upon them with disgust and malice. Besides the lords and the guard who had escorted her into the room there were no other servants, she was alone. She was led to a place a few yards from the table in which the lords feasted, smoked, and drank to perversion. Her head was bent low; her eyes closed, lips pursed, legs pressed tightly together, her arms limp at her sides, she waited for what was to come.

One of the lords, just finishing his drink and his fill of the feast, rose and hobbled towards her. He grabbed her jaw firmly in his meaty hand and turned her head from one side to the other, examining the delicate and defined features in her expression. Her dark hair hung ragged and tangled about her. "This is her. A fine object of use, perfect for your purposes my lords, perfect for the fouling." It was obvious this man had been one of the

---

spectators the night before and had recommended her for the fouling so he could have his own 'go-'round'.

Kaire had only heard rumors of the fouling, but once it had been done to a girl they never talked. They never shared the horrors of what took place inside this room on the occasions the lords chose to have a fouling. Every girl that had ever entered this chamber in the morning light of a new day had left it broken and destroyed. They literally became a shell of a human being; uncaring, passive, and utterly hopeless. Kaire was lucky she had not yet had to endure the torture of the fouling, so therefore had retained some of her hope. The fouling was merely a breaking of women instead of horses.

"You have brought us an excellent choice, Lord Bardi. We appreciate your selection." Lord Bardi released his grasp upon the ever silent Kaire Ra, turned to the lords, and bowed deeply with an almost theatric tone. As she had foreseen within her vision, like a memory, she extended a steady arm towards Lord Bardi, and gave a gentle tap on his shoulder. He turned abruptly startled by the firm but tender touch of the slave girl.

"I have something for you…" She said in a voice so solemn and sweet that its tone could only compare with the shuffling of the feet of angels. The lord chuckled, looking from her to the other lords with a slight embarrassment at his previous startle. "And what would that be my dear?" He said with a crooked grin.

"…a kiss."

The lords sang out in a roar of laughter. Such offerings were seldom willingly offered by the slave girls, and to see such a deliberate cooperation within a fouling brought a heated excitement to the thick bellies of the lords.

"Very well then, I will accept your offering." He leaned forward, readying to pucker his lips for the soft kiss of Kaire Ra. His fattened face flushed with the welling eagerness within him.

Instead of leaning in and kissing the revolting lord, Kaire simply brought the palm of her hand to her sweet lips, and kissed her fingertips ever so gently. A fire seemed to grow somewhere in the depths of Kaire's emerald eyes. As she withdrew her hand from her kiss, she extended it towards Lord Bardi as though offering a gift. The morning light within the room seemed to grow dark, and the room suddenly seemed to be shifting in a faint darkness, swirling with a mild haze as though the world itself had become *thin*.

Lord Bardi looked dumbfounded at her extended hand, his brow furrowed in utter terror and confusion. Her soft silent expression suddenly transformed. Her eyes went wild with fury as her hair suddenly began to tear about her in a sudden wind that seemed to resonate from her outstretched palm. The room was completely silent, as though it was a black void of space, and something startling even to Kaire happened. Upon the palm of her outstretched hand appeared a tiny glowing bubble of the purest white light. Lord Bardi's eyes grew with horror as the orb suddenly grew to the size of a fist, just sitting there, unmoving, residing upon her palm resonating its brilliant white light through the unnatural darkness within the room.

The lords were frozen with terror as she brought her hand to her lips and gently blew it towards Lord Bardi. The slight breath launched the bubble from her palm. It floated gently the few feet to the lord, dancing in the air as it went. Lord Bardi was paralyzed with fear and amazement, unsure of what was taking place before his eyes. He could only follow the

---

orb with his gaze as it drifted within an inch of his face and suddenly burst at the tip of his pointed nose. The light suddenly vanished and the darkness faded from the room. Kaire let her hand return to her side. Lord Bardi stood perfectly still.

"Lord...Bardi?" one of the lords managed to stammer as Lord Bardi suddenly swayed, and fell straight back. His head hit the stone floor with a cracking of bone and a spray of blood, the sound echoed throughout the room. His eyes were wiped completely white in his last moment of pure horror. Lord Bardi had died well before his brains were bashed out upon the stone floor.

The other lords were in shock. They were completely silent, unmoving, horrified by what had just befallen Lord Bardi, and before any could comprehend any action, Kaire moved across the room with such speed that few followed her movements. She leaped upon the table like a cat, sprang over the lot of them, and landed silently upon the Alter which had tortured so many. "This is where you want me is it not?!" She screamed like a great dictator inviting war. "Then come, take me! Take me and take me and take me 'til I am nothing but a ravaged shell of flesh, someone...*something* that was, but is no more." The lords began to shake off the fear she had gripped them in before and were rising from there seats to stand before her. They were mesmerized and *hungry* for the woman who stood upon the Alter of fouling.

The steady hum of the beam of light which surrounded the shrine of the scythe echoed in Kaire's mind. She felt drawn to it, like the lecherous hunger, need, *want* of the men before her. One of the lords took a few valiant steps forward. "We'll make you pay for what you did to Bardi, bitch!" He stammered in a weak shout as he approached with meaty hands

—

clenched at his sides.

Kaire put her hands on her hips, thrust out her chest, and let out a massive bout of laughter which seemed half-siren and half-hyena. "You're all damned fools!" She said after a final chuckle, and jumped within human dexterity ten feet backwards and fifteen feet up, back flipping with the angelic grace of a gymnast. Just before she landed, one of the lords spoke in a low tone meant only for himself and the ears of his comrades, "No slave girl, you're the fool. Death is instant for those who try to touch the scythe without the removal of the ward. Burn in your own hell little slave girl…burn."

As Kaire's somersaulting airborne form landed gracefully upon the pillar that the scythe calmly hovered above, the white light which had surrounded it suddenly shifted. To Kaire it seemed the light and air surrounding her and the pillar was changing somehow. Its substance seemed to thicken, the air felt hot, and it grew hotter. The vision of the room was now beginning to vanish as the swirling light and air changed form. Kaire was momentarily terrified by what was happening. She hadn't expected *this*. She hadn't *expected* a whirlwind of fire to suddenly burst into existence around her out of thin air.

Remember the words, remember the dream. What was it he said? "The ward, yes, there will be a ward. No spell, lore, or magick can break its strength in the haste you are burdened, but one thing you possess may be powerful enough." Think Kaire! What was it? "Your will…your will alone can break the ward which keeps you from your future, your new life." My will…alone.

Thoughts burst through Kaire's mind in an orgasm of possibilities of what real life could hold for her. A free life, one she could chose. She would do anything for that, even breaking a silly ward placed upon a

---

56

legendary weapon by the gods who made it, **anything**.

The red hot flames closed in upon her, licking at her tender flesh. *'My will alone…'* She thought as the flames made a final searing swirl before they closed in upon her helpless form. As the ring of fire engulfed her body she thought she could hear the laughter of the lords. *'Fools…You're all FOOLS!!!'* With flames engulfing her body, the silhouette of Kaire could be seen reaching a slender arm up toward the scythe hovering above her burning form. She seemed to be struggling against being pulled down by the flames, and just as it seemed her wavering form would fall, her hand found the ancient handle of the scythe. In an instant, as though being released from the power of the ward, Kaire's hands danced across the handle of the magnificent weapon, and in a flurry of strokes she seemed to be collecting the fires of the whirlwind with the scythe itself.

It was apparent to those who bore witness that the ward was broken. Kaire's previously engulfed form glowed with a powerful radiance as she continued collecting the fires upon the scythe and swirling it about her in an enchantingly terrifying display. In a single, fluid movement she thrust the scythe into the air. She held it poised above her as the powerful fires of the ward erupted from the blade of the scythe. The whirlwind of flames rocketed upward through the skylights in the center of the cathedral ceiling, shattering the glass.

Light from above danced off the falling shards of glass as they fell around her from overhead. The deafening roar of the inferno had ceased, giving way to the tinkling of the shards as they hit the stone floor. As the last pieces of glass fell to the floor, Kaire leveled the scythe with her line of vision upon the lords of Reum. "I will grant you no time to repent your sins, you will pay for that which you have inflicted and you will finally

---

understand the true power of that which you have supposedly spent your lives protecting! Your lives will satisfy the fury, the hunger within the Scythe of Vengeance!"

Part 3:

The Great Sword of Lindell

I

The firm grip upon Michael's arm was that of a beggar, a bum and drunken nightwalker of the street. "Got a few dars to spare, to buy an old man a drink?" Michael shrugged the man's grasp from his arm. "Yes, just…just leave me to my task." Michael said with a shameful tone as he fumbled in his pants pocket for a few dars to give the old man. He had plenty of money, provided to him by his assets of the living allowance he was allotted during his sentencing. He handed the dars to the old man and turned to knock on the door to the tavern. "Let the dishonored aid the cursed and the outcome is madness…" The beggar said.

"What'd you say old man?" Michael said as he turned to question the man's riddle, but he was already gone, vanishing back into the shadows from which he came. Michael tried to shrug off the suddenly tender feeling at the back of his neck, the feeling of something far too complicated for him to truly understand. So he returned his attention to the door of the tavern and pounded a heavy hand upon its dark wooden surface. The slot slid open for a moment, and all that he could see was the cold steely eyes of its keeper. Just as quickly, the slot slid shut once more, and Michael could hear the bars and latches being removed. The door opened inward to the sight of the man who had peered through the slot. He now dominated the doorway, his height reaching the doorframe, and his girth encompassed width.

The giant of a man peered down at him as though he were covered in manure, a scab upon society. "Three dars is the cover…my lord." The words *my lord* seemed to be said with utter vehemence, as though it was more spat than spoken, sticky with the saliva of disgust.

"I'm not here to join the bar scene. I only mean to purchase a flask from your keep. You see, the shops have already closed…" Michael had tried to sway kindness from the giant, but to no avail.

"I don't give a damn about what you want, what's closed, or what the fuck you plannin' on doin' tonight! All I knows is dat you gotta pay a six dar cover to walk through this here door." It was apparent that the giant had heard the wrong rumor about Michael Cross. The story, turned gossip, turned to tall tale, had already found itself several different first hand accounts and had made many enticing versions of its invitingly juicy tale, many of which made Michael Cross look like the villain of some drama.

"Six dar?! I thought you said three a moment ago?"

"I didn't say any such thing, but I guess you too busy flappin' them lips of yours to listen to what I been sayin'. Seems to me you need to make a decision…my lord…" He spat the words again. "So pay the six dar or get the fuck outta my sight!"

Michael did not have the patience to argue with the giant, nor was he stupid enough to even consider the confrontation. He fished from his pocket a ten dar coin piece and flicked it off his thumb into the air. The man snatched it from its spinning descent and took a gander at the coin in his large hands. He smiled a big unorthodox grin, which sent a chill down Michael's back. The man stepped aside, focusing mostly on the coin, but never really removing his eyes from Michael. Michael brushed past him quickly before the brute could change his mind and hold him out for more

—

of a 'cover'.

The bar was filled with drunken city folk, loud music from a piano in one corner, and there were several people playing cards at the table. A few young couples, blooming with the toxicity of love, were dancing in an area that had been cleared of the round wooden tables and chairs. They spun their beautiful companions in steps that proceeded and receded like a wave, and moved in an intricate pattern of lines across the floor. It was as though they were stepping gracefully across the surface of some map of a dance drawn out on the beer-stained wooden floor by cupids from times long past in an unknown fairytale. Michael actually looked at the feet of the spinning girls and expected to see the gnarled smirks of the love-weaving demons who had entangled them in the snare of such a disco. No demons glared at him from the floor, but from his thoughts he could see himself one day being tortured by such a creature that could make a man sick with love. He shuddered at the thought of a physical inflictor of such pain.

'It's hard as is, dealing with the war which rages in ones' heart over something like love.' He thought as he approached the bar.

A few of the conversations died as he approached. His square-toed black boots made a hollow click against the wooden floor, drawing the attention of those not interested in the conversations they were engaged. Michael ignored the glares and under-the-breath commentary as he took to a vacant part of the bar. He ignored the stools, and instead of sitting, leaned over the bar in an attempt for the keeper to notice him. The real problem was that he knew he didn't have to draw attention to himself; everyone had been scornfully glancing at him since he had first walked in the door. Even the keeper, himself had taken notice to the looks projected in his direction.

Regardless of the fact that the keeper had already seen him, he

—

62

pretended as though he had just noticed the presence of Michael Cross when he approached the bar, and gave an 'Oh, hi there! I'll be over in just a minute,' sort of look.

When the keeper had finally made his way over, his face shrouded with an evidently fake smile, he asked what he could get for him. "I need a flask of cashdun, strongest you got…" Michael said in a low voice to the bartender. "Ahh, good choice my liege, but I'm afraid I'll hafta go on down to me cellar to fetch ye that one, so it may be a moment or more."

Michael, wanting to be on his way, away from these people, safe in his room hidden within the bottle didn't care how much it would cost him at this point. That's what was set in his mind, and once set, with Michael Cross, it must be met. "I'll pay you an extra…five dar, if you could so kindly make that flask the first of your priorities."

"Aye, I appreciate yer kindness, but I isn't expect'n no special payment for the service to a good man who deserves a drink more than any of the trash I tend to hand and foot." Michael looked at him with confusion. *'Doesn't he know who I am?!'*

"I would just as soon steal money from me own good mum. Ta only reason I said it may take me a moment, 'tis because I got too much clutter bracing me door. It'll take me a moment to remove it to even open the door, and ta tell ya the truth…I have a hard time readin' them little labels on the bottles themselves," the jovial keeper explained as he pulled a glass from underneath the counter along with a clear bottle filled with a dark liquid. It was almost brown, almost red, but it looked smooth, very smooth. "Why don't you have a drink on me? I'll run off and fetch that flask for ya, and I'll be back before you finish." Michael nodded in approval, and took the drink.

———

"Thank you my friend." Before Michael could utter another word, the keeper was gone through the wooden door to the right of his bar. It appeared to have led to a pantry, and then probably the cellar door, Michael figured.

Taking the short, wide-rimmed glass from the bar in hand, he glanced around the room. The young couples were still dancing to the spell of the cupids, the players continued to deal cards, and the old dark-skinned man with a beard long since turned white, played the piano. Not just played, like any common bar musician, but seemed to capture the melody and rhythm as though they emanated from the depths of his very soul.

Michael was unfamiliar with the song the man played, but as he listened he was captivated by the deceptive melodies and rhythms. The melody was soft and light, yet quick and powerful. It appeared that the ebony-toned man's hands had been touched by the gods. Michael quietly wondered if perhaps his song was what had entranced the young lovers to their dance. Conceivably, there were no demonic little cupids firing their arrows and weaving their torturous dance of love. Maybe it was simply the old man, who seemed to play from the very depths of his soul and roused the spirits within the young lovers who danced. Perhaps *he* was a devil in disguise…perhaps.

Michael took the first swallow of the drink. The liquid went down smoothly, strong, warm…dark. The feelings drove his senses briefly to a standstill.

'What a taste! No wonder it's in such a short glass. I bet if I had a few more of these I'd be put away all night for sure.' Michael began to contemplate what his actions might be on this night, but as he took another swallow of the dark drink he finally caught the eyes of several of the people who were

talking about him under their breath. He would have heard it sooner, but the music had drowned the whispers. *'If I just keep to myself they've got no reason to bother with me. Just talk, I don't care if you talk. Just leave me alone. It's bad enough…It's…'* Michael's thoughts were interrupted by the sudden shouts of one of the men playing cards. "Ya dirty cheat! Ya skinny lounger! I'm goan-ta send ya ta hell!" The man this grizzly drunken wretch was screaming at merely sat quietly in his seat. Michael could see that he was dressed all in black, and he wore a large brimmed hat bent low. His face was decorated with no scars, but held a perfectly symmetrical structure. Michael would later recall that his hair was golden, like that of a sun baked field, but what he would always remember were his eyes. When the man looked up at his accuser, Cross could see that they were of the clearest blue. Like the sea Michael had only seen as an infant upon the coast, held tight in the arms of the king as his entire bloodline began their exile. Those eyes were narrow and focused, and yet clouded with a deep sense of understanding upon everything in consequence to what laid before him.

"Ya jus' goan sit there like a fuc…" His words were cut short as blue eyes calmly and almost too quickly for anyone's gaze to follow, drew a small black dual bladed dagger, and with a flick of his wrist, sent it skimming past the side of the screaming man's face. It hit and stuck in a wooden beam in the ceiling with a thud.

The men seemed to just stare into each other's eyes, but Michael knew, that blue-eyes was merely reading the fool. That man, the drunk, was frozen with sheer terror, but blue-eyes lowered his gaze to his cards face up on the table, and gently stood, leaving the winnings behind. As he had risen from his seat, Michael thought he saw the long curving shadow of an elegant sword beneath the shadowed shroud of his long black coat.

—

Michael wondered how easily *blue-eyes* could have killed the drunken man that stood in fear before him. A shudder ran up Michael's spine as the man's high black boots clicked against the wooden floor as he gently stepped past the man before him, as if he weren't standing there at all. He walked right past the fool who had called him a cheat, and a lounger, then stopped just below the place his dagger had driven home. He lifted his left leg while staring up at the dagger in the beam near the ceiling, and quite suddenly stomped his foot twice against the floor. The knife somehow pulled free from the ceiling and into the grasp of his quick hand. He sheathed the small blade and left the bar without a word, and gave only the faintest glimmer of a smile as he caught Michael's gaze. He flipped a token from a small purse beneath his coat into the hands of the eagerly waiting doorman, who quickly opened the wooden mass.

Michael turned back around, facing the bar. The people who had been using him as a prime target for their topic of conversation would probably have something else to talk about now, and so he decided not to draw any more attention to himself then he had to. So as though by impulse, repetition, or just plain nervousness, he removed his tobacco from his pouch he carried, along with his papers and a single homemade match Michael had forcibly learned to make. He let his focus draw on this task, and in the moments it took him to roll the cigarette and finish his drink the keeper had returned.

"Here ya are m'lord. It took me a moment to find it, seems we don't have too many bottles of that cashdun left down there." He handed the bottle to Michael to let him observe its dusty label. "How much?"

"Ten…uh, seven dar my lord…" Michael knew the old keeper was trying to show him generosity and pity for the scorn in which he had to bear, but Michael needed no generosity, there was enough in his coffers for him to throw to those who deserved it if he cut back on his own delights, which he never seemed to have the mood to dabble upon anyway. "I'll give you five for the cashdun…and fifteen for the drink you gave me a moment ago." Before the keeper could protest he had snatched his freshly rolled cigarette from the counter, placed it between his lips, and put several coins before the man. "Thank you for the wine and kindness friend, for I fear the later is even rarer than the wine." He solemnly said as he turned and left the bar. The door guard glared at him as he left, and just before he had shut the door on Michael and the dusty city street he spat after him. The saliva struck the ground with such force that Michael could actually hear it, even over the distance he had traveled down the alleyway. Then he heard the door slam.

A cold breeze blew hard against him as Michael rounded another street corner in the cold city of Lindell. *'The air has already turned cold. The Falling has come early this year… it will be even colder without her.'* The painful memories of love crippled his heart from within as he struck his homemade match against the side of a stone building he passed, and lit his smoke. *'A cold night indeed...'*

2

Michael's room was just as he had left it. His books of study were still strewn across the tables in the same disarray as before, and his bed was unmade, his covers thrown violently about the mattress. His nights had been restless and unnerving, always filled with dark mares of his recent memories and past haunting. In his waking hours, he suppressed the thoughts of his wife with the power of his conscious, but when he would

—

succumb to sleep, everything he was trying to avoid and forget would torture him to his limits.

As Michael undressed, he shuddered at the thought of returning to his slumber so early in the evening. He wasn't quite ready to deal with the nightmares of his life just yet. So instead, he went to the fireplace and attempted to conjure a flame as many people could easily do when using an existing will or ward. It was a task some children could even perform. This was yet another infliction of Michael Cross, his shame for the absence of talent in common tasks involving any form of magick.

Despite his constant failure, Michael never stopped attempting to use such simple forms of magick. He would always try the *correct* way, fail, and then use the primitive tools the lords had taught him as a child to aid him in his handicap. They were his replacements, '*...like a wooden leg for a paraplegic,*' he thought, disgustedly.

Michael removed the familiar flint and stone which had been rubbed with wear from use, and struck it once, twice, three times, and the kindling and wood began to blaze.

Accomplishing this tedious task, Michael fetched his bottle, the book he'd been reading earlier, a throw from the bed, and slumped into an ornate, but comfortably broken-in old chair in front of the hearth of the fireplace. He took a long drink from the bottle, allowing his mouth to be engulfed in the sweet taste of the cashdun wine. He set the bottle on the table next to the chair and wiped his lips. He tried to find the place he'd been reading in the book, but as his eyes grew weary he had to struggle to keep from closing them out of fatigue.

In an attempt to battle his lust for sleep he took several more large gulps from the bottle, but it only enhanced the blurring of the pages and words before him. After a final surrender of a swig of the delicious wine, Michael closed his book and stared intently into the fire before him. The flames seemed to be dancing the dance of the lovers, and he remembered the song the ebony-toned man played. With the music in his mind his eyes fell, and he found sleep.

3

For the first time since his fall from honor, Michael did not dream of his consorting wife or the actions and events that had taken place. Instead, his sleep was filled with a strange fantasy of the likes Michael had never known.

He found himself amidst blowing and perilous dunes, lost in an eternal desert. His skin was blasted with the heat and sand and his throat felt instantly parched, but this feeling quickly changed to the quite premature gland swelling of dehydration. The gritty pieces of sharp dust, the sand of the desert beat against him, and he felt as though layers of his protective flesh were slowly being stripped from his bones. His gasps for air were shallow, unable to draw enough oxygen from the sand blowing wind. *Where am I?* Michael wondered as he fought against the tearing wind, and started walking in what he found the most randomly appealing direction, straight ahead.

YOU ARE HERE… Michael thought he heard amidst the deafening wind.

It couldn't have been a voice…could it? No way I could've heard it that clear over this raging wind. Did I think it? Oh, course not, but I still don't know…where is here? Michael questioned again within his thoughts.

THE DESERT… was all that was replied.

—

Michael finally perceived the true lucid power of this dream, though he did not yet understand it. The sand and wind continued to relentlessly batter him. He squeezed his eyes tightly in an attempt to shield the sand from his vision, but every attempt to open them was utterly crushed with the blinding pain as raw sand ripped at his unprotected eyes. The desert was choking him, blinding him, beating him, and all he could do was stagger on, lost, confused, in pain. *How do I get out of this hell?!* He screamed within his mind.

COVER YOUR EYES...SIGHT CAN ALWAYS DECIEVE YOU.

Michael, confused and bewildered by the power of this voice, tore a strip of cloth from his already tattering shirt, and tied it snugly over his eyes. He stood solemnly within the desert storm, awaiting further instruction as the elements waged war upon his silhouetted form. He waited, but the voice said nothing.

Michael remained motionless as he was battered by the storm. The pain grew, it grew greatly, and just when he was sure he could bear no more, his heart bleeding out, boiling to let loose a cry of the pain of a million needles across his raw sensitive human flesh, the winds stopped. Everything of affliction ceased, and a feeling of calm fell upon Michael. The sand beneath his feet seemed to melt away as though an hourglass had been suddenly placed beneath him, but he remained, he did not slip away with the sand of the desert. He began to drift in the darkness of his vision. *What am I to do?*

'ALL YOU MUST DO ...IS FOLLOW YOUR NOSE...'

Michael awoke abruptly from his dream to find himself drenched in cold sweat, his throat aching with a dry thirst that felt several days old. His senses in whole were assaulted by the smell of burning. He reached for the

---

bottle upon the table next to his chair, and finished several large chugs, quenching his terrible thirst. He threw off the drenched robe he was wearing and donned the same attire he had worn previously that day.

He pulled on his loose breeches, *one leg at a time*, which was made of a thick dark blue material called denmen. Over time, they had faded in places and gave a feel that Michael always preferred over the hosiery of nobles, even though it was considered commoner attire. He wore a black leather vest which he buttoned over a long-sleeved white shirt. As Michael fastened the belt of his pants he looked quickly about the room for the remainder of his garb or clothing. He quickly donned his boots and fetched his sword from beside the bed. As he struggled to tuck the rest of his pants into his knee high black leather boots he left his room to seek out the burning smell. Once outside, he stopped in the hallway and looked out over the railing to the courtyard beyond. As he looked out over the enormity of the courtyard he was stricken with the sheer horror of the confirmation of the stinging smell.

Everything within the courtyard was being engulfed in flames. It had caught rapidly, even the magnificent pagodas Michael had once favored as a good spot for a days' reading, or an afternoon smoke. The trees and every single object that could catch fire, were ablaze. Michael rubbed at his weary, smoke-stung eyes, bewildered by the inferno just a few heartbeats away. Everyone was frantically carrying buckets, jars, washing basins, and anything that could hold water to the burning courtyard in an attempt to extinguish the blaze. No one had time to ask questions or seek out the root of the fire. They only frantically followed the example of the others, and just poured as much water on the blaze as possible. Michael, however, merely stood quietly outside his doorway, observing with an

---

expressionless gaze that seemed far too ancient for his youth.

As he watched the fire consuming the courtyard, he seemed entirely oblivious to the people herding to the aid of the attempts to fight the fire. The fire had entranced him, but something more, however, grabbed his attention within the back of his most hidden conscious senses. As he turned to look at what drew the attention of his mind's eye, he saw the fleeting form of someone who was *not* running to put out the blaze.

Cautiously, he followed the man who had drawn his senses. He seemed to recognize him in some way. It all came in a rush once the man passed beneath an amber lantern which hung above a doorway. It was one of the traders he had seen earlier that day. *'"Hello friend." I'll say. "What brings a fellow like you round these parts of the estate this late at night?" But he'd never tell me. "Oh I'm lost" will be his only reply. Its best to follow, but I wonder...did **he** start the fire in the courtyard?'* Michael pondered inwardly.

The random twists and turns of the inner house became disorienting. So much, in fact, that in the dark Michael could barely tell where exactly they were going. One thing was obvious, the man was trying to take extra care to avoid contact with any of the other people within the house, and he definitely didn't want to be followed. *I guess it's not your lucky day...*

He silently stalked the man throughout the houses' intricate rooms, halls, and stairwells, until at last to a single door at the top of one of the estates highest towers. The stocky, bearded 'merchant' briskly knocked twice. The door was opened from within, and the man stepped forward and disappeared inside. Michael moved briskly around the corner he was peering from and made his way to the door.

With a knot in his chest he approached cautiously The massive iron door was all too familiar to him. It was the entrance to the chamber which

—

72

held the true, legendary Great Sword of Lindell. It was a secret, Michael was one of few to be privy to, the location of the 'real' legendary sword. He shuddered at the sudden thoughts shooting through his mind as he noticed two small pools of blood next to the door. Michael instantly knew the fate of the two guards that had been on post. He listened and could make out the murmuring voices of those responsible.

"Were you followed?!" A strikingly rash and deep voice asked.

"No, I avoided everyone...well, except for the boy who guarded the alarm tower."

"What of him?"

"I don't think anyone's going to be noticing a dead body anytime soon. It looks like you guys didn't fare as well as I did. You look pretty messed up squid." He said to someone who Michael assumed was 'nicknamed' squid.

"Shut the hell up. Least we were quiet enough, and now we're here, so we can get this..."

"We have a problem." A booming voice interjected.

"You're talking about that ward ain' cha?"

"Yes. We're trying to break it as fast as we can, but we had a few mishaps...Jake and Rex are dead, the ward killed them."

"Shit!" The man Michael had followed said a little too loudly. "Hey! I think I figured this damn thing out!" The voice of a fourth person chimed in from what sounded like further back in the room, near the location of the sword.

"Then let's get that damn sword and get the hell out of here!"

He had heard enough. Michael shook with the painful twinge of some deeply buried cord within his heart, and ached at the responsibility which he still held. The oath, the only thing he had left, he had sworn to protect the sword. It was the only duty in his life that he was still bound to. *Besides, what are four against one half-crazed, half-drunk, dishonored lord? Last of the Cross, here I come…* He cursed himself as he swiftly drew his sword and threw open the door. He rushed into the room destiny had led him to.

As the view of the inner room was suddenly revealed to him, he was surprised to find himself at the attention of six men who appeared to all be the men he had seen earlier that day, the ones traveling from the mountains of Zwentor. Michael could now see that they were clearly not merchants. They were all large, muscled to the bone, most bearing beards and long hair. They wore a series of mismatched armor, which they had apparently hidden underneath their 'merchant' guises, and they bore large hunting knives the length of a small sword and axes of different types. The glaring lot of them quickly drew their sword-like knives and looked urgently from Michael to each other in looks he perceived to be total glee.

After being quickly surrounded, Michael prepares to fend off the first of many attackers with their blades and faces hungrily circling him. He lets loose his introduction as he stands at the ready, "I am Michael Cross, fallen of honor, broken in life, destined wielder of the sword before you, the sword you intend to take, I am the last of the Cross, and fool…"
To die…after all the pain dealt in this life…I suppose this will be a good death…dying to protect the sword…and dying with my own still clenched in my blood soaked hands…

The blades were already moving towards him, as though they were sick of his chatter. When the blades seemed a moment from a hairs' breadth away, Michael came to life.

His muscled, quick form moved like the flickering of a flame. The fine, thin steel blade of his sword rang out in a resonance echoing with the swiftness of his feet as he dodged and parried the onslaught of the blows the six men dealt. As he moved to dodge one blade, three more would come within an inch of his throat, but those he would turn with a shimmering glance of steel. As their efforts failed, the men grew fiercer, but Michael returned their intentions. He continued to turn the sword blades and faces of axes, and even managed to inflict several wounds to his attackers. Here and there, he managed to slice a wrist, cut deep into a thigh, and scrape a near miss of a stroke across another's chest.

Despite the mesmerizing footwork and flawless technique Michael seemed to possess, he could not hold back the thick knives and heavy axes that he battled against with the fine steel of his ornately crafted rapier. The blade was meant for the fencing and 'civilized duels' of the lordship of Lindell, and not for the battering of axes and short swords. Michael began to feel the inevitable pressure building within the steel of his sword, and as he turned yet another stroke of another plummeting blow of an axe, he could feel the strain as the steel began to fault. Another blow from above hit his blade and the pressure snapped the steel, breaking his sword. Michael managed to move his head aside from the plummeting axe that had demolished the blade, but still received a deep laceration to his left shoulder. Michael crumpled to his knees in pain, clutching his shoulder with his right hand, and forcibly dropped the remaining hilt of the sword from the impact of the axe. *You're a fool…a fool…a broken, dishonored, dead fool…*

The six men loomed over him. The leader, or what appeared to be the leader, the man who had dealt his defeating blow, lowered his heavy hand axe. "I will try to remove the sword from its shrine. Make sport of this valiant fool. Perhaps your target practice is in need of some fine tuning?" With this, the 'leader' turned and walked to the shrine holding the sword that was still sparsely protected by the dissipating ward.

The remaining men began to laugh as they all slowly formed a line before the kneeling, wounded Michael Cross. *It's punishment for my foolishness, a firing squad to end my days. If death has come, then upon my feet I shall meet it.* Michael Cross stood as the men readied their weapons like thunderbolts.

The first to throw was the man Michael had slashed across the wrist. Michael prayed somewhere in his thoughts for a true aim to his heart, so as to end his torment, but to his dismay the knife slashed perfectly across his forearm. It wasn't necessarily the wrist, and it was much deeper, but Michael got the message. *An eye for an eye…*   He suddenly thought, for whatever reason. He paid no mind to the slash across his arm, now painted red with blood. He merely stood there, ready for the next assault.

The second to throw his weapon was the man he had slashed across the leg. As the man threw, he grunted loudly. Michael tried to dodge the low throw of the whirling blade, and managed to escape with a deep cut rather than the loss of his leg. The pain it caused made him buckle forward. As he tried to regain his bearings, he had only a moment to see another axe spin once, twice, and then the handle of the axe hit him square in the forehead. He fell backwards, darkness clouding over his sight. As he fell he heard distant voices as though they echoed from within a well.

"…*Look at that! I think you did him in!*"…

"…*Yeah! What the hell, I didn't even get a shot?*"…

"*Quiet, you idiots! I can't get this damn sword to…*"…

As his mind drifted silently into the darkness Michael thought he

———

might be hearing a different voice, a familiar one.

CROSS...

CROSS...

Who's there? Michael replied with fear.

IF YOU ARE FOOL ENOUGH TO DIE HERE... THEN DIE...BUT IF YOU WISH TO LIVE...THEN TAKE THE SWORD...

How?! How can I possibly take it? I'm on the verge of death?! As if his cry was not heard the voice continued, TAKE *IT, AND SLAY THESE MEN WHO OPPOSE YOU...ONLY YOU CAN TAKE THE SWORD...ONLY YOU...LAST OF THE CROSS...*

How can I?

HATE THEM CROSS...HATE THEM WITH ALL YOUR HEART...HATE THEM, AND FIND WHATEVER MEANS TO DESTROY THEM...DESTROY THEM TO LIVE, TO REGAIN YOURSELF...TO AWAKEN THE CROSS WITHIN YOU...

...To regain myself...to awaken the Cross?

The last words whispered away as Michael's vision began to blur, and his world slowly drifted back to him. When the room came clear he was sure he had already died; he no longer felt the pain of his wounds. It seemed that they had simply been cut off from his mind. This brought a sense of resolve to him, and he remembered the words. "Hate them...with all my heart..." He muttered as he shuffled from the floor and then stood once again. The men turned swiftly, and their leader, who was distracted by this sudden mass attention shift from his work upon the ward, to the rising of the *dead* man upon the floor, was furious with the interruption. "You haven't killed him yet!?"

"We thought...we thought he *was* dead!" One of them stammered. Without even the slightest hesitation, and with soft, strangely passive

—

words, "I'll do it myself," he said as he pulled his axe from its place at his side.

Somewhere amidst the rage within his memory, thoughts of his wife, the Cross line itself, the lifelong frustrations and emotional baggage, and the destiny itself which lay before him like a line drawn in the sands of his life; Michael found the hate he required. He looked upon the six men with a fiery rage engulfed the form of his tattered and bloody body. The man who was front and center, the one who'd been working on the ward, threw his axe, a true aim lined with Michael's face.

The axe plummeted towards Michael with blinding speed, but with an equal rapidity, Michael moved to meet the axe, lunging head first at the oncoming plight of the spinning blade. As the razor edge of the axe closed in on him, he darted to the side like a flame in the wind. The weapon continued past as he lashed out with his hand and caught hold of the twirling hilt of the passing axe. Without hesitation, he continued his mad dash forward, now brandishing the axe in his right hand. The distance between them was cut in half with his charge, and at the last length between them, holding the startled gaze of the man who had thrown it, he leapt. The lunge took all of his might, but as he did so, he swung the axe in a brilliant arc, and clove through the skull of the man who had sought to destroy him. The man fell in a crumpled heap upon the stone floor. The other men went wild with rage as they turned in time to see Michael rush past the fallen man, and to the shrine of the legendary great sword.

The shrine was a masterpiece of artwork. An intricate twisting design of what appeared to be wrought iron, but instead of welds holding the black pieces firmly together, it was held in place by the ward. Upon the touch of 'unworthy hands', or those without the knowledge to unlock it, the intricate web of design would only tighten its grasp upon the sword, making it impossible to remove. If the unworthy pressed even harder, it would kill them with a current of some unknown power. As Michael made the last few steps towards the alter, he hesitated for a moment in the wake of its ominous form.

Although the alter itself appeared to be an artistically intricate design, the sword itself, Michael could now see, was less than impressionable. It appeared that the sword had been left to tarnish and grow dull. It was so tarnished in fact, that the blade itself had grown to become a marred, piece of blackened decayed steel. Its sheer size did not deceive the fact, that at one time the sword had obviously been magnificent. From the tip of the blade to the hilt the sword stretched to four and a half feet; a great length for such a splendid sword. The width of the blade reached seven inches at its widest point. Despite the poor condition of the blade itself, Michael could feel the power that the sword possessed, though he could not grasp it, he could feel it on the edge of his mind, and so placed his hands firmly upon the withered cloth wrap of its hilt, and pulled. Nothing happened.

Michael pulled again, confused. The sword remained within the web work of the alter. Fear, anger, and a quick snap somewhere in the back of Michael's mind, shattered his resolve. *'It is my **right** to draw this sword. I've heard it my whole life, and I've had to unwillingly live with that responsibility, and now, when I finally decide to fulfill that duty, this damn thing won't move?!'* He pulled again at the sword, and watched the web wrap tighter around it. The remaining five men rushed toward him with a fearsome look of determination in their eyes. *'Why won't this thing move?! Damn destiny, and damn the lore! I draw this sword on my own accord, on my life!'* As he pulled

---

79

harder at the legendary blade he stared intently at the twisting wrought iron moving around the entirety of the sword.

The deadly weapons of his foes were nearly upon him. *'Pulling straight up there is too much resistance from the design, but what if I move the blade **with** the design?'* Michael turned the sword one way and then the other, and as he did so several feet of the blade were freed from the clutches of the altar, until finally, the blade was free. As Michael pulled the last of the sword from the shrine it had rested upon for so many years, held in its intricate web of art, it all began to unravel. The wrought iron lengths merely twisted and fell like stalks of flowers which had immediately withered and died.

As he removed the ancient sword, he met the eyes of his enemies and pierced their souls with the hate in his heart. He could feel his blood pumping with the now familiar rhythm of the Cross, the true power within him. He shook for release, grinding his teeth with the pressure, until finally he could feel his life flowing into the sword he held. The sword took on his strength, and despite its decayed appearance, it radiated a feeling of certainty and warmth, a feeling of power. He continued to pour out his feelings into the sword, convulsively tightening and releasing his grip upon the hilt. When the blade could take on no more of his strength it began to seep out into the physical realm. The air around Michael Cross and the sword he held seemed to shift and contort like the ripple of heat above a fire. His aura had become as clear as anything could ever be to any who had eyes to see the true world around them.

Michael's eyes seemed black, his voice like a raver as he spoke, "See me…feel me…this is my life…this is my pain…my rage…my sword!" his voice choked the words, spat them as if crying out his last. His aura

---

suddenly raged, engulfing him and the ancient sword in the inferno of the shifting air. The remaining men took a single retreating step. The weapons they held were dwarfed by the great sword wielded before them.

Michael rushed toward the raiders like a lion leaping upon his prey. The first two fell quickly to a single stroke of the sword, defeated simply by the sure speed of the attack. Though the sword was unfamiliar in his hands and nothing like the sleek, thin blade he was accustomed to, it was well-balanced, almost perfectly, and he wielded it valiantly.

In a matter of quick steps, he was across the room again, already engaging the last three men at once. Michael was consumed with the euphoria of his release. Never in all his life, had he fought like this. His blood seared through his veins like fire, with a parry and another swift stroke, another raider fell. His footwork danced amongst the remaining two in a volley of steps coming within a hairs' breadth of the strikes of his attackers, but always moving gently aside as though dancing with death himself. The sheer agility he moved with, and even the massive sword itself seemed an enchantment. For such a man as Michael Cross, a man of less than average stature, lean with muscle, but lacking the shoulders of a man who would wield such a large weapon as the great sword, and yet he wielded it nonetheless. Without so much as a word, Michael defeated the two men that defiantly remained.

He stood solemnly alone amidst the carnage in his wake and tried to calm the fires burning within him. He refused to release any more of his rage, his pain, his Cross. Three times, he turned to one of the fallen before him and touched the hilt of the dagger he carried at his side. Three times, he battled against the urge to carve the cross into the faces of those he had slain. It was like a compulsion, an urge for something he had to do. Michael

—

could not fathom the origin of this desire, this malicious intent, but his thoughts were interrupted by the abrupt appearance of three high lords who unexpectedly burst into the chamber.

The light of the room struck the face of the leading man, and Michael could see in clear cut clarity the focus of his inner turmoil. The leading man was none other than Lord Raymark Lafey. His cross-wounded face just beginning to scab over.

As the three entered, Lord Raymark stopped dead in his tracks upon the realization of who stood before him. The other two lords briskly walked past him, and approached Michael. "Michael Cross! What has happened here? Who are these men?"

"They tried to take the sword, and I believe they set fire to the courtyard."

"And you stopped them, how?" One lord asked.

Lord Bervenmer, the true high lord of Lindell, interrupted without the slightest condolence to the other Lord.

"Clearly, you can see he has withdrawn the legendary sword, and that alone is wonder for questioning. But even still I believe this day was meant to come. I only hope that you have the control to wield yourself as well as the sword. The thing within the Cross line is a dangerous one, a curse perhaps, but if you are to relinquish the stains upon your name then perhaps the sword will guide you to that path…"

"What are you talking about?" Michael asked.

"We have a service for you, last of the Cross." Lord Bervenmer said, wielding a walking staff as though he were in council with the essence of fate itself. Lord Bervenmer had become the high lord at an early age, and his presence here served as chance, or fate. The other Lord, who was with them, whose question had previously been ignored, Lord Weston, spoke directly preceding the last words of Bervenmer's, "You have fulfilled your duty and oath in thwarting this treacherous attempt and I deem that in order to continue your service you must be allotted a chance to reclaim some of the honor you have lost. It would seem the Great Sword of Lindell is not safe in its present place. I sense something terrible will happen if it is to fall into the hands of whoever has planned this…deception." As Weston spoke, Lord Raymark made his way about the room observing the men who had attempted the assault. "They are from Zwentor…special military, disguised as merchants. It would seem we may be going to war." Lord Raymark said with a chill in his voice.

"We must send word to the kingdom of Jarum." Lord Bervenmer hastily spoke.

"We will send riders to Jarum, but as for you Michael Cross, I believe it is best to leave the sword in your hands for now. This will be a rather odd request for me to make of you, Michael, but I want you to carry it with you on a trek to Singe, the capital city of Trengar. There you must seek the high council and inform them of what has happened here." Weston spoke earnestly.

"He will go alone?" Lord Raymark asked, his words quelled with a deep anger.

"Yes, I fear only the three of us must know of the swords' true location…within the hands of Michael Cross. If we rally or debrief anyone, there could be a leak; he may be followed, and the one behind this may overtake him before he ever reaches Trengar. Unless, of course, Lord Raymark, you wish to ride with him?"

The mockery of this was known to everyone in the room, but Raymark seemed to actually ponder the question for a moment, rolling it over and over in his mind as though he consulted something much higher than himself. "Not a chance...I just find it fool-hearty to trust this *raver* of men." The counter, the words pierced the air, but had no effect on the stone like expression of Cross.

"I didn't ask for this...I didn't want this..." Cross muttered. They ignored him. "Michael, when you return to the main floor of the estate I want you to leave from the servants entrance-keep the sword covered, and make your way to the stable in the courtyard. Go to the one with a blue flag and the sign of a stag. Do you hear? A stag?!"

"Yes, I hear you, my lord."

"Good. Once there, you will find a chestnut stallion, the fastest in my stock. I want you to take him and ride until you can no more. Now go Michael Cross! Go!" Weston was gripping him by the shoulders as he gave the instructions, and now hurtled him toward the door. It seemed as though a fear stricken Weston as he spoke and somewhere in Michael's mind, he noticed the constant fearful glances the lord was casting towards Lord Raymark, but at the time Michael paid no notice. "My luck is with you, and all the blessings that god can grant." As the lords watched Michael make his way around the bend of the hall Weston turned to Lord Raymark, standing precariously amongst the bodies. A dark shadow was cast across the stern expression of his scarred face. Michael's footsteps could be heard descending the stairwell in the distance.

"What troubles you, my son?" The old high Lord Bervenmer said as he moved towards Lord Raymark. As Raymark let his eyes meet the gaze of the high lord, an evil leapt forth from within him, assaulting the high

---

lord's aura. "Lord Raymark?!"

4

As Michael continued down the stairs of the manor he thought he heard something, but when he stopped to listen he could hear nothing, and continued running down the stairs. He made his way through the estate, and along the way grabbed a few things he instinctually knew he would need. He took a dark cloak found upon a chair and a tablecloth from one of the dining rooms he passed through. In the tablecloth he wrapped the great sword, and tied it with the old belt and harness of his now-broken sword. He donned the cloak and made his way towards the kitchen. He hoped he could grab a bit of jerky, or some other provision he might need, but when he approached he could hear the scrambling of several people looking for pots, bowls, or whatever else they could use to send water to the flaming courtyard. Michael chose to continue to the service entrance and not to raise suspicions.

After retrieving the stallion Lord Weston had spoken of in the stables, he quietly moved through the city at a blistering speed. He ran wildly down dark alleys and amidst the shadows of the least populated streets. He finally came to the southern gate. It was apparent that no one knew about the fire in the courtyard, or that anything was amiss at all. Michael was actually thankful that the raiders had aided his own 'escape' by preventing the sounding of the alarm, but the life of the boy who guarded it was too high of a price for Michael's joy. Instead he dammed himself for even thinking such thoughts.

As he approached, he extended his right hand out towards the guard as he passed on the stallion. The silver ring upon the middle finger of his right hand, bearing the crest of lordship was all he needed, and the gates were opened without question.

Michael rode out into the open air of the land and let the horse unleash its pent up energy built from long days of rest. The stars loomed overhead like a million diamonds and the further he rode from the unnatural lighting of the cities of Lindell, the clearer the sky became. He rode hard through the line of trees which bordered the forests of Trengar, and only when he had distanced himself from the fading light of the cities did he slow his pace.

They rode all through the night, and when Michaels finally looked up, he realized in less than four hours it would be dawn. Michael had ventured well into Trengar, and it was a reasonable enough distance to stop and rest. Though tired, Michael rode on a little further, seeking a suitable place to rest for the remainder of the night. He had no sooner begun to spur the stallion forward for their final stretch only to then scream to a halting stop.

The horse had seen nothing of the cliffside; Michael had, but not until the last moment. He had been looking at the large lake of water that could be seen through the tree line, and in the center of that lake he had thought he'd seen a glimmer of light. It appeared to be solid, reflecting the colors of the water it rested in and the light of the moon and stars, but this was not what caught Michael's attention. The roaring sound, the screams of what sounded like a hundred lions echoed before them. It was the lake of water, it was pouring over the side of…and he saw it just in time, the cliff, which would have certainly spelled death for him and the stallion. They

—

stopped with inches to spare, and as the steed shifted its weight back from out over the edge, Michael could see a clear bird's eye view of what lay beyond.

The whole extent of Trengar stretched out before him, and upon its magnificent surface of thick forest were several vast waterfalls and tall plateaus covered in lush wood, but in their center was something he couldn't quite make out. Was it a tower built upon their plateau? No, it seemed to touch the heavens and glimmer with the light of the stars as if they were made of crystal. Michael had never heard of crystal towers, but they were there nonetheless.

Towers or not, they loomed in the skyline upon every plateau that had raised itself up from the forest like a scar, but the beauty of the waterfalls flowing from their peak alluded to an astounding magnificence.

The horse urged Michael away from the edge, taking him from the view and towards the shimmering water he had seen through the tree line. The horse didn't care about the scenery and had grown tired from the hard riding. Michael took hold of the saddle and reins and dismounted. He walked beside his newfound steed as they approached the river he had seen earlier.

As the horse drank, Michael followed the rushing water to the edge of the cliff and looked down out at the forest and towers in the distance. The waterfall roared over the edge of the cliff, thousands of gallons pouring forth; Michael hadn't expected such a sight. Michael came to the edge of the river a bit away from the cliff, and drank the cool, crystal clear water. It was refreshing. *'Best if I camp here tonight, and tackle that cliff face in the daylight. This is a good horse, but I doubt he makes a good mountain goat.'* He humored himself a little, trying to shake the near death experience from his

—

87

mind.

Michael spoke openly in his thoughts, trying to make sense of the days' events and his next course of action. He tied the reins of the horse to a tree near the river and sat down against the tree. He thought intensely until the fatigue of the ride, the battle, his wounds, and the wine he had drank finally caught up with him. He fell soundly asleep for the second time that night, undisturbed by any voices, visions, or dreams. Only the soft swelter of the flowing river and the roar of the falls lulled within his mind.

Part 4:

The Staff of Trengar

I

When the morning sun first dripped its rays upon the land, Michael's eyes went suddenly wide ripping him from his light sleep. He drank a buckets worth of water from the stream, mildly suppressing his early hunger. Once he had collected himself, he rose to his feet and untied the reins of the stallion. Michael led the horse from the crystal clear stream and walked back to the road they had been on the night before.

Michael could see the rough grooves where the hooves of the horse had drug hard and deep into the dirt road in order to stop from going over the cliff. *'That was a close one,'* he thought as he noticed how close to the edge they actually extended. He once again looked out over the cliff face, and out upon the forests of Trengar. The trees stretched for miles; he could make out several rivers in the morning light and the plateau like mountains he had observed the night before could now be seen clearly.

The plateaus were dotted across the landscape every few miles, varying in sizes. Most reached several hundred feet or more above the monolithic trees of the forests beneath them. Upon their flat peaks, which were several acres in diameter, were small lakes of water and in the center of the lakes were the towers which seemed to be scraping beyond the cloud line of the sky. The towers, Michael could now see, were not anything built by man, but a mysterious wonder of the world itself. They were

—

constructed of nothing more than ice, frozen water molecules of the atmosphere. The towers were constantly forming in the high pressure of the atmosphere as the water molecules froze in the extremely cold 'spots' in the sky which formed the towers. The ice would then grow more and more dense as the sky pressed greater amounts of ice upon it, and the ice towers had formed like stalactites in the sky.

The towers would rest in the center of one of these plateaus and form a lake, but since the tower was constantly forming at its top, and constantly melting at the bottom, the lake would overflow, and the waterfall would form along the lowest slope of the plateau. The falls would blast their freezing cold water thousands of gallons at a time over the edge of the cliff and down the hundreds of feet to the forest below. Rivers connected several falls together, and in some places a small lake would form.

Michael remembered reading about these anomalies of Trengar many years ago. Some of the wise men of Lindell had told ancient stories of many millennia ago when God had hurled massive 'arctic' stones through the sky and into the once barren desert land of Trengar. The 'arctic' stones were so cold that when they had pierced the sky they had altered it; creating an icy hole in the atmosphere where water would constantly freeze and form the ice towers, right down to the large craters the stones had made. The craters had been like giant bowls and the stones that had come through the sky were now hot from their plummet to the earth. They had been changed, the way the sky had transformed, and when the icy towers grew down from the sky and entered the craters which held the stones, they began to melt from its heat. When the bowls of the craters were full, the cycle continued and the water had poured over the sides and formed the falls.

Michael believed the story to be part truth and part legend. Whichever it proved to be, despite their glorious beauty, their mysteries pertained little to him or the task at hand. After clearing some brush from one side of the road, Michael found the path he had intended to take, mounted his steed, and continued his trek through Trengar.

After making his way down the winding road, which was little more than the well-used path of some animal of the forest, he found a sign stuck in the center of a forked road that the trail had led to. Pointing to the road at his left the sigh read: CAPITAL OF TRENGAR: SINGE. The one pointing right read: ROAD TO GREENHEARTH. Michael simply continued his path on the road to Singe He realized the road was well traveled and developed, so he let the stallion burst forth with a steadier gait once more and continued his hasty journey to the capital of the forest region.

2

Cross rode steadily for the entirety of that day, stopping only twice to allow the horse to graze and drink. Michael had cursed himself for not getting provisions from the kitchen of the estate, but his haste and secrecy was more important at the time, and he accepted this as fate. Drinking at the foot of the falls of one of the ice spire plateaus was very refreshing, though, and this made him think of a story he had heard of the significance of the falls. It was said that the stones that had fallen from the heavens had given life to Trengar, and that those who drank directly from their streams could be healed of all ailments. Michael wasn't sure the water had healing properties, but it had indeed seemed to dampen his hunger to a dull roar.

After continuing his ride late into the evening, he stumbled upon the ruins of a seemingly ancient temple. He was so fatigued from his trek that he found it difficult to dismount the horse. Once on the ground, he made his way to one of the starlit stone pillars that was poised for an eternity in what appeared to be a long dead and unused courtyard, overgrown with a soft mossy grass that offered some comfort to his exhausted body.

Michael settled against the stone, his back braced against ancient carvings whose inscriptions had been weathered to a decayed blur. Despite the wear, if he had wanted he could have read the inscriptions and lore of the old ways, but Michael's fatigue had long since consumed him. As the horse began to graze happily amidst the courtyard, Michael slept beneath the stars of Trengar for a second night, and for a second night he had a restful dreamless sleep.

3

When Michael opened his eyes to the morning light, he found himself staring at the engraved metal tip of a long wooden staff a mere three inches from his face. "I was wondering how long you would sleep with me standing over you- staff poised at your face and all- ready to kill you at a moments' notice," the figure wielding the staff said in a disturbingly jovial voice.

The staff was the first thing to come into true focus; it was intricately carved with all manners of mysterious and beautiful runes and symbols. The figure towered over Michael, his mere height was belittling to five and a half foot tall Michael Cross. This man was lean, lengthy, with all outstretched limbs entwined in muscles far too numerous to measure. His forearms were armored with black silken wrapping. He wore a sleeveless black shirt of a material Michael did not recognize beneath a dark green tunic that was the color of the forest, which was also sleeveless. His black pants were very loosely fitted at the hips, and fastened tight from the knee down with stealthy black leather boots. His tunic was form fitting, with a flowing sash matching his pants and the strip of cloth he had bound across his forehead, which pushed back the large spikes of black hair jutting from the cloth. His complexion was dark and mysterious,, and he was obviously younger than Michael. His stern, wide face seemed to conceal a blatant smirk just beneath its surface.

"I am Danube Drakendor, son of Ishlie Drakendor, High Lord of Trengar. Speak your business in the temple of Nalps, or be killed on the ground like a dog." There was a pause in his speech. "I do beg pardon if I seem rude, but it would appear the world has fallen upon perilous times, and therefore I am bound to ask these questions in such an inhospitable manner as this."

"You don't know the half of it…Do you always talk like that?"

"Like what?"

"Like explaining yourself before giving a guy a chance to answer a threatening question - if so, it wouldn't pose as much of a threat for long" Michael said, as he rose casually to his feet and pushed the staff away from his face.

"I suggest you answer the question before making another move like that" the man glared with the utmost seriousness.

"I am Michael…" His words fell short as the impending stare of Danube Drakendor pierced through his very heart. It was as though the man were looking directly at the grief and shame within him. Despite this, he swallowed his nerves and continued. "…Cross. I seek the council of Trengar."

And it was out of the bag so to speak, *Cross*, the match, to the fire which suddenly blazed in the eyes of Danube Drakendor.

"You…are Michael Cross?! The last Cross remaining in the land?" Danube continued incredulously after a brief nod of affirmation from Michael. "Then I'm afraid you and I have a far more pressing matter between us. I apologize, but I'm afraid I cannot allow you to leave this place."

Michael, well aware of his family's bloody history within Trengar, found the tone in the young man's voice to be suddenly very pressing with a venomous insistence as though he urged to release something he had held his whole life. It was the same feeling Michael supposed he felt when he finally decided to reach out and claim the sword. At the time, he couldn't have wanted anything more; Now, though, he second-guessed the decision he had made in those perilous moments. It was that look, however, that very feeling, that he could see surge within the eyes of Danube Drakendor. Michael wanted away from his gaze more than anything.

"I have no pressing matter with you, friend. I only…"

Danube snapped his free hand before him, cutting off Michael's words with the snap of his fingers. "You are false in your statement, Lord Michael Cross!" His words were soaked with disdain. "I am not to be mistaken as your friend!"

Michael was furious with his interruption, but still wanted more than anything to be away from the young man. "I give you one warning my…" He held his words before again using the familiar reassuring endearment toward the stranger, "…You do not wish to quarrel with me. I did not come to this place in order to settle some dispute we supposedly have. I only wish to deliver word to your council, word which pertains to the safety of

---

the land." Michael took a moment to eye the great sword still propped against the pillar behind him. The tablecloth had done well to cover the dull looking blade, but now draped over it in a precarious manner which reminded Michael of the large white cloths they would place over the statues in the city, just before their unveiling. Michael hoped that today the sword would go on wearing its shroud. *Sorry folks! There will be no unveilings today!* He thought, picturing a finely dressed bureaucrat of sorts sponsoring the unveiling of some great work of art.

"Fool! Is it really possible you know so little of your lineage that you know nothing of the Drakendor, of the plight of the Cross?" He demanded, breaking into Michael's frivolous thoughts.

"I know of the atrocities that my forefathers committed, but I myself am not responsible for the sins of my father. I am my own man, free from the curse of the Cross!" His own words struck deep within himself upon the recent realization of his own cursed susceptibility to his namesake's power. *'I did not ask to be a Cross, let alone, the last. The last one, to bear the sins of all those before me... so it seems...this will always be my fate?'*

"You are free from nothing. Your blood is soaked with the pain of my family, the pain of my father." An impossibly dark shadow, for this bright morning, drew across the face of Danube. "I swore in secrecy, when I was very young, that I would repay the Cross for their deeds. I am the last of the Drakendor, a marvel like you. The last of our lineage resides within us. Nearly all of my family was slain during the plight of the Cross, and those who did not immediately die suffered for many years until the end. My father, Ishlie Drakendor was the last to die. He suffered the remainder of his life after the war, bearing the *cross* on his face until his death.'

"You see, Michael, you and I are two of a kind, and we are left with

---

the burden of settling something we never started. It is our duty to end this, and fulfill our families' honor."

A look of anger dipped in shame dwelt upon Michael's face. "I have little honor left. Therefore, I do not believe the sins of the Cross will ever find atonement, but I will fight you nonetheless if it should bring honor to you, and to *your* namesake." Michael reached behind him and picked up the Great Sword of Lindell. With a jerk, he pulled the cloth from the blade of the sword and cast it aside, just as the finely dressed man would have done at his great gallery unveiling.

The blade was still tarnished, beaten, and as dull as it was the first time Michael had seen it, but he now knew the power it possessed. He held his breath in awe at the weapon in his own right hand. As Michael unveiled the splendid weapon, Danube's eyes grew with a frightening interest, totally focused on the now naked steel.

"Tell me Michael Cross…What kind of sword do you have there?"

"I hold before you, the legendary Great Sword of Lindell." Michael spoke low and to the point.

Danube's eyes narrowed with a cynical understanding of fate. "Ah, then my eyes do not deceive. It would seem then, that this battle truly is destined…" Danube swung his staff about him and just as swiftly brought it to rest, eye level with Michael. "What I hold before *you*, is the legendary Staff of Trengar…"

Before he'd finished his words, Danube lunged forward and made his first attack, it was light, just a tap to see if Michael was really a willing opponent. Michael reflected the wooden staff easily, and rushed in with his own weapon. Battle had engulfed the two young men, and only blood could ease the fury they both now felt.

———

The sword felt heavy and unfamiliar to Michael. He knew the power it held, and he could still remember how it had felt two nights prior, how easily it was to move the heavy steel. Then, he was righteous in his actions and it had felt as light as his rapier, but now, against this man, whose quarrel with him was of a justifiable cause, the sword felt like lead. And with a heavy heart he struggled to keep Danube's attacks at bay.

It was apparent that Danube was familiar with his weapon, and his laughter only emphasized the effect that his intimidating skill was holding on Michael. By the look in Danube's eyes, Michael presumed he knew this.

As their battle ensued with the clash of the legendary weapons, the whole world seemed to be bending to their battle. The sky overhead grew dark with black clouds. Thunder rolled in the distance and lighting shot down from the sky around the ice spires which pierced the heavens. The first drops began to fall just as the two warriors paused in their relentless battle, breaking momentarily from their unyielding attacks.

Cross could hear the faint ringing of the drops of water hitting the flat steel face of his readied sword. He could *feel* every drop upon the blade, and the tension of power that seemed to be increasingly growing between the two legendary weapons. It was as if they pulled towards each other, both crying out for battle. Danube's eyes locked with Michael's, and he understood that both warriors could feel the same tension of power between the ancient weapons.

In a flash of lightning, Danube moved the staff about himself once more, breaking the plummeting path of the rain before him, and lunged for Michael Cross. Michael blocked the first strike in a spray of rain water which shot from the colliding weapons. In dismay, he watched the rebounding staff change directions and gracefully turn as another attack.

The sword felt impossibly heavy, and still rang in his hands from the first tremendous blow. It now proved helpless in Michael's defenselessly open state.

The staff came in an arc which Michael only half-perceived, and with a clash of thunder struck the right side of his face. Michael fell to the ground in a spray of blood that shot from his mouth through clenched teeth.

The ground hurt, the gash in the side of his head hurt worse, but the grating of his not-quite-loose teeth and the ringing 'thud, thud, thud...' in his mind was the worst pain he had ever felt in his life. He spit the remaining blood from his mouth, then wiped a single streak which had found its way to his right eye, and stood readying the sword once more.

"It would seem, Michael Cross that you don't know the sword you hold. When exactly did you become its master?"

With another spit of blood Michael answered with a bloody and outlandish smile. "The night before last...I had never even touched its hilt until then, and as you can see...I've had loads of time to practice." His smile was outright sinister and soaked with sarcasm.

"Yeah...I can see that..." Danube answered with little favor to Michael's sarcasm, and an almost solemn feeling of disappointment.

Another bloodstained spit as he drew the massive sword back and struck more valiantly than before. The attack was true, his footwork precise as ever, but the blow was blocked, then his parry was blocked, and again, despite all his effort the staff once again rang against his skull with a thud. The strike was so loud and hard that he was certain he heard thunder accompany the sound. Michael dropped to one knee, clutching the left side of his head with his free hand and spitting more blood onto the rain soaked

—

grass before him.

"You're good Michael Cross, but you are far too slow."

"Fu..Ck...YoU!" Michael tried to say while choking on his own blood.

"I hate to see you like this Michael. I was hoping this would be an equal con..."

The pain and pounding in Michael's head had swelled to a point of reeling consciousness. All he could hear was the thudding of his own beating heart and the rush of blood through his skull. Danube's words were lost to him, drowned out. ...*I'm not...going to die like this...* The profanities rang amidst his thoughts, expressing his frustration.

The current situation seemed to weigh itself against life within Michael's thoughts and his raw emotion once again filled his heart in rage. Somewhere beneath the beating of his heart and the bloody liquid echo within his head he could hear a familiar pulsing, a different beat beginning to consume all else. It was the beating, shuddering rage of the power of the Cross.

"...You still in there Michael Cross?" Danube mocked as he lingered above the kneeling Michael Cross several yards away. "I suppose I should end your pain now and just get it over with, but I must say I am very disappointed. I always thought..." Danube let his speech trail away with the rain as Michael rose to his feet once more. "...I'll be damned. Looks like you aren't done after all..."

"Curse...you..." Michael said with his head hung low, his rain soaked hair hung like a madman over his face, casting a dark, impenetrable shadow across his eyes. The sword was clenched tightly in his right hand, its blade resting on the ground like a cane, supporting half his weight. The rain struck the steel with little 'pangs' like a ringing melody and gently streaked down its angled sides and face. Lightning flashed again, and its light danced fearsome shadows and reflections across the blade and Michael's form.

"Such profanity, why spoil a good fight with such words?" Danube was deliberately trying to turn his fear to insults, but Michael could still see the alarm slowly growing in the back of those calm eyes of the Trengar lord. Michael began to laugh with a comical lightning lit smile.

A thunderhead rolled out its song overhead, and Danube felt like cold electricity was running up his spine when he held the gaze of Michael Cross. In a flash of lightening, he could see what gave Michael his sudden motivation, his gall. Danube could see the faint glimmer of Michael's aura, but to his dismay, it was a sight that could not ever be unseen.

Now that he could see Michael clearly, and the aura of power flared amidst the darkest breeches of reality, he could not help but watch it take shape around his form as it grew in strength. Many people could *see* a glimmer of a person's aura, but they had to tap into their own *true sight* to possibly behold such a thing in its entirety. In another flash of lightening, Danube could see that comedic smirk once again, and could see even more clearly what was transpiring in Michael Cross. His body radiated light and the rain seemed to repel from him as though the water were his polar opposite. Danube could feel the pressure of Michael's power building against him, but before he could react to this sudden surge in strength, Michael raised his sword. Reaching the peak of his uncontrollable fury, Michael charged the unready warrior, his grey eyes flashing fear into the young Lord's heart.

Danube drew upon his ancient magick as quickly as he could, but his attempt to surpass Michael's strength was in vain. The great sword struck the legendary staff with such force that no presence of life or stone went untrembled. The echo of the collision resonated amidst the ruins of the temple, shaking the pillars, and freeing masses of loose rock.

The explosion receded and the earth stilled itself once more. The falling of the heavy raindrops once again consumed all sight. Michael and Danube remained alive, standing in the center of a clearing amidst the pillars, locked in the fierce void of their struggle. Both could see the auras, the blazing power which made the air around them ripple as though they were aflame. The two warriors remained in balance amidst each other's' power, neither giving way to any attempt to surpass the other.

Danube was stunned by the sudden *revealing* of Michael strange power. "I must ask you…" Danube said, still grinding his teeth with the strain of the hold. "…where'd you suddenly get your strength from? Have you simply been holding out on me all along? Say it isn't so?!" He inquired. Michael had no answers for the young warrior, he only surged more of his fury into the struggle as a response, but Danube simply matched it in magick.

"Impressive…I have never battled anyone who has come close to matching me in magick. Such a shame I had to beat this out of you. I really do apologize, but I can see that you are deaf to such things…I do have one question though. What is it that drives you? What element do you draw from to possess such strength? Never have I felt this kind of power. Tell me, who taught you this magick!?"

"That…was three questions…" Michael roughly pointed out to the younger warrior.

Danube gritted his teeth at such a foolish insult, but Michael's answer directly followed, and in a blast of strength the rage quelled within his form like a squall. Every image of hate and pain and sorrow filled his mind, fueling what Danube perceived as Michael's final release. The fallen Lord Cross blasted every ounce of power into Danube's staff, and in the wake of this oncoming force, Danube took a single retreating step. Then, quickly pivoting with his other foot, glanced all of the power which Michael had presented. Michael was taken off guard and fell forward, his attack following through on one of the ancient pillars standing in his path. The stone erupted into a showering explosion of dust and rubble.

Michael now stood amidst the rubble, completely off kilter. As quickly as Danube had taken his step, he suddenly leaped the distance between them, and with unnatural fluidity he thrust his staff forward like a spear striking, Michael directly in the chest and throwing him once more into the ground.

His lungs were on fire and he made hollow, lurching gasps for life, but was unable to catch even the faintest breath. He couldn't even cry out in pain. "A great power you possess Michael Cross, but I don't believe you understand it. It hinders me to think that such strange power is even remotely close to my own. It damn near frightens me. Especially since I've spent my life in the study of magick, and I can't seem to recall a single instance where I ran across anything like what you just showed me."

Michael continued to gasp relentlessly for air, clutching at his chest as though he thought to rip himself apart.

"You see, Michael Cross…you can't possibly match my magick. You may come close, but you cannot even hope to defeat me." As Danube spoke his eyes met with his, and Michael could *feel* how incredibly weak he was in comparison to the younger man. Cross shuddered as he caught his breath, and thought that very soon he would draw his last.

4

As Michael lay upon the ground, he struggled to regain his bearings amidst the agonizing pain as the storm began to recede overhead. Danube Drakendor stood over him like a specter. To his back, the temple overlooked a small valley bordered by a steady line of trees, and small cliffs upon which the temple resided. The large clearing was a field of waist high grass with what appeared to be some type of small bulbs upon the top of every other stalk. In the distance, where the sky seemed to be clearing, Michael could make out the peaks of the small mountains holding the ice towers stretching high from their tops and the great waterfalls pouring over their peaks. His mind had somehow been snared by the beautiful view before him, and his thoughts and fears of impending death seemed to roll away with the parting storm. Directly overhead, the sky turned an enchanting blue where the clouds parted in large holes and massive beams of fresh sunlight poured down over the forests. One of these rays of light happened to shine directly at the edge of the forest across the small valley of knee high grass, and what Michael Cross saw made his blood run cold.

Danube could see the vaguely disconnected look in Michael's eyes suddenly snap to another look of utter terror. He had no idea what Michael had been dazedly observing before, but he was sure he had knocked most of the sense from him. Now though, now he looked as though he had seen a ghost. Danube was sure by the look in Michael's eyes that death stood at his back.

"What are you looking at Michael?"

Michael only pointed with a trembling hand in the direction of the clearing.

Danube, well aware of age old tricks to get an enemy to turn their backs, did not think twice to actually look. He knew the fear in his opponent's eyes, and could feel it breathing at the back of his neck in the same way Michael's power had made him feel during their battle. A great force was approaching him from behind, and the stillness in the air made his throat catch as he turned. What he saw made an icy chill run through his blood.

At the edge of the forest, emerging silently from the tree line, walked a young and beautiful woman. Her long black hair tore through the wind, as did the tatters that were her clothes. She had a small bag slung across her slim form and in her right hand, off to her side, was a massive scythe gleaming in the sunlight. As she walked into the field, the beam of light seemed to follow her, surrounding her for about thirty feet. As the light from the heavens touched the grass stalks, the ones with bulbs instantaneously unfolded and their leafy exteriors exposed lovely flowers. The flowers' opening in response to the sunlight was by far the most beautiful thing Michael had ever seen. But as he took awe, the woman, who calmly walked amidst the blooming flowers, gently began swinging the massive scythe back and forth before her with the simplest of ease. She was decapitating the blooming flower bulbs in her path, which spoiled the scene entirely. Her aura seemed to strike the deepest cord of fear in Michael's heart, and he knew that more than anything he no longer wanted to be anywhere near the temple, Danube, or the woman who approached them.

"...Michael... She's got the scythe..." Danube said as he still stared in her direction. To Michael's relief, he lowered his staff, but what the young warrior did next he never would have guessed. Danube shifted his staff from his right hand to his left and stepped to Michael who had propped himself to a sitting position against one of the stone pillars. Michael looked up at the man who now held out his hand, but Danube's eyes were locked on the woman across the field. Michael reluctantly took Danube's firm grip and tried to get to his feet. As he rose, his head once again boomed out *THUD, THUD, THUD,* and his world swooned and began to spin. Michael started to fall back, and would have struck the pillar behind him with his head, but Danube caught him, and held him steady while Michael's bearings returned. Danube never once removed his eyes from the woman across the field still executing the blooming flowers as she approached.

"Are you all right Michael?" He said with a disconnected gaze, but for a moment Michael thought he heard true concern. It was almost like two childhood friends who had just had a serious fight, and after one had hurt the other they had returned to childhood chums, and concern had replaced anger. Danube Drakendor was not his childhood chum, nor was he a friend in any way, but he was perhaps a great ally, given the circumstance.

"Are you all right Michael? Can you ride?" He repeated.

Still shaking the image of childhood friends, Michael slapped an open palm to his forehead, "My head's stopped spinning, but I think so, why?"

"I'm afraid *our* battle must be delayed, but don't think I won't find you again..."

Michael nodded at this. "I know you will."

"I guess you can consider this a chance for you to become stronger, hone your power. I think we'll both need you at your best in the coming days."

"What do you mean? Do you really think that's the scythe from Reum?!"

"Aye, and I also believe there is something far bigger going on here..." There was a long silence between the two men. For a brief moment, one which felt like hours or days, they merely stood on the gully of the cliff near the edge of the temple courtyard staring out at the scene before them.

"I'm sorry we were interrupted. I will give you the chance to reclaim your family's honor someday if that is what you wish."

"Aye...but right now we both have more important matters we must attend to."

Danube placed a hand on Michael's shoulder and finally took his gaze from the approaching woman so that he could look into Michael's bloody and already swelling face. "A very large part of me hates you to an unjustifiable degree, but we are still two of a kind, and we are well met. I must tell you Michael...if you were any other man than the last of the Cross, because of what I've seen of you today I would consider having you as a friend."

"Aye, and you as well...if only circumstances allowed." Michael returned with a deep touch of emotion, and considered a moment. "...Two of a kind?" Michael gazed at the young man.

"Two of a kind..." Danube repeated, and they chuckled. It was a forced and awkward laugh, but it was still true.

Once their short bond was recognized and passed, Danube returned his gaze to the woman, who was now half the distance across the field.

"She's very powerful…" Michael half stated.

"…so she is." Danube's voice had grown dim and solemn once more.

"Would you have me fight with you?"

"No, I must fight her alone amidst the wood. She would slay us both if we tried to make a stand out here in the open."

Michael found this hard to stomach. He had just seen how far Danube surpassed him in power, and yet the young warrior held deep seeded fear in his eyes. *How powerful is she?* Michael wondered.

"Michael, you must continue to Trengar and seek the council. Tell them what happened here today, and that the scythe is near. Tell them you are…a friend. Show them this." Danube removed a small wooden medallion from an inside pocket of his tunic and handed it to Michael. "Take it. They will know what to do." Michael took the medallion from him and studied it a moment, running his fingers along the carvings and gold inlay with admiration before placing it in his own inner pocket.

"What about you?"

"I'm going to go see if she's lost." Danube let a loose smirk fly, but it wasn't out of place on the young warriors face. In fact, Michael thought it looked just about right for his age. After judging the concern on Michael's face, Danube continued. "Don't worry about me Michael. We'll meet again, and when we do…I hope you're ready." The smirk held, and he extended a hand to Michael. "Until then Michael Cross…"

Michael shook hands with a smile, but he couldn't help turning the thoughts in his mind. *…until next time.* Michael wondered if next time either of them would be so lucky as to shake hands and walk away.

Having said his goodbye, Michael placed two fingers firmly in his

———

lips and whistled the best he could. He had never really tried the trick before himself, but had seen many a rider just as easily summoned their horse in such a fashion. Luckily, the horse didn't make him look like a complete fool. It had run a good distance from the temple during Michael and Danube's battle, but had lingered back to the ruins as a well trained horse would, checking on its master. When Michael whistled, the horse emerged from the tree line next to the temple and trotted rather sheepishly to the center of the courtyard. It stopped and stared at Michael from a good twenty feet away, apparently not interested in coming any closer to Danube, or the approaching woman. Michael shrugged, "Well, close enough I suppose." Danube laughed at this and raised his hand in salute.

After mounting the horse, Michael made one final glance at the woman in the field, and then to Danube. "Until we meet again..."

"Aye...till then." was Danube's only reply. He was once again looking at the woman. She could clearly see that Michael was making a run for it, but it seemed she had no interest in hastening herself to stop him. *She'll find me anyway. Now or later, it doesn't matter to her. She must only care about the weapons. What else could it be?* These were his last thoughts as he spurred the stallion forward and was suddenly just a blur amidst the trees.

5

Danube stood like the stone pillars of the temple; unmoving, un-trembling in the oncoming wake of the immense power which emitted from the woman. She had made her way through the last of the flowers and now walked with an eerie fluidity up the slope of the hill. Behind her, Danube could see the long straight path she had 'cut' through the forest, the decapitated flower buds lay crushed and wilting in her wake.

Everywhere she steps is death…everywhere she treads is doom…behold her, taker of breath…she will not let the flowers bloom…for here comes reaping time…the widow to the moon…in her hand she holds her scythe…desolate is her womb… Danube heard the verse in his mind, an echo from his past, a song of lore from long ago. It was a long foretold prophesy of many thousands of years, and it played at this moment with such familiarity that he began to truly grasp his impending fear.

Somewhere in Danube's mind he knew that things would play as they were meant to, and he would do his part. Something told him that perhaps some of the old words of the world were not dead, and the things that were meant to happen were happening, playing out just as they had been set to play. He wondered if the old lore and the woman were just a coincidence, but the feelings within him told him otherwise.

As she made her final approach, Danube could now truly *feel* her power. It stuck within him like a knife with every breath. Her mere presence seemed to drive all sense from his reality, distorting time and space itself, skewing the perception of all things other than her. *Her and her power it's…beautiful…*

Every step she made towards him was another knife, another chill down his spine. Her emerald eyes, what Danube could now see were emerald eyes, were locked in place with his. At any moment Danube thought his mind would simply implode from the pressure. *How can she be **this** powerful?!* He thought.

Because I am… echoed in his mind. Danube drew a quick breath at the voice in his mind. It was a soft voice, but one filled with the same ice that froze his blood. Before he had a moment to question the voice within his head -her voice- she had come to a respectable distance and stood

---

silently before him. She held the scythe calmly at her side with ease.

Danube could now see her distinguished features, in her eyes he saw the familiar hardening of years of pain, and the slight premature aging the power she now possessed had inflicted upon her. In her eyes, he could see beneath the entire fiery aura of her spirit, and for just a moment, he could see the very beautiful woman that she was. For that instant Danube lost himself in her beauty and forgot all threat that was posed by such a woman. The attraction was short lived.

"I am Kaire Ra…I have come a great distance seeking the man who has fled from here." It was the same voice, pleasant and cold; direct, straight to the point.

Shaking off his previous disposition, and burying the fear of her power, he held the gaze of the powerful beauty before him and swallowed hard. His mouth had run dry, but he quickly found his 'Lordly' qualities and spoke with authority. "The one you seek…the man of Cross, holds an endeavor of my own which must be kept. Therefore, I cannot allow you to pursue him. For I am Danube Drakendor, son of Ishlie Drakendor, High Lord of Trengar, protector and wielder of the legendary Staff of Trengar. Tell me why is it that you seek him and not me instead? Is it not the legendary weapons you seek?" The words of Danube rang out against the stone and forest, commanding his authority.

At the mention of the staff, her eyes had seemed to take a sudden interest and she took a momentary gander at the staff he held, and then returned his gaze, her face as emotionless as before. "You have one chance to step aside, High Lord." She said High Lord with a hint of disdain.

Danube scowled. "What kind of weak fool do you take me for woman?!"

Kaire seemed to grow anxious and irritated by the delay, but the boldness of the strange lord seemed to intrigue her thoughts nonetheless. "I do not consider you a fool, Danube Drakendor, but if you do not stand aside, a fool you shall be."

Danube's anger only sparked a little, *Play it out, lure her in, use the emotion behind those eyes, don't get cocky...*

"You don't think I *know* how powerful you are, do you? I know the great force of will which surrounds you. It drowns me...chokes me, but I do not fear you, woman. Your power is truly imposing, and would make any run at the faintest glance."

"Then why do you stand before me in defiance? You only delay the inevitable. You are-" Danube cut her short.

"Because despite your power you are weak!" It was a bluff, but Danube was determined to follow through no matter the consequence. "You lack the experience of battle, your form is lithe, your guard is down, and despite the deep rage which burns in your fiercely beautiful eyes..." He had not intended on complimenting her, but it slipped anyway. "...there is fear. You fear bloodshed, you fear opposition, you fear the death on your hands, and that fear shall be your undoing." Somewhere he struck a cord.

"How can you even propose to know such things?! You know nothing of who I am!" Kaire showed her first signs of true emotion, he made her angry, made her frustrated, this was a warrior's greatest downfall, and Danube knew it. He knew the pain a single word could cause and intended to use it as his edge.

Kaire tightened her grip upon the blackened scythe. "I fear nothing!" She hissed.

In response, Danube spoke softly. "Then it would be very

disrespectful of me to hold back, even in the slightest. So, do you know what tells me who you are, and answers what I already know?" She looked at him with a puzzled gaze. *'She is off guard...'* he thought. "...your eyes. They tell me *all* I need to know, and if you try to say different then I shall show you...YOUR FEAR!!!" Before Danube had finished he lunged forward, closing the respectable distance between them. His staff ripped through the air with a strangely wooden and yet metal buzzing, it rang out with the ferocity of his true skill and force honed into the attack with monstrous precision. If such a strike were true, any who stood in its path would surely die. This cold mindset of true battle had slipped into Danube's mind at the moment he had sensed her power, and he had known then that only by trapping the woman would he have any chance of defeating her. Despite her beauty, he could not hold back even in the slightest.

The initial attack was so swift, so sudden, that Kaire had barely any time to react. Nevertheless, she blocked with the long curving black hilt of the scythe. As the weapons collided, Danube driving with all his force, the air between them began to ripple and shift. Physically, Kaire could not deflect, or even hope to block such a powerful blow, but with her will, with the magicks she had been unlocking by the teaching and *love* of the man in her dreams, she could hold back the great force of Danube Drakendor. As he began to overwhelm her with his awesome might, she drew deeply upon her magicks and forced them into the scythe, then countered Danube's attack with all that which she had focused.

The power within the scythe burst forth, the blade swinging in a devilish upward arch that would cleave a man in two, but Danube simply stepped aside, dancing from harm's way. His skill matched her power blow for blow. Instead of blocking most of her attacks directly, he would simply pivot in one way or another avoiding the immense power she seemed to unleash effortlessly. When the weapons did collide, they rang out against each other tenfold compared to Danube's previous battle with Michael.

Danube began to lunge forward like a shadow across the courtyard, making a swift lunge and retreat and a series of intricate attacks against the scythe wielding sorceress. *She still underestimates me…If I could only draw her into the forest I could lessen her magicks' effectiveness with her confusion of the unfamiliar terrain…from there, perhaps I can defeat that ungodly power of hers…*

Kaire wielded the scythe with a fury, casting blows at every angle, desperately trying to end Danube's resistance. Yet with every furious blow Danube would merely parry with his staff or dance aside like a flame. Unknown to Kaire, he was slowly luring her into the forest surrounding the temple, and she was completely oblivious to the change in her surroundings.

With another perilous stroke of the devilish scythe, Danube suddenly released his own magick, taking Kaire Ra completely by surprise. A blast of white light and a gust of wind suddenly burst forth from Danube's staff, and Kaire was forced back, shielding her eyes from the blinding light. When her vision returned Danube was no longer standing before her; in fact, he was nowhere to be seen. Kaire stood suddenly alone amidst the thick forest, scanning the tree line and foliage for any sign of the warrior, but could see no clue to where he vanished. Kaire stood at a loss, completely perplexed, and Danube could already feel the great reduction in her power.

"Have you fled High Lord Danube, shall I pursue the other now?"

———

She spoke with no emotion as she was trying to hide her confusion and fear.

"Nay! For I am here! Can you not sense me? Can you not feel my power, or are you lost within your fear?" Danube's voice echoed amidst the trees. Kaire scowled at his taunts, but regained her solid composure and closed her eyes. The great tension in her face relaxed and she reached out with her mind, looking beyond the barriers of all distraction.

Danube watched her with a fearful admiration as she let her lips turn to a halfhearted smile. She opened her eyes and released her power once more, Danube watched the flames of her aura consume her form; he had finally grown accustomed to seeing it and could no longer 'un-see' it, just as had been with Michael.

With a sudden burst of speed, Kaire dashed through the forest, darting over foliage and lunging off the sides of trees. She covered nearly thirty yards in two blinks of the eye, and when she reached a particular tree she used the building momentum to cut completely through its ancient trunk in a single perfect slash of her scythe. It appeared as though the attack had passed right through it, but as she stood, the tree groaned with the sudden shift in its weight as it began to buckle and fall.

The tree crashed to the forest floor with a deafening thud. Kaire stood poised next to the remaining trunk with her halfhearted smile still strewn upon her face. "Nice attack...but I'm afraid you missed..." The voice of Danube came from a branch some twenty feet up in a nearby tree. Kaire glared at him with her fierce emerald eyes and lunged forward once again. In six steps she ran up the side of the tree, defying the very gravity of the world with her display of skill, but Danube merely waited upon the large tree limb. Kaire flipped off another branch and landed squarely in front of Danube, a respectable distance once again between them. Danube was leaning casually against the main trunk of the tree his arms folded across his chest in relaxed defiance. He wore a vicious smile. "You know something Kaire..." She returned his gaze still in her stance upon the tree limb poised for attack. "...you really don't look very pretty when you're angry." His smile became a wide grin and she swung for him in a hot rage.

Danube blocked her scythe and held it in place with his staff. His grin turned grim and he shook his head. "That's not very nice. I wasn't done speaking." Before Kaire could blink Danube spun his staff, still locked with her scythe, in a precisely calculated spin. The scythe was ripped from Kaire's hands, and launched through the air of the forest until its blade struck a tree and it halted with the *TWANG* of vibrating steel. Fear had finally engulfed her eyes, and she looked at Danube with dumbfounded shock. "How did you..?"

"It doesn't matter *how* I did it. What matters is that I did it, not with my power, or magick, or any other aid, but simple skill. It would seem you're the second person I've encountered today who has obtained immense power without the burden of a lifetime of training and grueling effort." Danube said, with what sounded like resentment.

"YOU KNOW NOTHING OF WHAT I AM OR WHAT I'VE BEEN THROUGH!!!" Kaire was screaming. She apparently did not know what to do, and Danube knew he was about to make her burst with emotional strain. He knew this was a woman who obviously wanted to bury the pain she had endured, and bury the emotion that came with it. But burying something would only hide it for awhile; only subdue the harm it would bring.

Danube had long since lowered his staff once more. His hands were on his hips in his most defiant and yet relaxed of gestures. *'Peter Pan...'* he thought though, he didn't know quite why. He watched as Kaire stood before him, head bent low, her hands balling into fists, hair hanging down over her tormented face. He could see the fire of her aura suddenly beginning to flicker its flames once more, but before she could entrench herself in her power once again, another option suddenly dawned somewhere in the depths of his mind, a little voice which told him to act with such authority that he never had a chance to stop himself.

…As Kaire stood before him, her power readying to explode once more, to retrieve her scythe, and slay the man named Danube Drakendor. She heard a familiar voice tell her that this defeat was acceptable, and that things were already in motion. She did not fully understand, but she knew that now, the other man no longer mattered, but Danube, Danube Drakendor, was someone whom her interests concerned. But as her fiery aura continued to bloom, Danube did the most unexpected thing…

The young warrior of Trengar stepped towards her along the branch, held his staff out to one side, and as he breached half the distance between them, let it fall from his hand. She heard it fall into some bushes below, but she had closed her eyes, the fire in her heart was still burning. *'How could he have disarmed me so easily…Why is he walking towards me…? What is he going to do to me…please not again…'* she thought as Danube broke the distance that separated them.

He took Kaire in his arms, ignoring the searing heat of her skin and the force which surrounded her. He could feel her pain like a hot flash. He could see her life in an instant when he drew her close, one hand at her back the other buried in her long black hair. For a moment she beat at his back with her balled fists, but he only pulled her closer, pressing her face tenderly against his chest. *'Why am I doing this? I don't know this woman…but*

———

somehow…somehow I do…somehow this is right…somehow, I love you Kaire, my widow of the moon…' The images burning in his mind were of all the torment, all the rape, beating, and degrading she had endured. He saw it all, but amidst the memories of her mind he saw a single man, but not a man- more so, a shadow, who had consumed her soul as payment for her revenge. As the last of her images swept through his mind he felt her shudder from utter release, felt the fire of her aura die down, and her skin began to cool. "I'm sorry Kaire…I'm so sorry…" He could no longer see her memories or hear her voice in his mind, but he could feel the heat of fresh tears and the muffled sobs as he held her close to him high in the branches of an ancient tree in the enchanting forest of Trengar. In the distance, he could hear the singing of birds and the rushing of the falls of the ice towers, and the sunlight beamed down upon the two of them from the forest canopy above. Trengar really was Danube's home, and always would be the most beautiful place in existence from this moment on, the moment he held the widow of the moon within his arms and the world stood still.

Part 5:

The Great Apology

Michael Cross rode with a burning fury from the ancient ruins of the temple. He rode towards Singe, the capital city of Trengar, the place of council. The fear which had gripped him upon the sudden presence of the woman in the field, the woman with the scythe, remained. He took a final look back at the two warriors who were no doubt far superior to him. *'Even a fool such as I, who can sense nothing of magick, can tell they are gods among us...'*

The little voice in the back of his mind told him that his only chance of survival lay ahead, to the city of Singe. The distance he did not know, but as he rode, the wounds Danube had previously dealt him slowly took their effect. The blood had stopped pouring from the wound in his head, but he struggled to remain conscious. At several points along the way he had nearly fallen from his horse and sustained even worse injury, but he happened to catch himself each time.

Despite his injuries and his battle for consciousness, the ride proved far less difficult than he had anticipated. It seemed that the young warrior Danube had walked the distance in just under a few hours of the early morning. With the speed of his fresh horse, the time it would have taken Danube on foot was cut to a forth, and he arrived at the edge of Singe in little under a half hour. Michael brought the stallion to a halt at an overhang of a small gully which overlooked Singe. The city lay before him with astounding beauty. Michael had heard many stories of the cities within Trengar, but he himself had never seen such a sight in all his life.

The city consisted of three levels; two of which were built, or grown, Michael wasn't really sure, into a collection of three massive trees. The three trees seemed to dwarf all others in the forest by the sheer diameter of their trunks. They towered over the rest of the forest by several hundreds of feet, easily matching the height of the ice tower plateaus, which there also were three of in the distance. The trees had been planted millennia ago in the middle of the triangle the ice towers made, forming a smaller tri-force of the massive trees.

The first level of the city was like any other, for it resided upon the ground. Roads and streets, shops and taverns, stables and barns, all the things a normal city had, but this was a massed populace, and everything seemed to be blended perfectly around those three trees. It had a natural feel to it, and it reminded Michael of a large nest or hive, everything in its place, though random, all had a purpose.

Massive and intricate wooden stairs had been built leading to the second level of the city, and Michael noted that the stairs continued to the third level and even farther into the canopies of the trees. What struck him as the most interesting development was the unique system of pulleys and wooden platforms; even at this distance he could see moving people and goods from one level to the next., Michael did not know the word 'elevator', but that's what they were, wooden elevators.

Michael couldn't quite tell what all of the different structures that were built into the trees purpose were, but he could see that much care had been taken in their design, and that every element of construction was completely and utterly a work of art. It seemed the culture here was bent on it, and their most prominent medium, of course, was wood.

After looking at the city from his hillside perspective for several moments, Michael noted that he had drawn the attention of a few people in passing, and when the throbbing in his head returned in full once more, and he nearly lost consciousness again, he determined it was a good moment to get moving.

As he led his horse through the dirt roads of Trengar, he unwittingly obtained the attention of many people. He did not know if it had been the blood caked upon his face and brow, or the large sword slung upon his back, wrapped once again in the tablecloth he had acquired, but it seemed that many, far too many people were looking at him.

A red bird suddenly took flight from its perch upon one of the local shops, and flew rather low and close to Michael and his horse. He let his gaze follow its flight, and when the bird flew past Michael looked back, seeing just where it might be headed, and saw the reason for the attention he'd been given. Behind him, twenty paces back, were two men on horseback, slowly approaching.

As soon as the two riders saw that they had been noted they galloped the remaining distance between them and Michael, and rode next to him, one on each side. "We are guards of Singe, we must know your business here, or you must depart immediately." One of the guards said. His face was hidden behind a black strip of cloth tied tightly from the bridge of his nose to his chin; he wore red armor of a material Michael had never seen. The other wore a similar mask and armor, but his was of a light blue. "I am, Michael…" Cross wasn't willing to risk another revenge attempt at this time and therefore had no immediate intentions of giving his full name. "…I have come seeking the council of Trengar on a matter of grave importance to the state of the land…I am a friend of High Lord

Danube Drakendor." With the mention of such a name the guard in red suddenly squint his eyes as though trying to see through some lie Cross had told.

"Is that so...a *friend* of Lord Drakendor. What if I told you our lord has no *friends*?"

"Then I suppose I'd have to call you a liar..."

Michael continued forward upon his horse never breaking stride, he'd dealt with the likes of guards many times. *'Guards, cocky soldiers, and overzealous barkeepers, some had just been doing their jobs, most just insist on being an ass...'*, but Michael figured this one was doing his duty.

"What'd you say to me?!" The armored guard was so shocked by the response that he had brought his horse nearly to a halt.

"I said I'd have to call you a liar, because it just so happens that I *am* a friend of Danube Drakendor, and if you seek proof then I suppose I'll have to show you." Michael snatched the medallion Danube had previously given him from his pocket and held it out to the guard who had once again brought his horse to pace with Michael's. At the sight of the medallion the guard seemed instantly humbled, as though the creator of existence had just tread upon his grave. "I beg your pardon...I didn't..., but I just...don't understand it."

"Pardon given... If you could be so kind, would you show me the way to your council? It is prudent I get there as quickly as possible."

As they spoke, a third rider approached upon a gallant steed coming from the opposite direction and halted their passage. The two guards saluted the new presence before them in unison, standing at attention.

"Well, well, what do we have here?" The man said. He was a broad shouldered man, who sat high upon his steed. His hair was long, pulled back into a neat ponytail, the color of autumn twilight, brown with a reddish tinge. His jaw was defined, that of a man of high decent. His face was lined with a fine beard and 'stache which complimented his confident brow and his penetrating hazel gaze. He wore a fashion of mismatched leather armor and a pair of denmen jeans similar to Michael's.

"Captain Albright! This man seeks the council. He proclaims to be a...*friend* of Lord Drakendor..." The guard spoke in an informative tone.

"Hasn't anyone told him that our Lord has no friends?"

"Aye sir, but he, had this..." The guard showed the medallion which Michael had carried, apparently a well-known artifact of their esteemed high lord.

"How did you get this boy?" Albright said with a suspicious glare.

Until this time Michael had held his tongue, waiting to see just how this would play out. "Danube gave it to me...after we underwent a rather heated encounter ...he gave it to me so that I could bring word of the peril that not only inflicts my region, but your lands as well."

"Aye, then I shall show you the way to our council...personally. As a *friend* of Lord Drakendor it would be my honor to serve you." Albright seemed to believe his story of deluded details without question.

"Would you have us accompany you sir?" One of the guards asked.

"No, I can handle this business myself...return to the edge of Singe and keep up our patrol. You may wish to find another to replace my own patrol for today or at least until my service to this man is finished, but keep your eyes keen and your judgment clear."

"Aye Captain Albright. I shall find another man, don't worry about the rest of the perimeter today. I will take care of it personally. I have a feeling this man is going to need your aid." He nodded and gestured at the gash in Michael's head.

"Spoken true..." Albright said in agreement. As the other guard turned his horse Albright seemed very distant. "What's on your mind stranger?" Michael asked.

Albright frowned. "It is not my place to ask about your wounds, but I must ask you if he's all right...Lord Drakendor?"

Michael sighed. The truth was he didn't know if Danube was 'all right'. He sure as hell hoped so, but that woman's power... "I know that when I left him he was in far better condition than I." Michael said while gesturing at the wound in his head and the swelling of his face. *What else should I say...? Oh he's fighting a sorceress right now who's wielding the legendary scythe of Reum, and well he's...uh...probably dead now, and she's on her way here to cut off all our heads like fuckin' dandelions...But talking like that would get me nowhere way too fast.*

"Aye...suppose that's all a man can say when he's not really sure himself. Would I be right on that?" Albright said without much enthusiasm.

"Aye...I suppose so..."

"Never mind all that. Does your head need attendin' to?" Albright gestured.

The horses continued their march down Main Street, Singe, never breaking stride. Michael let the horses cover a few yards before responding to the question, he appeared lost in thought. "...When we get to the council..." Michael said faintly.

Albright found the sudden change of Michael's condition disturbing. Someone must have dealt a mighty blow to him indeed. Michael seemed vacant, glassy eyed, *knock-knock, nobody's home.* Albright suddenly wondered if the man would stay conscious on the trek up the many ramps and streets of the three levels of the city. He figured he wouldn't, and decided to use the supply lifts instead. *Why not? It would be a lot faster, and it is 'okay', in emergency situations, to use the lifts as transport. Besides, I'm the captain, and who's going to say no to the captain of 'the guard', **especially** in an emergency?* Albright figured this easily counted as an emergency, and took the reins of Michael's horse, and led the barely conscious Michael to the nearest lift.

For Michael, the lift ride to the second level was nothing more than spotty images and shapeless blurs. Darkness seemed to trail at the horizon of his vision, he felt like sleeping, like dying, but each time thoughts slipped that deeply, he would be blinded by another beautiful sight of himself astride the steed which had bore him many miles already, and the forest of Trengar slipping past him as the lift bore them upwards, passing the second level platform without so much as slowing down. There were several people who had been waiting for the lift, waiting to transport goods, equipment, or whatever. Albright could see the frustrated glares as the lift continued its trek upwards. Michael, on the other hand, saw none of this. He had only grasped a few blotchy moments of the world slipping by him, and then he was out once more. Out for the count...

Michael didn't rouse once they'd reached the third level, the level of council. Luckily for Michael, the level of the city devoted to the pursuit of knowledge and specifically that of the medical field. Albright took Michael to the nearest practitioner, which was about the distance of a city block from the lift platform. The polished white wooden building was carved from the trunk of one of the many outstretching branches of the massive tree. A woman wearing a green and white gown emerged from the archway, appearing just as they approached, as though expecting them.

"Quickly now, bring him inside!" The woman said in a stern yet tender voice. Albright dismounted, and handed the reins of the horses to a young apprentice boy who stood nearby. Albright lifted Michael off the horse, and seemed surprised by the sure weight of the man and the sword he bore upon his back. The boy quickly tethered the horses to the post and fetched them cool water for the trough.

Albright managed to haul Michael's limp form into the healer's place of practice and aid the woman in removing the sword and other restrictions from Michael's body. They laid him in a bed of a soft pine, it smelled wonderful, like mint, or menthol, but it was not sharp, nor sticky. Michael rested very easily in this bed of pine as the woman tended to his wounds.

Albright sent a message to the council via the young lad who served as the healer's apprentice. The boy knew how to earn a few dar if he was good. It wasn't much of a notice to the council, but it was better than nothing. He figured Michael would be feeling wonderful in a few hours thanks to his secret mistress, the Lady Annabel, one of the most well versed healers in all of Trengar. He knew how good she was because her magick had saved his life more than once. It was one instance in particular that drew the two lovers together, not many summers ago, when Albright had been wounded in a hunt, and Annabel had been his healer. The wounds from the boar had been arduous, and he had lost a lot of blood. His men had taken him to Lady Annabel in hopes that there was a chance he would survive. In the time of his healing they became lovers, but such a love was forbidden. For any who practiced the white magick of healing were to remain celibate and unwed for the entirety of their lives, this was law. Law was what Albright was made for, but such hypocrisy of love had cut him deep into his own tortuous secrecy. And it was this that troubled his daily thoughts.

Michael was sure to be healed by her in less than a few hours. He assumed that Michael was suffering a concussion, but something of that caliber was nothing to his mistress. He was sure Michael would be fine. The council would still have plenty of time to prepare, rally the people, so to speak, and when he was ready, Michael would meet them all, and tell them what was to be told.

In the meantime, Albright decided to sit down on a bench outside, leaving Annabel to her healing. With a small kiss he took his leave, and exited the place of healing to the old wooden bench outside. It was here that he had longed to sit and grow old with his love, watching the sunsets of their life together as time passed on.

The third level was high above the forest canopy overlooking the horizon of seemingly endless forest and ice towers. Albright removed a small pouch from his belt and unfastened the flap with the fluidity of ritual. From the bag he removed a wooden pipe that he had whittled himself the day he had become a man. He pulled a clump of tobacco from the pouch and packed it tightly into the pipe.

"Need a light?" He mumbled to himself as he snapped his index and middle finger together. He is not certain why such phrases suddenly leap to the front of his mind, but he says them anyway, as he always has and always will.

A single tiny flame flickered into existence from the very air amidst his fingertips. The flame danced upon his hand as he let it move across his knuckles and onto his thumb. He then placed the pipe to his lips and

---

dipped his thumb to the bowl of the pipe. The tobacco grew cherry red as Albright puffed small clouds and rings into the air, and the few hours went by with a waning drag like the smoke of his pipe.

2

Michael woke to the sounds of a faint music, but the further he drew into consciousness the fainter the sound became, until the music was no more. A woman wearing a green and white gown sewn with thread of gold came and sat at the edge of his bed. "How are you feeling Michael?" she asked in an angelic voice. At the moment Michael found it impossible to respond, too taken by the sunlight glow of beauty which surrounded everything in the room, but especially her.

She touched a tender hand to his brow where his wound had been, but there was no stinging pain, no jolt of lightning shooting into his skull from the open gash, nothing but warmth. "The wound has healed nicely, but I fear it may have… jarred things a little." She said with a lithe smile.

"Sorry, I'm fine. Just, a little confused."

"That's all right Michael. You have nothing to fear. You will see that all of your physical wounds are healed, do not be alarmed, it is the power of white magick that has touched you. Although, I can still see that many wounds have yet to be healed within your heart… I will tell you of what has transpired." She got up from the bed and went to a table next to it that looked like a very ornately carved tree stump. She poured a glass of water into a cup from a wooden pitcher, and returned to Michael with it. "Here you are, drink this." He took the glass and drank it down quickly.

"Who are you?" He said once he had finished.

"I am called the Lady Annabel. You lost consciousness when you were on the lift with Albright, so he brought you to me. He has already sent word to the council of your arrival, and they are preparing a gathering so

---

129

you may address them, but it will take some time yet. Do you feel up to speaking with the council?"

"Aye... I must."

"Aye, then you will. Take it slow while gathering your bearings. I have a small meal prepared in the next room. I will go fetch Albright once you have finished eating, and you will have your time with the council." At that she turned and moved to leave the room, but at the doorway she stopped. "It was a pleasure to aid you along your path Michael Cross, and may you find more healing and atonement within our city. For it would seem you have much weight to relieve from your heart."

Before Michael could respond she left the room. Michael took care when making his first efforts to stand, but he had no trouble. He made his way to the kitchen and found his meal laid out for him complete with dining utensils and folded cloth. The meal was a bowl of soup, companioned by a series of meats upon freshly baked bread. Michael ate slowly until he was full, and put the rest aside. After taking a moment to refresh himself, and redress in his outer clothing and gear, he walked outside with a renewed sense of self.

Outside, on the little bench where Albright had smoked his pipe, sat the Lady Annabel. Albright was holding the reins of both Michael's horse and his own. It appeared as though he were engaged in a rather intimate conversation with the Lady, but at Michael's sudden presence the intimate gaze between the lovers' eyes was broken.

"I see you are well. Are you ready to address the council?" Albright said at once.

"Aye, as ready as I'll ever be, I suppose." Michael said this as he stretched in the yellow glow of the afternoon sun. He looked to Annabel, who sat quietly with her head down, collecting her thoughts. She returned his gaze. "We are well met Lady Annabel." She did not reply, simply nodded in approval. Michael returned the nod, and moved to mount his steed.

"Me thinks we should walk, get your blood circulating again before we get there. What do you say?" Albright posed.

"Aye, a good stretch would probably do me good."

Michael had agreed to the walk, and it did him well indeed, but something made him want to run, to hurry as fast as he could to the council. He wondered if Danube was all right, and if the woman was on her way here. Would they be able to stop her if she did come? He wasn't quite sure they would be able to.

Albright was quiet for most of the walk to one of the third levels' three massive center points. This massive trunk stood before them as the place of council. They would be there in a matter of minutes.

"Michael..." Albright said with his head hung low.

"What troubles you?" Michael replied plainly, as though no longer aware that the man was still with him now that the council was in sight.

"Lady Annabel...she told me who you are...that you are the last of the Cross."

Michael continued pace, never breaking stride.

"I just wanted you to know...that I am to serve you through your journey." Albright said solemnly. Michael stopped and turned to the man.

"I...don't understand? Serve me?"

"It is not yet for you to understand. I merely want you to know that my allegiance is now with you, for whatever trial may lie ahead. This is all I will say on the matter at this time. I just- wanted you to know." He turned

———

and continued toward the council. Michael was taken back by the sheer suddenness of what had just happened. Regardless, he found himself again and followed.

Now that the trunk was in full view Michael could see its detail. The trunk was several hundred feet wide, and in its center was an archway which had been carved fifty feet high. At the gated entranceway were two guards with spearlike staffs. They wore armor of a glistening brown and green, and Michael had a difficult time seeing them even at such a close distance, it was in fact an illusion of sorts, camouflage.

Carved into the trunk, on either side of the archway were torches. One on the left that flamed a dark red, one on the right which was yellow, and another torch at the top of the arch way which flamed a bright blue. It was unclear to Michael what the purpose of these torches was, but it was obvious that they were of significance in this culture.

Something Michael found peculiar about the trunk were the large bulbous balconies which seemed *grown* into the tree like giant knots. Michael could see how people were seated high in these hollowed-out balconies, and it seemed some of them were simply there to allow more light to pour into the inner chamber. Michael could see the arena-like meeting chamber of council through the open doorway. It was like the one in Lindell, except that everything was made of polished wood in different colors. The chamber was incredibly, breathtakingly beautiful.

As Michael approached the guards at the entrance to the council, he thought he heard Albright say something under his breath.

"…All the lies must right their ways…to live, to die, to become of sage…blessings lie in broken paths…all atone…for fear of wrath…"

Before Michael could question what he thought he had heard the introductions began.

3

The clicking of Michael's black leather boots echoed through the deathly quiet hall of the Council of Singe. The silence was unnerving, but from somewhere Michael heard music playing and it compelled him forward. The click of his heels seemed to grow louder in his mind, drowning out the thoughts of what he would say and how he would say it. The sheer amount of people in the colossal arena-like chamber was enough to unnerve anyone, but Michael felt an even greater pressure from them. The weight of the name *Cross*, amidst the council of Trengar. *Surely*, after giving his message of what he had seen and bringing the sword here for protection, Michael thought to himself, after completing his task, *surely* he would be killed. Murdered in his sleep, drugged at dinner, or simply stabbed in the back right here in the presence of all the lords of Trengar.

Despite this paranoia, Michael felt something else, something deeper.

It was something digging at the back of his mind, screaming to be let out, to be free, and in the open, but he didn't know how to begin.

Michael continued down the long walkway lined by the pews of commoners and lower officials, all full, brimming with every interested ear that had caught the news. Whether they knew him as a Cross or not, he was still a messenger bringing news from Lindell. Above the commoners' pews, surrounding the whole council circle, were three levels of balconies carved into the tree along with stairways, and massive windows with balconies and walkways leading outside the trees trunk. These balconies were also full, every seat. He tried not to think about that, and walked to the center ring, the speaking circle. It was a three feet high platform that was placed in the center of the floor between the commoners' pews and those of the council members, which wrapped around the circle so that all could see the present speaker's face.

Michael walked up the three steps to the top of the platform and to the center. Here, he bowed low to the council. The man in the center seat, directly before him, spoke. "Welcome to the council of Trengar of the city of Singe, may we hear you well, with just hearts and just minds."

"Aye, till the end of sage!" The council spoke in unison.

The man in the middle spoke again, "You may state your name and speak your fill for our ears are open to you."

Michael felt his heart take over, and he no longer had to think of what to say. For his heart knew what this was, the chance to find forgiveness, if any was really possible. This would be Michael's chance, his great apology.

"I say thank you. Before I may address the matters at hand I will address myself in a matter all can respect." There was a pause as Michael drew in the air of the room, air thick with rapt attention. "I am Michael Cross, wielder and protector of the legendary Great Sword of Lindell," At this, it seemed the whole assembly gasped and took their first glance at the heavy blade upon his back. "Last of the Cross, and bearer of the sins and atrocities committed to you and your people by my forefathers. For the symbol, of which I myself am guilty of using…upon the face of the man who bed my wife. A crime for which I have been stricken of my lordship, my marriage - my life as I knew it, and left only with one charge…to safeguard this sacred sword that I possess and guide it to the safety of your council. With this, I also offer myself to you, once my words are spoken, you may have me as penance for all the pain the Cross ever plagued you, and you may do with me what you will, for their blood runs with mine, and I am as guilty of the *Cross* as they." The council remained silent, everything was silent. Michael hung his head low, the shadows of shame shrouding his face in darkness. This moment was the most difficult in all his life, even more than his fall from honor in the council of Lindell. This was the exposing of the darkness in his heart that he had held since first thought. Something in his soul he thought would never be clean. His life now rested in the hands of these people. The very people his fathers had inflicted so much pain upon. The people who had been robbed of loved ones by those of his blood.

For the moment, with his head bent low, he thought the silence was the calm before the storm. On the verge of his mind he could hear the wail of their screams as he pictured them seizing him from the platform and burning him alive upon a pyre for their revenge, but the room remained silent. He let his gaze rise from his feet, and met the eyes of the hundreds of people around him. Not a single eye was dry, they all wept.

A young Lady of the council rose from her seat and walked down a small staircase to the platform. She walked gracefully towards Michael like a symbol of judgment, like a goddess. Michael fell to his knees, and the emotion within him erupted into tears before the woman. The Lady knelt with him, taking his face in her hands and brushing aside the tears from his cheeks.

"Hear me and speak true Last of the Cross. I have waited my whole life for someone to blame. Someone to place the entirety of my sorrow, but such a thing should not be so, but now I see that it is. And for that, I am sorry." Her elegant voice paused a moment. "I ask you this as I speak for all...Do you...Michael Cross, ask forgiveness of the sins of the Cross, and to be cleansed of all the pain it has caused to so many?"

"Aye, I do..."

"And do you swear, to only use the *Cross*, if it so must be used, the reason must be just and pure, on your life, on your honor, on your blood, of the Cross?"

"Aye, I swear..."

"Then I proclaim, that from this moment on, you are forgiven and cleansed of the sins of the Cross. There is a phrase here in Singe, 'NaCros...NayCros...' which means, god given...god forgiven, this is your forgiveness Michael. Live with it in peace." With her last words, she bent forward and kissed Michael's forehead and then his lips passionately, breathing new life into a part of Michael that had long ago turned to stone. As she kissed him the entire council and spectators of the assembly shouted in unison, "NaCros...NayCros...To live, to die, to become of sage..." was like a song within the chamber.

The Lady returned to her seat and Michael Cross stood to meet the song of those who had granted him with more than just mercy, but forgiveness. He then spoke of the reason for his coming. He told them of the raiders who tried to steal the sword, and how they had set fire to the courtyard as a distraction. He told them of his first time wielding the great sword, and of his battle with Danube, which ended with the woman bearing the Scythe of Vengeance. After discussing all of what had occurred, the council made a private concession of the mind through the life force of the forest spirit.

The council would immediately dispatch riders to Jerum and to find Danube and the woman. After discussing this publicly, they invited Michael into an adjacent chamber where he and the seven lords and ladies of the highest part of the council could speak with him in private.

4

Albright sat in the corner of the room, his face sullen in the shadows. He snapped his fingers together, and produced a tiny flame, his face lit with a brilliant orange glow. The shadows danced as he let the flame roll back and forth across his knuckles until he turned the flame to light his old pipe. Michael watched as the smoke started to dance in the air with its ever mesmerizing wane.

Behind the now-closed doors Michael could hear the remaining council, and the spectators being vacated, and the final adjourning of the meeting being undertaken. Michael was seated at the head of a large table and poured a glass of wine. Soon everyone was seated with wine in hand. Albright had even switched from his seat in the corner to the one at Michael's right side. The council members spoke amidst themselves for a moment, and Michael figured they were just waiting for the echoing sound of the departing people to cease. Albright, still smoking his pipe, leaned toward Michael. "You did well…you are a good man, me thinks." Albright said as he held out his pipe, offering it to Michael.

"Thank you…" He said as he took a drag from the pipe. "I am happy you found forgiveness Michael. For many, clemency is something they can never achieve." As Albright finished, Michael could hear the last massive wave of footsteps leaving the chamber, and the lords turned to the attention of Michael.

"Michael, we have decided. We are to immediately dispatch the riders to Jerum and to seek out Danube. We also think it best due to sudden presence of this woman with the scythe that you and the sword are kept on the move as well. We believe there is a great danger brewing in the land, and we have allies whom we believe will come to aid when the time arrives."

The Lady who had offered him forgiveness spoke to him now in her elegant voice. "We want you to travel to the island of Laotia. Inform them of what is happening here, and that Trengar may be in need of their aid."

Another Lord spoke, "The Island of Laotia has been our trustworthy ally for many generations. It is our belief that you and the sword will be safe there, and in secrecy. It will be free from corruption, thievery, and other harm."

The Lady spoke up once more, "You will embark on the later day of the morrow. Albright and two others will accompany you on your journey, and you will make your way first through the wastes of Gell."
Albright broke in, "Only the four of us? I thought we would have more?"
"Aye, we believe it is prudent that we keep the location of the sword as secret as we can. If we were to move as a massed group it may draw

———

138

suspicion, but as a group of four riders, you will appear as nothing more than a band of travelers on some less than important mission. Wouldn't you agree, Captain?"

"Aye, you speak true. I withdraw my statement." Albright seemed too relaxed. He questioned the council with fluidity, not surprise or misunderstanding. He asked his question simply to hear the lord's responses. He wanted to make sure *they* knew why they would only go as four. With their answer now resting on his mind he took a humble, satisfied drag from his pipe.

"We will make preparations this evening for your journey; you will have the best of equipment, clothing, and rations. We were wondering, however, if you would accept a sheath for the blade of the sword, if we were to give you such?"

"It would please me greatly." Michael said as formally as he could.

"Then it will be so. For now, take leave, and rest Michael Cross…for you are amidst the sage…" The Lady said.

Michael was led out of the room by Albright, who had put away his wooden pipe and had just downed his second glass of wine in a single chug. Albright took him back to the Lady Annabel's home and refuge of healing. There was a small one-room home carved into the tree next door, that was currently vacant and up for rent. It was here that Michael found rest for the evening, and he rested very easily on a mint-scented pine bed once more. Somewhere nearby, the smoke of Albright's pipe wafted into the night sky after enjoying the tender love of his Lady of Secret.

Michael woke to the singing of birds and the warm glistening glow of the morning sun's rays. The dew still lay upon the leaves, and in the distance he could hear the sound of people rising to greet the day, and perform the tasks of their daily life.

He dressed slowly, donning his familiar clothing and all the while he gandered at the room in the fresh morning light. The room was spacious, with many furnishings, even a desk with fresh quill and parchment. He found this intriguing, but before he could dabble a little ink, there was a light knocking at the door. Michael pulled on his second boot and called out to the visitor, "Aye, it's open." His hand instinctively went to the hilt of the small dagger in his belt, but it was Albright that entered the room, bringing with him a breeze of fresh morning air, the hint of spice tobacco lingering about him like a perfume.

"Good morrow Michael. Did you sleep well?" Albright asked as he entered the room and walked briskly to the table beneath the window sill. He left the door open, and the fresh morning smells bombarded Michael's senses. In the distance he could smell fresh bread baking, the blooming of a thousand flowers, and the greatest smell of all…the scent of sage. It was at this moment that Michael finally saw the jug and cups Albright carried.

"I slept well enough. What do you have there?" Michael gestured at the dishware.

"It is a special brew of tea. It has an *awakening* effect. It is calming, soothing, and unlike alcohol it increases your awareness instead of impairing. It is a good way to start the day. Will you join me in this practice on this morning?"

"I would be honored," Michael replied as Albright finished pouring his own glass. With his approval, Albright poured a glass for Michael and handed him the steaming liquid within the brown clay cup. Albright took a seat at the table and Michael did the same. Several birds took flight from branches just outside the window as Albright pushed it open, letting even more of the aromatic morning air into the room.

"It pleases me to see you well rested Michael. It would seem that you and I have a long journey ahead of us, do we not?"

"Aye, so it seems." Michael held his train of thought to sip the hot tea. "Albright, do you mind if I ask you something?"

"Feel free…" Albright's smile faded slightly.

"Did I do well yesterday? Do you think they spoke true, am I really forgiven?" Michael looked at him with penetrating, concerned eyes. It was a look with a touch of madness.

"Everything that brought unease to your heart may now be forgotten. You are the one to decide whether or not your past destroys you. We have forgiven. It is up to you now, to forgive yourself." Albright returned a mighty gaze, one which would pierce the soul of any man, and it was this moment that would inevitably drive Michael to the solution of his inner turmoil.

"Let it trouble you no more this morning. We have matters at hand I would like to discuss with you."

"Such as..?" Michael took another strong sip of tea.

"The trek ahead of us will be difficult. I just thought it would be wise to confer with you before we embark." Albright reached to the pouch at his side, and removed a rolled piece of parchment. He unrolled it, and Michael was impressed to see a map that very accurately depicted the land of Selador. "As you know, we are here." Albright pointed at the area on the map marked Singe, within the region of Trengar. A black dot in the middle of three trees and three ice-towers represented the magnificent city they currently sat within, drinking tea. "We will ride north, crossing the river Cash, and enter into the region of Gell." He gestured on the map the route they would take. "Have you ever been to Gell, Michael?"

"I have seen it, but never have I actually journeyed its lands."

"It is a rather arduous place to travel. A place of large spans of dry land, volcanoes, petrified forests, sulfur pits, swamplands, and I believe the word is geysers…or gushers? Either way, they are dangerous."

"What are they?" Michael seemed intrigued, he had never before heard of such as geysers, gushers, or whatever they were.

"Aye, they are curious creations indeed. They appear as just small formations of rock, or a stagnant pool of water, occasionally spraying streams of water into the air, until, when you least expect it to happen, a rumbling comes from its hearth and a blasting stream of boiling hot water, hot enough to strip a man of his flesh in an instant's breath, explodes several hundred feet into the air, raining down upon the earth and those foolish enough to stand near. I have seen these many times on my journeys through the region, and if you know what to look for, they are easy to avoid."

"This whole trek sounds pretty arduous all right."
"I'm not even finished. The region of Gell is a mountainous and ever-changing region. One minute you are in the middle of a forest, the next you're standing knee deep in a swamp infested with who-knows-what. On some days, the sky grows black in the middle of the day - others, the sun never even rises."

"Albright, I think I'm getting the point…it's going to be pretty bad."

"Yeah, well, I just thought I should let you know." Albright held a wicked smile that unnerved Michael a little. *'He's playing with me,'* Michael thought.

Albright pointed at one last place upon the map. "This is where we go today. We'll make camp around this area, which should give us a good start for the first day." The place he pointed to on the map was a cluster of stones marked 'Rook's Rest', that looked to be nearly a fourth of the journey along the map.

"Looks like quite a distance for one day, wouldn't you say?" Michael asked skeptically. From the look of it, he thought it was almost double his trip from Lindell to Singe, that journey alone had taken him three days.

"I see the concern in your face, but not to worry. Tonight we travel the hardest that we will through the entirety of our voyage. I just want us to have a good start on things." Albright produced the tobacco pouch from the belt at his side, and started to load his pipe.

"How long will it take us to get to Laotia, roughly speaking?"

"It shouldn't take over four or five days if things go well." Albright lit his pipe, and took the day's first drag.

"When do we leave?" Michael asked after he had finished his glass of tea.

"Whenever you are ready to do so, but if you're asking me, the sooner the better." Albright offered Michael a hit of the pipe, which he took.

"Could we leave now?" Another smile formed upon Albright's thin lips.

"We'll leave as soon as I finish my pipe, and you, your tea."

"But I've already finished my…" Albright poured Michael another glass of the tea.

"After this glass then…" Michael stared at the now-full glass of steaming brew.

"Aye, finish your drink, Michael Cross."

6

After finishing, Albright took Michael to the chamber where they had met with the high council members. When they entered the room they were greeted by the same seven lords and ladies. Once formal introductions were aside things turned directly to *business*. Michael was given a full formal swearing in to the undaunted protection of the sword, and the secrecy their movements would require. They went over a larger version of Albright's map, and the entire route they planned to take. From Singe to Laotia, the entire span was discussed in formal detail.

This took a little under an hour, but to Michael it seemed like moments. *'SO much ground covered in such little time,'* he thought, incredulously. All the details, all the instruction seemed to slip past him until he could take in no more, and he simply hoped Albright would catch the finer details.

Once this was over, the three ladies left the room, and in a matter of seconds returned, bearing a collection of items for the departing men. Albright was presented a new addition to his armor; it represented an increase in his rank from captain. He had become a Lord Guardian, a title only bestowed upon the best. At seeing the piece before him, the promotion, he fell to his knees, bowing, and accepted the great honor.

Michael was touched to see the large man take a knee. Despite Michael's little time with the man, he had determined a few definitive things about Albright's character. One was that despite the fact that Michael was a lord himself, or former lord for that matter, it seemed as though this man, until now a mere captain, had always seemed far more in authority during the time he had known him. Albright in Michael's mind was 'the big man', a father or older brother figure he had always wanted to look up to, but hadn't had, and here he was in front of him…kneeling. It only then occurred to him that Albright called him by name, and never by *lord*. Such thoughts always dawned on Michael at the wrong moments.

The lady who granted his forgiveness the day before carried before her the sheath they had spoken of making. The blade fit perfectly. The sheath was designed by the specifications listed within the scrolls of history. Its dark colored wood shimmered black in the sunlight and was cut to the perfect measurements. It had mirrored steel braces upon its edges, and was bound with an intricate weaving of white braid made of a fine thread

Michael did not recognize, but was told it would never break and would be difficult to cut even with the sharpest blade. The strap which fastened the sword across his back was made of the same braid, and could be adjusted to a desired position.

Michael examined the sheath closer, and upon the exposed wood he could see intricate patterns carved and burned into its grain. Upon looking up from the inscription he caught the gaze of the lady who had given it to him. "It is a blessing…NaCros…NayCros…God given…God forgiven…to live, to die, to become of sage…Please accept it as our forgiveness and blessing to you Michael Cross, for you have brought a most wonderful gift indeed."

"I have come with only grief and terrible news. What gifts have I brought you?"

"Peace…in our hearts. That is a gift that is worth our debt to you."

"I thank you." Michael's voice was thick as he fought emotion that quelled within him, but it felt as though he would burst. Then he did the only thing he could think of, and fell to his knees. He took the hand of the lady before him, and kissed her hand. "I thank you, my lady."

"Such humble thanks is noted Lord Michael, now accept these for the journey ahead." As she spoke the other two women brought forward what they were carrying. One brought him a long dark brown coat they called the 'Coat of the Highwayman', or the name Michael found more to his liking, a 'duster'. It fit him perfectly, falling just below the knees in length, and it was loose enough not to restrict his movement, and yet snug like a nice glove. He thanked the woman, and took what the next woman held after donning the 'duster'.

She handed him a satchel. Inside was a week's rations, a large canteen of water, and a large length of the same cord upon the sheath, only thicker. There was also a bedroll, and a shaving mirror and knife. Michael smiled at the Lady and accepted her gift. After sliding the sword into its new sheath and pulling the satchel full of his belongings over his shoulder, he said his thanks one final time, and bid goodbye to the lords and ladies of Trengar.

Michael and Albright made their way back in the direction of Lady Annabel's abode. When they had reached her place of practice, Albright went inside and said goodbye to his love, his precious Annabel, whom he could never truly give the life he wanted for them. Michael waited outside, studying the engravings and braids upon the sheath until Albright returned. His cheeks were flushed, and his eyes vacant and glazed with some deep pain he refused to release. After a moment, his eyes returned to their stony steel gaze, and by then he and Michael had reached the lift that would take them to the lower level of the city. Michael had suggested walking down through the other levels, but Albright immediately refused, explaining that the fewer the people that saw them leave the city, the better. Michael buckled under Albright's instincts and followed.

Once on the ground, Albright led them to the stables where two men stood inside holding the reins of four horses, two of which Michael immediately recognized. "Is Siren ready for me to ride?" Albright questioned one of the men.

"As ready as he'll ever be for ya, old man!" The man who said this actually appeared to be the same age as Albright. They both had the same light lines of crow's feet at the edge of there eyes, and a fine line across the brow from plenty of stressed thought. Yet neither man could be mistaken for the other's brother, for Albright had medium length auburn brown hair and a grey blue gaze which sometimes looked green, his jaw was almost always set, and his lips held thin beneath his light moustache and beard. The man who spoke however, he had hair as black as night reaching to his shoulders, and eyes as brown as earth, his face was scruffy but not bearded, and his mouth was creased in a manner that he always seemed to be smirking at the world. He wore a light armor similar to Albright's, except it was black and green.

"Still the wiseass I see. Didn't your ma ever teach you to respect yer elders?" Albright snapped back with a smile.

"Bah, elder my arse, I be a full day and a half older than ya and ye know it!"

"Aye, right you are. Michael let me introduce you to my best friend Jayce. We grew up together here in Singe, there's nobody better I'd want with us on this trip." Albright said proudly.

"Why Albright, how can ya say somthin' like that wit me standin right here? Have you lost all sense of your manners through the haze of that pipe of yours?" The other man holding reins chimed in.

"Ah crap, who invited you, ya damn cuss?!" Michael could hear the accent of Albright's voice shift to a childhood slang he had obviously shared with his friends.

"Who're you callin' a cuss, king of the cusses if I've ever have seen a more stubborn, self-absolved and strangely honorable cuss as you?"

"Shut yer trap an' give this *ol' timer* a proper handshake."

Michael watched in silence as the three old friends exchanged familiar greetings and puns at each other's' expense. The laughter from such men came in strong bellows that seemed more like a roar to Michael.

"Michael this is Willum, another, *old* friend of mine." Albright explained.

Willum certainly did look like an old friend, in fact, he looked twice as old as Albright. His hair had once been black but was now mostly grey, pulled back into a single braid which ran down his back. His eyes were slits that had squinted out the sun for many years, and his skin was like tanned leather. Crevices marked his face around the eyes and upon his brow, and his mouth and grey 'stache' was framed by thick lines. He wore a black herd keeper's hat and attire similar to Michael's, only many years faded, and instead of a white shirt he wore a faded blue.

After all the introductions were made, and the horses mounted, Michael took one last glance at the city of Singe as they bolted from the stable and charged through the city's lowest level. The last look back was the hardest. Michael wished that he would see it all again, but somehow knew he never would.

7

The four men rode through the forests of Trengar in a few hours of the late morning until they came upon the embankment of the Cash River. The other side of these rushing waters was the region of Gell, a place of birth and a place of death. Albright and the others made to water their horses as Michael Cross once again stared out over the region of Gell. It was place he has always wanted to see, but never dared to travel, and now lay before him just on the other side of the rushing river. Michael finally realized in this moment he had never truly lived until the recent events which had taken place in his life had forced him to this point.

Part 6:

Beneath the Ice Falls

I

Danube holds Kaire amidst the trees, amongst the sage, beneath the starry sky at the edge of the falls of an ice tower. The crystal clear water falls with a peaceful roar. Kaire is lying in the nook of Danube's chest, looking up at the pillar of what is first rock, then ice, which reaches straight up into the sky, piercing the very heavens. Danube and Kaire lay with their weapons within their grasp, but they hold each other with a tender comfort that defies any suspicions.

"Danube…" Kaire spoke just over the sound of the falls, "Something terrible is happening to our world, and I'm afraid that fate resides in our hands now." She gently squeezed the dark wooden handle of the scythe instinctively as she said this; she had not intended her comment to be so literal, but what was done was done. "Danube, I think we need to go to Jerum."

"We can send messengers to Jerum, you and I can reside in my city. The council of Trengar will see past what's been done."

"I still think that you and I should take the scythe and staff to Jerum. Something tells me…something in my dreams…that they will be safe in Jerum. I believe this to be true." Kaire seemed dead set on the idea.

"Let me think on it…" Danube said distantly.

Kaire seemed to be chewing on more than just going to Jerum, "Do you really believe your council would forgive me for taking the scythe…and killing those men…?"

Danube was silent a moment longer than she had expected. For that moment he recalled the things he'd seen within her mind, the things that were burned upon her soul.

"I believe...the council will grant your forgiveness. It's another that may not be so lucky."

"The man you'd been fighting just before I entered the clearing...this Michael Cross I was told to...?" Kaire asked, but cut short.

"Aye, it is he of whom I speak. But who was it that told you to seek him?"

"The same man who told me to take the scythe, the one who showed me the power to obtain my freedom." She replied.

"Who is he that told you these things?" Danube pried.

"He is but a shadow. He comes to me in my dreams as I sleep, and speaks within my mind. I know not if he is a perception of my own desperate imagination, or if he is in fact *real*."

"You know nothing of who he might be? His name, perhaps?" Danube was scrambling for answers, and he knew he was close, but he did not believe Kaire was lying. *'Perhaps she doesn't know who he is?'*

As the thought passed through his mind, Kaire broke to tears as she spoke, "No, I don't know. I'm sorry, I just...I..." Tears streamed down her cheeks and Danube pulled her tightly to him.

"It's alright Kaire, I understand...just shadows. Don't you worry I've got you now, I'm not going to let anything happen to you.

With her beautiful emerald eyes, green like the lush forests of his home, she looked up at him. "Who is he? The man he made me seek?" Kaire asked as she looked up at him from the comfort of his arms.

Danube told her just who Michael Cross was, and what that meant.

———

He told her of the banishing of the Cross bloodline, the sins committed upon his people, his own father. He told her how he was the last Drakendor, and Michael, the last Cross. She slowly fell asleep listening to the stories of his life, resting comfortably in the safety of his arms beneath the falls of the ice tower.

He stroked her hair until he heard her breathing slow. Danube pondered many things on this night, but soon after drifted to sleep with his newfound love.

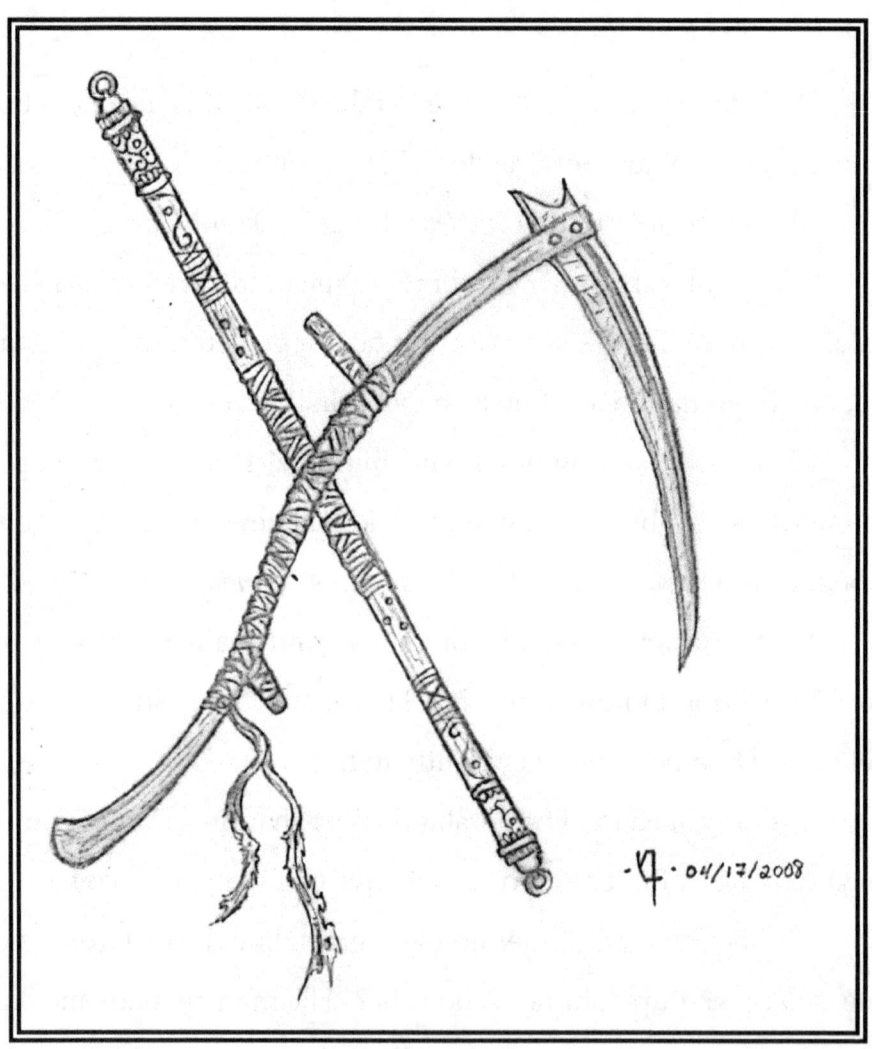

2

It was shortly past the middle of the night when Danube woke to the sound of several sets of hooves striking the nearby road. They carried torches, but Danube doubted they would see them lying together beneath the falls through the mass of trees and brush which separated them from the road.

Danube waited until they had passed before he gently shook Kaire awake.

"What is it?"

"Riders on horseback...shall we see who they are, and why it is that they are treading on the paths of our heaven?" Danube charmed.

"We shall." Kaire feigned to kiss Danube, but quickly leapt to the side and started her eerily silent sprint across the forest floor. Danube moved swiftly after her. Together, they stalked the men until Danube was certain of who they were. At that instant, the two of them broke from the tree line, some twenty meters behind the riders. They walked to the center of the road, and stood side by side. "Hail! Riders of Trengar! Turn and meet the face of thy Lord Drakendor!" Danube spoke like a king. The riders turned, and at seeing Danube they exclaimed in joy, but several looked to the woman with a nervous gaze. "This is my...Lady Kaire Ra, she has pleaded her forgiveness to me and I have seen to her pardon. May you treat her as my special guest to the forests of Trengar, and with the highest of respect. For as far as I can tell she is the rightful protector of the Scythe of Reum and is in need of aid." Kaire looked at Danube with wide eyes conveying half-fear, and half-love.

The men on horseback rode forward and Danube at once recognized the seven men as the city's best trackers and rangers. As they came close they dismounted and bowed upon one knee. "Hail, Lord Drakendor!" they said together.

Danube nodded and the first of the men in line stood at once, the others swiftly followed example. "It is good to see you well my lord, we bring news from Trengar."

"Aye, then speak."

"Michael Cross came to us, and told of the situation he had left you in. We were immediately dispatched, but not before we were told of the thing that this Michael Cross has done."

Danube's interest instantly blazed, "Tell me…what has he done…"

"The people are calling it 'The Great Apology of the Cross'. Before he spoke to the council of the events at hand, he apologized in humility for the sins of the Cross, and he has found forgiveness by the council. NaCros…NayCros…Is what they're all saying."

Danube appeared in shock, but shook his look and turned to Kaire, "I don't think the council is going to have any problem with my pardon."

"I was told to deliver this to you, my lord. It is from the highest seven of the council." The man produced a roll of parchment sealed with a green wax seal. Danube noted and instantly recognized the stamp of the lady who had given Michael her pardon.

He broke the seal and read it quickly. In the letter he learned that Michael was going to be heading through the Wastes of Gell by morning on his way to the Island of Laotia. To Danube, it seemed as though his council had done well in protecting the sword and its bearer. Danube knew it was wise to keep Michael as far away from him as possible, because, forgiven or not, they had a pact that would be kept.

Danube finished the parchment and tucked it in his vest so that he could burn it later. Best not to tell anyone else just where Michael was going, just in case anyone might be listening or looking. He didn't like the figure in Kaire's dreams, and didn't like the idea of telling her if somehow she could be used to get to Michael, and the sword.

The lead rider spoke again, "My lord, other riders have been dispatched to deliver word to Jerum."

Danube asked, "How many riders?"

"Three of Singe's fastest."

"That's good, very good." Danube seemed distant, as though wrestling with a decision.

"Will you be returning with us my lord?"

Danube looked to Kaire. Her eyes pleaded with him, and pulled at his heartstrings, "No...I'm afraid we will be going north, to the kingdom of Jerum. I believe there may be a chance we can group with the other riders, but I will need horses, provisions, and quill and parchment, if you have any."

The riders looked to each other, and two of them offered their reins to Danube and Kaire, the others packed the two horses with satchels containing several days' worth of rations. The main rider who had spoken went to the satchel upon his own horse and produced a quill and fresh sheet of parchment. He gave them to Danube, who went straight to work on a letter proclaiming the council temporarily in emergency power, and an order to double the defenses of Singe's perimeters. He included thanks in the letter for the well treatment of Michael Cross and the pardon bestowed upon him. He also included directives in regard to Kaire's pardon, making it official, with wax and seal. The seal was of his father's signet ring; he had worn it since the day he had spoken his vow many years ago to take revenge on those of the Cross.

3

Once the seal had dried, the riders mounted their horses, each of them doubling up with other riders, and rode back in the direction of Singe at full steam. Danube led Kaire to the ice tower falls where they had left what little things they had with them. The horses drank from the pool beneath the falls, and the two lovers gathered their belongings. Once everything was packed tightly on the horses and extra clothes were layered to protect them from the chilled night air, Kaire and Danube stood beneath the falls once more looking up at the pillar of ice stretching into the sky. They let their gaze fall and meet each other's eyes, and they kissed.

It was long and passionate, and when it was gone, it was gone. It became just a single frame of memory in the treasured depths of Danube's mind. He handed her the reins, and she waited for him by the path. It was at the foot of these falls that Danube burned the parchment containing the destination of Michael Cross and the Great Sword of Lindell. But what Danube didn't know was that burning such a parchment no longer mattered when it came to the secrets of this world.

Part 7:

The Wastes of Gell

I

The sun reached its afternoon wane and started to make its descent toward the horizon. Michael and the three men, Albright, Willum, and Jayce, had been riding for several hours. They had long since crossed the Cash River, and were now far beyond the borders of Gell. Trengar was no longer in sight, but in the distance, the pillars of ice which scraped the heavens could still be seen upon the horizon.

Michael watched the terrain of the world change before his eyes in the course of an afternoon. He saw the trees change from firs, pines, and oaks, to the white birch and Blackwood trees of the nearly colorless forests they now rode through. He watched as streams and ponds turned to geysers, steam beds, and sulfur pools that bubbled noxious fumes into the air. The sulfur stung the sinuses, choked, and at times blinded with its stench. Some pools and streams were worse than others. Some were as docile as a hot bath, while there were those few that emitted gas that could neither be seen nor smelled, and it was these that could kill a man before he even knew what was happening to him.

Albright and his companions did their best to navigate the pools and places that emitted the reek of death, and once a path was found it proved to be fairly easy to make their way at a decent charge. Michael found this forest of black and white disorienting and confusing. He looked to the sky for guidance and assurance, but to his dismay, he could no longer see the ice towers in the distance, only the fading light of day. Ahead of them the sky seemed to be growing darker. Black clouds loomed in the distance, constantly shifting and changing place, distorting the sky.

Michael found the growing darkness threatening and returned his gaze to the forests in which they led their steeds. Michael noticed that for many acres they crossed through a section of forest that had been burned. Michael had no idea how long ago the trees had been engulfed in flames, becoming burning towers of fire, but it seemed he felt the pain as if it were present at that moment. He could feel the pain as if the living wood had been stripped of life, consumed for fuel to the fire, but now all that stood before them was the remaining skeletons of what once was; blackened, charred, forever changed, and left only for the earth to consume. Michael could sense this agony as they rode through the forest of ghosts.

Albright did his best to move the men quickly through the burned acres of woods. He fought to find the quickest trails and paths through the loose soot and foliage of the forest floor. There were no roads in sight, and it was preferred that way. Albright had long since decided it unwise to use the public roads and trade routes because it was best to avoid any unnecessary attention from the rare passerby.

Despite Albrights efforts, the burned trees seemed never ending, the stench of sulfur around every bend, and now and then the group even stumbled upon strange sections of forest that seemed…petrified, as though the wood had turned to stone. The group continued riding, bent on reaching their destination for the night, still not having even the slightest inclination to rest.

After a little over an hour of steady riding, all of the trees started to look as though they had turned to stone. The forest had once again changed before Michael's eyes. This transformation, however, was not as disheartening as the previous, and yet it was still just as lifeless. These trees had been dead for hundreds, maybe even thousands of years, and they were silent to Michael. He felt nothing from them except a gentle peace brought with age and time.

The riders continued into the petrified forests, as the light of day vanished into the pre-dusk haze of the darkening sky. The darkness allowed no starlight through and the moon was nothing more than a dull blur behind a blanket of layers of black clouds. The men stopped at a small clearing to break camp for the night. Michael stretched his aching muscles for a moment after dismounting his horse. He watched as Albright walked off into the woods, obviously to relieve himself, as the two other men undid the packs upon their horses. They laid out bedrolls, and built a circle of stones in the center of their camp. Albright returned from his 'walk' and quickly removed his pack from Siren. He never bothered to tether the horse's reins. Siren knew never to leave his master's side, and so he would not, unless told otherwise.

Michael watched as Willum and Jayce each removed a set of three stones from their pack and placed them like a pyramid within the circle of stones.

From his pack Albright pulled his own set of stones, which he built into the pyramid the other men had formed. Once he was finished he stepped back for a moment. "You do the honors, old man." Jayce said in a solemn tone.

"Aye, it is the first of our nights upon the road, may it hav' da blessins' of a *good* man." Willum agreed with his dry humored voice.

———

Albright chuckled as he snapped his fingers together. The flame appeared instantly, and he let it roll across his knuckles, over his palm, and onto his wrist. His eyes fluttered as a single word inaudibly dripped from his lips. He suddenly flicked his wrist ever so surely, and the flame shot into the circle of stones and onto the pyramid. The stones instantly burst into a raging fire, and then settled down to a subtle flame.

"I noticed a pool over there, looks like a hot spring, the docile kind. I thought maybe your expertise could tell us whither it's usable or not?" Albright spoke to Jayce and Willum with a friendly sarcasm. They agreed to check it out, and after confirming its safety, each of them washed in the hot springs. It was once proposed that the hot springs could bring about healing and enlightenment, but Michael doubted in such things. It was because of this doubt, that on that evening Michael was given no visions from the spring, but another of the group saw very true on that night, as the smoke from his pipe waned into the steam of the spring, he saw very true indeed.

2

Once they had all bathed in the revitalizing hot springs, Michael and the others sat around the fire made of stones and ate a light meal. The wind had died down, but it still cut sharply, bringing an unnatural cold to the night. The men sat close around the fire, blankets around their shoulders, hands outstretched to the flames before them. This was a time better than any to speak, to find resolve, to learn, to tell tales, and to counsel. The men spoke on the current state of affairs in the land of Selador. They spoke of the journey ahead, and the troubles they would no doubt endure. It was the sort of discussion implying, linking, and tying itself into a singular web of conversation. Michael needed his own answers, and though he had long kept them to his own private thought, he let his questions scrape the surface of the conversation from time to time.

"Is this the place you showed me on your map Albright? The place called…Rook's Rest?" Michael said the name with uncertainty.

"No, we are actually seven miles west of it, but close enough to consider it an established goal. I'd say we put in a good first day of riding." Albright said, leaning in closer to the flames for warmth as another gust of wind picked up.

Willum took a long draw from his flask and offered it to Jayce, who took a slightly smaller drink. Jayce then offered a drink to Michael as Willum suddenly spoke. "Since it's our first night on the road with one another, we might as well have a story told o'er the fire like da ol' days. Ye remembers, don't ya Jayce? The spirit stories we used to share on cold nights much like this." His voice spoke with a long draw, an accent Michael couldn't quite place.

"Aye, I remember such, but I also remember that most of yers was a bunch of chicken fodder. I was always the better teller of the tale, and I reckon I still am." Jayce gloated.

Willum was about to retaliate to match the jab that Jayce had made, but Albright intervened, "Nobody wants to hear your malarkey of made up fairy tales that couldn't scare the jibs off an infant. How about a real spirit story? Something pertaining to the very region we travel. How about a story of a man…"

"…a man named Raven Warlack?" Jayce finished with a suddenly very serious tone.

"Aye, Raven Warlack." Albright replied, returning the gaze with a looming stare of his steely ever-changing eyes.

"Who the hell is Raven Warlack?" Michael said with a shiver after finally taking a drink of the flask Jayce had handed him. It tasted sweet like cider and warm all the way down, but strong like whiskey.

"Don't matter! It's a story bout nothin'. In fact, Albright shouldn't have brought it up a'tall. An' Jayce shouldn't encourage him any more than he already has." Willum spoke up with a sudden rashness in his tone.

"Ah, give it up ya drunk piano player. It was bound to come up. Wit' us talkin' about the land and all, and tryin' ta figure out what's about to hap'n. I'm glad Albright has brought it up. This way *I* didn't have to." Jayce said once again slipping into the childhood slang the friends were accustomed to, but Michael didn't quite catch the bit about the piano.

"Michael should know this story. Hell, everyone should know this story!" Albright solemnly stated. "If you don't mind, I believe I'm going to take the time to tell him. An' the two of you cusses can either shut yer traps, or I'll shut'em for ya!"

"Alright...I think ya know, Willum here may be an ol'timer, an' you an' I both may be ol'men, but by far, out of all of us... you've been a damned cuss the longest." Jayce remarked with a wide grin.

"Shut up, and let me tell the tale." Albright said smiling as he took the flask from Michael and took a shot.

"The stage is yours, my friend." Willum blessed.

Albright handed the flask back to Willum who took another swig, returned its cap, and placed it neatly in his inner vest pocket.

"Many years ago, Raven Warlack was born into the world. Some say he never existed at all, but he did, and I know the price his father paid for playing with the fates upon his birthing. His mother was lost in the labor.

They say her soul just seemed to pour out of her body, and into the stillborn child which suddenly breathed life with the consumed essence of his mother.'

"His father, Lord Randall Warlack, High Lord of Gell, and one of the most prestigious men of magick in all the land, was said to have cast a spell over the mother's womb before she had been impregnated. Many believe it summoned the soul of a devil into the child, and this devil was the very cause of his mother's death.'

"Years went by, and Raven appeared to be a normal child. That was until the mutilated corpses of small animals and rodents kept turning up hidden in his room. Not to mention the countless incidents when he would be discovered in dark corners in the towers of Gell, torturing the life from tiny creatures, using his prematurely well developed abilities to manipulate the creatures' mind until the animal would…do terrible things to themselves, leaving them dead or dying as malformed, broken atrocities of their former selves. Of course though, him being the High Lord's son, such things were severely forbidden to speak of, but like everything else, stories and rumors have a way of seeping through the cracks of secrecy and out into the public ear and debate.

O' course, the adults who discussed these things over the dinner table or with their spouse inadvertently spread the rumors to their children. And, as the story goes, many children that were peers of Raven in his early life learned of his darker secrets, and some say as fate would have it, several of those children happened upon the wandering little Warlack in one of the lower level halls of the commoners. The children, three sons and one daughter, of the lords of Gell found Raven Warlack coming from a dark room, blood from a fresh kill still upon his hands, painting them a dark crimson. The boys immediately surrounded him and began to mock him and tease him, calling him a freak and childish names. The girl spit at him and called him disgusting and evil. And that was when the evil truly reared its ugly head.

They say that when they found the children, the young girl sat amidst the corpses of the three boys, the blood still steaming upon the cold stone tiled floor. She was covered with blood and screaming over and over. She screamed that he entered her mind…entered her mind and had eaten her soul. She cried that he made her kill them with her bare hands. As all this transpired Raven Warlack simply stood and laughed at the scene before him."

"What happened to him?" Michael questioned as Albright took a moment to remove his pipe and tobacco from the pouch at his side.

"He was locked in a special tower and placed under strict observation by his father and colleagues. He spent several years in that tower, until his father discovered the evil which had inhabited his soul, and personally banished its hold upon him.

In the wake of his father's death, Raven Warlack was elected as High Lord of Gell. As the new High Lord he brought prosperity to the desolate region. He helped establish trade commissions with the cities of Lindell as well as other neighboring regions. He also proposed massed projects of industry, and introduced new forms of technology to the people, establishing the means necessary to harnessing the power of Gell's volcanic eruptions, minerals, and other resources. He brought forth a new era to his people as well as to the land of Selador.

Yet as what remains as the strangest thing, was that when he was at the height of his reign, and strangely enough, around the same time the

———

Cross were sentenced to be banished from the land, he disappeared. Some say with the legendary weapon of Gell. Although most are rumors, there is a constant mysticism about the government of that place. No one has ever seen the new High Lord except for the king and highest of officials. Such said, no one truly knows what became of Raven Warlack, only the hearsay of his story remains." Albright placed his pipe to his lips with the sudden conclusion to his tale.

"Did you say that he took one of the weapons?" Michael asked.

"It's a rumor…" Willum spoke up.

"There are those that believe he does indeed possess the true legendary weapon of Gell…" Albright paused to take a drag from his pipe. "…and there are those, who do not." He finished, taking Willum's comment into consideration.

"Do you know what happened to the girl?" Michael asked.

"Girl?" Albright said, taken by surprise at the unexpected question Michael had chosen to ask.

"The young girl Raven Warlack forced to kill the boys who teased him."

"No one knows…" Albright said in a forlorn voice.

For many moments separated only by the fierce crackle of the fire and the sound of the wind, Albright, Michael, Jayce, and Willum sat in silence collecting their thoughts around the blazing campfire breathing from the strength of the magick within the stones.

"Well Albright, old pal, that wasn't entirely what I had in mind for a spirit story, but hey, you get props for realism. But as for me, I'm checking out and hittin' the hay, so goodnight all, and hopefully good morrow hence its comin'." Jayce spoke up suddenly. Albright nodded, and bid him a

---

goodnight as well.

"Well, reckon I'll a' be crying off as well." Willum said. "Good evenin' then…" He too made his way to prepare for sleep.

Only Michael and Albright remain. Their faces hold the distilled glow of the ever changing flickering flames before them. Michael struggled to hold Albright's piercingly steely gaze. It was a look that said, *'I can read your every thought and know your very soul.'* Michael held the gaze and refused to let his determination falter.

"What did you think of the tale Michael?" He finally asked.

"…Very informative…" Michael said truthfully, but unsure of how many of his thoughts he felt obligated to give away in a single evening.

"I believed it was something you needed to hear. You could just say a little birdie told me."

"A little birdie?" Michael looked at him with the utmost epiphany of utter confusion.

"Nevermind, Michael. It's late, and we have a long day ahead of us. Get some rest. I'll take the watch for now." Albright spoke with sincerity.

"Thank you…goodnight Albright."

"Goodnight Michael." Albright said as he packed his pipe full once more and watched Michael walk away. He lit the pipe and collected his thoughts as he always did, his smoke joining that of the great fire before him, and drifting off as a wane into the eternally black sky of Gell.

3

When Michael woke early the next morning, he was surprised to find that the sky was nearly as dark as it had been the previous night. The black layer of clouds above had not receded with the dawn of the new day, and Michael could hear a deep thunder rolling in the distance.

Albright, seemingly untroubled by the dark sky, sat on a nearby

———

stump smoking his pipe. The stump was all that remained of the ancient tree, long ago turned to the cold stone familiar to the petrified trees of the forest. "Good morrow Michael, did you rest easy?"

He hadn't. His body ached and his bones were stiff, frozen through from the chilled night air. He knew complaining would get them no further along the road, and such talk would only bring discouragement on the already bleak day. "Aye, slept as easy as one could in such a place."

"You speak true Michael Cross, but I can see the darkness in the sky has brought worry to your thoughts."

Michael wondered just how easy he was to read. "I was wondering…why is it still so dark?"

"It seems that darkness seeps from the very heart of Gell. It is a combination of the natural and…unnatural elements of this place." Albright puffed at his pipe as though in deep thought.

"Unnatural?"

"It is believed that the byproducts of the industry that has grown so prominent in this region have somehow melded with the very chaotic and uncontrollable nature of the eruptions and emissions this land seems to be constantly trying to vent. Those inhabitants of Gell who have clustered together to form a single massed city took it upon themselves to exploit the raw power of this land. Using its gases to generate power and drive the machines they use in the elements of their massed production of many products which are traded all throughout the land. They have even been said to have mastered the very eruptions of the volcanoes and have learned to redirect and pressurize their heat in order to form massed forges to create even more of their damned machines."

"I've heard very little of this from where I come from. I mean, I've heard of the industry there, and have even seen the machines they have produced and delivered to Lindell, such as the devices which heat water, and much advancement like stoves, and other devices which have made life easier for the people. But most still rely on the magicks of the ancients over the new found power of steam."

"As they should...but tell me something Michael, have you heard anyone in your parts speak of something called...electricity?" Albright took another drag from his pipe as he looked intently to Michael's reaction to the word.

"Electrick...iciety...?" Michael struggled to form the word. "I've never heard of anything of the sort."

"Perhaps not... In the city of Gell, which ironically is called Gellor, there is a form of power that has been discovered. It is not magick, nor is it the power of the gods It is some form of energy which can be conjured through something called...generation, or maybe generated. I'm not quite sure. All I know is that it is extremely difficult to control, and it is extremely dangerous."

"How did you hear of it?"

"During my travels I have made a few stops to the city of Gellor; mind you this was before my rank as captain in Singe. Anyway, on my visits to the city I saw many things. Massed clusters of glass which seemed to illuminate from their core and create a light which could outshine a thousand lanterns. These lights cover nearly all of the city and its black towers, bringing day to their endless night. When I asked about it I was told that they were powered by this...electricity. They told me that it was in fact the power of the land, transformed to be put to use by man."

"Sounds fishy to me." Michael said.

"Fishy?" Albright asked, being unfamiliar with the context.

"It's something my friends and I used to say when something just didn't seem right. So we said it smelled fishy, and I gotta tell ya Albright, transforming the raw untapped power of Selador doesn't sound like that great of an idea to me. Otherwise, why else would the ancients have given the people the magicks to better their lives?"

"That's exactly the same thought that I had. When I asked you if you had heard of this new power I was hoping that you hadn't and that it had indeed remained in Gellor for the most part. Rather then spreading to the other regions as so many of their other products have, and with a catching enthusiasm that brings me to worry."

"I wouldn't worry about their other devices, such as the steam engines and pumps, they seem to be a good balance between the ingenuity of man and the power of nature."

"Aye, I agree some are indeed well balanced, and I myself must admit I am rather partial to the idea of indoor plumbing as well, but what worries me…what scares me…is that the rewards their success brings them from their simpler devices will only give them the means to further their pursuit of this new power. And what I fear the most is that it will undoubtedly change the face of Selador forever. For example, since Lindell has received many of these devices that heat or pump water, and the things you called…stoves, I want you to think about the people who now possess them. Since they have a machine which replaces even the simplest forms of water and fire magick, and now that the convenience is within their grasp, do you see those people using the magick anymore?"

"No…they just use the machine, but what's wrong with that?"

"Because, Michael, over time what other kinds of machines are these

---

people of Gell going to create, what other needs of magick will be replaced and what ancient lore will become obsolete? And what's going to happen if those machines break down someday and no one remembers how to do things the 'old way'?"

"So what you're saying is, what if these machines not only change the everyday lives of the people, but erase the very magick from the world?"

"Aye…what happens if no one remembers how to tap into the true power of this land? What kind of society, what kind of people will we have become?"

"It's a scary thought…one that makes me wish that I, myself had the ability to use the lore of the ancients…I almost feel guilty for having welcomed the idea of machines because of how it would have made my life easier."

"You mean to tell me you cannot use the ancient lore?!" Albright seemed stunned.

"Never have, no matter how hard I've tried…the closest I've ever come to that kind of power was when I…" Michael thought of Lord Raymark and the cross which would forever be carved into his horrible face, but chose to keep his inner turmoil just as it was, within. "…first took the legendary sword. The only problem is I'm not sure if it's me or the sword conjuring the power I have used in my battles."

Albright looked to him with sympathy, unsure just how to respond. "Refresh me again on how you first came upon possessing the sword, and the details of your battle with Danube Drakendor. Perhaps I may be able to provide some insight as to how this power of yours is summoned." Albright finished his pipe and began to pack fresh tobacco into its bowl. He offered Michael the first drag, and Michael inhaled gratefully before beginning his tale.

When he had finished, Albright was smiling and seemed rather excited, like a child having just heard a magnificent story of legend. He even chuckled, which Michael questioned. "What's so funny?"

"My apologies Michael, I only laugh because of Danube. The damned fool just wants his big battle, and yet he chooses you as his only friend. It's simply irony is all, but it's like they say, you can never truly know someone until you have fought them, and I would suppose that Danube Drakendor knows you very well Michael. He knows you so well, in fact, that he even stated that the two of you are indeed two of a kind, each the last of his lineage. I only wish that he can put the past behind him much in the same way you have put yours behind you. Perhaps he will see in time that revenge is never the answer and will forgive your forefathers for what they had done."

"I can only hope. I've grown to liking the idea of having him as an ally in these strange times, and would rather not have that change upon our next meeting."

"Aye, spoken true…despite all that, I believe I may have an answer to your earlier question. From what you have told me, I can only gather that it is your own power which you have used in these battles. In fact I think it may indeed be the power of the Cross bloodline running through your veins. However, I believe the sword was indeed what initially unlocked this power of yours, and it is the sword allowing you to channel that energy under dire circumstance when you are…emotionally driven to that form of resolve where you find the determination you need to defeat your enemies."

"So in a way the power of the Cross is my magick?"

"I wouldn't say that necessarily. I think perhaps the power of the Cross is one of the rawest forms of magick still in existence. Magick before there was magick if you get my meaning."

"So if it's not magick then how can I hope to master the lore to control its power?"

"I don't think there is any lore to learn that would teach you the ability to control it. I think that this form of power quite simply reacts to the amount of will you have to conjure its potential and be able to withstand the strain it will put upon your aura, body, and mind."

"So mind over matter, right?"

"Aye, if you wish to look at it that way, but more so the state of your resolve, your determination to act." Albright said finally finishing the second pipe full he had shared with Michael. Jayce and Willum were returning from a morning scout of the area, and Albright made a gesture which Michael immediately took as, *'we'll finish this later'*, and he abruptly changed subjects.

"How far do you suppose we'll travel today?" Michael asked as openly as he could, leaving the question for any of the three men to pick up as they pleased.

It was Jayce that answered first. "Reckon today'll be as slow as molasses by the looks of it."

"Why do you say that?" Albright immediately questioned his old friend.

"Oh you know ya old cuss, just our favorite part of the journey through this godforsaken place."

"You don't mean…" Albright seemed immediately disgruntled.

———

"…swamplands…" Jayce finished.

"Swamplands?" Michael questioned.

"You'll see…" Albright said as he tucked his pipe back in his pouch and rubbed the place where the bridge of his nose and his forehead met. Michael could see that at the mention of the swamplands Albright had suddenly grown very worry stricken, so much so that if any other man had known what poor Albright had known on this day they would have fled from such swamps. Fled their destiny and never looked back.

4

The swamp Wastes of Gell. Such petulant, murky, uncharted land as this was never meant to be traveled by the likes of men. Acres of stagnant water stretch infinitely before them, shrouded only by the fog and abyss of tangled ominous shadows and life lurking just beneath the surface.

Albright led the group upon his old horse Siren. Annabelle always favored Siren, and if law one day allowed he would pass the mighty horse to her as a wedding present. *'One of many…'* he thought wistfully. Siren made his first plunge into the murky moss-covered water, wading up to his knees. The horse gave out a light whinny of disapproval at the cold slime-covered mess. Albright tightened his grip upon the timeless leather of the familiar reins, and led Siren on.

With a steady pace achieved, Albright laid off a bit. He let the fingers of his free hand trace the grooves and cracks that had worn into the leather of his saddle over time. He knew every crack as though it were his own. A physical reminder of those miles he'd wandered in his life, and the cracks upon his soul that had formed along that journey. His breath was heavy as he thought of his past transgressions.

The air was thick and humid, sticking to the lungs longer than one would hope. His skin ran gooseflesh with a sudden chill. His thoughts returned from reminiscing. It was then he saw the darkness in the corner of his eyes. His world seemed to be moving forward along a set path driving to a set point. These feelings he's had before, these feelings of following...

They have come nearly halfway through a series of mile-long stretches of murky stagnant water and moss. The horses are chilled from the cold water and lack of food. Albright makes a move to rest the horses on a nearby patch of dry land. He steers Siren for the patch of land, thinking once again of the dreams only a lover can have, of marriage, of children, of happiness, but the sad truth of all is the fate of such men.

As Siren struck hoof into the bank of the small island, Albright was sure they'd struck solid ground, but a little farther and he knew the source of his 'bad feeling'. He felt the shifting of the horses' weight, heard the deep guttural sucking of the pressure escaping from the deception beneath him, the false lands. The ground and moss peeled away beneath him as the ground began to swallow them up. The horse panics, driving them further in as they sink. Albright, still gripping tightly to his faithful horse, has sunk to his waist and the horse is at its neck. In a matter of seconds there is nothing more of the rider and his steed above the surface of these false lands of Gell.

Darkness is all around him now. He feels his final breath being spent with every moment. The pressure is building around him, he is bound to the weight of his old friend beneath him, and it is dragging him further and faster into the darkness. The vision finally comes clear in his mind.

He sees the dragon...he sees his Lady...his Annabelle...he knows what he must do...he must save the Cross...death must wait for me. These are his final

———

thoughts as one old soul sinks to the depths of darkness abroad his mighty steed…once more.

5

The twists life can throw are sometimes too complex, too tightly wound on the spectrum of one's assumption to the solidity of the world around them that when something happens that doesn't fit the mold they so easily settle their minds to a point where they ask 'why', or proclaim that it is 'unfair'. Michael Cross knows that such thought, such places of comfort in one's mind, when all seems to be well and fine, and the great things your life were meant for are surely on their way. It is this mindset that Michael knows is the most dangerous of all, because in an instant…all can be taken.

Such may be said, and perhaps was said, for the fallen Albright as he disappeared from the sight of the world, and the sight and help of his friends. It was in these moments that Michael was held back by the likes of Jayce and Willum. It was in these moments that *he* spoke with the thoughts of 'why' and 'unfair'.

"You must cease your efforts Man of Cross! You can do nothing for him now! Those kinds of horrors are only one-way. There is no escape for him. He is gone!" Willum spoke with the deep rasp of a man aged by the land and driven by discipline long turned to stone. His voice commanded, and Michael obeyed. He quit trying to run to the place where a man he was beginning to call a friend in his mind, had disappeared. Jayce and Willum still held their grasp on him a moment longer, but soon released him.

Michael looked ahead of them to the false lands. The now brown crust covered still pool that could easily be mistaken for a dried mud puddle. He felt sick to his stomach for a moment, but it passed. *'Such a shame...'* was the only conscious thought he held, but he never spoke. No one spoke for the remainder of that day. Michael was never sure if it was out of respect, a moment of silence. He just never felt like anyone needed to say anything at all. It almost felt like the simplest thing said could cause a serious rage amidst the group. Anger forged from pain, frustration, sadness, and fatigue of the journey they pledged to make that day despite the loss, a silent pledge.

Such silent trekking can sometimes stand still the fabric of time, making each hour stretch infinitely into the horizon, or make the day slip so incredibly fast that there simply isn't enough time to accomplish that which should already be achieved by the reasoning of the mind. In this case, however, time seemed to slip past Michael Cross so smoothly, that Michael had no idea that they traveled nearly thirty miles through the swamps of Gell.

When the travelers broke camp that night they gathered plentiful amounts of roots and wood, and everything they could find that would burn, and built a pyre in honor of their fallen comrade and friend. Yet even as the fires climbed into the night the silence between them was not broken. The three men sat in silence as the demons of the fire danced before them. Michael felt entranced by the mystical flames and the noises around him. His head swam with the fumes of the swamp, the heat of the blaze before them, and the song the fire made with the creatures lurking there.

It seemed as though days passed before anyone made a sound, but all too quickly Michael began to hear what started as a whisper, a humming beneath the breath, and became a song which bled from the hearts of Albright's oldest friends. Michael remained silent, a lone spectator to the death song, sang between brothers. The words he did not know, the dialect was alien, but the power it breathed, the emotion that quelled within it, was all too familiar. His skin broke to gooseflesh as the song reached a peak, his mouth ran dry, and a strange numbness ran through his body. The world around him spun, his stomach clenched as the dizziness entered his mind and the world began to blur, he could hear the thinness of the world pounding in his ears with the retched warble of some estranged instrument. Despite the warbled, disoriented way Michael Cross viewed the world as he began to collapse from a mild narcotic-induced seizure to his brain, the song of the brothers still echoed in his heart.

6

As Michael collapsed to the ground in a spasm of what appeared to be a seizure, the still conscious friends looked to each other with horror filled eyes. Realization had struck. They had lacked on the inspection of all the kindling wood and had no doubt neglected to inspect Michael's. Considering his unfamiliarity with the land, something in the fire was burning that could poison them, and probably already had.

Yet as fate deals with the affirmation of all that which forges destiny, so it does the fate of its 'heroes'. As Jayce and Willum catch each other's gaze one last time their worst possible nightmare comes true. They were too negligent to realize where they had broken camp. They had seen the dry spot and thought it well enough, but what they had neglected to see in the darkness was the random array of spouts all around the area of the swamp. In a glance of the eye one could easily catch a hundred or more. Each one served as a let off valve for the massed array of volcanic chambers beneath the swamp and all of Gell. The valves sprayed invisible clouds of gasses which under normal circumstances were odorless, and induced a general 'high', but with the presence of the flames…the burning of the pyre…those gases now erupted into flames.

The little island where they had willingly selected to host a bonfire of praise and honor for their lost brother quickly became the fiery depiction of hell. Walls of fire shot up through trees and in turn erupted larger clouds of gasses raining fire down from above. Each spout that caught fire caught the next one, spraying flames fifteen feet and higher. The entire area had become an inferno, and would later become known as 'The Devil's Gateway'.

Jayce dove to Michael's collapsed form as quickly as he could, pushing him from falling into the blaze which now surrounded them. Willum helped him carry the slowly stirring Michael Cross. Through fire and hell the two men managed to carry him far enough away from the burning area to escape harm. It was here that the effects of the gas and burning thin roots released their hold upon his mind.

He remembers seeing the scorched and singed figures before him. He remembers the oldest of them turns back for the horses. He remembers the look on Jayce's face as the swamp exploded into a single massed blaze, engulfing Willum in the brightest light he had ever seen. He feels himself being pulled to his feet, he sees Jayce next to him, and sees the terror and pain upon his face. Jayce is screaming at him, but he cannot hear him over the roar. In the depths of his mind he is still hearing the 'brother's song' as though it is now permanently transfixed in his thoughts as though forever burned into his mind. Yet the fiery hell he sees before him, and the realization at what has happened to Willum brings his mind snapping dangerously fast into the heat of the moment. He has no control, but simply acts.

Willum lies in a burning heap upon the ground, his blue eyes looking up at Michael Cross with a cruel dignity that still commands him in a way he has never known. This burning, melted heap of flesh, which only resembles the man he once was, his eyes giving the only clue, lifts the remnants of his arm, and points to the legendary Great Sword of Lindell driven into the ground upon the island their pyre stood, like a great Cross standing witness to the fiery hell which burned around it. Michael understood that Willum had not gone back for the horses, and that they had valued him first over the sword.

Jayce looked to Michael, having seen the gesture to the sword, he knew not what to expect of the man of Cross. But as he gazed upon this sullen man's face, and saw the way the fire danced shadows across his expression, he needed not to say a word, for he knew that Michael Cross was born to walk the fires of hell.

Without a word spoken Michael waded through the swamp waters to the fiery island that held his namesake, his right, his destiny. Clouds of gas erupted into flames above him, and all sorts of fiery debris fell around him, but he never slowed his pace. Jayce watched as Michael approached the island as it once again erupted into flames, bathing darkness with light. He watched as the flames enveloped the man Cross.

Michael felt the searing heat gather at the center of the island, he felt the explosion grow and burst, and in this moment he could see the way the sword created a sphere of energy around it protecting it from the blast. It was as the explosion concussed its flames that Michael's instinct truly took control. His aura poured out the power locked within him, something beyond the Cross, something of another life. The flames engulfed him, and he felt the pain of its heat, but he was not burned. He forced himself forward, driving towards the sword, to the center of the flames, the hottest point. He swore the heat and pain would kill him, but neither did, and he pushed on.

He was upon the island where their campfire once stood, and where the sword had somehow been driven into the ground blade-first, sheath and all. The fires burned hotter than anything he had ever felt in his life, but the sight of the sword pushed him on. Just as he thought he could bear no more, his fingertips touched the hilt of the legendary sword. He had closed his eyes, blinded by the pain, but now as he touched the sword he felt sudden release as if he had peacefully died and drifted elsewhere. The air around him was still blazing hot, but it was a *different* kind of heat.

Michael Cross opened his eyes to find himself once again in the desert of his dreams, and yet it was real. The sand beneath his feet, the blue sky of the horizon, and the hot sun beaming down on him was all real, even the voice he hears.

'*EVERYTHING YOU FACE, MICHAEL CROSS, IS A TRIAL… CONSIDER THIS YOUR TRIAL BY FIRE, YOUR BABTISM AMIDST THE FLAMES …*'

The voice was familiar, a voice that had visited him before in the darkest depths of his mind. Part of him wanted to call out to the voice, but before anything could be said the voice was gone, and the desert transformed into flames that suddenly were once again engulfing him. Michael drove forward, pulled the sword from its sheath and held it to the sky letting loose a valiant cry as he released the power within him. In a blast of blue light a shockwave of energy ripped out through the inferno, and the flames of the fire ceased. All was darkness.

182

7

He drifted through images and time, until he found himself in a grey world amidst a wheat field. The day is bright, and the light brings color to the wheat and into the world. The blue and white fades slowly into the sky, and the wheat slowly comes to life as it sways in the wind with the sunlight shimmering from its, once grey, now golden stalks. In the distance Michael can see a house. It is of no design he has ever seen, and yet appears to be centuries old. There is a small shed in the back. Michael cannot see it, but he knows that the doors to this shed are sealed and locked.

He walks towards the house, but as he takes his first step in this new world he can feel it suddenly shift, and fade. Somewhere in the distance he thinks he can hear the brother's song and an overwhelming beat accompanying it. A beat that drives steadily into his mind like a hammer; "THUD…THUD….THUMP…THUD…THUD…THUMP…THUD……." It drives all thought from his mind and a sheet of white hot pain rips through him.

8

"THUD…THUMP…" Michael opens his eye's to find himself unharmed, lying in the back of a cart full of goods and items of trade. He can see that many of the items had been restacked making room for him to be laid in the straw. Michael, as always, struggles to see in the pitch black darkness of the nights of Gell. He tries to sit up despite the strange pain

183

still echoing in his bones.

He can see that the cart is driven by an old man who sits hunched over with his back to Michael, reins in hand. Michael looked around for any sign of Jayce, or even the barely alive Willum. As though to cue, Jayce rode his horse up to the cart, somehow the horse had managed to escape the blaze.

"I see that you've returned to the land of the living."

"How long have I been out for?"

"Most of the night, it will be dawn soon."

"Where are we?"

"I found this unmarked trader's route a short trek from where we were. These carts are owned by an old trader I knew in my days as a convoy guard. He was happy to help me with you and dear Willum."

"You mean he's still alive?!" Michael had managed to lean on the edge of the cart, enabling himself to hear the news better.

"Yes, Willum still lives. We are on our way to the city of Gellor. Once there we will find help for him, healers, leeches, and such. I hear that despite Gellor's remote location, it is by far the most advanced city in all of Selador. They are said to have greatly advanced medicine and technology beyond the likes any have ever seen...." Jayce seemed to trail off. He rode close to a lantern hitched to the wagon and Michael could see the delirium entering the man's face.

"...They must have a way to help him...I cannot lose two brothers in a day's time..."

Michael saw the tears begin to well in the man's eyes just before he turned and rode further up the rode to scout ahead.

Michael knew that no such magick or science could mend the burns

———

that had been dealt to Willum. He had seen him himself, what was left of him. The fact that he had not died from shock was a miracle alone, but having the hopes that they could possibly save him was…madness.

Michael settled down in the straw bedding of the old cart and wrestled his thoughts to a silent standoff.

Somewhere in his thoughts he lost his train, lost his point, his focus, and in turn drifted slowly to sleep. He would not dream in this sleep, nor would he see the visions of places yet to be, but his sleep was restless nonetheless.

9

Michael woke to the black towers of Gellor looming in the distance, scraping the sky much in the same way as the ice towers of Trengar, but falling far short in comparison. While the ice towers had always been a welcoming presence, the towers of Gellor proved to be ominous, deceptive, in size and height, and black as the hearts of the evilest of men. Black smoke trickled from the peaks and spires of some of the towers blanketing the city below in thick fog. The metropolis was a magnificent towering giant of mechanical ingenuity and industry. Metal, stone, and fire reflected the true nature and heart of this land. Its buildings were built upon buildings that crossed and crisscrossed with the girders and supports of other buildings, making up a maze of strength and power. Even at the distance from which they now approached, Michael could clearly see huge flames roaring at the tops of several of the towers and in the center of platforms high in the air. The flames appeared to be fifty feet in places, but at all times in a state of control, of purpose. It was a place of darkness, and yet was the most spectacular display of lights Michael had ever seen.

As they neared, Michael noted the strange luminescence emanating from the dark sky overhead. As they rounded a bend in the path he could see the source of this unnatural light. Each building, post, and tower was lined with strange mechanical lights, each seemingly the strength of a hundred lanterns.

Michael sat quietly in the back of the cart as they approached the city gates that loomed ahead. Mesmerized by the sheer infrastructure, machinery, and strange glowing lights of the city, the remaining events were like a blur to the exhausted and troubled Michael Cross.

They were accompanied by guards to the city's main tower. It was here that they found the great healer of the city and entrusted the burned form of their fallen friend to his care under the assurance that everything that what could be done, would be done. But Michael had his doubts, even *if* the poor man was able to live from his injuries he sustained, he would still be a walking freak the rest of his days. Michael could almost see in his mind the way women would cover their children's eyes as they screamed, and hear the harsh words of the men who would cry, "*My god, what is that?!*" as he would walk by. It pained him greatly to think of this, having experienced much of the same shame himself after his fall from honor, but the shame Willum would know would be far greater than Michael had ever known, and far more arduous than he would ever be able to imagine. For within the mangled scarred flesh of the man that was Willum, though old…once handsome in his own way, had the heart and soul of a good man. A man of honor and courage, only to be shamed with disfigurement in the eyes of those he served and loved.

When Michael and Jayce were taken from their maimed comrade they were led to separate rooms. It was here where they could freshen themselves before a meal that would be held as their welcome. It was in this time of collected solitude, these few moments which he spent alone with his drifting thoughts that Michael wept for the fallen, wept for those who had sacrificed everything so that *he* could continue on. It is a hard thing to see a man cry, but see it well. See the tears for those who die.

10

Michael and Jayce have been led to the entrance of a fine dining hall by a tall wiry man named Vincient. The hall in which he has taken them is ordained with grand paintings of lords, ladies, and great tapestries depicting the rise of industry in their 'great' city. There is a large table, stretching thirty feet in length, its wood is as black as the sky and carved with richly elaborate whittlings. Michael and Jayce are led into the room through a set of giant double doors, and the table before them is lit by several beautiful candlesticks alongside a feast worthy of kings. At the opposite end of the table is a massive stone fireplace, its hearth spanning at least ten feet across.

Michael is surprised by the elegance of the dining hall and simply stands just outside the door, purely taken back by the sight of such extravagant food. He could not remember the last time he had actually sat at a dining table to eat a proper meal. The doors had been opened by two figures wearing opposing garments that now looked to him in question at his bewilderment. One wore white robes and a black mask which reflected the flickering firelight of the hallway and the dining hall before them. The other wore robes of black and a mask of the purest white, and their movements were fluid and precise. They moved in unison; at the same moment, the same way, only on opposite sides, creating mirror images of one another.

Michael and Jayce were escorted into the dining hall where they were shown to their seats. Michael was seated at the head of the table, his back to the fireplace with the great sword resting on the arm of the chair at his side. Jayce was seated at his right. Wine was poured and a light entrée lain before them. "Be pleased, Lord Michael Cross. Feast and enjoy yourselves. Your entertainment will ensue momentarily."

"Entertainment isn't necessary this meal is more than enough. We thank you."

"Aye, you are quiet welcome my liege, but I must insist on the entertainment. For it is not often we receive such honored guests as yourselves, and we always keep to our traditions of hospitality. I must bother you though…with a request."

"Go on…" Jayce replied immediately, clearly rushing the small talk to move on to more nourishing things.

"It has been requested that a certain lord accompany you for your meal…as well as I?"

"We would be honored, of course. You are our hosts after all, right Jayce?"

"Aye…"

"Very good, then we shall join you momentarily. Until then, help yourselves, and just ask if you need anything." As he said this, Vincient poured a glass of wine for both Michael and Jayce. Michael watched as the dark liquid rippled and swirled within the crystal as it was filled, and for a moment his eyes connected with their courteous host. Michael felt something pull in the back of his mind and felt the most dreadful feeling. As one always does, he convinced himself of an overactive imagination and thanked the man for the wine. Vincient swiftly left the room.

Once he was gone, Jayce immediately turned his attention to the steaming food before them. Michael was hesitant at first, looking first to the two servants who stood 'guard' at the doors, and then to the dark wine before him. He recalled the last glass of wine he had taken the pleasure of drinking, back in Lindell, in his room in the estate, just before his life turned to the perils of his duty to protect the sword. *The sword*, he thought, *Damn this bloody blade. It has brought nothing but death and pain to those who have sought to help protect it, or perhaps that is simply **my** failure.* He couldn't muster the desire to fill his plate with the food before him. He had lost his appetite with such thoughts. He did, however, once again long for the taste of wine. As he sipped from the fine crystal chalice, Jayce devoured his meal, swallowing his own wine in large, overindulgent gulps. The wine was strong, and hit his palate very well. He took another sip and then quickly downed the entire glass, an old habit he knew he'd never be rid of. He felt the strength of the wine, the warmth it brought to his heart, the emptiness it momentarily filled, and so he poured another glass. He sipped it a little longer than the last, already feeling a slight tingling in his head, but soon enough he downed it too in a mighty shot. He wanted to rest his mind from his thoughts, to let go of the death of Albright and the infliction which had beset Willum. He drank a third glass and his head began to swim, his terrible thoughts began to return to the depths of his unconscious mind, and his appetite slowly returned.

He reached for the bottle of wine to replenish his glass, and then perhaps he would find a morsel or two to feast upon, but as his mind made the message to move, something kept him still. He was suddenly and completely paralyzed, a cramping numbness ripping through his muscles. He tried to speak, but found he could not. He could only look, and see that Jayce was in the same terrible position as he, only Jayce had still been eating, and was now seemingly frozen in place as he was reaching for another leg of meat.

Michael watched from the corner of his eyes as the two servants in black and white knocked three times on the door.

At once, the doors were opened and two figures entered the room.

"Ahh, I see you enjoyed the wine my friends. Good…very good." Vincient said as he approached the table with the second figure that Michael couldn't quite make out except for a long dark cloak the color of blood. He could tell it was a man, but his face was deeply shadowed by a hood pulled down low over his eyes. The man at first appeared as a cleric or wizard, but as soon as he had reached the table, and Michael's direct line of vision, the man removed his shroud. The strings of Michael's heart broke loose at the sight of the man before them.

The firelight danced across a familiar wound upon the man's face, a wound that would forever burn with the hatred of Michael's heart, a wound in the shape of a cross.

"Let me introduce you, my lord and good man, to the esteemed and great High Lord Raymark of Lindell." Vincient proclaimed in an exocentric fashion.

"Oh, I'm afraid that our dear friend Lord Cross here has already had the pleasure of knowing me on more than one occasion…just as I have had the pleasure of 'knowing' his wife." Raymark's devilish grin tightened the muscles in his face, creasing the wound and no doubt causing him great pain, but he relished in his joy nonetheless, and smiled even wider. Vincient chuckled at his remark.

Michaels' eyes once again returned to Jayce, who was struggling to do something, *anything*, but his efforts were futile. No matter how hard either of them tried, they simply could not move or speak, but could only watch in horror as the trap was unfolded before their eyes.

"It is no use to struggle, for the poison we have given you will not lose its effects for many hours to come, and not even the mightiest of men can break its hold upon the physiology of your body. You are truly helpless." Vincient said this with a certain sick satisfaction.

"Just as your friend Willum, was, lying upon his cot, so helpless and maimed. He could only watch in wide-eyed horror as we plunged dagger after dagger into his still beating heart." It was Raymark who said this, his malevolent smile framed with crimson lips.

Michael saw the sudden fury in Jayce's eyes, and the helplessness as he struggled against the poison which pumped through his veins. Tears began to flow from the corners of his eyes, red hot against his skin, but still Jayce could not move.

"You have done very well here Vincient, *he* will be most pleased. But enough of these games. Have your guards take the sword and his belongings, and take him to the worst cell you can possibly find. *He* won't be pleased with the ill treatment, but, well, I guess you can consider this a little payback Michael. Although, I really have *you* to thank for everything…"

———

Michael looked at him with eyes that could burn a hole through the soul of any man.

"You see Michael, not only did I get the chance to have the best fucks of my life again, and again, and again, but once you were given the sword by the high lord…well, after you left for Trengar, I killed them, and once all that bloodshed was discovered, do you know who I blamed it on?" He gave Michael a second to let things roll in his mind. "That's right, you. I told them the other bodies, the raiders from Zwentor, were those of a secret guard exonerated for the protection of the sword. I told them that you killed them all and that when the high lord and I discovered you in the act, you killed them as well." Michael could feel the rage of his ancestry boil within him. "And, if you're wondering how I explained my survival. Well, I simply told them you had knocked me out with the hilt of your blade, not wishing to kill me, so that I may live on forever bearing this god forsaken curse upon my flesh." Raymark traced the wound with his fingertips as he spoke.

Michael couldn't help but let his ancient blood flow within him. His body broke out in a cold sweat, his muscles began to spasm, he could feel his heart exploding with hatred, but yet he still could not strike out against the man.

"You know what Michael? They believed every word I said. Not only that, but they elected me as the new High Lord of Lindell. For having endured so many hardships for the sake of the land and honorably risking my life against the mad man Michael Cross. They could think of no better way to honor me. It is a strange twist of fate Michael. I only wish that I could thank you properly for the wonderful things you have brought into my life, but then again, there is this." He gestured to the wound upon his

———

face. "Eye for an eye I suppose. What do you say we call it even...huh? Whadaya say?" Raymark mocked. "Ah, well, perhaps another time. Get him out of my sight Vincient. Put him in that place we discussed earlier, I must prepare for *his* coming. See to it he isn't harmed...much. *He* wishes for this man to be intact upon *his* arrival.

"Aye, my lord, but what shall I do with the other one?" Vincient asked.

"Kill him. We have no use for him." At that he turned, his cloak flashing out behind him like a cape of blood, and walked back to the doorway. The two guards at the door approached the table. When Raymark reached the door he stopped abruptly as though forgetting a final task. "Oh, and Michael, I'll give my love to your wife for you." With that, Raymark at last disappeared from sight, his maniacal laughter echoing through the halls.

This was the epiphany of pain, of frustration, of helplessness, of hatred. So much the young man Michael wished to do, but nothing could be done. No matter how hard he tired, he could not move. He could only sit and watch unblinking as the guards approached the table, the one in black robes and white mask towering behind Jayce's frozen form, the horrible look in his friends eyes as his head was jerked back by his hair and his throat was slit by the blade of a fine silver knife. Jayce's life spilled out over the table before him, coloring the white linen cloths and food in crimson. Michael would be haunted by the look in Jayce's eyes for the rest of his life.

At that moment Michael had strained himself to the point where his body could fight no more. It was no longer a matter of paralysis. His body simply shut itself down from the stress and poison. Michael collapsed, his body swiftly taken by the form of the guard in white, its black mask still gleaming in the firelight. The darkness of the mask took him to a dreamless sleep filled only with shadows and pain.

II

Michael saw no wheat field, no desert. He heard no guiding voices...all was darkness. A thundering was present in his mind like the quake of a thousand echoes crying out at once. He thought perhaps the darkness would never cease. When he opened his eyes, he found that it was not only his dreamless unconsciousness that thundered in the black void but the world around him as well.

The ground which he lay upon was damp and cold. His eyes struggled to adjust to the darkness before him but refused. He could smell soot and ash, and for a moment thought perhaps he had indeed woken in hell.

His body ached, his muscles were slow to react, his head felt beaten and bruised, but still he found his feet and gained some bearing about himself.

Once he had regained himself, he felt his way through the darkness trying to create some mental image of just where he was. After a few moments he determined the inevitable truth. The cell was four by six, three sides of it, iron bars, the back a solid wall of stone. He couldn't quite determine which side, if any, had a door but if he had to guess he would've chosen the wall of iron bars adjacent from the stone wall. Yet before he could test this, he heard something moving close by. It was a sound unlike the relentless dripping of water and the pounding of the furnaces and machinery beyond his walls. It was the shuffling of flesh - movement, perhaps in another cell close to his. A knot formed deep in his thought. There was no telling what sorts of malformed demonic things might lurk in the dark dungeons of Gell and Michael had no desire to find out. Fear took him.

"Is anyone there?" Michael projected his question into the darkness. There was silence, and then another shuffle, farther away this time. "Is someone there?!" Michael's voice began to sound desperate with fear creeping onto his tongue like the taste of blood.

At last, when he was sure his fear would consume him and force a scream bellowing from him like a child awakening from some ill begotten nightmare, a soft voice spoke from the darkness.

"Are you the one whom they have spoken of? The one *he* fears?"

Michael was so startled by the womanly voice that he nearly stumbled back, but his hands firmly grasped the iron bars before him. "Who are you?" He asked the woman in the darkness.

"It matters only to me until you can make me see. The man you are, the man you're not doesn't matter if you forgot."

"I haven't forgotten, woman, but I have recently made it a point not to give my name lightly."

"A wise decision to make, but trusting the hospitality of Gell was your first mistake…speak your name or hold your tongue, either way you'll remain 'cept by blanket hung…there is no escaping the prisons of Gell. Besides, who'd you rather have as company, the rats, or a beautiful woman who's been alone for a *long* time?"

Michael thought about this for a long moment, trying to picture just what the woman he was speaking to might look like, and judging by her voice he decided a good deal better than the rats.

"My apologies my lady...I am Michael Cross." He put his hand between the bars in the direction of the woman's voice. Almost immediately he felt the soft touch of a slender delicate hand which could be no more than a decade older than his. Whatever reason this woman was in this cell, she was only in her thirties at most. What surprised Michael was how quickly she had found his hand in the darkness, but he quickly passed it off that his eyes had not yet adjusted.

"I am Eleanor Stevens-Priory, undoubtedly the last of the Priory. I thank you Michael Cross, we are well met."

"You're not rhyming anymore?"

"Pardon?"

"Before...when you spoke it sounded like a riddle or a song...it rhymed."

"I take no note of such."

"I see...Where are we exactly?"

"We are in the western tower, the second highest tower of Gellor. It is here, in its highest chambers that they hold their prisoners, test subjects, and farseers alike. The rest of this tower is an installation which both serves as one of the main exhaust let-offs for the volcanic eruptions beneath the city, as well as the center of all scientific research. Once in this tower, there is no escape."

"Farseers? What is a farseer?"

"You are not of Gellor are you?"

"Nay, I am...was, a lord of Lindell, but it would seem deceit has stricken me of that position."

"I see... a farseer. It is a creation of *he*. Those who are 'touched' by the gods, the special ones, are taken and changed. Changed, to see the distance over the land, to see the future of life and events, to hone their psychic abilities and perceive with their mind pieces of the events destiny has preordained the flow of our lives. They are connected to machines of *his* creation, and made slaves within their own mind and thoughts."

"Who is '*he*'?"

"Ssshhh! Not so loud you fool, or they'll turn me head to gruel! To speak of *he* is to speak the key. To say his name is to play his game! If I touch you then you touch me and what an awful thing we'll be." The woman's rhyming was broken by her outrageous laughter into the darkness. When the cackle had subdued, the woman's voice seemed to return to its natural and almost beautiful tone. This change preceded in a mere moment when Michael did nothing but wisely listen.

"Are you not the one who has carried the weight of the sword of the gods, the great sword which is now in their possession, no doubt?"

"Aye, that was my burden."

"So you are the man I thought you to be…the one…*he* fears?"

"Who is this '*he*'?" Michael asked in a whisper.

"The dark one, my lover, my bearer of onslaught upon the heart of my bosom, the one who's slippery fingers delve within mine mind raping mine thoughts and dreams, taking from me mine innocence, mine sanity, mine virginity, mine white. The one cast in the shadows of this world…mine…mine Raven Warlack."

Michael felt an icy chill race its way through his spine as the name was muttered so softly, so slowly like a secret pronouncing doom between lips once undoubtedly sweet.

"I have heard this name before…from stories along my journey…" Michael holds to the painful memories of his now lost friends and the

---

198

campfires they shared along their journey through Gell. He sees them very well, their ending moments captured and framed in his mind like murals of the recent past, but though both Albright and Willum passed on beyond his view, one death held fast and fresh in his mind.

He could almost smell the stink of Jayce's blood as it had poured from his throat and onto the massed plate of food before him, spraying across the food and linen dotting it in a mosaic Pollack style painting, of speckles and splatters of crimson. Such memories were very clear, and very fresh in his mind, as were the few told tales of the infamous, but not quite 'known' Raven Warlack.

"…rumors, but nothing more. You speak as if you've known him…personally."

"Aye, so I have… he always took a certain 'interest' in his first victims, especially me. He found it a way of understanding his purpose in this world and honing his abilities. You might say I was his greatest…manipulation."

"Manipulation?" Michael was confused by the way the woman spoke, but tried with all his efforts to follow what she was trying to say.

"His greatest power is that which confuses the mind. He can place thoughts in your head which you would never have. Drive temptation into your body to commit acts you would never even consider. He can make you think you want something so bad that you would kill to obtain it, and frenzy over the actions you just made to do so. He can twist and bend and contort a person's desire to the point that it is so malformed so disfigured that you have lost all recollection of who you were and why and how you came to be the way you are. He is the darkest master of manipulation, the purest of evils in the land, and yet in appearance he is a saint, a god send, a beautiful figure whose features could only have been carved by the deity itself. The worst and most horrible thing is he can make you enjoy every second of every action he manipulates you to perform. He can make you love him and the things he does to you."

"I thought that the evil within Raven Warlack was exorcised by his father?"

"Extradited?! Ha, that's quite a sense of humor you've got there Michael Cross! The evil within Raven Warlack was never removed! In fact, the ceremony which the High Lord Randall Warlack performed as a supposed exorcism of evil was in fact a ceremony of coming to the terms of manhood, focusing the powers given to him in order to hone *his* purpose in the world. It was an ancient ceremony performed originally by the Priors of magick, descendants of my family. It is meant for one to truly master their abilities and take the first step towards their true destiny, whatever that may be."

"So you're telling me that Randall Warlack, Raven Warlack's father, not only didn't remove the evil from his son, but increased the power of darkness which resided within him? Why would he do such a thing?"

"Because Randall Warlack summoned it forth into the child in the first place when he cast the spell upon his wife's womb, calling forth the powers of darkness to aid him in impregnating her with a child who would become more powerful than anyone in all the world, and deliver the people of Gell from their eternal darkness in the inhospitable region they had been bestowed, and help them rise to power. Obviously he got his wish, but the price he paid cost him everything, including his life and the mortal soul of his wife and only son."

"All these machines, this industry, and…electricity… are all of *his* design, *his* invention?" Michael asked as he prided himself in saying the word 'electricity' with the correct pronunciation.

"Yes, in a way…they are *his* ideas. He gets them from somewhere though…the 'other' place, and once he understands them to a point, he explains the ideas to others, and how he proposes they will work. The people built it, and after some modifications the machines inevitably perform substandard to expectations. He quite literally raised Gellor from the depths of the wasteland of Gell little over thirty years ago over the span of a single decade."

"It sounds to me like he did quite a bit for his people."
"They paid a price…" She suddenly hissed in response to Michael's misplaced comment.
"You said before, that you knew him, something about him taking a certain 'interest'…?" Michael changed the subject.
"Aye…I was his first…just a childe…he drove his thoughts violently into my mind. You see…we had teased him…'cause he liked to play death with the rats…" The woman began to sob.

Michael felt her wrap her hands around his. He felt hot tears striking his skin, and pitied the terrors of her life as she told them.

"…He took me…in my mind…took me, and made me his…I didn't want to, but he made me hungry, made me angry, made me kill, and eat…and drink the blood of those I killed as he laughed before me, laughed with the heart of darkness beating within his chest as I feasted upon the three boys, the three sons of lords, three of my childhood friends…"

Michael realized at this that she was the young girl of the story Albright had told him over the campfire that cold night in the petrified forests of Gell. She was the daughter of a Lord of the Priory.

"I have heard your tale Lady Eleanor Stevens-Priory, and how you

201

were manipulated by the power of the young Raven Warlack. I must ask you though, how could your family stand by as the ceremony was performed and lied about? How could they let him imprison you and keep you here all this time?" Michael asked in disbelief.

"Why do you think I am the last of the Priory?" She said in a cold tone.

"You mean…they killed them too…"

"…To attain their goals…to keep them quiet…it doesn't matter now, they're dead, and he is god in my world!" She finished his sentence with an alarming display of emotion.

"What is Raven Warlack's goal? What does he want with me, and why do you say that he 'fears' me?" Michael asked.

"I do not know his ultimate goal…but I know the hole…the hole within his blackened heart…because he knows you'll play your part…seek the sword, seek the dragon…find your way within the wagon…" She spoke again in her archaic riddles.

"What did you say?" Michael asked.

"When?" Eleanor said in puzzlement.

"Just now, that riddle, what did it mean?"

"I know not of what you speak Michael Cross, only that I long for the gentle touch of your lips. You are the only man I have spoken to in countless years and I long for your pleasure." She said in an encitingly sensual tone which seemed to come out of nowhere.

Something in Michael snapped and he lost control of his more primal nature, and his prodding of questions ceased. He could feel her hands moving over his hands and arms and then one moving up to his neck the other down his chest and stomach. She bent his head close to the bars where he could feel the slight static electricity of her body and face close to the bars, and close to him. She whispered to him through the bars, "I want you Michael Cross..."

Michael felt cold and hot shiver down his spine, and despite his honed focus on the offer which lay before him and the feeling of her hand moving down past his belt, something, somewhere in the back of his mind went off like an alarm. He heard a distinct tapping at the wall behind him. "What's that noise?!" he said, pulling away from her embraces slightly, her hand still heavy at work beneath his belt.

"Michael! Is that you?!" He heard a muffled but familiar voice coming through the wall.

"Michael, don't answer him, it's a trick! Stay here with me, and I'll give you pleasures you've never known! You can do anything to me Michael!" She pleaded with him in the darkness as she touched him in ways he had not felt in a long time.

"But I, know that voice...Albright, is that you?!" Michael replied in a wavering tone, trying to rip his mind and body away from the seduction of Eleanor.

"Yes Michael! Thank god you are still alive!" Albright said.
"Thank god I'm alive? How the hell are you alive...?" Michael thought aloud.

"What was that!?" Albright hollered.
"Nothing...just...can you get us out of here?" Michael said.

Before Albright could respond Michael suddenly felt the firm grasp of a slender hand and lengthy fingernails digging deep in his arm to the point of drawing blood.
"No Michael! Please, don't leave me! Don't leave me in here to die alone!"

―――

She pleaded again.

"Don't worry. We will get you out. It'll be alright, I promise." Michael tried to reassure her.

"You don't understand Michael…I want you to stay…with me…together in our passionate darkness…Please Michael…Stay!"

"I…can't…I can only take you with me…"

"You don't get it do you?…*I CAN'T LEAVE*!!! *He* won't let me, and *he* doesn't want you to leave either! *He* wants me to make you mine, make you mine to please and toy with until our darkest days are done!" She was screaming and pulling him painfully into the bars as if she was trying to pull him through them. He struggled to free himself, all the while hearing a strange noise coming from the other side of the wall, the wall Albright spoke from.

The noise was like that of the machines only louder and faster paced like a small engine, then came the sound of steel scraping against stone. Sparks began to fly from the wall with chunks of rock as a circular piece of steel spinning at a blinding speed penetrated the wall. The blocks began to crumble around the cuts the blade had made and light began to envelope the room. Michael was momentarily blinded by its brilliance as Eleanor released her grasp and fled screaming to the darker corners of her cell, untouched by the new light.

Albright finished his third cut and shouted out to Michael, "Stand back!!!"

Suddenly the wall of stone fell forward and broke into several blocks of rock and chunks of mortar. Dust formed a cloud which made the lights behind the figure appear as beams. The shadowed form of Albright stood amidst the debris as a silhouette, a strange device held up by both his hands

---

still chugging out its mechanical sound, as the jagged edged circular blade spun to a halt in the front of the device.

The dust cleared and Michael could see that the saw blade was caked with blood as well as the dust from the stone. "How did you…?!" Michael stammered.

"It's a long story, but we don't have time, we have to move *now*!" Albright shouted through the haze of dust still lingering in the cell and the hallway Albright stood.

"Ok, but we have to free her too." Michael said as he turned to gesture towards Eleanor. "She's the girl from the story you told us about Raven Warlack, the girl who he forced to kill those boys!" He finished saying as he turned to look upon the face of Eleanor Stevens-Priory for the first time as she emerged from her shadowed corner.

Her hair was white, her eyes, they too…were white. Not just white, but ghostly white. Her skin, however, was the color of milk, a bit more pleasant with just a hint of the color from the blood which undoubtedly still pumped through her veins. The only thing that wasn't white were her lips…they were the color of ripe black cherries. She looked at Michael with her blank eyes as she walked slowly from the shadows of the corner of her cell. She looked at him with longing, her lips quivering with a deep-seeded lust. Her body flowed across the room with a eurhythmic beauty; she held the perfection of the womanly form beneath the rags she wore which covered only the bare minimum of her private being. Michael stood open-jawed at the unrelenting and strangely beautiful form of the woman who approached the bars of the cell which he still stood dangerously close to.

"Michael…Michael, I'm yours for the taking, open the bars, and take me here…take me now…again and again…"

"I will free you my lady, but we must go now!"

"NOOO!!!" She screamed as she rushed forward, her arm reaching through the bars and grasping Michael's throat in a death lock. "You don't get to go Michael! I have to make you stay, and I will! By temptation or force you will be *mine* Michael Cross! It is his command! I have to…make you *mine*!!!" She squeezed him tighter, both his hands desperately trying to pull away the insanely strong grip upon his throat. Her free hand grasped one of the bars and she pushed against it. The bar began to bend. Her white eyes seemed to fill with blood the same color as her cherry lips, and she hissed, opening her mouth to expose fangs which protruded from her bottom and top rows of teeth. She pulled Michael to the bars and licked his face with a perfectly pink tongue. "I want to taste you Michael…" She whispered to him as her fangs dripped with glistening saliva. She opened her mouth wide and leaned toward Michael's neck ready to taste his blood.

Michael heard the chug of the engine from behind him as the circular blade once again spun violently through the air. He pulled back from her as hard as he could, keeping the bars she desperately tried to bend between them. He watched as the spinning saw blade swept down from over his right shoulder and sawed through the arm which held his throat just below his grasp upon her wrist. Blood sprayed, and Eleanor screamed in sheer pain and horror as she fell back clutching her mutilated arm.

"NNNOOOOOOOO!!!…Why?!!!" She cried, her eyes suddenly returning to their colorless white. Michael wiped the blood from his face. "Fuck, Albright! Did you have to do *that*!?" Michael yelled as Albright finally turned off the chugging machine-saw and dropped it with a clatter to the ground in a splatter of blood.

"I had to Michael…she meant to kill you…she is nothing more than a shell of the woman she once was…a puppet of Raven Warlack's to play with and manipulate at his very whim. The only humane thing to do now would be to put her out of her misery…to end the torture he inflicts upon her mind, and no doubt has inflicted upon her body as well…" Albright spoke with an absolute tone, and a matter-of-fact sensibility too apparent to deny.

"We can't just kill her?" Michael asked incredulously, looking from Albright to the huddled form of Eleanor Priory, still clutching what remained of her arm.

"I can…and I will…" Albright spoke with resolve as he reached to something at his side tucked neatly into his belt. Eleanor looked up, her white eyes expressionless as ever, but her brow furrowed in pain and pleading sincerity.

"Michael…Please…Don't let me die…" She spoke in the gentlest of tones.

As Albright pulled the weapon from his side, Michael made a move to stop him, but just as he did, Eleanor leapt forward. Her eyes flashing crimson as blood once again filled them. Her mouth gaped open once more, exposing her lengthening fangs. She screamed like a banshee as she threw herself between the bars, struggling to reach for the weapon which Albright now brandished before her. He leveled the barrel with her head, pulled back something called a 'hammer', and squeezed another thing called a 'trigger', the weapon let loose a noise like thunder with a small trickle of flame from its end followed by smoke.

Eleanor flew back. Her head separated in an explosion which Michael did not take care to witness. She lay lifeless on the cold stone floor of the cell she had called home for so many years. Michael turned to Albright, "I'm sorry…I just thought…"

"There was something left of the woman she once was. No Michael, I'm sorry, but this is a place of monsters and evil. They have created far more than just machines within these dark towers of Gell, but sadly, I don't have time to explain, we have to move quickly."

"What are we going to do?" Michael asked.

Albright looked at him with a sternness only a father could embody. "Fetch your sword Michael..."

12

Michael and Albright made their way down the massed corridors and halls which made up the many floors of the western tower. On the way, Albright explained that he had found the saw earlier on a lower level of the tower. This level was under some reconstruction, and he used it to make his way through the tower, where he dispatched one of the guards carrying the weapon he called a 'gun'. They made their way through the tower climbing higher and higher through its massed infrastructure. It was the largest thing Michael had ever seen created by man; so vast and intricate, and he did not understand how he and Albright could possibly hope to find the sword amidst the labyrinth.

"Albright, do you have any idea where you're going?!" Michael finally asked after they climbed yet another set of stairs leading to another set of hallways displaying vast laboratories, and machinists' rooms. The whole place was one giant collection of all the darkest dealings of Gell, brimming with all the darkest evils Raven Warlack could dish out.

"I got ahold of a strange-looking guard close by where I found you. Killed his twin then questioned him. They were garbed in all black and white...weird lookin' too." Albright started out, not even breaking the rhythm of his speech as he ran.

Michael again had a painful thought back to the dining hall, Jayce's last meal, and the contrasting guards. Albright continued, "...It took me some time, and a lot of....persuasion, but I eventually made him talk. Yeah, once I got to him, he spilled all the beans..." Albright's eyes seemed to take on a different hue as he spoke, flashing a precariously bright blue instead of his regular green and brown. "...He told me 'bout Jayce and Willum, and even told me where to find the sword...which is in the secret weapons armory, where they keep most of these…" Albright waved his muzzle loader so that Michael could see it. The 'gun', as Albright liked to call it, was part wood, part steel, and it could only fire one shot at a time. Once the shot was spent, it was a tedious process to reload, requiring packing a black powder and a steel ball into the muzzle or 'barrel'.

"…The only thing I couldn't get out of the poor bastard was where *you* were. Took me using the saw on him quite a bit till he proclaimed that he would die before he told, because *he* would inflict pain upon him that I could never imagine…It was only by his behavior, the way his eyes kept lingering down the hall, and the way he tried to whisper and go without screaming when I took his legs and arms. It was by these clues that I discerned that you were nearby. It seems to me Michael that you are very important to Raven Warlack, perhaps even more so than that sword of yours." Albright finally finished.

"I see…Sooo…you do know where you're going?" Michael asked again.

"Not a clue…" Albright said in a serious tone. Michael looked to him in utter shock as Albright's lips cracked into a devilish smirk. "…Just kidding…The armory is on the highest level of the tower, all we have to do, is go up." Albright jested as he sprang up another flight of stairs.

"I should've figured that…Hey, where is everyone if this is an installation?" Michael questioned aloud.

"Normally there would be a small number of those working the night shift right about now…that is, if it is actually night, but it would seem the entire city is on alert and taken to home. The whole city's been quarantined, something about an outbreak of gas, but I'm pretty sure it has something to do with you."

"With me? Why in Selador do they think I'm so damn important...?" Michael started to ask, but was suddenly cut short as they topped another level of stairs.

Outstretched before them was a hallway made of a crystal clear glass supported by steel beams. The hallway stretched between a mass collection of platforms and rooms, with both glass and steel doors to enter into. Each had a glowing box next to them displaying many buttons labeled with a numeric code. The rooms were filled with people, strange looking people. Some appeared mildly disabled while others looked almost normal. They were simply sitting and staring intently before them with faces vacant of any emotion. In one of the rooms, some of the most deformed and disfigured examples of the human form were strapped into chairs constructed of a strange metal, wiring, and padding. Masses of wires and plugs were jutting from the hairless oddly-shaped masses of flesh they had as a head, grotesquely swollen to three, even four times the normal size of a human skull. Bulging veins pumped a strange liquid injected into them through a tube from a clear sac attached to the ceiling which flexed like a muscle as it pumped the strange substance through their bodies. Behind these poor souls, sitting just above rows of control panels were massed screens displaying images Michael didn't fully understand, some were like dreams, others of places far away, and still others of people he didn't know and would never encounter. Amidst all of the screens displaying images, only one caught the eye of Michael Cross.

In one of the farthest rooms, almost out of sight, Michael could see one of the lesser deformed of the creatures, significantly different, because of the scar upon his face, a scar which stood as the mark of the Cross. Why this poor wretched soul bore the sigil of shame he could only wonder, but it had done its job by attracting his attention. Michael looked upon the screen which flickered and fuzzed with spots of black and white - the images of this creatures' mind until finally, the storm on the screen ceased and an image became clear…it was the desert. And amidst those white hot dunes displayed on the screen Michael saw a dark figure struggling through the sands, leaving a trail of blood in his wake, bearing upon his back the Great Sword of Lindell. The dark figure was him, and just as the scene became clear to him the black and white static resumed its charge and the screen became a blur of images from the past, present, and future, all entwining to form a complete mess.

"By God, what are they?" Albright asked.

"I think they are called 'farseers', Eleanor mentioned them to me earlier when I was in the cell with her." Michael replied.

"More monsters…" Albright muttered to himself.

Michael turned to Albright, who had slowed to a walk and then came to a stop with him in the center of the glass hallway. Albright looked around to the many people, some painting, some scribbling or writing, some appeared to be entertained by small, childish toys. He shook his head in disgust and met Michael's gaze. "What, Michael?"

"We have to get them out of here. We have to free them…"

"No, we don't…You are my only responsibility, and we must first get you out of here with the sword, then we'll worry about freeing them another time. I mean, just look at them Michael! If we opened all the doors, which I wouldn't recommend trying, and yelled to them to run for freedom, I guarantee you they would simply stare at us, if they would even be able to understand what was happening."

"You're probably right…I don't understand though, why do they act like they don't see us?"

"Because they don't…the glass…it only works one way. We see them, but all they see is a mirror."

"How do you know all these things?" Michael asked.

"We don't have time." Albright said bluntly as he turned and continued down the hall.

At its end were two sets of steel double doors locked and controlled by large square panels similar to the panels on the other doors. This keypad had a clear rectangle which had six small squares to display the numbers selected for the intended occupant's guess of the code. Above the doors hung a sign reading, 'TO WEAPONS DIVISION CODE: 3-417 KEEP LEFT; ACCESS ENROUTE EXPERIMENTAL WEAPONS ARMORY KEEP RIGHT', next to the different destinations were handy little black arrows directing which way to go.

One glance at the electronically locked keypad Albright suddenly grew angry, "Damn!!! How the hell are we going to get past this?!" he pounded a heavy fist against the steel doors which resounded with a muffled solid 'thud'.

Michael felt a strange pull in the back of his mind like someone had just plucked a loose hair from his head. He turned around, and looked to where his mind's eye directed him. There, across the many lost souls bumbling about was a single small young boy. His hair was tuft and tasseled, and his face was slack and empty, bearing a few freckles around his oddly wrinkled lines in his face where his brow furrowed. From across the many rooms through the 'one-way' glass, the boy stared directly at Michael, and held an outstretched arm in his direction, pointing at him with the tip of a piece of chalk in his hand. Behind this boy, in large white lines upon a large chalkboard built into a metal frame, was a series of equations and mathematics Michael would never understand, but beneath it all was a series of numbers written out as the solution. The boy pointed at him with the chalk, and then turned and circled the series of numbers again and again. Michael counted them in his head, exactly six numbers.

"Albright, I have an idea as to what the code is…" Michael began, but knew full and well that there 'was no time to explain'.

"…You just have to trust me…"

"You do realize you can't just take a guess at it don't you Michael? You pick the wrong numbers and I guarantee you this thing is rigged to set off an alarm…" Albright warned.

There was a long silence until Michael finally spoke, his back still to his friend, his gaze set upon the chalkboard where the boy still stood, thrusting his piece of chalk at him with an increased vigor. "Trust me Albright…the code is…" As Michael spoke Albright moved to the keypad next to the right door and began to enter in the numbers as they were cited.

"…3…7…13…17…21…33…" A bead of sweat fell from Michael's brow as Albright punched in the last number of the numeric code. To his relief, the door hissed with pressurized gases, and he could hear the clanking and grinding of gears and wheels and cogs moving within the infrastructure of the walls, generating the leverage and power needed to move the massive steel doors.

The doors stood open before Albright and Michael, revealing the hallway that would take them to the armory. Albright turned to him, bewildered, "How did you know?"

Michael was beginning to feel the same strain on time as Albright felt and wittily replied, "As you keep saying, no time to explain."

Albright grinned, a hard look at Michael, who was gesturing a look of thanks down one of the halls. "I believe this is the way we want to go…" He said.

13

The armory was unyieldingly vast in comparison to any Michael had ever seen. Experimental weapons and prototypes long-forgotten lined the surrounding walls, strange looking 'guns' covering the left half of the room. The right half consisted of various types of swords, spears, halberds, crossbows, and the like, axes, scythes, war hammers, knives, and every other type of weapon imaginable neatly cataloged in rows of shelves filling the room.

On the farthest wall was another door, this one more wood than steel, a kind reminder of the way things were in the rest of the world, outside this terrible tower and outside the city of Gellor. The door was flanked on either side by two shelves containing multitudes of armor. Some were polished to perfection, appearing as though they had never even been touched by any but the smith who crafted them, whilst others lay tarnished and beaten with untold ages of use.

Michael and Albright approached the door at the far end of the room. As they walked between two of the aisles, Albright took the liberty of replacing the empty muzzle-loader with two of a weapon labeled on a small gold plaque as 'REVOLVER SERIES SEVEN- MODEL RAVENCHESTER .66'. The guns were enormous works of metal. They were made of a dark alloy, which made them black as coals, every part of them except for the light hue of sandalwood grips, carved by hand to fit the hand precisely. Encased in its mechanics and workings near the grip, and between the trigger and hammer, was a large cylindrical casing which held seven rounds. Albright marveled at the fluidity of the mechanics of it, and how the cylinder in the middle spun freely when its hammer was half-cocked. He took two and tucked them neatly into his belt at his sides. They felt strangely comfortable to him so he took one more and held it at ready in his hand. He checked all the cylinders, making sure they were full, seven rounds each, twenty one of the odd creation of black powder and lead tipped capsule-like bullets in all. As far as Albright figured it would be plenty, but would consider the other three that remained on his way out. He was disappointed, however, that there were no extra bullets - only enough to fill each of the guns.

Despite Albright's apparent interest in his newly found weapon of choice, Michael's sole focus was upon the steel braced wooden door unlocked and unguarded before them. Behind it, Michael could feel a familiar surging of power, and knew that behind that door was the great sword of Lindell, 'his sword' as everyone seemed to call it. And yet despite the sudden flare of excitement rising in his blood, he felt a chill run through his mind, *what else is behind that door?*

Michael moved to open it when Albright suddenly grabbed his shoulder. "Michael, wait! It doesn't feel right - in fact, it feels very *wrong*. I think it may be a trap." Albright said with the faintest fear of the unknown trickling into his face.

"I *know* it's a trap..." Michael replied as he opened the door.

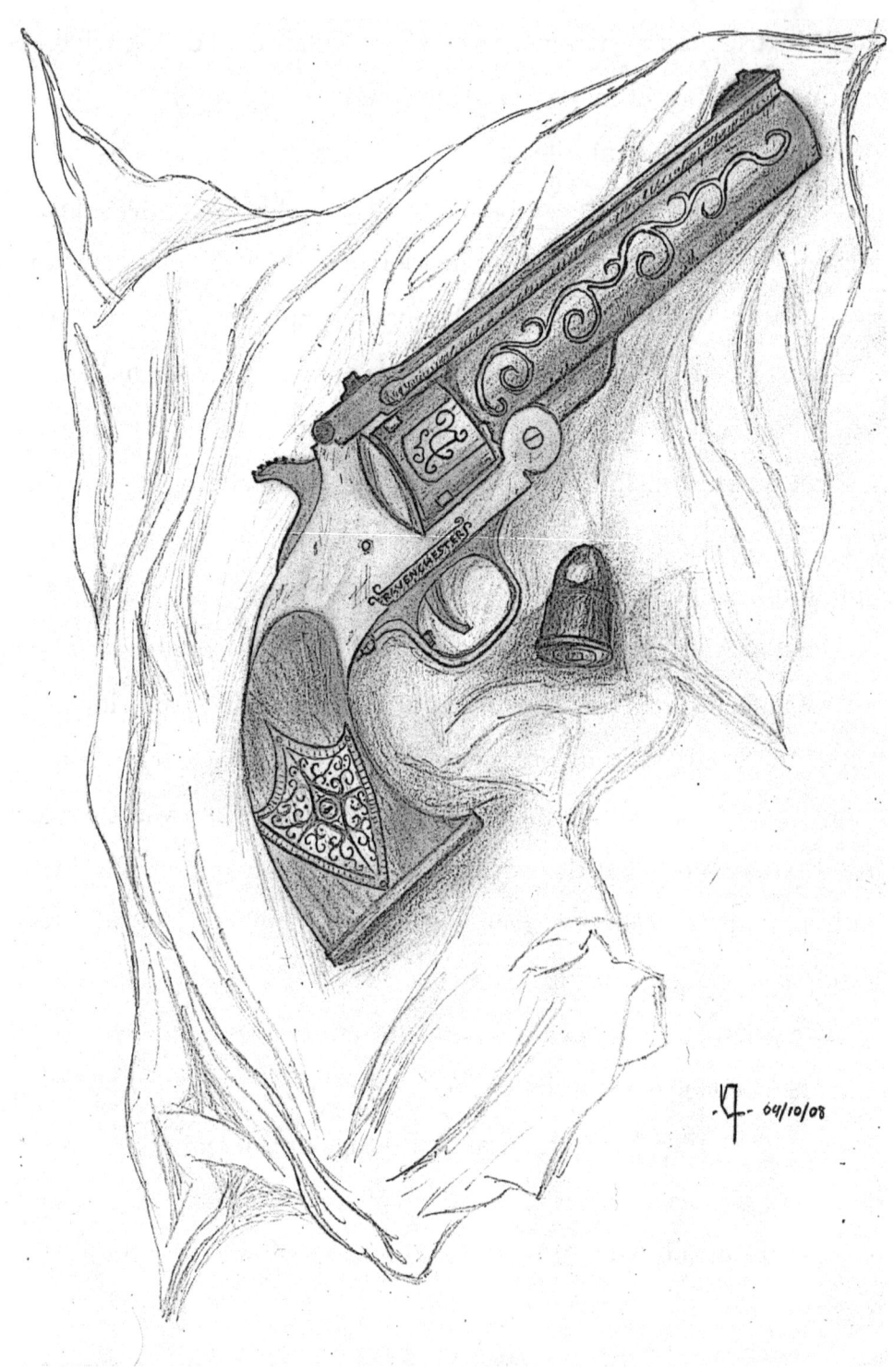

The room was circular, the walls covered in three massed tapestries of the arcane and ancient lore. Between the tapestries stood three black suits of armor, each bearing its own unique shape and ominous poise about them, all holding a different weapon, seemingly alive despite their statuesque state. In the center of the room were three black pedestals, elaborately carved from a shiny obsidian stone. Upon the first of these pillars was yet another gun and its ammunition, a single silver bullet similar to the kind in the guns Albright now carried, only much, much larger. The second pillar held the great sword of Lindell, the third, the sheath, his bag, and all of his belongings. Despite this and all the other aspects of the room, the only thing that immediately drew Michael's attention before all else, was his sword, hovering above the middle pedestal suspended by some unknown magick. The blade of the sword pointed towards the ceiling looming above as one massive clock face.

The clock was accurate to the milliseconds and driven to that accuracy by a massed of spinning gears and cogs which could be seen going to work at a hypnotizing speed behind the orange hued stained glass of the clock face. The massive hands of the clock moved steadily over the thirteen numbers displayed upon its face. Somehow Albright managed to watch the second hand of the giant clock make three small clicks, three whole seconds before the wooden door behind them slammed shut and the three suits of armor came suddenly to life.

Michael took off in a dead sprint for the sword, Albright firing his new found revolver at the closest of the three. The gun roared like thunder as he fired, three shots rang against the suit making whatever was inside retreat a few steps back as sparks flew from the black steel. He pulled his second gun and began firing with both hands simultaneously at all three as he covered Michael's dash for the sword. The bullets showered sparks in all directions as they ricocheted off the suits of armor and through the room, the smoke from the guns bellowing as Albright unloaded round after round into their attackers, but yet they seemed to have no effect.

Michael was inches from the sword, as Albright dropped his first gun, the cartridges spent and left as only hot shells in the cylinder, he drew his third gun. Michael reached for the sword, but as he touched it he was instantly washed over by a white hot pain which ripped through his spine and throughout his body. His teeth grinded together to the point he was sure they would break, and his muscles convulsed and spasmed. Hot tears began to pour from his eyes as his hand began to smoke and sizzle with the immense electrical current which ripped through his body, but still he reached for his sword.

The suits of armor looked battered and beaten, but still they came unscathed by the many bullets fired against their solid forms. Albright dropped his second gun, and took care not to waste the remaining five shots left in the last gun. He aimed for their helmets, and what he supposed were eye slits. The five shots rang out as Michael screamed, his hand finally taking hold of the sword. Each shot hit its mark, but only pierced one of the suit's defenses. Black liquid shot from the visor of the one he hit, and it fell forward with a clatter.

The other two suits of armor were close enough now to hold their weapons high, preparing to strike down on the now defenseless Albright, whose only remaining weapon was now spent of its ammunition. Just as the great axe and halberd the suits wielded came swinging down, the Great Sword of Lindell swung to meet them. Albright ducked as the steel rushed towards him; the sword blocking both of the weapons, and held them poised for a moment, forming a cross over Michael's blade.

Michael suddenly thrust the sword into the air, flinging the weapons upward and throwing the black knights off balance. Michael then spun gracefully on his toes and whirled the sword down and around his body in an impossibly swift arch which gave the impression that the massive sword was light as a feather in his hands. The suits of armor split in half and fell in pieces to the floor, black liquid spraying from their joints and slits made in the blackened steel. The blood formed pools upon the floor and slowly trickled towards a large metal grate in the center of the room. There the dark liquid drained away leaving only the reek of death and evil.

Albright approached one of the fallen suits of armor, kicked it over, and found that only the faintest residue of the black liquid remained in the hardened steel, they seemed to just disappear into the darkness of Gell from which they'd come. Albright gave a shiver and muttered to himself, "More damn monsters…"

Michael returned to the pedestal next to the one he had retrieved the sword, and found that his bag was intact and possessed all it didbefore, except for one new addition, a small scrap of parchment, torn at the edges, but folded neatly. He unfolded it to the finest hand script he had ever seen, it read, 'See you soon Michael Cross… Sincerely, Raven Warlack…. P.S. Hope you liked Eleanor…' Michael crumpled the note in his hand. *This whole thing is just a setup, another part of his plan. Is there nothing I can do to prevent myself from following the path which he has no doubt already foreseen?* Michael pondered to himself as he tossed the ball of parchment aside and began to pull the sheath over his back and adjust the fine cord which held it in place.

Albright gave him a curious look, but it fell on unseeing eyes.

"Raven Warlack…" Michael muttered.

"What did *he* have to say?"

"Just the confirmation that this was all *his* idea…"

"Let it go Michael…he hasn't foreseen everything. We decide our own fate, and it is by the choices we make that we can change the predestined to a different path…" Albright caught Michael's gaze as he continued to speak. "You have to trust me Michael…I will make sure that you make it out of here with that sword…"

"I trust you Albright…" Michael said as his attention was drawn to something else in the room. Michael sheathed his sword and approached the first pillar, the one displaying the black gun and single silver bullet. It felt as though it was calling to him, he did not understand why, only that there was a significance about the weapon, the kind he could not deny. His only reasoning was that it must have been left there for a purpose. Perhaps another part of Raven's plan, or mayhap a piece he overlooked, something he wasn't *supposed* to find. He decided there was only one way to find out, and that one less destructive weapon in Raven Warlack's control could only be of good measure.

As he reached for the gun upon the pillar, he heard Albright shout from behind him, yet something clouded his mind, and told him to take the gun. He touched its dark wood grip, stained with a red dye and polished to smooth perfection that formed admirably to the hand. He traced the grain of the wood with his fingertips, and marveled at just how cold it was to the touch. He let his fingertips linger to the bullet, and it too felt like ice to the touch. They called to him with a strange desire he had never felt before, and with one in each hand he picked up the icy objects which lay before him as Albright placed a firm grasp upon his shoulder, and Michael at last heard what his friend had been saying the entire time, "...chael! Stop Michael! It's a trap!" Michael had time to turn and look at Albright, the gun and bullet held outstretched in his hands like a child who had taken something that didn't belong to him, and had just been scolded.

Horror swept over Albright's face as the orange hued light emitting from the clock above them suddenly transformed to a dark red. The screams and bellows of alarms began to resonate throughout the room as the red light from above began to flash. Albright grabbed Michael by the arm and pulled him hard, "Now we really have to get out of here!!!"

Michael was ripped from his trance over the weapon he held "Umm...sorry?" he said. He then quickly wrapped the gun and bullet in a piece of cloth, and stuffed it into the bottom of his bag beneath his other belongings. Albright jerked him out of the room by his arm as he struggled to close the bag. Everything was bathed in the flashing blood-red light of the clock as the two ran from the inner chamber of the armory.

As they passed through the first room and between the shelves they had passed before, Albright grabbed the other three .66's that were left upon the shelf, tucking two into his belt as he had before. It had only then dawned on him that there were originally six total of the Ravenchester prototype. *'Huh...six .66's...I wonder if that's lucky?'* He thought to himself as they ran

They ran through the arsenal and down the hall, returning to the massive room containing the farseers and the glass hallway from which they'd come. The alarms blared and the red light flooded over the room, illuminating the terrible scene in one horrific collection of chaos.

The farseers were frantic, most of them screaming, clutching their heads and holding their hands over their bleeding ears tightly. Some ran in circles, others pounded their heads against the walls and glass. There were those that flipped tables and threw chairs, but none of them striking any of the others, none of them turning to violence upon one another. The ones who were sedated, or hooked to machines seemed to convulse violently, their bodies shaking in spasms, mouths spewing foam.

Albright pulled Michael by his arm once more, trying to get him running again, but Michael held. "Wait Albright, look!" He pointed to the farseers strapped into their chairs, convulsing and foaming, the tension on the many restraints and plugs and wires upon them growing by the second. He pointed to the massed collection of screens behind them, all displaying the same thing, all from different viewpoints.

Albright stopped pulling at Michael and looked at the screens. The displays showed the stairwells which led up the tower – that led up to them. Upon those stairs, climbing them with a massed fury nearly bordering panic, but no doubt the discipline of duty, were scores of men. Armored and not, guns, spears, and swords alike, crossbows and axes and strange fireless torches, the soldiers came. Ten, twenty, thirty, and more, they had been waiting for the alarm, waiting at instruction of one Raven Warlack no doubt.

"We have to get to the lowest level of the tower we can before they reach us! We still have a little time to try and escape, but we've got to hurry!" Albright yelled over the alarms, and the dulled thud of several of the farseers who banged their heads against the glass.

Michael and Albright made a mad dash for the stairwell at the end of the hall, and sprinted down the stairs from which they'd come. They ran through the passages and down more flights of stairs, and through the levels they had already seen. They passed by experiments and machines, Michael would have no doubt wondered what their purpose, or what made them work, but he had time for no such thoughts, his mind was panic, escape, run. He felt assurance from the fact that he once again had his things, had his sword, and that he was not drugged or hindered in any way that would keep him from making a stand., Still, though, he held fear in his heart as any man would, and he relished in the idea of making a clean getaway from the darkness of Gell, but he knew in his heart of hearts, that escape would not come without a price.

15

They had come to the main stairwell. The clamoring of armor and the shuffling wavelike roar of footsteps rose from only a few floors below them. They looked down the many flights of spiraling staircase to see the wave of soldiers rising like a tide to meet them, their many lights shining sporadically over the walls and stairs, casting dark shadows of menacing figures like demons dancing their way closer.

Albright looked to his right to find a steel hatch-like door with a turn crank in its middle, and a very faded plaque labeled, 'LV. 33 MAINTENANCE'. The door was rusted around the edges and the sediment on the wheel itself made it nearly impossible to turn, but together they managed to loosen the long dormant crank and unlock the mechanism which held the door in place. From inside the door they could hear the gears turn and groan as the jam slid from its long held resting place, just as voices shouted from below, "There they are! Get them! Take the man of

Cross alive and kill the other, we can't let them escape!"

Shots rang out from below as Albright rammed a hard shoulder against the steel door. The door shook and groaned, but didn't budge. Several bullets whizzed past them and ricocheted with gallant sparks against the wall as the report from the guns echoed after them.

"Together!" Michael yelled, and he and Albright drove themselves into the door once more. The blunt force heated Michael's muscles with fresh pain and he grimaced at the impact. The door once again groaned and moved slightly on its hinge, but still held. Albright took hold of the railing behind them, and bracing himself, began to kick the door as hard as he could. Michael moved to do the same and together they assaulted the slowly giving door as the bodies of their enemies charged ever closer to capture them.

By the third kick, the door flew open, its hinges groaning as it swung and crashed to a halt against the wall on the other side. Michael and Albright rushed through the opening and slammed the door behind them, locking the wheel in place with a steel bar which lay in a pile of scrap metal just inside the door, buying them some time.

Michael turned with his breath heavy in his chest, to find himself on the outside of the tower, the black sky of Gell looming above them like an eternal nightmare. Before them was a maintenance walkway stretching the distance between the tower and a circular balcony on top of one of the many connecting sections of the tower that served as release regulators for the exhaust of the power plant deep in the heart of Gellor. Spikes and pyres decorated the exterior of the tower and its many steel plates, crossbeams, and panels had long since been scorched black by the heat and pollution of the smoke and ash bellowing from the industry of the city. In the center of the circular platform, this balcony of sorts was a pitted ring like a cone which came to knee height and led down into the tower and to the heart of Gell. Ten foot flames roared from the opening spraying sparks, and a constancy of fire which illuminated the walls of the tower casting Michael and Albright's shadows against it like specters.

Albright rushed forward running across the walkway and to the balcony with the fire in its center. Michael followed him hoping, and praying that his friend, his rescuer, had a plan.

Albright came to a stop at the far edge of the connecting rooftop of the tower, and looked out over its spike-covered edge, thirty three levels down. His heart sank at the thought that hope had been lost, but he knew, deep down, that by will, there would come a way. Michael joined him at the edge looking down at the perilous descent before them and he staggered back slightly at the nosebleed height. Michael cursed under his breath and reached for the hilt of his sword.

"I guess this is where we make our stand..." Michael said as the first rapping came upon the steel door from which they had emerged.

Albright stood in silence for a moment, his face growing grim and resolute with the satisfaction of things to come just as things were meant to be. "No Michael...this is where I make *my* stand."

"What are you talking about? There's no way out of this, and I intend to fight! You helped save my life, and I'll be damned if I don't get to return the favor!" Michael shouted as he began to draw his sword. The pounding upon the door across the walkway grew louder and in greater force.

"Sheath your sword Michael Cross! *I'll* be the one who's damned if I cheated death for nothing! I came here to free you, and to get you and that sword away from this godforsaken place. I knew it would come to this and I have accepted my fate, and am ready to meet the face of destiny. You must do as I say, or we will both be unmarked graves in the swamps by morning, and that sword will once again be in the hands of Raven Warlack!" Albright said with a cold sternness in his eyes that Michael would never forget.

"Albright, I don't understand…"

"It's like I keep telling you Michael…there's no time to explain. Now, do you trust me?"

"Aye, my friend, I trust you very well…"

"Then give me the rope given to you by the sage."

Michael rummaged through his bag and pulled out the finely woven cord and handed it to Albright. Albright took it and made a noose with one end, which he looked at uncertainly, as if foreseeing some event of the distant future. He took the loop and placed it around one of the spikes upon the edge and lowered the rope.

"There is a small ledge twenty feet or so down. Climb down to that ledge, and I will untie the rope and drop it down to you. You have a long descent ahead of you, and speed is dire. You have to get down as fast as you can Michael, without being seen, and without getting yourself killed. I'll hold them off as long as I can, but know this Michael, no matter what you hear or what you see just continue climbing down."

Michael looked at Albright with the lost sincerity of the truest of friends and he held out his hand. Albright's eyes flashed from a hazel green to a cool and collected blue, he smiled, and took Michael's hand, shaking it with the steadiest grip he had ever felt, a grip which lingered with the sense of brotherhood, friendship, and the sense of a father Michael

---

had never known. He held Albright's gaze for a time, and struggled to form words he didn't know.

Albright could see the conflict in Michael's face, and so he spoke for him, "We are well met Michael Cross…I hope to see you again someday…perhaps in another life…"

"Aye…Thank you Albright…I will never forget you."

"I don't reckon you will…" Albright said finally releasing the long held handshake as the metal door across the walkway began to groan and give as its last resistance was spent. "…Now go, Michael! May the angels give you wings!"

Michael nodded his eyes screaming with the conflict growing within him, "Farewell Albright…until we meet again…" Michael said as he took the rope in his hands and began to make his descent.

"Aye, Michael Cross…until we meet again…" Albright said as Michael disappeared over the balcony's edge.

Michael made it to the ledge without much difficulty and shouted to Albright above who untied the rope and dropped it down. "Goodbye Michael…" Albright called after him.

"Goodbye Albright…" Michael returned wholeheartedly, though the words were filled with pain. He remorsefully continued his descent, making it only halfway down one level before he heard the steel door above finally buckle and pull from its hinges with a crash. He could hear the first falls of footsteps as the soldiers poured out onto the balcony and made their way across the walkway to the incandescent flames and where Albright undoubtedly stood in defiance of their wake. At last, with the broken twang of Michael's heartstrings, he heard the first shots of the roaring gunfire overhead and knew that soon, sooner than he had ever hoped, he would lose another friend…for the second time.

16

Albright stood alone out of initial sight behind the stack still spewing flames reaching fifteen feet into the air.   The first flood of men poured out of the stairwell and onto the maintenance walkway. Albright counted in his mind a stretched out 1…2….3, and then pulled the second pistol from his belt with his left hand. He took a deep breath, and turned, his colorless overcoat flashing about him like the flames of the fire.

The first of the soldiers came into sight, and Albright drew a line with his eye, leveled the gun with the man's head, and squeezed off the first of many rounds to come. The man's head exploded, spraying fragments all over the men behind him. Albright had a single second from when he fired that first shot, and took in the scene before him, the thirteen or fourteen some-odd guards and soldiers who came pouring from the doorway cluttering themselves as Albright aimed his next shots carefully, both guns leveled with his enemies, the sights at the end of the barrels gleaming with the light of the fire. Albright began to scream as the bullets roared from his guns. He made each shot count, just as he had been trained to do with any weapon he had ever used. He sought his target by instinct, lined his shots, and fired without hesitation. He moved like a killing machine, one way and then the other, ducking low, and then rolling to one side as bullets, arrows, and crossbow bolts whizzed past him, narrowly missing their mark.

Three…Six…Nine…He dropped them like flies, but still they came. Right gun was empty, its seven shots spent, he let it drop. Then he was firing the last round of his left gun into the chest of another soldier about to pull the trigger of a long gun leveled with Albright's head, but as the soldier flew backwards from the blast of Albright's .66 the man's gun went off, sending its stray shot into the abyss of the black sky of Gell. Before the man hit the ground, Albright was already pulling the last gun from his belt and dropping the now-empty revolver from his left.

With his free left hand Albright fanned the hammer as he squeezed the trigger with his right. Seven more men fell to the ground stone-dead in rapid succession. His last gun, now empty, felt hot in his hand. He realized he had been screaming the entire time, and now stopped, his blood seemed to pump with a strange resonance pulsing through his body. He threw the gun aside, smoke still rising from the tip of the barrel. Twenty-one bodies lay before this single man, and yet despite his skill, despite the abilities he processed, he was greatly outnumbered, and knew that there was no chance of survival. He was left with one last trick to pull, one last stand before his life would end. For as his final gun struck the ground with a clatter, the twenty or thirty more guards and soldiers that had rushed out onto the balcony to replace the twenty one he'd already felled, leveled there weapons as one, and fired.

Bullets ripped through Albright's body as three crossbow bolts buried their tips within his flesh. Dealing him mortal wounds, the guards and soldiers ceased their firing-squad attack, and watched as Albright staggered, hot blood pouring from his wounds. He leaned forward with the pain, blood seeping from his clenched teeth, his knees threatening to give out beneath him, but he held himself, and slowly, very slowly he managed to stand up as proudly as he could, his teeth clenched in a menacingly twisted smile which spoke of death and the sick humor one can feel when they know that they are about to die. He thought to himself how good the heat of the fire felt at his back…warm…the way Annabelle used to

---

make him feel…but no more…never again.

He looked to his right hand which was covered in the blood of his wounds. He wiped the blood from his mouth and muttered to himself, "Need a light?", and the familiar flame came to life at the tip of his thumb. He let the flame roll across his knuckles and over his fingertips for a moment, and then he rolled it into the palm of his hand. He closed his hand over the flickering light, making a fist. His entire hand burst into flames and the soldiers muttered to one another in alarm. It was apparent that, because of their new dependence on machines, they had truly begun to forget what the magick of the world really was, and had grown to fear its mysteries and power. Albright began to laugh at their sudden fear.

His laughter carried over the crowd with a resonance which grew to a height unnatural for any mortal man's voice. As his laughter grew so did the flames within his hand. The flames grew brighter, changing from a fiery orange to white, and then to a flickering of white and blue which began to consume his arm as well. Albright's laughter subsided long enough for him to say these words, "To live…To die…To become of Sage…To seek the maker…To wake his rage…Bless me father and God above…For I be reconciled of my love…" The fire consumed the late Albright Eldred Cane and he became a towering inferno of power. The soldiers of Gellor turned to flee back the way they came, but too many blocked their only escape.

Albright's form became a blinding white light for a short moment before the entire platform erupted in a massive explosion. Collapsing the main stairwell of the tower, as well as the walkway and the tower top with the flames, all was instantaneously transformed into burning debris and shrapnel. Nothing remained of the man called Albright or the many soldiers of Gellor, everything had been completely and instantaneously incinerated.

17

Flaming debris began to rain down upon Michael from above as he scrambled to climb down the edge of a balcony several floors below. He looked up in time to see a large piece of spiked steel, still engulfed in flames, hurtled down toward him. He didn't have time to attach the rope, to try and swing, nor would he be able to climb out of the way in time. He did the only thing he could do, and jumped. He jumped as hard as he could, straining to make the distance he would need to clear the falling rubble. A narrow spike upon the lower outcropping at the bottom of a balcony was his only hope. He strained to reach it. trying to have a chance at saving himself from the fall, but he missed it, falling just short, over three feet from where he aimed.

He freefalls, the darkness of Gell has become a spinning abyss of death, fear, and confusion. Michael struggles to gain his bearings as the world around him rushes towards the sky. He hears a distant voice in his mind, it sounds like the voice in his dreams, and yet, in a way, it sounds like Albright... *'DRAW THE SWORD MICHAEL CROSS! DRAW THE SWORD AND DRIVE IT FORTH INTO THE BANNER OF GELLOR AND SPLIT THEIR SHROUD IN TWO!!!'*

At first Michael did not understand, but as he looked below him he suddenly saw what the voice spoke of. Several hundred feet down, attached to the railing of another balcony was a massive banner-like tapestry which seemed to stretch nearly twenty feet wide and nearly the entire distance to the ground, displaying the colors and crests of the region.

Michael reached behind his back and pulled the legendary blade

———

from the sheath those of Singe had given him. The blade hummed with the resonance of air rushing over it as Michael struggled to steady the blade as the air rushed furiously passed him.

The balcony grew larger in perspective as he plummeted down toward it until at last the railing came within grasp as he flew past. For an instant, he thought to reach out and grab the railing but he knew that at the speed he traveled it would break or more likely rip off his arm. Yet as that instant of thought passed another came to play as the banner flashed before his eyes. Its pattern, colors, and sequins became a blur as they whizzed past him.

Michael leveled his blade, taking care to place both hands firmly upon the hilt. Carefully he aimed and waited…for the precise moment, and then forced the blade into the banner. The edge bit deep and slashed into it. The first ten or fifteen feet went by in a blur, the slash just becoming visible above him moments later in the gust of a breeze. The banner was thick, and the resistance that built against the sword started to slow his tumble, but he knew it would not stop him. He kicked out his legs, sliding his feet against the banner, almost riding it down as he guided the sword through the shroud.

Michael watched as the ground suddenly began to come into clearer view. He couldn't make out what they were, but he could see buildings beneath him at the edges of the tower and built up around it. The sword suddenly became very hot in his hands. Michael looked to his blade, and where the banner met the sword. Friction had built to a momentous point. Sparks began to flicker from the steel of his swords tip against the stone of the tower behind the shroud, and then, as Michael expected, the banner began to catch fire. The slash he cut burned upon both edges of the banner, leaving a trail of fire behind him as he slid down the side of the tower. On the ground it would have been an astonishing sight, one almost worthy of fulfilling a long ago foretold prophesy already long ago forgotten.

Michael descended the last levels of the tower far quicker than he had hoped…floor thirteen…floor nine…floor seven… Michael could now see that the building directly below him was a straw roofed stable and barn. He assumed the roof would help cushion his landing, but he did not account for the fact that the banner ceased three levels above the roof of the barn…floor six…floor five… Michael braced himself as the edge of the banner rushed up to meet him as the blade of the sword seared through its last inch, leaving the flames in its wake.

Michael fell the remaining three floors to the straw and wood lattice beamed roof, where his body ripped through in an explosion of wood shards and straw. He struck the hayloft, and ripped through its floor as well, finally coming to a rest as he landed in the straw of an unoccupied stall. Straw fell down on him from above, and he lay there for a long moment, struggling to regain the breath ripped from his lungs.

Once he was physically able, he managed to drag himself from the stall and out of the barn. Outside was a large cart fixed with a team of horses and loaded to the brim with a barrage of machinery, machine woven clothing, beddings, tablecloths, and rugs. Michael suddenly remembered something from the ramblings of rhyme Eleanor had spoken…something about a wagon. Michael hoisted himself into the cart. He moved the things around until he formed a kind of pocket, which once he was inside of, he covered over with the bundles of clothing and rugs and other materials. He was perfectly concealed.

Moments passed and Michael could hear the hustle of the city as it

235

suddenly came to life. Alarms brayed and soldiers marched in the streets, fire brigade scrambled to put out the flaming tatters of the banner falling from the sky as well as control the damage caused by the rubble from the destruction of the tower above. Michael heard two men approach the cart.

"Damn it Stevenson, I don't care what's going on tonight! I want you to get yer arse behind the reins of that cart, and get it the hell outta here! I want you to be at that market by tomorrow morning!!!"

"Alright boss, but if I get arrested fer tryin' to stick my neck out fer ya don't think I'm goanna be keeping my yap shut bout *you*…"

"You won't have to worry about that…Here's five hundred dar, a three hundred advance on yer pay, and two hundred to bribe the guard…Now…get out of my sight."

"Reckon so boss…reckon I'll see yas in a week." The man replied as his footsteps approached the cart.

Michael heard a faint murmur from under the other man's breath but he couldn't understand what was said.

Michael listened carefully to the sound of the man climbing aboard the cart and taking up the reins. Soon the cart was moving, and Michael finally relaxed a little as they weaved through the city. It was only when they reached the outer gates that Michael grew nervous once more, but the need for worry was easily avoided with an accepted bribe by a greedy guard. The gates were open and Michael was on his way safely in the cart of goods bound for the market.

Michael's injuries finally weighed on his body, and then his mind as he curled up in a nest of blankets hidden from sight in the bottom of the cart. His thoughts quickly faded from his exhausted and bruised form, and found rest beneath the shroud of his eyes as the wheels of the cart rolled over the terrain.

Part 8:

The Riders of the Sage

I

The cash river roared before them, its rapids smashing against jagged rock faces sending sprays of crystal clear water into the air. This far upstream the river was tremulous and dangerous to cross without boat or bridge. Danube silently cursed Michael for having had it much easier further downstream, closer to Singe. At that point the river could easily be crossed on horseback, but Kaire and he would have no such luck.

"Should we look for a bridge?" Kaire asked Danube from atop her white mare. Danube stands at the edge of the river.

"There are none nearby. We would have to go far out of our way to find one, and that would make it nearly impossible for us to make any gain on the riders from Singe. If we cross now we may catch up to them by mid-day tomorrow."

"And just how do you propose we cross, oh Great Lord of Trengar?" Kaire smiled with her new found love for the man, and she had finally found parts of her personality awakening that she had never known, such as sarcasm and humor.

"God will guide us..." A sudden seriousness seemed to blanket over the Danube's aura. The muscles in his face grew lax, yet the muscles in his body seemed to tighten. He stepped forward, approaching the rushing river before him. In the depths of his mind he had learned to awaken a part of himself that was far more attuned to the true power of the universe. It was as if he counseled with something far greater than he himself, an essence that flowed through not only him, but everything in existence. In the depths of his mind, he trusted that deity of all to give him his strength. At this moment, he let this deeper part of himself take over.

Kaire sat astride her mare watching the tall, lean form of Danube as he began to let the power flow through his body and the staff he held in his hand. Her trained eyes could make out the shifting of the world around him as he focused his life force and channeled it to form.

Suddenly, in a blur of movement, Danube moved the staff in an arch, and with a deep throated yell, he struck the ground with it.

The earth shook with the blow; birds took to flight from nearby trees, even the wind seemed to be changed in course, but more importantly, the river collided with an unseen wall of force, its waters were stopped from continuing its path down the Cash River.

The water was held in place by the invisible wall, but soon began to spill around its sides and over its top. It would not hold for long.

"Hurry we only have a moment!" Kaire had already spurred the mare forward before Danube had finished shouting over the rushing water. He swung up onto his horse as quickly as he could and rode on after her, down into the riverbed which would soon be bombarded once again by thousands of gallons of water. Danube knew that if they weren't on the other side by the time the walls of his ward failed they would surely be swept away and drowned.

The river bottom was a mess of thick mud. The horses struggled to make their way through it and at many points were nearly stuck. Each time Danube was sure they would be permanently trapped in its grasp, but still the brave steeds managed to climb from the muck, and push forward through the river bottom as quickly as possible.

Just as they had climbed upon the bank of the other side, the invisible wall cracked and broke. The water roared like a tidal wave as the river bottom was once again covered from sight.

"Impressive, but cutting it a bit close aren't we?"

"Thank the Lord above, my love." They held each other's gaze amidst the last sunny day their eyes would ever see together in the forests of Trengar.

2

They rode all that day, breaking camp late in the evening. When the distant rays of the morning sun had just seeped over the horizon they headed out again, another hard ride. Danube was bent on catching up to the riders of Trengar and joining them in their trek across Gell. He did not, however, anticipate the haste at which the riders had traveled.

By mid-morning they stumbled upon something that Danube found rather disturbing. He first found it by the faint lingering smell of smoke in the air and followed its source cautiously.

It was the campsite of the riders. They had picked a narrow clearing amidst the black and white trees of the forest. Several stones were set in a small circle around the smoldering remains of their fire. Danube dismounted and approached the fire ring, instantly aware that several firestones were still present within the ashes. He bent low resting his weight upon the balls of his feet. It was the position of a tracker, to hunker.

He placed an outstretched palm over the smoldering fire, judging the heat.

"What is it?"

"It's their fire...You can tell it was them because of the firestones they used, but what's disturbing is that it's still burning."

"That's a good thing isn't it, that means we're not that far behind them?"

"Judging by the heat we are not that far behind, but that's not the problem."

"Then what is?"

"There shouldn't be a fire in the first place. No one from Trengar leaves a fire like this. We are taught as children to always remove the stones, douse the flames, and stir the ashes until nothing of the demons of fire remain. It is the teaching of the sage."

"What would make them leave it as it is?"

Danube looked around the site, observing other elements out of place. He even looked at the tracks on the ground.

"There is more here than I anticipated."

Kaire's eyes grew with anticipation.

"They left in haste. Barely finished their morning meal, and there…" Danube pointed to a moist spot on the ground. He touched his finger to it and when he withdrew it, it was stained with blood. "One of them was wounded, and these tracks show signs that they were pursued…We have to hurry there may still be time!" Before anymore could be spoken, Danube had mounted his horse in a blur and they were off once again.

In their furious ride they stopped only twice to water the horses and check the tracks which they followed. By mid-day they found the riders of Trengar.

The black and white forest had turned to flatlands. The swamps lie to the east of these barren plains, and the stench of sulfur lingers even here in this place of dry, cracked earth. The sun no longer shines through the thick masses of dark thundering clouds overhead.

Here in this desolate place, Danube Drakendor finally finds his riders of Singe, the riders of the Sage, bearing their grave message to the king. He finds them no longer as men, but as a permanent part of the desolate place in which they lie; their bodies broken, their life blood long since poured from vicious wounds which will never heal. Such a sight as this brings a lord to his knees.

Kaire was moved by the compassion he held for each member of his land, his home, and how he prayed for the souls of his men, whom he praised with rightful honor for dying in the line of duty.

In Trengar, such men would have been given a proper and ceremonial burial so that their bodies could return to the earth from which all things grew, to nurture and feed the new life of the land. It was the birthright of all who lived their life by the Sage.

However, to Danube's dismay, the dry earth of the barren landscape would offer no such possibility for such a right. The ground would not turn, and no amount of water would loosen such parched soil.

Instead, Danube collected all the dry foliage and wood that he could find. Kaire too, once she understood what he was doing, and by nightfall they had built a stack of pyre over the forms of the three men. Danube took the men's firestones, still in the packs at their sides except for the one who had left his behind at their previous encampment. Danube set them around the logs.

The wind howled in this dark barren place, the kindling before them. Danube felt the sudden heat of Kaire's touch, her hand on his, and he could feel the way it warmed his blood and warmed his heart. Yet he still felt cold, cold for the death that lay before him. He said a final prayer to the three men setting their souls to peace, to Sage, and muttered the words of the firestones.

The pile was instantly engulfed in flames. The heat it emitted was astounding and Kaire was forced to move behind Danube for fear of it burning her tender skin. Yet Danube stood fast, never taking his gaze from the fire, before him, the fire which consumed his men.

Kaire had not expected such a sight and was troubled by the light it cast across the barren plains. "Will the fire not attract those that did this? If they see it, do you think they will come?" Her eyes pleaded to Danube for comfort.

"Aye, they may, and they may not, but if they do…they will die." Danube's voice was morose, distant, and emotionless. He hated what was happening to Selador; the betrayal, the murder, the thievery of such sacred relics to all. A fire he had never felt before began to spark within him; a fire that quelled with ancient blood that none knew the power it could possess. None except for one, his only rival, Michael Cross could understand what lingered in the man's heart. Kaire could see this fire begin to rage in the depths of her lover's eyes. She pulled him from his thoughts in the only way she knew how, and for the moment Danube's fire was quenched by the tender passion of the only woman he would ever love.

Part 9:

The Region of Reum

I

Michael is jarred awake in the cart of goods, and when he moves some of the rugs and machinery aside fresh, clean sunlight seeps through the small opening he has made. It is the first true sunlight he has seen since he embarked from Trengar with Albright and the others, and it is dazzling. At first it blinds him, but his eyes eventually adjust, welcoming the fresh light.

When he peers from the cart, he can see the dusty roads behind him and the telltale signs of the markets of Reum. Everywhere he looks he sees people wearing the garments of the region the long colorful jellaba.

The marketplace is filled with all sorts of goods and mercantile. Woven baskets, intricately woven rugs, instruments made of reeds and wood, beautifully formed glass vases and bottles, vials of unknown potions, spices, and perfumes. There is food by the cart full. The smells of fresh fruits, vegetables, fresh poultry, meats and dried pork make Michael's stomach groan for something nourishing, but yet he pushes this aside to better focus on his surroundings.

There are performers in the streets, juggling, snake charming, and performing great feats of dexterity and human flexibility. Beautiful women wearing ceremonial shawls over their faces as they twirl with ancient exotic belly dances and Michael can see that some of them are even being auctioned to lords who have the dar to pay.

Michael finds the women extremely striking. Their skin is tanned to a dark caramel and their hair is as black as night. But what he sees as the most enchanting trait of these women is the fierceness within their eyes, like a hidden fire which seems alluring and yet dangerous, but sadly kept dormant amidst the control of their captors. Michael wonders how such slavery has been able to survive the rule of Jarum after its abolishment several hundred years ago. He is faced with the familiar conclusion that where there is money and power there is always corruption. 'Thistles in the roses...' He thinks to himself.

As the cart rolls on through the streets of Reum, Michael waits for the proper moment to make his escape

The cart passes close to an alleyway between two nearby clay buildings that are scarcely populated. He takes the opportunity to climb from underneath the goods and leaps from the cart. The driver sees him at the last moment as he bolts down the closest ally. Michael hears a distant cry of cursing, but takes no time to listen to what was said.

He makes his way down the alley passing under the Koubha archways above. He has read in his studies that the archways once symbolized prayer, this was in a time long before the corruption of the lords. A time when the gods and the weapons were the primary focus of everyone's everyday life, but with the coming of man's need for 'the good life' and its increase of population, expansion, and consumption, such things were long forgotten.

Humanity grew and with it they paid a price. Michael recalled the unnatural darkness over Gell, and the poverty he had seen in Lindell, his own backyard. The corruption in this place was having much of the same ill effects, he could see as he passed by sleeping beggars and diseased outcasts hidden away here in the alleyways of Reum's cities.

As he walked, he adjusted the sword upon his back, tightening the strap just a bit to ensure it was secure. As he did this, he passed another beggar who wore tattered rags and a large brimmed black hat pulled down low over his face. He sat with his back against the wall, the classic siesta position. "Dar for prophesy masseur?" the man asked.

Michael felt bad for the man and wished he hadn't lost his coin purse back in Gell. He stopped, thought a moment, and looked to his hands before him. "I have not a single dar my friend, but perhaps this will do you just fine." Michael pulls a ring from his left hand. It is made of gold and in its center is a fine emerald gem which glimmers in the light of the day. It is the ring his wife had placed upon his hand on their wedding day so many years ago. "It is no king's ransom, but it may fetch a handsome price, and perhaps open a new path for your life."

"Thank ye, this is a most generous gratitude masseur, but are ye sure ye would give me such a precious thing?"

"…it no longer has use to me…"

"As ye wish, and for such I give ye prophesy in return." The man took the ring from Michael with a curiously young, but dirty hand, and placed it in a wooden cup he held. He shook the contents of the cup until he seemed satisfied, and then emptied it onto the ground. Small bones, a few coins, and Michael's ring spilled out onto the sandy alley floor. The man leaned close, the shadows from the brim of his hat casting across his face in a manner that made it impossible for Michael to see his face. The man peered at the items before him for a few moments before he spoke.

"They speak your path very clearly me lord…ye path nears to its end…truth will come very soon, and all will be clear as Laotian days…must beware though of he who holds ye heart's old love. Ye will have to face the witness of the doves' final embrace, and in its time will face your true self. In all these things, old prophesy will be fulfilled and the doors will be open to a new path…" When the man was finished, he scooped up his tokens and placed them back into his wooden cup.

"I do not understand what any of that means, but perhaps with time it will speak true and I will find the enlightenment I need. If you know, can you tell me which way it is to the Council of Reum?"

"Aye kind sir, just continue down this alley until you come to a fountain in the shape of a star. It will have eight points, come to this and ye will see a building with a spire upon its peak. Upon this spire will be three spheres. That is the building ye seek. I must warn, not many suns ago a slave girl stole the weapon of these lands, the Legendary Scythe, and with it she slayed the High Lord and his closest of command. As a result, Reum's Council is in great turmoil with only the lowest of lords to replace command. Some hope that with the coming of the new lords perhaps some of the corruption and belligerence will die with their predecessors, but I myself will have no false hopes."

"Thank you…may you be blessed along your path." As Michael said this he turned and began to walk away, but as he distanced himself he heard the man call out once more. "I will…but such is not meant for you Michael Cross…" In utter alarm Michael abruptly turned only to find himself alone in the alley. The man had vanished. Michael stood in between the two clay buildings, the sun beaming down overhead, a light breeze blowing gently at his back. He shakes the feelings that take him, and continues down the alley thinking on the prophesy he was given.

He finds his way to the fountain of the eight pointed star, and to the building with the spire upon its peak. It is here he is greeted by the guards

247

of Reum.

The two guards at the entrance to the estate hold pikes, and though they look nothing like the two guards from Gell, the ones at the feast, he is still shaken by their presence. As he approaches they cross their pikes and speak with a deep authority. "Speak your name and business stranger, or you shall come no further."

With a twinge of hate brought from the familiarity of his previous encounter, Michael speaks with a solid heavy voice. "I am Michael Cross, last of the Cross, bearer of the legendary Great Sword of Lindell. I seek the lords of Reum. Step aside or I shall make my own path through you."

These were cowardly men and they withdrew their pikes at once, looked at each other, and motioned Michael through. "Straight ahead my liege...we would show you the way, but we are instructed not to leave our post...inside you will find a man servant who will take you to the council...and I apologize for our..." Michael brushes past the guards without a moment's hesitation and without a word. He proceeds into the estate of Reum.

2

Inside he finds a man wearing the traditional jellabab of the region. The man is more than happy to take him to the council chambers, and along the way he instructs several passersby to carry out tasks for the arrival of the Lord Cross. "Thank the gods they've sent us someone. Our region is in quite a fix with the loss of the scythe. I only fear what sort of reprimanding we'll all receive for losing it...*wait*..." The man stops Michael in the hallway of an upper level of the estate. "...You're not the one who's been sent to punish us are you? With *that* sword nonetheless? Oh please have mercy Lord Cross! The High Lord and his men were corrupt. More than corrupt! I had nothing to do with the dealings of the lords, I swear I am just a simple house servant! Have mercy!"

"Have no fears friend…I am not the one who brings justice to your land, let alone salvation. Show me to the council." Michael reassured him.

The man simply looked at Michael with sheepish unbelieving eyes. "Oh, I see. This way then…"

The council hall was surprisingly similar to that of Lindell with its high cathedral ceilings and images of the missing scythe burning overhead. It was a familiarity Michael had no appreciation for.

The room was empty except for five men who sat around a long table obviously meant for more, and a sixth man who was standing at the head of that table directing their frustratingly exhausting discussion. It was apparent the men were flustered with their new responsibilities and duties to the region. With the loss of the scythe and the death of their predecessors it seemed they would no longer be able to relish in the finer things of corruption. In essence, these six men were left to clean up the garbage that had been left behind.

The massive double doors were shut behind Michael and the servant who had brought him to the council, but none of the lords seemed to notice. It was only until the accompanying servant spoke that any took heed to the new presence. "My lords, I apologize for the interruption, but…" The lord who stood at the table instantly snapped his head around in fury. "It had better be damn important for you to interrupt our council…" Michael stepped forward as the lord interrupted the servant. He had grown tired of formality, tired of titles and lords and government when it was quite obvious that no one's council was getting anywhere nearer to the truth of what was really happening right before their eyes. No more deceit from anyone, no more beating around the bush. Action was avoided by diplomacy and reasoning. The fools had failed to protect the scythe because of their corruption, and he intended on letting nothing be taken lightly anymore.

Michael drew the legendary great sword from his back and held it high so that all could see its entirety. The sunlight shone through the stained glass from above and glimmered off the ancient blade. The lord who spoke was instantly silenced in the presence of the legendary sword so far from its home of Lindell, so far from its resting place. Michael let the tip of the blade strike the stone floor with an echo of ringing steel. The lords before him were astounded.

"By the Gods! Our reckoning has come…"

Another spoke, "If that is what I think it is…then you are the last of the old blood…the last of the Cross."

"That would be correct, humbled lords of Reum. I am Michael Cross, and this is the Sword of Lindell. I have traveled many suns and many moons. I have trekked the darkest places of Selador, been imprisoned by enemies of the land and lost many a friend. I have lost my patience for formality and ask you to excuse all before we continue." The lords nodded in agreement. "I have seen your scythe, in the Forest of Trengar wielded by a woman with hair as black as the skies of Gell. She battled with the High Lord of Trengar, Danube Drakendor as I made my escape to Singe. The outcome of the battle I know not. I have been sent by their council to journey to the Island of Laotia; it is there that I will keep the sword in safety, far from the threat of whatever darkness envelopes our land. I need your help in reaching my destination, because every asset I have had, my guardians, my friends, my resources have all been lost. I have nothing but what you see."

"You say the Council of Singe gave you this command…" The standing lord asked.

"…and that the High Lord of Trengar battled against Kaire Ra?!"

"Who?" Michael asked.

"The woman who took the scythe, her name was Kaire Ra."

"Yes, what I have said is true, he battled her so that I may escape to Singe."

"Then I'm afraid we have made a terrible mistake…" Michael looked to the lords who now were all standing with a look of grave confusion. Beads of sweat broke out on the forehead of the main lord and he fell to his knees, dread creasing his face in terrible realization. "…We have sent every available guard, soldier, and man-at-arms to retrieve the scythe. We sent them to the city of Singe…They have been given orders to retrieve it at all costs…even if they have to burn the city to the ground."

Ice ran through Michael's veins, his hot blood nearly slowing to a stop, his breath held with a wince in his chest. "You did *what*?!"

The lords looked to Michael and then to each other, none knowing just how to respond.

"What gave you the idea that Trengar was responsible for taking the scythe?"

Again, the lords looked to each other before the apparent leader spoke. "We were given the information by a high leveled diplomat of the kingdom of Jerum who came to us two days ago claiming he had received vital information to the whereabouts of the scythe by the use of the kingdom's Falcon scouts. He said he was the representative of Gell for the highest council of Jerum.

"What was this man's name?"

"He called himself Lord Raven Warlack." Michael felt his stomach drop at the name. He remembered the women in the dark prison of Gell. Her vacant white eyes looking at him through the darkness, and the things she told him of the man called Raven Warlack.

"We have made a grave mistake, have we not Lord Cross?"

"Aye, but I do not believe you are the first to be misled by the one you speak of." Michael returned the sword to the security of its sheath. His head was spinning with the realization of what was taking place before him. He could feel how close behind, how tightly raveled he was in the intricate plot that was laid out before him. It was right in front of his eyes, an illusion, a riddle, yet to be solved or viewed from the right angle. So many pieces of the puzzle were slowly falling together, and yet he could see nothing of the big picture. It was the true plot which eluded his mind and would torment his nights and days for much time to come. Only one part of the riddle was deciphered, and this he knew for certain. Raven Warlack…it was he that drew the pieces together. Somehow, he was behind it all. For what purpose he did not know, but the land of Selador would suffer greatly for the actions and manipulations of this one man, and many innocent lives would undoubtedly pay the price, as some already had.

If such suspicions were indeed on the mark, taking the sword to Laotia would only postpone the inevitable and do nothing for the sake of the land at all. If what Raymark said was true, that he indeed was the new High Lord, and in league with Warlack, then it would only be a matter of time before they found him and the sword. With Singe burned to the ground, Reum's forces no doubt depleted, and the armies of Lindell, Zwentor, and Gell in the hands of Warlack, nothing would stand against him and the kingdom of Jerum. Nothing except Laotia, and whatever remained of Trengar and Reum's forces if any. Michael could see the possibility of all-out war in his mind. The mayhem, the confusion and destruction; all caused by the manipulations of Raven Warlack. The worst thing of all was that he was the only one who could see this.

Even Danube Drakendor, so many miles from his rival, had no knowledge of the dark man named Raven Warlack. He only knew of a man who visited his lover's dreams.

Michael had become the sole bearer of the knowledge of what came to his mind. The only one who could catch a glimmer of what was really at stake. He had to change that, he had to try. Even if they didn't believe him he had to tell them what he knew before it was too late.

"You must send riders at once, your fastest horses! Send them to Trengar! Send them to your men on the march to Singe. Stop them from making this a complete disaster!"

"How do we know he was not telling the truth? And that you are not in league with Trengar in some twisted plot to overthrow the land yourself?"

"I'll tell you why!" And he did. He told them of his entire journey and the steps of Warlack's twisted game he had managed to piece together. He left no part of his story out, from his decree of dishonor for carving the cross into the face of his wife's lover, Raymark, to the traitorous hospitality of the servants of Gell and the atrocities of Warlack's childhood powers of manipulation upon a gorgeous young woman he encountered in the dark prison cells of Gell. He even told them of the beggar's prophesy earlier that day.

By the end of his tale he was stricken with exhaustion, with grief, and anger for the time they were wasting to have to gain the trust of these fool-hearty men. The tale was told and the men had seen the genuineness in Michael's eyes, the compassion of a man who has endured and lost much in so little a time, they asked his forgiveness for doubting him.

Riders were immediately dispatched to halt the procession of the army in course of Singe, though such an effort may already be in vain. They then made arrangements to take Michael to the coast by the swiftest carriage for the following day.

The lords of Reum had taken and taken throughout their time of service, but at seeing the weariness in this hard-traveled man they instead took the time to care for his every need. He was given the treatment of a king, a fine meal with the company of light music and an entourage of the loveliest and most elegant of dancers. They performed hypnotizing, rhythmic belly dances which Michael found mesmerizing. It had been ages since he had seen such beautiful women, all wore a series of sequined silk garments of a revealing style with scarves and those enchanting dark eyes he so loved to fix his gaze upon. It had indeed been a long time since he had felt the tender loving touch of a woman, unlike the lustful wanderings of the woman in Gellor. He longed for such, but his heart still mourned and he would find no comfort from the forcibly given love of a slave, no matter how lonesome his weary heart was. Michael slept alone in the estate of Reum, his heart aching deep in his chest with the weight of depression and growing sickness as only the last of the Cross could know. A sickness, that one day, might claim his very life and soul.

3

Michael once again dreamed of the burning white sands of the desert he had never seen. He could hear his name being called in the distance, carried by the wind, the voice he had never known, but that he found familiar nonetheless.

This dream was by far the most real he had ever experienced. He could almost taste the dry grit of the sand around him. When he finally woke from his slumber, his skin still burned from the beaming sun and the dry sand-filled wind.

Darkness still covered the land and Reum had yet to stir for the morning chores. He found his way to the tiled room adjacent to the one where he had slept. It was filled with the recent marvel of what many called plumbing and he used it with great satisfaction. There was a fountain mounted to the wall pumping fresh water in a steady stream, and above this were many mirrored tiles that had been set into the wall to form a decorative mirror which blended perfectly with the motif the tiles made.

He let the water flow gently into the palms of his cupped hands and he splashed the cool liquid across his face. Streams of water spilled down his cheeks and neck as he splashed the water on his face again and again until he felt thoroughly cleansed. He reaches for a towel left of the fountain but hesitates and stops as he catches a glimpse of his image in the mirrored tiles.

The water beads and continues to streak down his rough face. He looks deeply into his grey eyes, the eyes of his own image, eyes that would always bear the deepest secrets of his tortured soul.

He suddenly realized how long it had been since he had last seen his own reflection, and how much he had changed in that time. Instead of the accustomed clean shaven face of lordship; his face now bore a thickening beard and mustache. His hair had grown mangled and disheveled, and his skin was pale from his time in the darkness of Gell. He looked…unhealthy. His cheekbones had sunken out of malnutrition, and his skin seemed worn thin from exhaustion.

Michael felt compelled to change his drastically grim appearance and searched the room for lather and blade. He found both in a nearby basket set upon a wooden stand. Among these he also found oils and perfumes, a brush, and other tools of a lord and lady's private grooming.

He lathered his face and steadied the blade of the knife, judging the sharpness with his thumb. Once he had determined it held a true keen edge he began. It was a meticulously well practiced ritual, one that his foster father had managed to teach him. His foster father was a harsh yet loving man in his own, stern fashion. A man of many lessons that helped to forge Michael into the man he was today. Relishing in memory, he took swift steady stroke after swift gentle stroke and cut away the thick facial hair he'd obtained through his days of journeying. When he was finished he washed his face again, and was satisfied to see his familiar mug once more.

He brushed out his mangled hair and with a strip of leather tied it neatly back. He looked himself over a last time and marveled at the improvement of his appearance. Satisfied, he returned to his chambers and dressed for the day. He strapped the familiar weight of the sword upon his back and left his room just as the sun broke over the horizon bringing forth the dawn of another day.

It had been a day's coach ride for Michael to reach the coast. Lord Abari had purchased Michael passage on a sail driven sea schooner that delivered supplies to the Island of Laotia. Michael awaited its departure, scheduled for the next morning. He stood upon the shoreline looking out over the Sea of Belle. The wind blew against his dark, lean form which stood upon the sand of the beach. He stood as a silhouette against the afternoon sky, the tide beginning to rush the shoreline with sprays of foam from the relentless breathing of the ocean waves. He could smell the sea in the air, taste the salt with every breath. He became entranced by the sound of the sea. So much in fact, that he did not hear the footsteps of Lord Abari's approach.

"Lord Cross…"

Michael turned, his hand reaching to the hilt of his sword with such speed it was nothing more than a blur, but he did not draw once he had seen who it was. Lord Abari seemed alarmed but quickly eased at the lowering of Michael's hand.

"My apologies Lord Abari…it would seem I'm a little more on edge these days than I used to be."

"Quite alright my lord… It's the lady ocean. No matter how many times I am within her presence, I never get over quite how easily one can become entranced by her beauty and song."

"Aye, such is time. What did you come to say Abari?"

"My men and I have taken leave at a tavern called the White Stag. It is there that I have prepared a room for you as well. In the morning we shall see you off and then return home."

"Thank you. You have been a great help to me along the path of this journey."

"My service is to the land my lord. I only hope that my assistance to you has brought some atonement for the ill reputation of Reum and its previous lords. We will try to make things right. This is simply our first step."

"Aye..."

"Will you join me to the tavern, or do you wish to listen to the lady's song a while longer?"

"I believe I'll be hearing it enough on the morrow to suit me. I might as well join you for a drink."

"Very well Lord Cross, follow me."

"By the way, Lord Abari..."

"Yes..."

"Call me Michael."

"As you wish...Michael." Abari said as they began their silent trek to the pub.

5

The tavern is scarce of many, but Michael is never one to seek the comfort of a crowd. Abari orders a round of drinks as Michael finds a table in a far corner next to a table of several fisherman playing a game of cards he does not know.

A piano player beats out a strong and steady rhythm accompanying the melody of the mariachi band which sings a deep and heartfelt song that Michael finds soothing to the deep innards of his soul.

Abari sits down with the first round of drinks with a smile upon his face. "Seems you've caught an eye, my friend," he says as he gestures to a lovely young woman who is taking orders at the bar. "Play your cards right and you may find your belly warmed by more than a strong drink." Michael can't help but laugh, a laugh dispelling all nervousness. The idea of being in the arms of a woman after so long is appealing, but his stomach still quells with the anxious longing of a young man unsure of his ability to pursue such prospects.

Abari's expression turns to a slight concern. "I know the things that trouble you Michael…"

"What do you mean?"

"You still hold to the pain of your wife, I see that clear as day." Michael is silent and Abari continues. "I mean no disrespect Michael, but perhaps it is time you let go of such things. That is, of the past. I feel that destiny has touched you my friend, and you must follow its winds to whatever land or events it takes you, but you must learn to enjoy yourself along the journey." Abari finished the last of his drink, wincing with satisfaction slightly with its strength. He pats Michael on the shoulder and rises from his seat.

"Don't dwell on the things you've lost Michael, but honor them with your perseverance. Continue down the path, and perhaps someday you'll meet them again." He turns to leave.

"Where are you going?"

Abari chuckles, "I'm getting too old to have more than a single drink in the evening. I'm going to check in early for the night. I'll see you off in the morning. As for you, I suggest you find yourself some company, and enjoy it to its fullest."

And Michael did.

It had been so long since he had felt the embrace of a woman, and it

———

proved he had missed it much more than he had thought. Time had a funny way of making a man numb to more human desires, making it easier to cope with the responsibilities at hand, but it was always nice to discover that one was still capable of such pleasures. Even in the arms of a woman he would never have a chance to love or even see again.

Part 10:

The Hero of Trengar

I

The fires of the cremation wood had long since died to smoldering ash that blew fiercely in the wind of the barren plains of Gell. Danube was the first to wake, though he had never truly slept on that cold night. His mind never once slipped to the deep consciousness of sleep because his nerves were frayed. His mind was searching deep in the noise of the night looking, listening, for any sign of approach from the murderers of his men. He had been certain the light of the bonfire would have been seen by them if they were still close, and he was also certain that if they had seen it, they would come.

Yet no one came, and Danube felt his anger fueling even stronger with the lack of resolution of the murdered riders. He found comfort in the perception of his true surroundings, the warmth of Kaire's body against his, the sound of the last flames flickering from existence within the pyre, and the soft whining of the horses grazing on the sparse patches of foliage.

The sky retained its darkness though the sunlight struggled to pierce its haze. In the distance, Danube could see the blue skies upon the horizon, and the ice towers piercing the heavens. Danube quietly moved from his lover's side, taking care not to wake her. As he rose he felt his bones cry out in protest, and felt the deep ache within them. He had not spent this many nights sleeping on the ground since he was a child, when he camped deep in the wilderness alone. He remembered the hunts, and how it was in those times he learned about the land and how to survive. The pain in his bones seemed premature for age. Such aches should not inflict the young and righteous, but getting older was a sad fact of life that Danube would never willingly accept even in his eldest years.

Once he had dressed, he took another glance at the woman he had come to love by such sudden impulse that he feared it trickery at times. She was still fast asleep, wrapped in the thick, warm blankets they had come to share. Danube simply admired her, as he found himself doing on many occasions. When he could not sleep he would look at her, trying to burn every line and detail of her form within his mind. He would look at her as often as he could, stifling an embarrassed laugh when she would catch him staring, but in his heart he knew that she truly appreciated his admiration of her.

Something about this sleeping beauty disturbed him though, putting his nerves on edge. It was the way she stirred, the way her lips quivered, and things she whispered as she dreamed. *Who was the dark man within her dreams? Her true lover? Her master?* Danube didn't know. He found it ever frustrating when he could not get answers from Kaire about the man in her dreams, and when he would ask she simply couldn't answer. As if she was unable to, and that part of her mind that knew was blocked and inaccessible. Danube feared that inaccessible information may indeed be his, and maybe even *her*, undoing.

Danube turned from his sleeping lover and walked to the horses still grazing a short distance away. In the distance, across the plains of Gell and into the very distant Forests of Trengar, Danube could see the blue sky upon that horizon, the ice towers just barely visible upon that skyline. Something caught his eye in this glimpse, something so distant, so far away, that only one of great skill and of the sharpest eye ever could have perceived, for amidst the ice towers and the blue horizon were the blackest, thickest clouds of smoke reaching to the heavens from the forest floor beneath it. Trengar was burning, but no, not Trengar as a whole, but something more specific. Only Danube's trained eyes could see that it was his home which burned, it was Singe.

Dread came over Danube like a sheet of ice, freezing his blood in place, catching his breath tight in his chest, slamming his heart with pain like a sledgehammer. He was lost in the sight so far beyond him, so impossibly far that nothing could even be done. He wanted to move, to leap upon his horse and blindly charge forward to the horizon beyond. How far away were they now? A day's ride, two perhaps? How fast could he get there and would it make any difference if he went? He was lost amidst excruciating thoughts, frozen in his inner confliction. He did not hear Kaire rouse, he did not hear her approach him softly from behind, and did not expect her touch.

When Danube turned around he looked like a ghost, his usually dark skin was deathly pale, and his eyes were wide with terror. Kaire was shocked to see him this way, but knew what was wrong…she'd seen it herself; only she had seen it in her dream, the way she had seen many things that Danube would never know. She had not expected him to have known, had not expected him to have seen the smoke on the horizon, but that wasn't quite right. No, she knew he would see, just as she knew he would have to go back. It was his duty, they were his people, Singe was his home. She could only play her part as she always had and always would, but she hoped that perhaps when everything was said and done, in the end, she would live out her life with this man.

"What is it Danube? What's wrong?" Danube was silent, his eyes

———

unfocused, he did not know how to form the words.

"Singe…its…burning."

"Your home…I understand Danube, but the messengers are slain. We alone carry the message to Jerum."

Danube was slow to respond, weighing the responsibilities before him. Yet one duty weighed upon his heart with a force that could not be ignored. He was the High Lord of Trengar, the wielder of the Staff, the protector of all who lived of the Sage; he could not ignore that responsibility.

"I can't just turn away…I have to go back."

Kaire grew solemn at this, but after a long moment she held Danube's gaze, then took his hands in hers.

"Would you have me carry on the message alone? If you ask it of me…I will bear it."

2

He did, it was not the last time such a choice would be made in Danube's heart, but it would be a decision that would haunt him for many years to come. It was something he could never take back, and never could have chosen differently in the first place, it was destiny. It was unavoidable in the grand spectrum of all those finite decisions and events leading to the ultimate climax one man had spent his life manipulating in order to achieve.

Danube, Kaire, Albright, Michael, and all the others along the path are simply the pieces in which *he* plays his game of chess. So much would be lost, so much sacrificed, all in the end to attain a single goal. With such said, one can only say 'sorry'. Sorry for what Danube, a man of honor, a good man, must face along his path, and the price he'll pay for true honor, something that is slowly dying in the land of Selador, as it dies in every world, and may be lost forever as the true of destiny die. Ride forth Danube, ride forth upon the winds of destiny.

3

Kaire stood beside the smoldering remains of the fire as Danube disappeared from sight. Her long black hair tore through the wind as it always did, but something was new in this picture. She wept. Her hands never reaching to her face to wipe away the tears pouring from her eyes. Despite her pain, her sadness, she remained firm and steadfast, her face showing no signs of the squall of emotion tormenting her from within, no sign except for the tears.

She stood this way for a long time, looking out over the horizon that had swallowed the silhouette of her lover. She knew she should have warned him and wished that she could have, but darkness had ensnared her soul that she could never hope to break, but only wish to be free of.

If only she'd known then what she knew now? If only she'd known what Danube would awaken within her, these feelings she had never known. She damned the man of her dreams, damned him for bringing this upon her, but no, that wasn't right. It had been her decision, her choice; he had simply offered her freedom, life, power. It was she that ultimately chose to carry out his commands, just as she continued to do so.

She knew she was a fool, knew she was simply being used just as she had been used as a slave. Her freedom was a lie. She had never attained her freedom. She wasn't free when she killed the lords of Reum, wasn't free when she battled Danube, or when she willingly fell into his arms and into his love. She was simply fulfilling the commands of him, the shadowy figure of her mind. *He* whispered promises, but brought only death, and she remained a slave, to *his* power. But, what other choice does she have? *When the only gain in life has been brought by the following of such a darkness. If it is the only true opportunity one is presented for freedom then how can such a decision be condemned?* Weighing the costs was all she could do. To remain a slave of Reum she had no chance, but with this opportunity, perhaps, she could find her true freedom through Danube, but until that time she remained a slave, to the man in her dreams…her nightmares.

These things weighed upon her heart, and he only hoped Danube would return to her as swiftly as he had been carried away. Until then she could only continue, continue with *his* commands, and continue to Jerum.

She packed the few supplies she had and saddled her horse, then riding north along the path which she had been shown in her dream.

As she rode further into Gell, the darkness upon the barren plains continued to thicken like the darkness within her. No escape was presented from the path she'd chosen, and she came to realize that the one she had taken she would regret for the rest of her life, however short it may present itself to be.

4

The darkness of Gell was behind him now, but the setting sun cast an ominous cascade of red and orange hues across the Forests of Trengar. He could feel the pain of the forest crying out to him even now. Its cries called him, drove him forward, drove him home.

The Cash River came within sight, and he held his staff high crying out as he summoned his power, never slowing his speed for a second. His horse crashed into the descending rapids as the river parted by his power for passage once again.

As he made his way along the winding paths and trails of his homeland, his mind began to slip. The trees and familiar landscape began to drift past him faster and faster until he could see nothing of the peripheral world, only that which lay ahead. The forest itself seemed to be pushing him forward, and Danube became lost to space and time. To him, what seemed a blink of the eye had been the worth of a day and half's ride, but even time can bend to the will of God. A great distance was traveled that day in an amount of time Danube's mind could never recollect, but needless to say, the winds indeed blew at his back and aided him, the Lord of Trengar, to save his people.

5

When Danube reached the place in the road where the path widened and gave the full view of the city of Singe, he halted the quick advance of the horse he road. What Danube saw was the most horrific sight he had ever witnessed in his twenty-three years of life.

The great city of Singe, which stood like a monolith amidst the forest on every side, had three massive, ancient pillars made from trees. These trees were as old as time, and covered acres of space upon the forest floor, casting the first level of the city beneath it in a continuous state of cool shadow. Three levels of the city were built into the very trees themselves, and packed with residences and establishments of trade, market, government, and study. This wonderful and beautiful city, so at peace with the natural world around it, so elegant in structure and design, was now the victim of the largest assault of troops the land of Selador had ever seen. It was the largest ever cooperative assault of ground forces. The very forest itself was littered with the masses of bodies striking forth against the city in regiments of deadly precision.

Danube could not count how many men were before him delivering the onslaught against his great city. But he knew those colors, and knew the reason they had come, for the soldiers that were present were sent from not only Reum but from the massed cities of Lindell as well. He even saw several men bearing the red armor of those of the mountains of Zwentor. It was as if everything had been played perfectly into the hands of his enemies so precisely, and that he had not been here at the time. Not been home to protect his people, instead he was misled into delivering word to Jerum, misled by… his only love.

He watched as his people fought from the security of the treetops, firing arrows, casting stones, and throwing spears, but for every man they had killed three more seemed to take his place. The effort seemed futile, for only perhaps 500 warriors of Trengar remained in the safeguard of the city, but every man, woman, and child did their part to protect their home. Those who could not fight helped the injured or doused the fires below with the reserves of water that they had within the trees themselves. Everyone was in a swarm of frenzy to help their approaching Lord in whatever way they could. Death rained from above, the guardians of Singe unleashed hordes of arrows and stones.

It was in that moment as Danube sat gallantly abroad his horse, his staff at his side, overlooking his great city as its first two levels burned, his people screaming as the soldiers overtook them, that he came to realize just how big a part Kaire had played in what was happening right before his eyes.

A million thoughts went through his mind at once, playing back images and softly spoken words from the past several days. He had been foolhardy in trusting her, but even now he still loved her, hoping perhaps all would be explained when he'd seen her again, *if* he'd see her again.

At the moment, such things could not be pondered, forward was at hand, his people were dying at his feet. *Most of them probably crying out for their lord, their great High Lord Danube Drakendor, to save them, and where was he? Off to the king to chat about world events with his newfound love? Had he abandoned them in their greatest time of need?* Danube did not need to wonder if such things echoed in the dying thoughts of his people, he knew they did. Even at this very second, as they died upon the battlefield, the third part of his mind could hear their cries, could feel their pain. They had all counted on him, and he had failed them in their time of need. At this very instant, Danube felt like Michael Cross…dishonored, and yet despite that failure he felt the greatest, most powerful feeling any man could ever feel. At the realization of his love's betrayal, and his own failure, it brought about a final breaking point within his soul. Once all is lost, and broken, within a man, only then his true strength and determination will reveal themselves. It is in these moments he realized that the honor he fights for is not for himself. What a man desires in his life can be given and taken away. His achievements pass with time. All the things he can reach for gain nothing for the life of the world, but only fulfill one's own desire. What is truly important, what really matters, is that which aids the side of righteousness. It is those sacred few who are willing to sacrifice everything to do the right thing that find themselves in moments such as this. In this moment, actions can define the kind of man one is destined to be; a fool, a coward, a hero, or a king. Only in the lowest moment can one truly see a man's courage, and in Danube's moment of silence upon the overlooking crest of the hill, he found his.

To see this is to see legend, a single man, astride a faithful horse, wielding high a weapon forged by God himself, charging forth into the fray of hundreds of men at arms bearing down upon his home, his people. In this moment the world seems to stop, wave rushes over the hundreds of soldiers as they turn, their many colors of red and orange and blue rippling like a mosaic tile. They see him, this single man, this last of Drakendor, and for a moment every one of them is filled with fear as he cries out to the people of his land, the people of the Sage, and they return the cry.

"Hail Trengar! Hail ye people of Sage! I come to deliver you from thy enemies!"

Danube could see his people gathering at the balconies of the remaining second and third levels. They had all suddenly ceased in their tasks for that moment in time to see the approach of their lord, the only hope the city had. Together, the hundreds of people cried out in a single voice so great it shook the world.

"Hail Drakendor! Hail Lord, savior of the Sage!" Their words brought courage and power to the brokenhearted Danube, who charged forth toward the onslaught which awaited him. Danube was met in his charge by a wave of men whose sheer numbers seemed colossal in comparison to the single figure who rode towards them, he was like a single ship against the terrible forces of the sea.

But if Danube was such a ship, then the wind which blew his sails was destiny. This great wind seemed to charge with him, starting low and soft, but as the gap between them closed it grew in strength. The staff could feel the will and the heart of the last Drakendor and with such compassion it drew upon the strength of its creator and bent its will to the aid of the Sage. The power radiating from the ancient wooden staff engulfed Danube's form, blasting him forth into the masses with such force that soldiers were literally thrown aside, striking the ground with cold death residing in their vacant eyes. Their archers fired a barrage of arrows, so many that as they fell upon Danube he was certain his life would end. Yet as the black cloud of projectiles screamed down upon him, the blazing wind engulfing his form blew them all from their mark, breaking some and even returning several in the direction of his enemies.

Those trying to rush him were trampled into the earth and those who tried to flank him were cast aside with disturbing ease. Bodies flew in all directions, limp limbs flailing wildly as they hit the ground with stomach wrenching sounds. Danube had become a whirlwind of destruction.

But despite the many falling at his feet, there were three times the number charging to face him. He had charged deep into the sea of warriors and was on the verge of being engulfed by the sheer number. The horse slammed hard into the ranks, tossing Danube far from his mount.

He used the power of the wind raging from his staff to right himself in the air before striking the ground. He landed with the grace of a cat, his knees poised to lunge at the first of his attackers, his staff held defiantly ready before him.

Focusing, he watched as the soldiers moved around him like a pack of wolves, ready to lace their fangs within his flesh, but cautiously waiting for the right moment when they could all spring upon him and make their kill. Danube Drakendor stood amidst the eye of a hurricane with no perceivable end to the faces of armored men who pursued only death.

A great and heavy breath was drawn, and the enemies of Sage drove upon him. Danube stood poised like a mountain as they dove, closing the distance. Eight, ten, twelve, twenty, thirty, they all poured toward him one after another. He did the one thing he knew how to do... he fought.

The ancient, hardened wood of his staff struck violently in every direction, striking steel, bone and flesh. His martial skill was insurmountable, his movements too quick to follow. He danced amidst the bodies, his staff whirling wildly, deflecting strikes and redirecting blows to and from his enemies. Countless bodies fell at his feet and yet still the onslaught continued.

Danube, cool minded and deadly, reached a state of responding purely on instinct. He could feel himself gaining through the crowd. He knew he was driving closer to the base of the tree top city working his way through the masses of soldiers.

He knew he could not hope to fight them all alone in the midst of those blades and arrows and axes. Surely one would get lucky, one would slip through the perception of his skill and run him through, but at the base of the first of the trees he could hope to make his stand. Perhaps he could even retaliate against them with his own surviving soldiers and create a resistance, but before he could place such a plan into action, his greatest fear became reality.

As he fended off both a soldier of Lindell and two of Reum, pivoting their swords in a fashion bringing the three together and down to the ground. He spun the other end of his staff around striking another man in the jaw before landing three lightning fast strikes upon the skulls of those before him, and then he saw something glimmer out of the corner of his eye. He swung the staff as quickly as he could, just barely connecting with the head of the axe wielded by a large man of Zwentor and glancing the axe blade from a true blow. The hardened steel of the axe head drove hard against Danube's skull and blotches of strange light pulled across his vision like a curtain as he felt himself falling.

Somewhere amidst the ranks he heard a commanding voice cry out "I want him alive!" and instead of the hundreds of blades he expected to pierce his body, he could feel himself being beaten. The staff was ripped from his hands and he could feel the ground rush upon him with blinding quickness.

Once they had their fill of destroying his body, he felt himself being hauled up and partially dragged across the ground for a distance, until he was again thrown upon it once more. His only thought was, *'I have failed.'*

When he opened his eyes, he found himself looking at the feet of not a soldier, but of a lord, and by the attire an honored lord of Lindell. "High Lord Danube Drakendor I suppose?" The man inquired, as Danube spit blood.

"Nevertheless..." He said as he took the staff from one of the soldiers who had seized him. "I suppose this is the great Legendary Staff of Trengar as well. Doesn't really look like much, does it?" Some of the men around him began to chuckle. Danube's vision, even with one eye sealed by blood, began to clear enough to see the face of the man who spoke. "I suppose a thank you is in order my fellow High Lord. As you can see..." the figure gestured towards the burning city. "...We've been going through quite a bit of trouble to obtain this little item of interest." Danube continued to struggle to clear his vision to see the man who spoke. He struggled hard and found the focus he needed, only to find himself face to face with something he had long since thought gone from the world. Upon the malevolent-faced man who towered over him, cloaked in a cape and hood of crimson around his shoulders, was a scar and yet not a scar, but a wound cut deep into his face. It traced from the right top of his forehead to the bottom of his left cheek, and across from his right cheek over the bridge of his nose and under his left eye, forming a cross.

Lord Raymark could see the reaction on Danube's face as his eyes traced the cross he bore. A deep-seeded red-headed anger leapt forth from the man but he quickly quelled it. "My apologies, my fellow lord and *friend* of the land, I have forgotten to introduce myself. I am High Lord Raymark Lafey of Lindell, seemingly your equal here in our great land of Selador, and yet it would seem that I have the upper hand. Perhaps, however, as a gesture of good faith between the regions we can have a bit of a…peace conference and find a civil negotiation regarding your fateful city which will indeed lie in ruins if you do not fully comply." Raymark paused briefly to gesture two of the soldiers on either side of Danube. They brought him staggering to his feet.

Danube struggled to look his captor in the face. His eye stung from the fresh blood beginning to trickle its way into the cuts on his face as well, he grimaced from the pain. Raymark smiled at this with a row of pearly white teeth that seemed to clash with the morbid red of the cross upon his face. Raymark continued, "I think you know why these armies are here Danube. It is something your involvement with has been quite vast no doubt. The armies of Reum are here in demand of the scythe which was unjustly stolen from them by the slave girl Kaire Ra, who no doubt worked as a spy of your faithful sect of Sage.

In a similar indication, my armies of Lindell are here seeking the legendary Great Sword taken from us by the traitorous bastard Michael Cross. The armies of Zwentor are simply here because of a great allegiance to the land and the wish to abolish any threats which may arise to oppose it." Raymark paused briefly, letting this settle in Danube's mind for a moment.

Danube knew this was a setup. Despite his limited vision, he could still see in Raymark's eyes that he indeed was lying about everything. He knew that Michael Cross had not stolen the sword and that the whole thing was a setup, a dastardly plan to overthrow the region of Trengar and claim the staff as part of the true scheme to overthrow the land. Danube held his silence and listened to Raymark's lies, playing his game.

"Now that we have confiscated the staff from you in the name of Selador we wish for you to surrender *our* weapons as well. As you can see we are willing to do anything necessary to retrieve them," Raymark continued.

"Your weapons are not here..." Danube spoke solemnly.

"You lie! We know they are here and our people demand their return. Do not deny us our right!"

"I deny you nothing I possess..." Danube again spoke in a solemn and disciplined tone.

"I will ask again Danube Drakendor, and if you do not comply then I will be forced to allow these armies before you to rip Singe apart, kill every man, woman, and child, and burn it all to the ground until our weapons are found! Where are the legendary Scythe of Reum and the Great Sword of Lindell? Where are Kaire Ra and Michael Cross?"

"You play a sick game, but I can tell you're just a puppet. I do not know who has done this or why but I know that you, Lord Raymark are his prized piece indeed. For it is you who lies, and knows as a fact that the weapons and people you seek are not in this place nor are they spies of my Sage. I know that no matter the answer I give you, no matter what I say, Singe will burn to the ground, and the Staff of Trengar will indeed be in the hands of evil. These armies, these people are pawns of he who plays you, and will unknowingly aid the darkness which is brewing to destroy the land. Only a fool couldn't see it!" Danube's voice rose like a king in waves over the armies upon him. Raymark leaned very close to him, and in all but a whisper spoke, "There are many fools in this world Danube Drakendor, and you are right. I am going to destroy everything you love no matter what you do or say. Why? You may ask, because it is what I do. Just ask Michael Cross… when you meet him in the afterlife."

6

Annabelle healed another of the injured warriors burned from the fires which had raged upon the first level of the city. He had been lucky to have escaped with his life and he now struggled to keep it, having received burns to nearly forty percent of his body. She struggled to use her quickly draining abilities to help ease his pain and keep the damage to his flesh from killing him.

Hundreds of people frantically rushed around them. Archers stood at the railing and edges of platforms firing barrages of arrows, only to be struck by those of the massed clouds returned by the enemies below. People scrambled with water, keeping the fires from climbing any higher than they already had.

Smoke was everywhere and she could hardly see through the chaos around her. The people were choking on smoke and screaming in pain, the children crying out in fear. There seemed to be no hope in sight. There were just too many of them. All seemed lost...until he came.

Danube Drakendor, the young High Lord, staff brandished high as he cried out to his people. Even over the noise of the chaos she heard his voice. She felt it rip through her with the authority of a king, a mortal chosen by god himself. She ceased what she was doing, everyone did. All returned his cry and watched his legendary charge upon their enemies.

There were cries of joy and judgment; a few whispering thoughts of his obvious insanity for charging one man against so many, but all were silenced as he unleashed the power of the staff which he wielded. The people stood in awe at his power, and no one who witnessed that day would ever forget these moments.

Nor would they forget the great sadness, the great pain which ripped through them as they watched their hero fall. His charge was terminated and his staff taken. Their High Lord, their young Drakendor…was defeated.

Annabelle watched as the red-cloaked, scarred man so many hundreds of feet below began to speak with Danube. She listened with her mind to the truth of what was said, and she could see the folly of what was happening. The deceit, the betrayal which this…Raymark, she *heard*, was bringing upon them all. Danube would die no matter what he said or did, and so would Singe, that much was clear.

She looked around her, looked to the people of Sage. They merely stood in disbelief, no one doing anything to save their fallen lord. What could they do? They did not know what was happening or why, but Annabelle did. Somehow deep in the recesses of her mind's eye the place no one can every really understand, she knew. She knew it all, and knew what had to be done.

She thought of Albright, a man she had cared for so passionately as a lover and as a kind companion of the likes she had never known. He had come to face his destiny, and played his part in this world so that Michael could carry on. She had seen this very well, and she now saw her fate just as clearly. Through all the smoke and chaos and mosaic of colors of the soldiers in the armies below she looked at one man. The dark skinned young lord Drakendor.

She thought to Danube with the power within, '*Albright died to save Cross and I die to save Drakendor. With our deaths, let your discrepancies die and let the last of Cross and Drakendor stand together at the end of your paths in this world…save the Sage, Danube, save your people, and hold strong to the honor in your heart…*'

A single tear rolled down her cheek as she climbed onto the railing at the edge of the balcony overlooking the world below. She whispered the words as a familiar flame appeared in her hands, "Need a light..." She let the flame roll across her knuckles as she smiled with the soft but slowly fading memories of Albright. He had taught it to her well, though at the time she did not know why. Yet all things come clear in time, and in this moment she finally understood just why she had learned the enchanting secrets of her lover.

One last time she looked at the flame she held within her hand and jumped from the railing of the balcony of the third city level of Singe. She plummeted thirty three feet before the flames began to engulf her form. She did not scream out in pain but in glory, in righteous rage, in power. She cried out to Danube Drakendor.

7

Danube could hear her voice in his mind, so familiar and yet so different in resolve than the tender voice of the lady Annabelle he had known. She spoke with command and dignity in his thoughts. *'Albright died to save Cross and I die to save Drakendor...'* Danube looked up to the sky as he heard the screams of those who had seen her jump. She was a beautiful haze of white and green, her long golden hair tore through the wind, but she seemed un-phased as she plummeted. Danube's heart strings tore at the sight, for he knew the figure plunging. This Lady Annabelle Stevens, daughter of Roweland, master of the white magick, and seer of life. She had helped guide him through his life as she had helped so many others.

Raymark turned his back to Danube to see what was happening. Many of the other soldiers, in fact, most of them, stared at the sight of the apparently suicidal beauty, falling to the forest city floor. Danube understood what she was doing and knew that this would be his one chance to reclaim his staff and stop this senseless destruction.

As he made his move, pulling the two men who held him smashing them into each other, he heard Annabelle cry out, "Long live the Drakendor!" as her body became engulfed in flames. Danube didn't completely understand how this was happening or why, but he understood that all that mattered now was his staff. He reached across Raymark's turned body and caught hold of the staff, simultaneously catching a grip on the hood of his red cloak with his other hand. Just as Raymark yelped in utter surprise and terror at the stern, cold killer's eyes of Danube Drakendor, Annabelle's flaming form struck the ground part-way into the middle of the armies.

The ground erupted in an earth-shattering explosion tearing through hundreds of soldiers. Fire swept up their fleeing bodies as they tried to escape the unexpected blast. Those who were not killed by the explosion itself were internally liquefied by its concussion, or mortally wounded by the masses of shrapnel bursting through them in clouds followed by smoke and fire. Hundreds of men cried out in pain and agony, many fled, unsure of how far the destruction would radiate.

As Raymark was pulled backward, and ironically tripped by his own flashy red cloak, the legendary Staff of Trengar was ripped from his hands by the darkened figure of Danube. He glared upon him with the fires of Annabelle's explosion raging in the background of his steady and resolved form. The staff grew dark in his hands and around his stature his aura became visible to the physical world. It rippled like the heated air around the fire at his back, and Danube remained untouched in the wake of destruction. Soldiers all around ran to escape its power, but no one was willing to stop and help Lord Raymark in this moment of terrifying danger. Raymark looked to the man before him frozen in time and grew so terrified he couldn't even scream. Raymark struggled to flee, crawling away like a crab into the tide.

Danube looked at him with the same fiery blaze of the explosion echoing in his eyes. "High Lord Raymark of Lindell! Your lies have deceived these men into becoming nothing more than murderers! The sign of the *cross* upon your face was rightfully placed, and therefore should be respected for the warning it heeds. Traitor! Liar! Murderer! I see you for what you are!" he shouted as Raymark shuddered in fear and guilt.

The earthquake had stopped and the explosion receded to reveal the massed trail of destruction which surrounded its eye. Burning corpses, wounded men, and scattered blazes of debris upon the blackened earth stood as a scene all of its own, an indignant serenity to the words that now echoed in its wake.

Danube continued to speak, never turning to gaze upon the destruction behind him, "The last casualty of my people, the people of the Sage, has died in sacrifice to help end your sinful treachery! I swear the Lady Annabelle has been the last innocent life you will claim on this day! If I have to kill every soldier here- every one of you, I will! But you will die no matter…" Several soldiers rushed to Danube at once grabbing hold of him tightly and trying to wrench the staff from his hands. The six men struggled to grapple him, but it was as though they were fighting a wall. For a brief moment Danube merely stood there unwavered by their efforts, and then the anger crept abruptly into his face. His muscles tensed and the shimmering, clear fire surrounding him burst forth from his body and the six men were sent flying in all directions.

Luckily for Raymark, he had taken this opportunity to desert his followers and flee. He had mounted the nearest horse after pulling its unsuspecting rider from its mount, and rode away as fast as he could.

Danube cursed him under his breath as he watched him escaping through the crowd of chaos stricken soldiers. "You are a marked man Raymark, one way or the other, be it Cross or I, your life will be finished!" he roared as Raymark cowardly rode off with his back turned.

Danube now looked to see the damage Annabelle had done to their men and marveled at the fact that the soldiers had been dropped by a third. He could also see his own soldiers repelling down from the now quenched, fire-ridden first level of the city. Hundreds of them came, massed in one last rally to stand against the enemy.

After seeing the retreat of Lord Raymark, a majority of the remaining soldiers of Lindell, fifty or more having been killed by the blast out of the original one hundred and fifty strong, fled in retreat as to the example of their lord. Those of Zwentor also fled, seeing the battle would soon be lost by the lack of leadership on their part, and no doubt the impossibility of taking the city with the dwindling numbers of their original onslaught of sheer force.

These people were defending their homes, and would give everything they had to protect what they held dear, and yet still nearly two hundred of Reum's finest remained ready to do anything necessary to reclaim the scythe which was taken from them, two hundred against one hundred and seventy seven of the Sage and one young High Lord wielding his weapon of legend.

The last of Reum's soldiers and those few of Lindell who remained formed a line of their ranks in preparation for one great charge against the defenders of Trengar who had also formed their own defensive line at the base of the city. Danube joined the ranks of his men who greeted him in gathered voices.

No speech was necessary, no triumphant dialogue giving the commands necessary to deliver the message of the importance of the battle standing before them. They all knew what they must do, what was at stake, what valiant and fervent effort must be put forth by each and every one of them. Despite this common knowledge, this silent understanding between them all Danube spoke, "Hail ye brave men, Hail Trengar, Singe, and Sage. Hail true defenders of Selador. Let us fight and die with honor."

"Hail!" The men sounded together.

They awaited the expected onslaught of the army before them, awaited the beginning of their first move, their first step of the march drawing the two armies to war. Then it came, like thunder rolling across the plains; two hundred soldiers of Reum and few blue garbed soldiers of Lindell charged forth..

Danube counted the steps as they marched towards them; 30, 31, 32... suddenly out of the corner of his eye, Danube caught sight of a white horse bearing a rider of Reum wielding a flag held high upon a staff as he rode into sight...33. The rider cried at the top of his lungs, "Stop! End the march, men of Reum! Soldiers under the yellow sun, men of the plains, we are deceived!"

Danube felt the chill run through his body as the miracle transpired before him. Word was delivered from Reum, proclaiming the mistake in their actions. The army halted its forward momentum and receded, observing the scene with a stunned silence, overcome by the strange absence of impending battle so abruptly taken. The feeling was replaced with feelings of disgrace and shame for what they had unwittingly been fooled into enacting upon these people.

The messenger spoke with those of the highest ranks and explained the situation in its entirety. At last, the messenger and the highest ranking officer approached the center of the field of destruction that lay between them. Danube and his commander in chief rode out to the center on horseback. The two representatives of Reum came slowly towards them. Their heads hung in shame.

When the men spoke, their voices were low, tones honest and apologetic. They offered to help extinguish the fires, bring aid to those they had cut, burned, and pierced with arrows. 'Help', to offer 'help' is what they gave. Danube was the only one to speak the remainder of the meeting, and it was all that needed to be said.

"I venture not at the reasons for you to be ill content with my people. Even if it was suspected that we had indeed deceived and tricked our way into obtaining the Legendary Scythe and Great Sword, would you not in accordance wait until given direct order from Jerum before setting to blaze the city and risking the endangerment of innocent lives? Is it simply because our home is made of wood that you wish to burn it so hastily? No matter... You are excused of this in the sense of the endearing term 'mistake', but I mark my words you are indebted for seven generations to the people of Trengar. We ask not for your aid on this day, for the sight of you any longer would burn our hearts and pour scorn into our veins, and we *will* kill you. This is why you must leave now, with not another word

285

spoken. Know only that one day the Sage will call upon you for our cause."

Neither man spoke a word, but merely nodded and rode away. The men sounded their horns for the troops to fall back, and head home. Danube's commander in chief looked at him with glassy turquoise eyes and spoke, "Something should be said."

"What can be said, say sorry? I know not what to say, only what must be done..."

Danube knew he couldn't stay, but he did everything he could to try and convince himself that he would. He called for the fastest, freshest horse that could be found and a week's ration for two. He rallied his men, set the defensive perimeters, and appointed his most trusted in charge. They asked him why he must leave, but they all knew why. He no longer held the people's gaze as he mounted the fresh horse.

He bid them farewell, they bid him good luck, and he turned his horse and rode.

8

Danube reached the outskirts of Gell, just at the edge of the line of trees ending the border of the forests of Trengar, as the sun dipped serenely over the horizon. It was the perfect sunset, and Danube took a moment to admire its glory before gathering the resolve he would need to cross the Cash River once more.

Once he did, he would ride the horse as hard as he could through the night in hopes of seeing his lover's face by morning, but what Danube would find on that following morning would forever haunt him through the many years of his life.

Part II:

The Island of Laotia

I

Michael did not enjoy his time at sea. In fact, he had spent most of his time on deck leaning over the side of the ship relieving his stomach of all of its contents. Luckily for him, the journey was not a long one. It only took them a day to reach the island, and the sight of it overjoyed Michael. Due to the preceding events of his quest, the darkness of Gell's ever black skies, and the damage his time of imprisonment had caused to his internal clock, he wasn't exactly sure just how long it had been since he had first embarked on his journey to the distant island. He figured it had been roughly ten to thirteen days since he had left the city of Singe back in the Forests of Trengar. Even so, it felt as though a lifetime had passed. Time has a funny way of changing perceptions.

Nevertheless, Michael was truly happy to see the palm covered island in the distance. He marveled at the sheer populace of it, and even at the distance the ship still sailed from its shores, he could see the great infrastructure of its single massive collaborated city.

2

As the ship pulled into dock, Michael could see several men approaching along the many wooden scaffolds and planks. They all wore the same uniform which consisted of long, flowing white robes and a peculiar yellow wrapping upon their heads. They appeared to have no hair on either their face or extremities. Michael assumed that their heads were indeed shaven as well beneath the wrap.

Michael counted seven in all and marveled at the discipline they held even in the way they made their approach. Forming two lines, their hands tucked into their sleeves in front of them like some awkward position of prayer, each one stepping in unison. Michael found uneasiness in the fact that their hands were hidden in those big sleeves and couldn't help but imagine them all pulling knives from them at the simultaneously, but they did not. They simply waited patiently upon the wooden dock as the sailors tied their ship and began unloading supplies.

Michael checked the sword upon his back and stepped from the ship. The two lines of men parted and bowed deeply to the Lord. Michael returned the bow. One of the men Michael could not distinguish from the others stepped forward. "My lord, I am San Judashni, we have been sent to welcome you and ensure your safe delivery to the Ja Mahaul and our High Lord Nieon Sulton. If you'd please, follow me."

"It would appear as though you were expecting me," Michael said slightly unnerved.

"The redtailed hawks of Reum do far more than hunt field mice, my lord. Come, come, we have much to speak of."

Before Michael could voice thanks, the man turned and began his march across the dock. The others remained in their two lines following only after Michael had passed them.

Michael found it unnerving, having so many mysterious men he did not know following so close behind him, but he thought it best to follow his host's wishes.

The men led him to an interestingly decorated cart driven by a large

288

man instead of a horse. Michael climbed aboard and was rather startled once the man lifted the front of the cart and dashed forward, making his way swiftly through the crowded streets of the port's marketplace. The speed of the man who carried them was amazing and Michael found it marvelously intriguing, but didn't really take to the idea of a man being used as a horse. When he questioned the strange man that accompanied him in the cart, the man simply replied, "Horses are sacred here…we have none as captives." Michael chose not to question the hard-faced man anymore and simply tried to sit back and enjoy the sights as they passed.

3

When they arrived at the main estate of the island city, Michael was not entirely surprised to see another, even larger, welcoming party of what he assumed were soldiers or perhaps royal guards. They once again stood in two lines, giving a space between them like an aisle. The silent man he rode with gestured Michael to get out first. Michael got out of the cart, checking the strap of his sword as he did. There were more than he had expected there to be.

Michael walked side-by-side with San Judashni, the man with the red turban top. Michael had long since thought out the significance of the differently colored top caps of the turbans these men wore. Judashni was obviously the highest ranking of those he'd seen, and he was the only one with a red top upon the yellow turban wraps they all wore. It reminded him of the sun, and he wondered if this was coincidence, or perhaps a religious belief of the people here. As for the orange and white toped turbans, he only figured one color were the elites of the group, the best, the individual squad leaders, and another made up the soldiers of those squads.

Before him and the captain, the line of men stretched a whole 50 yards to the entrance of the estate. As they walked past these rows of guards, the rows collapsed and the guards they had passed before now followed them.

Aside from the guards following behind them, everything about it reminded Michael of a game he used to play in combat training as a youth. All of the trainees would line up in two rows, and one youth would walk between them. The boy walking between them would be attacked by several of the people in the rows along the way, but the catch was he didn't know who. It was called Dark Alley, dark because the walker wore a blindfold.

At this moment Michael wore a blindfold of sorts. He had no idea if suddenly he would be attacked by one or all of the guards surrounding him, their many hands tucked neatly into their sleeves. *Are they my protection, or are they all a threat? I have never seen so many guards massed for such a greeting other than for a king, or a prisoner. For the king it is protection, for the prisoner…so he can't escape.* Michael felt his world close in on him. *The possibilities of so many incredibly fast hands with so many daggers?* He knew he would be killed at once, all at once, in a single second…gone.

Yet before Michael could be cut down by his own thoughts of being mercilessly slain by the numbers around him, red top and he were safely inside the estate. It was a massive villa, with the majority of its structure upon a rock face overlooking the sea of Belle on one side, and on the other side were the forbidden lands where no one traveled, the lost desert. The edge of this lost desert was said to be the end of the world. At one time many explorers ventured into its sea of fiery white sand, but no one ever returned. The cliff the estate sat upon was one part of the long stretch of cliffs separating the lost desert from the rest of Laotia.

Michael could see that many of the buildings in this place were cut into the same shale stone as others, connecting them in a random maze of uniformed style of construction.

"What is this stone?" Michael asked red top.

"It is kiyoke stone, given to us by the lady of the sea long ago."

San Judashni continued to lead Michael through the richly decorated estate. Many of the halls and rooms were extremely spacious with ceilings which were no doubt three, even four stories high. Massive white pillars throughout were carved from the common stone of the island.

"It was said that in the old days, the sea gave the stone to a man who lived alone on the island. His only company was the sea and the goddess who reigned over it. Each day, the man would walk along the beach and sing to his lady of the sea, the goddess Belle. Over time, the Lady Belle fell in love with this mortal man, but since the gods were forbidden to love the beings of creation, the humans of the world, she could only admire his songs from afar. Yet each day, this single man who had been stranded on the island for many years grew lonelier and lonelier. His songs turned to sadness and hope for death. One starry night, when his loneliness had reached a point no man could bear any longer, he stood upon the very cliff on which this palace was built, and as he sang his last song to the Lady Belle, he plummeted to the sea below. Had this been any other man he would have surely drowned and his life would be at rest. Instead, because the goddess so loved this man, she returned him safely to shore. When the man finally woke he was astounded to see the Lady Belle."

"In her presence he sings to her, and in return for his mortal love, she gives him everything he needs. She teaches him to fish and gives him the kiyoke stone to carve and make a home. She even makes love to him, but what he wants most is a woman of flesh and blood and a family of his own, children to live in the home he had built and friends to bring him joy and company. Out of a deeper love than many could understand, she gives him these things just so that she can see the man happy. And even though the man went on to have a family and establishing the community that founded the region, the man still loved his Lady Belle, and would continue his songs to her until the day he died. She named his people Laotians, the lions of the sea. All this happened in the time before, the time of the gods and the beasts and creatures of the land, when man was new to life, and the weapons had not yet established the order of the one true God. It was a time before the beginning...of the end..."

Michael marveled at the power in the man's voice and his fortitude for storytelling. The man seemed somewhat more open once he was away from the presence of his guards, but he was still as thick and emotionless as the best of soldiers were.

"I see ...a fascinating tale." Michael said.

"One of legends..." San Judashni said as he let the faintest hint of a smile drip upon his lips.

They continued through the massed estate until they came to a set of doors that loomed in magnitude over all others Michael had ever seen in his life. "Here we are. I can go no further Lord Michael Cross, for this threshold you must pass through alone. Inside you will find many answers...nothing more I can say last of the Cross. I bid you farewell. Do not be hasty in your choice..." With these simply spoken words, the interesting man turned and left him standing at the final set of doors, rich wooden twins of mass and girth shrouding the things which lay beyond the frame of its set walls, beyond the grain of its thick, once living, core. Stripped and shaped, sanded and stained, made in to two of the most ornately but yet beautifully simple doors he had ever seen. They were doors which led to his destiny. On the other side, fate stood in the flesh. Michael Cross...opened these doors...

04/09/08

Two men stood just beyond the stained glass cathedral ceiling which covered half the observation deck. The closest was of dark complexion, wearing a white robe and a black turban upon his head, the top part a bright blue. *'Blue top...High Lord Nieon Sulton?'* Michael thought. At the man's side, resting with his lean form, was what appeared to be the legendary Spear of Destiny. His face was expressionless.

The dark figure that stood beyond this man was dressed all in black with a large brimmed hat tipped just beneath his eyes, shrouding most of his face in darkness. His coat flowed about him like a shadow, it became shadow. At his side was a sword Michael had grown to fear. He knew immediately that it was the legendary Katana of the place that would forever haunt his nightmares, the place called Gell. He knew this man not by his face, but by the aura which surrounded his presence, the darkness carrying his sin upon his exterior like an impenetrable shroud. He knew this man to be Raven Warlack.

The two men held time still, like two statues chiseled with the echoes of past, present and future. Their features were carved like men chosen by destiny to oppose the fates, to oppose the god's *design*.

At the sight of Michael, Warlack's long face stretched to bear a handsomely welcoming and yet maniacal smile which made Michael want to flee and strangely, come closer. The man's eyes were blue, but not just any blue, but the same blue as someone Michael had seen before. *''Blue-eyes', the card player in the tavern at Lindell, the same night the attempt on the sword was made...'*

"Michael Cross, we meet at last. It's been a long time coming. How do ye like the trials I've set before ya? Certainly not enjoyable, I assume. I can only fathom the hatred ye must hold for me." He took a few steps forward as he spoke. Michael readied himself.

"But I want you to ask yourself one question, Michael Cross, what do ya want...Do ya want your wife back? Your happy...normal life? Do ya want your lordship, or perhaps forgiveness for sins which ye never committed, or is it power ye seek? The ability to control that which is in you or the power of the sword which you've bore upon yer back, like a cross, ironically enough, so many miles the physical embodiment of that which weighs upon your heart. I can give you whatever you desire. And I've already set ya upon the path of yer destiny. Ya know this to be true..."

"Think about it Michael, without me you never would have left your beautiful home amidst the decaying cities of Lindell. Without me ya would never really have known yer true purpose. You would never have the answers that you've always sought. I need ya, Michael. The future of the world needs ya and a grand future it could be. Join me, and rule at my side, the last of the Cross at my right hand. This is my offer to you Michael Cross, do we have an accord?"

"Do you take me for a pawn?"

"By no means friend, you are surely a greater piece in this game than a mere pawn." Raven chuckled lightly, his body language friendly in his gestures.

"But a piece to be played by your hand, nonetheless, I reckon..."

Warlack chuckled at Michael's response, but despite his deliberately forced humor he seemed unsettled.

"Ya got it wrong, Michael. I'm not trying to manipulate ya in any way. I'm simply asking yer help, yer allegiance. I want only the best for ya."

"Is that why you took away my life and sent my wife into the bed of the scum Raymark?"

Warlack let a long sigh escape his lips, his shoulders relaxed; his appearance was that of a frustrated friend. He took a bold step towards Michael. His guard was alarmingly down; it was too empty of a threat for Michael to reach for his sword, because he spoke with open gestures.

"Michael, Michael, Michael…it was not I who sent your wife to the bed of Lord Raymark. She did so on her own accord…I can honestly say my hands are indeed clean of that. Yet I will not lie to ya when I say that I did set other circumstances into motion, the fires, the attempted taking of the sword, which by the way…was a win-win for me. They succeed in taking it, it's in my hands. You stop them, and pull it yourself…it merely sets prophesy in motion. Ya must know that at some point in yer life it was destiny for you to claim that sword as your namesake…it just so happens I moved things along, so to speak…"

"Don't play coy with me Warlack, I see through your façade. Cut through the bullshit and get to the point. Why do you want the legendary weapons?"

Warlack chuckled again. His distance to Michael was now that of a handshake. "Why Michael, I can't tell you that unless I know you're with me, and if I were to tell you the true reason…why, you would be the first, everyone else that has been pulled to this has been by their own reasons, their own desires, but all with one inevitable goal in mind, a better world for all."

"Bullshit! If anyone's going to do it, then I will be the one to call your bluff. I know the evil inside you, and I've seen more than anyone what you can do, what you have done. So don't pretend to be a saint before me, because I see that the only desires and wants you care about are your own."

"How instructive Michael. Your knack for the 'true-sight' piques my interest. Please, continue." Warlack mocked.

"Let me ask you a question that you seem to be so obsessed with…What do *you* want Raven Warlack?" Michael spoke with a great power in his voice, it was a dignified clarity fueled by a confidence he had never felt in the face of such great opposition. He could no longer feel the slippery, wormlike fingers of Warlack's mind probing at his thoughts. It was apparent he had struck a cord and broken the hold that Warlack was trying to form upon his mind.

For Warlack, he had never faced any man or woman with the will and heart that Michael Cross possessed. It made his mind slip, made his cold heart tremor and pulse a fearful excitement like one would have on their first time in the arms of a woman or the rush of adrenaline as they run into their first battle. This feeling was totally new for Raven Warlack, who had taken everything he had ever wanted with such effortless ease that he continued to seek and consume greater and greater things looking for that challenge which brought him his sick joy. This was that task, Michael Cross was that challenge.

"You ask what I want…I want you to join me. I want the power of the Cross within you at my command. I want the sword ye yield and the potential it holds within its ancient steel to open the way to my new world. I wish to see ya as my equal, my friend, and to take whatever things we desire as we bask in the glory of our victories, our laughter echoing throughout the worlds as the most powerful beings in existence! No lies my friend! No deceit, for I can see that such cannot touch yer perception.

You are different from the others Michael; you are the last of the Cross. Can you not see that I am the only true way?! I offer you everything…can you not see that my influence is everywhere? I have already won, and I am asking you to join me, to pledge your right hand and the great sword of legend to my cause! Will you not join me, Michael?" Warlack's voice held a genuine cord. His eyes pleaded with Michael's in a way that any lesser of a man would have sold his soul in the same breath as the question was asked, but Michael Cross was no ordinary man.

"I see that much of what you say is true Warlack, and I am grateful to be given such an offer. It would seem that such a choice would be obvious, all or nothing, who would choose nothing? I know that your influence, your control, your manipulation spans across all of Selador, and that you may very well indeed have already won. There is nowhere left to run, nowhere left to keep the sword safe from your hands. If this is true, then who is left to oppose your power? Who could possibly hope to stop you, to even find you and get close enough to stop you? You've done well at covering your tracks Warlack, and in my heart I believe I may be the only one who truly knows that you are behind it all. For me, a man who has reclaimed the little honor this world has to offer him, a man who has faced trials and fought so hard for what he has thought was right, I cannot possibly tarnish my name in such a manner by accepting your offer. I choose my honor over my life, but if I am to die and the sword be taken then I will at least end your influence on this world, Raven Warlack." Michaels hand went to the hilt of the Great Sword of Lindell with the thought that this would indeed be the final time he would ever fight again in his life, and that it would indeed be a decision worthy of reclaiming every last bit of honor he had ever lost.

As Michael's hand neared the hilt of the Great Sword, Warlack's kind expression turned to malice. His eyes grew dark and his long face tightened as his eccentric smile all but disappeared.

"I see that you have made your decision, and are set in your choice. A pity, but perhaps I'll have luck in another world. Nieon Sulton, if you would please."

Michael drew the sword as Raven spoke, but he could see no reaction on Warlack's part to draw his own sword or even step out of danger's way. Under any other circumstances Michael wouldn't strike an unarmed opponent, but figuring he had one shot at the infamous Raven Warlack, he cast his rules of engagement aside and swung the heavy blade with all of his might.

He watched as Raven's dark eyes followed the movement of the sword, he could see Nieon remove a single hand from his ornate spear and snap his fingers in the air. In the same moment, the sword passed within a hair's breadth of Raven's neck and would have easily decapitated him. Instead, Michael watched as his cruel lips formed a sinister smile and he disappeared in a flash of black smoke. The swing went wild nearly throwing Michael off his feet, he caught himself. He could not believe what had happened, or what happened next.

In his right ear he felt his breath and heard him whisper "You should have joined me Michael, now you leave me no choice." He felt Raven grab hold of him from behind, felt his weight shift, and suddenly felt himself being lifted off his feet and thrown into the air. He caught a single glimpse of Warlack before he hit the stone tiled floor; he felt his left arm getting caught beneath him, dislocating his shoulder. Warlack stood, smiling like a mad man, his blonde hair flying out from beneath his large brimmed hat, casting shadows across his dark blue eyes as his black coat flared about him like great black sails.

Hot pain ripped through Michael as he tried to force himself to his feet. As he gained his bearings and his vision cleared he was startled to find himself staring at six pairs of sandaled feet. Just above these feet were the white flowing robes of the guards he had seen before, as well as the same yellow wraps of the turbans and belts, but these six wore black masks with black tops upon their turbans. The masks reminded Michael of Gell and the shimmering, expressionless masks they had worn, but these masks each had a different pattern of white, yellow, and blue dots. These six stood in the same fashion as the others Michael had seen, their hands tucked neatly into their sleeves as though they prayed, they were evenly spaced around him with statuesque stillness. Despite the apparent danger, Michael rose to his feet and tried desperately to reset his shoulder into its socket.

"One more chance Michael, reconsider, or at least give up the sword, and we'll let ya be on yer way. Ya don't have to die here." Michael heard Raven grant his twisted mercy one last time.

"You can all go to hell!"

"So be it, goodbye, Michael Cross." The silent, still guards at last came to life, and with such speed Michael would never have expected, and never would have been able to counter had it not been for the sword he refused to yield. Its power pulsed through his body with a resolve unlike any other. It was his honor, his courage, and his purity of heart which awoke the sword in this moment. It was in this very same moment as the masked guards of Laotia removed their knives and rushed towards him, that the power of the sword took him.

Time itself seemed to slow as the six guards bore down upon him

---

like wolves upon their prey. The sunlight from the balcony gleamed brilliantly from the blade of the Great Sword as it moved with an unnatural speed, reflecting the many blades wishing to claim its master. In one swing, it clove through two of the attacking guards, their bodies hitting the floor in pieces. In the next, it took the hands of the man behind him, the knives still tightly caught in his grasp despite being separated from his body. Another guard leapt high into the air like a diving hawk coming down on Michael from above as the remaining two came at him from either side, but in a matter of seconds, they too fell to the swiftness of his sword, and joined their companions upon the blood stained floor at Michael's feet. Such carnage, such fierceness, all one-handed no less, was already over just as it had begun.

As it is told by philosophers and warriors alike, one can wait a lifetime for such battles and have them passed to memory in the blink of an eye. Yet even still, some battles can seem as though they themselves last another lifetime all in their own...it seemed for Michael that the battles in his life would never end.

Michael stood amidst this circle of death, his body stained in the blood of his enemies, his sword pulsing in his hand as he fixes his shoulder at last. He hung his head, the wind from the desert beyond the balcony catching his form in long, steady breaths, blowing his clothing and hair in an ominous fashion. Before him, Nieon Sulton and Raven Warlack remained. A sense of fury crept upon the High Lord Nieon Sulton's face, as a twisted grin formed upon Warlack's. He could see Nieon's expression as he began to ready the spear at his side, but as he did, Warlack caught his hand and held him fast.

Warlack removed his large black hat, tucked it under his arm and began to clap, a very slow and obnoxiously loud applause. "Very good Michael, quite a show. I was wondering if ya had actually succeeded in awakening any of the power within ya or the sword, but I see ye have done quite well." Raven cut his applause and took the hat from under his arm. He shoved the hat into the un-expecting hands of Nieon, who seemed distant. His emotions were suppressed by some greater purpose or power. "If ye would be so kind my good man, keep my hat for the moment and fetch me some of that smoke and wine yer people so often enjoy with such praise. I believe I'll need a spell of the simpler relaxations once I'm finished with our guest." He spoke with a heavy and slightly jovial voice, and without a word, Nieon carefully took the hat and left the chamber, his gaze meeting Michael's only once, and with the coldest absence of emotion imaginable. A chill ran down Michael's spine.

Raven stood beneath the archway leading to the balcony overlooking the lost desert. His blonde hair now flew wildly in the wind and his blue eyes gleamed in the sunlight. If not for the darkness of the aura surrounding him, Michael would have assumed he was an angelic creature, but he knew that the man's physical appearance was only a perk to his ability to manipulate and confuse.

"Come Michael, I have something I wish to show ya."

Despite his lack of trust, Michael followed the black cloaked man out to the balcony before him, his grip never loosening upon his sword.

When Michael stepped out onto the balcony, he was surprised to see just how large it was and the view it possessed just over its carved kiyoke railings. The balcony itself was over sixty feet wide and stretched at least forty feet from the archway he had passed through. The sun beamed down from above, and he could feel the dryness in the air blowing in from the desert.

The desert itself stretched farther than the eye could see. It appeared to be an infinite distance covered only by white sand and dunes which rolled and changed shape with the constantly blowing winds. Michael could see nothing upon the horizon, no end to the lost plains. He had never seen such desolation, nor absence of life. There was no mistaking the desert before him. It was the place he had seen in his dreams, the place he had heard his guiding voice so many times along his journey.

"It's magnificent, is it not? Such untamable vastness - lifeless, and yet so raw with the power of that which used to be. So many have risked their lives to venture amidst those white dunes, but none have ever returned. Makes ya wonder doesn't it? Did they not return simply because they died, or were killed, or did they find something far greater than anyone could've imagined, and just decided to stay and leave all this behind? I've always thought that as an alternative to my ambitions. I, too, would venture into that desert seeking atonement for what I've done, and perhaps put to rest the evil hunger within my heart, but I'm afraid its hold upon me is too strong. Darkness is my nature, my calling, and I cannot deny who I am."

"I don't understand…why are you telling me this?"

"Yer time in this world is short Michael, yer end is a mere stroke of my sword away, and considering my position, I don't get the luxury of speaking plainly with anyone. Consider it my last confession before I strike the final blow to you and to this world. You are witness that somewhere inside me I do indeed have a human heart, despite the material it may consist of."

"Ice, steel…or stone?" Michael muttered.

"Something like that; I only wish that things could have been different Michael. Perhaps in another lifetime they will be, or perchance they will be much worse. Regardless, I thank you for your patience; I truly have enjoyed our mild conversation on this beautiful day." As Raven spoke, Michael took the opportunity to calm his thoughts and prepare himself, reaching deep within his core, for the strength and power to be able to deal the damage necessary.

"I'm afraid our time has run out…are you ready Michael Cross?"

Michael could feel the fear of his impending doom begin to well up inside of him, and he knew that killing this man was the only option he had, and that he was the only one who would ever have the opportunity to end Raven Warlack's life. Hopefully, before his own concluded. Michael cried out with his mind to the sword he held and to the power of the Cross within him, he cried out to his God, he cried out for aid and succor.

Raven's bright blue eyes seemed distant, clouded by some thought which quelled within his being. Empathy seemed to have taken him, the look of one who deals in death mercilessly drawn upon his face. Michael could feel the sudden shift in power as Raven Warlack drew upon his own inner essence.

"Are ya ready Michael?"

"Aye, let us end this…"

"I'll try and make it quick…a mercy I've seldom granted."

"Whatever makes you feel right about it...?" The two men's shadows were cast long and dark against the stone tiles of the balcony, their opponent's stances and intentions unknown. Warlack held his hand at the hilt of his sheathed blade, the legendary Katana of Gell.

Michael stood with both hands upon the hilt of the Great Sword, the extraordinary energy of its ancient steel pulsing through his hands and into his body. He could feel the pull of the two weapons longing to clash, yearning to defeat each other, to draw blood, to destroy. Despite Raven's obvious advantage of skill, strength, and power, Michael could only hope that the Great Sword would help him compensate, and aid him in his time of need.

They stood in perfect stillness, waiting to reach the peak of power they could summon within their forms. The winds seemed to blow harder from the desert beyond. Dark clouds formed above them, a storm of power conjured from the legendary weapons of God.

A light rain began to fall, and the drops cooled his skin. Even as the rain began to increase neither made their move, they cherished the moment as though it were their last. The dark clouds thickened, and in a flash of white-hot light faster than any eye could see, a single bolt of lightning shot down from the heavens and struck the place between the two men.

Michael felt the heat of the blast and was nearly blinded by its sudden brilliance, but he knew this was the moment he had waited for, knew that as the blast returned to the heavens, the onslaught of Raven Warlack would soon ensue upon him. Despite the heat of the flash and the fear welling up inside, he drove himself towards the blast, knowing that Raven was on the other side driving towards him in full swing.

As the lightning ebbed, Michael was indeed met face to face with Raven Warlack, his ominous blade at last pulled from its engraved black sheath. Time again seemed to slow as the two swords cut through the air, breaching the distance between them. A field of energy poured out from the swords, pushing back the rain and charging the air around them with electricity that numbed the wielder's hands and arms.

When the two blades met for the first time, it was as though the universe bent to their initial impact. A shockwave ripped through the air and the floor beneath them cracked and buckled. Michael was so enveloped in battle and the power flowing within him that he simply ignored the pain that tore through his body from the force of the impact against Warlack's sword. They pushed against one another until finally Raven overpowered him, blasting him back fifteen or more feet through the air.

As Michael was hurled through the air he managed to gain his bearings, and at the last moment caught himself just in time to see Raven rushing forward with unnatural speed. Michael had barely enough time to raise his sword and block the attack, but was overpowered once more.

Raven drove him back into the railing and Michael could feel the stone cracking under the strain. He caught a glimpse of the balconies and cliff faces lining the mountain walls the structure had been built into, and quickly judged the distance survivable if he were to fall. White sand was piled high in a massive dune against the rock face at the foot of the mountain and would serve as a cushion if he were to choose escape. The only thing he was not sure of was where he would escape to. *'The desert, an even slower and more agonizing death than the one Warlack promises?'* He surely couldn't hope to make it out of Laotia alive, not with Raven's influence everywhere. His only option at the moment was to fight, and hope by some miracle he could hold off Warlack's attacks long enough to form a plan that Raven would not expect and hopefully decimate him with it. He knew if such were the case he would only get one attempt to pull it off. *'One attempt…one shot…one shot, the gun? The gun from Gell, but…'* The gun was wrapped neatly in a handkerchief in the bottom of his bag, safe and secure, inaccessible for the battle at hand.

As the railing at his back started to crumble beneath him Michael could feel Raven shift his weight and pull Michael back. Before he could completely adjust Raven had pivoted his blade in a manner which Michael couldn't hope to block. He felt the cold steel sear into his flesh, cutting a deep gash in his side and a deep rip in his long black overcoat.

Michael gritted his teeth as hot blood shot from the fresh wound. He swung hard trying to land a blow that would send Raven off his feet regardless if he blocked it, but Raven simply danced aside from harm's way. Again, Michael swung, but Warlack seemed to be too fast. The more he missed, the more frustrated he became, pulling more and more of the power from the sword and into his body pushing himself to his limit. Yet with each incredibly powerful attack, Raven simply moved aside, waited for an opening, and drove his sleek sword to its mark creating more and more small cuts and wounds, weakening Michael bit by bit.

"What happened to ending this quickly?" Michael taunted out of frustration. Warlack chuckled in response, his maniacal smile twisting back into his face. "I changed my mind. I can sense the power yer continuing to draw. I want to see your limit before I destroy ya. Besides, this is more interesting than if I were to just..." As he spoke, Raven Warlack remained in place as Michael took yet another powerful swing. The blade passed within an inch of Warlack and he yet again he vanished from Michael's view. "...kill you in a single blow." Warlack yet again whispered into Michael's ear from behind him. This time, however, instead of hurling him across the room, or across the balcony, he drove his fine edged sword into Michael's body. The blade pierced between bone and between his vitals, shooting out the other side.

"AGGGGGHHHHHH!!!!" Michael's scream echoed with the thunder overhead as blood sprayed from his wound and mouth. Involuntary tears lined his face. The pain was agonizing, but he knew he would not die from such a wound.

Warlack placed his knee in Michael's back, pushing him forward and pulling his sword free. He slashed the sword to his right, the remaining blood splattering on the tile floor, cleaning his blade. "Come now, Michael. I know yer better than this. Ignore the pain, ignore the blocks within your mind, unlock the power within ya, and free the potential of the sword. Use it Michael! Use it to strike against me! Show me ya have some will over yer destiny and fate! Don't just lay there and bleed Michael!" The storm raged with his words each heartbeat driving to a pivotal moment.

As he lay there, bleeding, his hope of even landing a single strike upon the man Raven Warlack dwindled to nothing. He knew he was being played, and knew that Warlack was indeed too powerful.

This was why he toyed with Michael. Played him and tormented him with pain and degradation in hopes that Michael would provide some sick entertainment or unwittingly, unknowingly accomplish some task for him by pouring all of his strength into the sword, prematurely unlocking its true power before he truly comprehended its use. If Michael were to do so, perhaps in his destruction Warlack would indeed absorb that power as he had drained the life from his mother in his birthing, the same way he had consumed the soul of the white-eyed beauty of Eleanor. Such would be worse that just dying. Not only would Warlack have the sword, he would have his soul, honor, and power as well, a fate far worse than a slow and painful death amidst the white sands of the desert beyond.

Michael Cross rose from the crimson pool of blood that had soiled the remainder of his exposed shirt and vest. His tattered black coat blew about him like the rippling silhouette of the fire of the power consuming him. He drew upon his body's strength enough to raise the sword high above his head. Warlack watched in approval as Michael Cross at last unlocked the power within himself in its purest form. The air around him became a torrent of power. Shards of kiyoke stone from the broken railing and floor rose from the ground, levitating in the air with the immense telekinetic force of his power's release. The floor beneath him cracked and buckled, and Michael became outlined in a shimmering skew of fiery rippling air. He could bear to hold back no longer as he screamed from the depths of his soul.

"Now that's more like it!" Warlack said as he too readied himself in stance and stature.

Just as Raven was sure Michael would rush toward him with a hopelessly powerful and misguided attack, the main supports of the balcony snapped. Inch thick cracks shot through the tiles along the floor until the entire platform became a web of breaking cracking stone.

But instead of Michael driving forward with yet another attack, he did the most unexpected thing. He brought the sword down, hard, smashing its power into the spider veined cracks that covered the floor. The force that struck was so great, so sudden that Raven Warlack was thrown off his feet. The cracks became breaks, and the stone floor broke into massive chunks as the platform began to crumble and fall to the desert below.

Warlack managed to catch his footing and at the last moment leapt back through the archway into the grand hall. As Michael fell, tumbling with the shards and chunks of rock and stone, he could see Warlack standing at the edge of the remaining section of balcony, sword in hand, his blonde hair and black cloak blowing in the wind. He could see Nieon Sulton approach him from behind and hand him his hat and wine. Warlack placed the large brimmed hat upon his brow and tipped it courteously to the plummeting Michael Cross as he took the bottle of wine and drank.

5

The hot white sand did indeed cushion Michael's fall, but not nearly to the extent that he had wished it would. As he tumbled end over end down the steep incline of the massive dune the sand scraped away at his flesh as it bruised his body with each impact. The fine grained sand got into his many wounds dealt to him by Warlack, and they burned far worse than when they were first inflicted. He at last slowed his descent and rolled to a sudden stop at the bottom of the dune. He struggled desperately to find his footing in the deep sand and found himself crawling and staggering as he got his bearings and went further into the desert. He could hear Warlack behind him, hundreds of feet up, still on the remnants of the balcony. He was shouting something in an ancient tongue, his hands outstretched to the sky above. Nieon was no longer in sight, but Michael figured he too was still nearby and could feel the great power that Warlack conjured.

Above, where the highest towers of the estate met the sky, the dark clouds summoned by the legendary weapons grew darker and more violent. The wind was picking up at Michael's back and it was cold, unnaturally cold compared to the heat of the desert which still blew fiercely into his face.

The two currents seemed to be colliding, battling for leverage against each other, the dark clouds massing together. Their fury was unnatural, and yet it was the greatest power of nature Selador would ever witness. It was a storm Michael had heard tales of his entire life; a myth, a legend…like the tales of the Cross, and the seven weapons. It was the Dark Wind.

Michael struggled to flee from the brewing storm. He tried to run but found he lacked the strength. In his wake, the desert sand swallowed his footsteps. The only sign of his passing was the steady trickle of blood dripping upon the shifting sand, hissing from the heat with every drop that fell.

The winds raged at his back, and he knew there was no hope of outrunning the storm. He could only hope the storm itself would not only destroy him, but cast the legendary sword into the abyss of the desert buried beneath several thousands of tons of sand. The chances of that, however, still depended on how far he managed to push himself into the lifeless desert. The farther he got, the harder it would be for Raven Warlack to find the sword. It would take years to dig through all the sand.

Michael drove himself harder trying to distance himself as quickly and as far as possible in the little time he had. His pain was unbearable, the sand stuck to his skin and dug into his wounds. His stomach clenched and cramped from the loss of blood, while his muscles burned from fatigue growing worse by the second from the weight of the ancient blade. His head swooned and his eyes felt as though they were being ripped from their sockets by the echoing force from the pounding of the migraine enveloping his mind.

Michael thought it certain that he would die here, with the great Lost Desert stretched out before him. Somewhere in the distance far behind him he heard with the recesses of his mind that still listened, Warlack cry out the last of the words. "Novas eh vertouse da requme aus Naudaous."

The sky rippled with the shockwave of power surging from the eye of the storm above. Hail began to fall, lightning clashed in the sky, and the great Dark Wind was summoned into the world once more. Like the wall of a tidal wave, the fierceness of the sandstorm, and the power of a hurricane, the Dark Wind roared across the menial patch of desert Michael had managed to cover. It lifted the sand from the desert and destroyed all that was in its path.

Michael could hear the rage behind him, a roar like that of a thousand lions. He knew that death was upon him, the great power of the Dark Wind rushing at his back, and that anymore running was useless. He had come far enough. He felt the first rush of the cold wind upon his sand torn face as he turned to see his demise.

The Dark Wind was the most terrifying thing Michael had ever seen. It crossed the desert with such speed, such mass, such violence and a terrible blackness. He shuddered in pain and fear, but he would never cry out. He simply stood in the wake of death, feeling its cool torrent blowing against his form, reenergizing his body and easing his pounding head for a moment. Then he felt its power, it was a mere quarter of a mile away and it moved faster than anything he'd ever seen. The great blast of power he felt surging from it nearly brought him to his knees, but still he stood in its ever closing wake.

Then, as suddenly as the blackness roared upon his unmoving form, another great wind seemed to swell up from nowhere. The space remaining between him and the Dark Wind erupted to a halt against a wall of wind far greater than the force of even the ancient spell Raven had cast. An explosion of great force erupted from the colliding winds, and Michael was blasted back over three or more dunes of sand. His body was hurled through the air like a child's toy across a room. As Michael was falling, he could see the Black Wind battling with the invisible force which held it in place, ending its advance. Then he saw the ever approaching dune of sand that his body hurtled towards. His back hit first and the air was ripped from his lungs. He was slowly consumed by blackness as the cool breeze from the battling storms rolled across the dunes and blew gently upon his sand lacerated face.

Part 12:

Blinded by the Light

I

After her first night alone since meeting the High Lord of Trengar, Kaire awoke to the sounds of horses nearby. From a distance, Kaire counted twenty one men bearing armor of yellow accents proclaiming their allegiance to Zwentor. She wasn't sure if they'd seen the smoke from the fire she had carelessly let burn the night before, or if they had simply come upon her by chance, but she knew it was only a matter of time before they would see her.

As she turned to gather her belongings, she heard one of them cry out, and several of their ranks on horseback rushed forward to overtake her. She frantically grabbed the scythe and ran towards the horse she had tied to a dastardly excuse for a tree out where it could graze. She undid the reins and leapt onto the horse's back in one swift motion, spurring its sides just as she landed in the saddle.

Her mare sprinted forward, surprised and fearful by the sudden presence of its master and the strange horses riding fiercely behind them. Kaire looked back to see the riders advancing, the morning sun gleaming off the polished steel of their armor. She knew it would be only moments before they overtook her, but still she feverously rode as though escaping the confines of a nightmare. There is no escape, she hears the twang of crossbows and feels the rush of air as it skims past her, narrowly missing the back of her head. She hears a rasped voice cry out, "The horse you fool! Shoot the horse!" Before she can turn her horse to avoid their next attack

---

she could hear three simultaneous twangs echo somewhere in her peripheral. Two arrows missed their marks near the sudden cold and fearful eyes of the horse and one struck it in its haunches. The horse stumbles and falls, spilling Kaire across the rock littered, barren earth of the wasteland. The horse rode off whinnying from the pain in its behind.

Small rocks dug and tore at her skin, her belongings flew in all directions, and she yelped in pain as her side caught the jagged edge of a large stone. Yet even though her nerves screamed, she still held the scythe. She rose to her feet as quickly as she could, hoping to have a second or two to gain her bearings and prepare to flee or fight, but they were upon her. Seven soldiers of Zwentor mounted high on their steeds drew short double edged swords with fat faces, an accustomed weapon of their people. They held these to Kaire's throat.

She could hear several more of the ranks riding up on more horses and she feared as a single woman, beautiful and alone here in the wasteland of Gell she would be overtaken as she had been so many times in her life. Taken and used in whatever fashion desired of her captors. Circumstances change, but she knew the yearnings of evil men never would. She could only hope they were here for the aid of the land, on their way to Jerum themselves, upholding the honor of their people, but the feeling in her gut told her to extinguish such childish hopes. These were more likely the very men who had slaughtered the riders of Trengar, and her only hope was to fight.

But as she stood there bringing about the resolve and strength from within herself, she felt a familiar tremor race through her body from the scythe she held. She had felt this only in the presence of the Great Sword of Lindell and Danube's staff. It was the calling of the legendary weapons, and another was close, growing ever closer with each breath she took. She held the gaze of the soldiers, hoping in the recesses of her mind that the strange feeling she felt racing up her arm was a sign of her salvation, her lover perhaps.

She heard the mass of horses stop and several of the riders dismount. She felt the blades of the swords being withdrawn from the back of her neck, and the riders themselves retreating enough to make an opening in the circle of death she had been ensnared in. She turned slowly to see who approached her; a larger man of average height took the lead of two others. His hair was long, as was his full beard, both were a jet black customary of those from Zwentor. Unlike the others of the group, he wore very minimal armor - nowhere bearing the colors of his people or any symbols or medal signifying his rank. Instead, he wore a heavy vest of a grey and black fur tied by a black leather belt at his waist. He wore tanned leather pants and heavy boots which bore a furred brim at their top. His wrists held the only armor he wore, heavy steel bracers lined with a fine cloth and adorned with many engravings. Upon his back was what appeared to be a large double faced axe with a spike on the end of its four foot handle. At the sight of him and the axe which he bore, Kaire knew that the feeling coming from her scythe was not because of the approach of her lover, but rather because of this man and the weapon he held.

Her feelings of hope were suddenly dashed with his presence. She looked at him with her deeply intense emerald eyes, holding his gaze as he began to speak, her hand tightening upon the ancient wood of the handle of the scythe.

"What a beauty ye turned out to be... 'Tis a shame ye ran lil' woman, for those who run be guilty of something on most accounts. I reckon ye were just afraid of all me men, so many bodies, so lil' time. I kin understand yer nervousness, but I kin assure ya it'll come with time. I wouldn't let a fine piece 'o' meat like yerself go to waster out her' in the middle of nowhere. I kin assure me men of that..." The man held a straight face, blank and void of all emotion. Kaire's eyes flashed in response, a familiar power fueled with the rage she held towards what had been done to her in the duration of her short life. Her essence began to summon forth and awaken the power of the scythe. A black aura began to materialize from her form and surround her body. The green of her pupils seemed to expand until the whites of her eyes vanished.

"Ah, such power! Such immediate anger as yer response, well it looks like we've got ourselves a feisty one boys!" The men around him laughed. "There's no sense in gettin' all worked up lil' woman," he continued. "We haven't even had proper introductions yet, although it would seem our weapons know each other very well if ye ken." The man reached behind his right shoulder and grabbed the axe, pulling it over his shoulder rapidly, pivoting it with the weight of its double sided blade, creating inertia out of the arc he swung. He struck the ground between them, and small crackles of electricity ripped out of the strange metal it had been forged from. The ground buckled with the impact, and the man shouted out over the sound of cracking earth. "I am Hilgon Minge, bearer of the legendary axe of Zwentor. These are those of Zwentor sworn to my allegiance and to the cause set forth by someone we've both become very familiar with, Kaire Ra."

Kaire's face flushed white as Hilgon Minge spoke her name. Yet what brought the most dreadful fear was the mention of a familiar host. Someone she had only seen in her dreams, in her nightmares. Hilgon could see the realization dawning upon her face, and his thin lips formed a smile exposing his jagged, unhealthy teeth. "Yes Kaire, my lil' woman, that's a-righty, our friend in black, but me wonders if ye've even had the pleasure of knowing that of his calling?"

Kaire held his gaze stayed silent. "Yes well, I reckon ye wouldn't know, not now anyways. 'Tis Raven Warlack. That be his callin', and my, aren't ye his prize indeed! Took extra care ta make sure ye got to Jerum intact and untouched, but I don't see why we need ye at all. In fact, I can't think of any better idea than enjoying ye as a little bonus to all that we'll gain from our arrangements with *him*. What be *he* to ye anyways, I wonder? Yer lover, yer master, yer savior,…eh, no matter, yer nothin' but replaceable meat lil' woman, and my are we gonna' have our fill. Then I'm gonna' kill ya, leave ya for the birds and take that scythe of yers ta Jerum meself and get twice the money. Do ye ken?" Hilgon leaned in close to hear the response of the fiery beauty before him, this 'lil' woman trapped with only one option she could hope to take. Only one chance, by using the two things she had ever been good at - seduction and killing every bastard who had ever touched her in some sickly sinful way.

She looked at Hilgon Minge with her deep green eyes, and quelled the black aura which surrounded her body. She forced herself to do what she had to do, just to give her the edge she would need. "Why Hilgon, why would you threaten me so? Don't you know you can't rape the willing?" she asked with a devilishly seductive smile. It was a look that would bring any man to his knees, but Hilgon simply gazed at her with part lust, part total and utter confusion.

"How about a kiss…" she said, as she slowly brought her hands to her lips. Hilgon's confusion turned to an uncontrollable hard on and a flush of the blood in his face, but before her fingers could touch the sweetness of her lips, to everyone's sheer horror, the darkness of her aura erupted forth once more. This time, though, the black rippling air consumed the area as her body moved in a blinding blur. Her scythe cut down the seven riders initially surrounding her. Seven bodies, their heads severed in a single momentous sweep of the legendary scythe which reaped the souls of the wicked, the Great Scythe of Vengeance.

"Ye rotten bitch!" Hilgon yelled as the headless bodies fell from their horses and clamored on the ground noisily. In the span of a heartbeat, another swift blur of black, she rushed past the falling bodies at an incredible speed. The two soldiers at either side of Hilgon Minge fell to the ground, kicking up small clouds of dust. She had killed them faster than was visible to the human eye. Hilgon blinked in this split second, and felt an unfamiliar pressure at his back. Hilgon Minge stood back to back with Kaire Ra and was both enraged and ready to turn and strike, but still relaxed with the cold dignity of fearlessness that such power brings.

"Impressive, but yer naïve beyond comprehension, and because ye have just pissed me off!" Hilgon turned, whirling about with alarming speed, striking fast and hard with his heavy axe.

"I didn't like you before!" Kaire gracefully spun, catching the head of the axe with the blade of her scythe, bringing them close in a death locked hold. "I've killed your men, a fair price for the insults you've bestowed upon me in the short time we've been acquainted, and now I teach you a lesson in manners towards a lady." Kaire's irises expanded to the fullness of her round eye, once again consuming the whites with green. They flashed momentarily with a great power before growing dark with the dilation of her pupils until her eyes grew completely cold and black.

———

Hilgon at first seemed terrified by her gaze, but then laughed it off. "Yer pretty strong, I'll give you that, but ye shouldn't boast so quickly." As he said this, a great power lunged forth from his axe and blasted Kaire backwards, her feet sliding in the dirt, stirring up dust as she struggled to keep her footing. She stopped and stood poised, indignant on the battle she had been entangled in. She gazed at the man with hatred and began to unleash the power of the scythe.

Hilgon again laughed at her black eyed gaze and unleashed his own power. The sky overhead, already dark, grew even darker. Thunder raged within its black clouds and lightning began to strike down against the barren landscape of Gell. The storm had begun.

2

The electricity of the storm reached its peak, so thick, so powerful, the remaining horses and men fled from the immediate scene. Only Hilgon Minge and Kaire Ra remain. They stand a distance apart, weapons held at the ready and all the power they can conjure raging within their forms.

When lightning cracked overhead, they both dash forward with blinding speed; weapons held high, swung with precision, the warriors make their move. The weapons clashed and were applauded by the sound of thunder across the landscape.

Hilgon seemed to match Kaire in strength, but his blows came with a speed that she struggled to fend off. The blade of his axe seemed to dance with an enchantment, flashing one way and the other, misguiding and directing, blocking and seeming to disappear at times. He showered blows upon her with haste, never once stopping to make a comment or grant mercy or jest. He simply fought through clenched teeth with a seriousness and resolve about battle Kaire had never seen before nor expected from the character of his previous boasts.

She struggled to evade his attacks using the length of her scythe, an advantage that allowed for some range helping to keep him at bay for the moment. He pushed harder, striking with increasing vigor, solely bent on sinking a blow into the sleek form of Kaire Ra.

As he struck again in haste and deliverance, Kaire hit in return with blinding speed, causing his attack to go high. The hook of the scythe caught the underside of Hilgon's axe as Kaire pivoted her weight and stepped into Hilgon's momentum and swung down with all her might, trying to grapple him to the ground.

To her dismay, he releases the axe and with great force it is flung to the ground in front of them. Hilgon quickly squared his body and reached to grab her. The failed maneuver left her pitted against Hilgon's raw strength and she could already feel the pressure building in her arms as he pulled the hooked scythe up with one arm against her two.

Hilgon laughed deep and loud as he grabbed a handful of her hair with his other hand. He jerked her head back, which forced her to look at him from behind; he leaned over her, meeting her gaze. His hand released her hair and gripped her neck just beneath her chin. He smiled, exposing two rows of yellowed teeth and leaned forward, a strong smell of rot coming from his open mouth, and licked Kaire's cheek with a decayed and fleshy tongue.

Kaire refused to let go of the scythe, but she could not bear to be in his grasp any longer. As quickly as she could she released her right hand from the hilt of the scythe, pivoted on her heels, and slammed her elbow into Hilgon's stomach as hard as she could. She heard the crack of ribs and the gasp of air leaving his lungs, but just as she had released her hand on the hilt of the scythe it had slipped through her remaining left hand, and was pulled from her grasp by the immense force of his grip.

The scythe was flung into the air, spinning deadly and swiftly until it found its mark in the ground some twenty feet away.

Kaire ducked swiftly around the bellowing form of Hilgon Minge. She sprinted to the scythe, sliding to a stop the last five feet, kicking up even more dust. Her hand found the old wooden handle of the scythe and she pulled it free.

As she turned to meet her enemy she was met with the sudden presence of liquid pain swimming through her whole body like a burst of fire. She was brought to her knees with the sheer agony of it, and all she could see was a blue fire dancing before her eyes. Just when she thought she could bear no more the pain receded, and she could see again.

Hilgon Minge stood dignified against the stormy background. His eyes flashed with the lightning of the storm, one arm clutched his side, and the other held the axe pointed at Kaire like an accusing finger. The faintest trickle of lightning, like a spark of static flickered along the blade of the axe.

In a booming voice Hilgon cried out to her, "You have cost me far too much on this day Kaire Ra and you will pay for your insolence. It's time I had you fixed!" as he said this, the small static sparks along the blade of his axe grew larger, erratic, and finally began to torrent with bolts of lightning. He held the axe to the sky as the heavens boomed. A bolt of lightning reached down from above striking his axe, and he became consumed in its power. Kaire tightened her grip upon her scythe in defiance of the man before her, her black hair blew wildly around her kneeling silhouette as her blackened eyes transformed back into the fiery green of her lover's fancy. These soft emerald eyes held dread as they took in the last images they ever would.

3

Danube Drakendor closed in upon the eye of the storm raging across the desolate plains of Gell. He can see Kaire, scythe held high in defiance of the awesome power the strange man unleashes with his axe. The rain and hail beats against him as he charges towards the scene, desperately trying to force the last bit of speed from the horse he has ridden all through the night, he sees Kaire lock weapons with the man. He sees her try to grapple him to try and throw him. He sees the attempt fail and the disgracefulness of the man she fights.

He tightens the grip upon his staff as he watches Hilgon lick his lover's face. He spurs the horse forward knowing the poor creature has long since crossed the threshold of its physical limits. Blood falls in thick clots from the nose of the handsome beast as it shudders and gasps from the strain and the cold of the storm, but Danube pushes on.

He watches as Kaire escapes his hold and moves to reclaim her scythe. In horror, he sees the man conjure the power of the heavens and strike her with lightning from his weapon.

He can see her kneeling before him, her hand still upon the scythe, and he watches with gut wrenching agony as the man conjures the power of the heavens unto his axe once more and fires blue lightning into Kaire. She has no time to do anything except cry out in pain as the fiery bolts of electricity rip into her beautiful green eyes, into their sockets, burning them out forever. The lightning ravages her body, but she doesn't drop the scythe, just endures the pain.

Danube closes in on them and summons all of his power into the staff, firing forth at the man. The blast strikes him full on, halting the tormenting of his beloved. The man is blasted across the ground, his body scraping over the rocky terrain.

As the last remnants of electricity flicker amidst her flesh, she at last releases her grip upon the scythe. It falls to the ground at her side, dispelling its own remnants of blue electricity that still linger. Kaire holds her head back as though she were looking to the heavens above, but she sees no more. Her eyes are nothing more than steaming, charred and blackened holes. Her mouth gapes open, but she cannot find the strength to scream. She remains this way as Danube leaps forward and glides to the ground with the winds of his chakra just as his mighty steed dies out from under him, giving its last breath to deliver the lovers together. He mutters a prayer of Sage to the fallen beast, thanking it for its sacrifice. Danube took Kaire in his arms just as she grew limp and fell unconscious.

The man she had battled got to his feet and dusted himself off. Danube set Kaire gently on the ground, and rose to his feet as well.

"Nice shot! Who the hell are you!" the man yelled.

"I am your Angel of Death!" Danube yelled in response.

"My name is Hilgon Minge, but I believe my axe shall decide whose fate falls on this day." Hilgon said as he leveled his axe and began to conjure his lightning once more. Danube dashed towards him, staff readied at his side. The clouds above stirred and circled them as the power gathered once more.

Lightning shot down from above and once again entered Hilgon's

---

blade. He fired the blast of blue lightning at Danube, but just as he did Danube leapt swiftly into the air, unnaturally high by the power of his staff.

He raised high over the attack and blotted out the single beam of sunlight shining through the eye of the storm. His body eclipsed this light, casting a dark shadow over Hilgon Minge. Danube cried out with all his heart and all his power. With an upward turn of his axe, Hilgon channeled the electricity to intercept Danube's descent, but just as Danube came within range of the blue lightning he unleashed his power, blasting through and continuing his plunge. It was not the power of Danube's staff, but from himself, his heart and soul, driving his own inner God-given power into the physical world. Danube came crashing down with the legendary Staff of Trengar. Such power rose from Danube that Hilgon would've sworn he had met a god on that day.

Hilgon Minge lay in a shallow crater littered with stones and dislodged earth, bloody and beaten, broken and bruised. The axe lay just out of his reach, dark and sapped of power. Hilgon Minge was never meant to wield such a weapon. He was nothing more than a selfish man driven by the pursuit of power and wealth. A dishonorable wretch unworthy to even be in the presence of the legendary weapons, and yet despite his crushed and damaged frame, Hilgon Minge somehow managed to climb his way to his knees and found himself at the feet of Danube Drakendor.

"What was your purpose here Hilgon Minge, and how did you obtain this weapon? I see very clearly you are not one of the chosen of Zwentor and this weapon does not belong to you." Danube held the axe of Zwentor by its hilt in his left hand, his staff in his right.

"I recruited enough men to take the axe by force... I was promised many things if I could pull it off…"

"Promised by whom?" Danube demanded.

"…you mean to tell me *she* never told you?"

Hilgon asked incredulously, gesturing towards the unconscious Kaire Ra. Danube kicked him hard in the face and Hilgon spit blood and a tooth, but remained at his knees. He wiped the blood from his mouth and spit a few times before clearing his throat and voicing his response.

"..The dark man, the master of Gell, and the Legendary Katana, he will soon be the new ruler of this land, and there's nothing you can do to stop him!"

"His name?!" Danube said holding the point of his staff at his face.

"…Raven Warlack…" He finally answered.

"What does he want with the legendary weapons?"

Hilgon laughed "Ultimate power? Immortality? How the hell should I know? I only know what I get out of the deal!"

"How is she involved in this exactly?" Danube asked as he gestured towards Kaire.

"Her? She's just his favorite puppet. Believe me, oh so mighty High Lord of Trengar, she's his number one play thing and you're all playing right into his hands." Hilgon mocked.

"At least I'm still playing…" Danube said.

"Yer nothing more than a pawn…"

Danube ignored him. "Was the attack on Trengar's city, Singe, collaborated by this…Raven Warlack?"

"Undoubtedly it was, but as far as I know, everything of any significance in the last several decades could have been his doing."

"I saw soldiers of Zwentor there and killed many of them. Your men bear the same markings and garb as they. I think you're withholding something." Danube again kicked him, this time in the stomach.

Hilgon nearly lost the contents of his last meal but found the nerve to hold his kneeling composure, one arm clutching his stomach, the other braced to the ground, holding his weight as he leaned forward.

"Alright, alright, yes, he was behind the attack on Singe, and those were indeed my men, a third of them to be exact. And it was *he* that instructed me to do such. *He* said that Trengar would be the last remaining challenge that would stand in our way."

"Why?!" Danube demanded

"I…I'm not sure. Something about a prophecy, something about the coming of a new king, and the Sage being the last hope this land would have. Honest 'tis all I know!" Hilgon, by now, was broken to the point of pleading for his life, and he did so as humiliatingly as a man could possibly imagine.

If it had been any other man, perhaps he would have acted differently, but after seeing the burning and assault upon his home and the pain inflicted upon the woman he loved, he would not find it in his heart to forgive the man who knelt before him. Instead of forgiveness he gave him lent, and gave the people he loved most the justice they deserved.

"Is that really all you know Hilgon Minge?" Danube asked one last time.

"Yes it is, for the most part, everything else is just frivolous events and meetings that led up to these moments."

"Aye, so they must be. Do you repent of the things you have done Hilgon Minge?"

"I've lived my life as I've willed it, and I reckon I don't regret

———

anything I've done."

"You are so certain?" Danube asked finally. Hilgon simply nodded with a devilish smirk.

"So be it…" Danube pointed the tip of his staff into the center of Hilgon Minge's forehead. "As High Lord of Trengar, I hereby execute you Hilgon Minge, in the name of the Sage, of Selador, and of the King…" Danube shouted as he thrust the Legendary Axe in the air. The sky overhead brewed and rumbled. "What do you see Hilgon Minge?" Danube whispered to the man as lightning shot down from the sky and entered the axe. The electricity channeled through him, and Danube's own power shot out as a pure white beam of light from the tip of his staff. So bright, pure, and defined, was the beam that pierced through Hilgon Minge's skull and ended the darkness festering there. Just as the beam of light had appeared it was gone, and Hilgon still kneeled and stared before him as though lost in deep thought. He muttered his final words…

"…I see…I see…nothing…"

His words trailed off and his body fell forward, a steaming hole now made up most of what was left of the back of his head. Danube turned and made a superstitious gesture, something old and lost from his childhood about making a cross of his head, heart, and each shoulder. Something about it warding off the evil of the curse of the Cross, and the misfortunes of their dead.

Danube leaves the body to rot in the wasteland so that it can be picked at by vermin and creatures of disgust. Then he turns to his lover and sees her wounded body lying upon the ground. He takes her in his arms, cradling her limp, burned form. He bandages her eyes and the burns upon her hands and feet where the electricity had exited her body.

4

Once Kaire has been cared, for Danube fetches the cart of goods drawn by the strongest team of horses he can find. He empties it of everything except the supplies they need, and makes a place with blankets for Kaire to comfortably lie down in the cart.

He sets her into the bedding as gently as he can. He can hear her murmuring something in her unconscious state but only two words are clear... "Raven...Warlack..." and she would return to her senseless ramblings.

Danube secures the gear and climbs to the seat at the front of the cart and cracks the reins of the horses. Their little coach lurches forward and begins to roll. The team is a good one, and they work together, moving faster and faster until they've reached a steady pace. Danube lets his mind wander with all the possibilities of the things at hand as the sun begins to set over the horizon and the skies seem to be growing clearer.

Kaire's condition worsened through the night. She burned with fever and screamed relentlessly into the crisp, quiet night air of the desolate Gell. Her screams echoed for miles as nightmares and days passed.

5

Danube and Kaire stand at the edge of the White River looking out over the beautiful kingdom of Jerum. She has recovered much of herself over the past days, and has found her bearings in the new darkness of her

———

world.

"I wish you could see it Kaire, it is amazing."

"I just wish I could see your face..." She whispered.

Danube felt a twinge of pain at the obvious realization that she would never again see his face, let alone anything else, and he had yet again unwillingly made a point of that fact once more. He pulled her close to him and held her tight.

"Do you want to continue on into the kingdom, or do you wish to go in the morning?" he asks her gently.

"No, I want to stay out here with you, just this last night together under the open sky." She found the open sky a luxury in comparison to the infinite nights of her life spent in the cold dark of her cell during her life as a slave of Reum.

"Alright Kaire... we'll go on the morrow."

They kissed and spent this last evening together underneath the open sky between the desolate plains of Gell and the beautiful kingdom of Jerum.

6

The following morning, Danube and Kaire crossed the White River over a handsome bridge of white stone entering into a lush green forest. This lasted for a time, the great spires of the castle city of the kingdom of Jerum growing ever closer to them. The morning sun shined with a brilliant glow from the white towers and walls. Following the main road, they came to a series of magnificent gardens leading all the way to the castle walls and the main gate administering entrance to the great kingdom.

The massive seventy foot opening was protected by a series of watchtowers and a fully garbed garrison of knights patrolling the nearby area. Kaire and Danube entered into the kingdom of Jerum through these massive gates and were immediately intercepted by four guards. They were knights of the kingdom and were adorned in full plate mail, bearing long swords and shields with the crest of the king. Once their business was stated, and the weapons of legend recognized, Danube and Kaire are taken immediately to the kingdom's main estate. It is here, once their presence is known, that they are granted a private meeting with the king himself.

They are brought to a set of twin white oak doors forged from the same section of tree from the forests of Trengar many millennia ago. Danube marveled at the sight of them, but the other twins were what really grabbed his attention. The two guards that stood on either side of the door reached well over six feet tall. They were more statues than men, with their mismatching black and white armor and helmets glowed ominously in the torchlight of the corridor. One wore armor of black and a cloak of white, the facemask of his helm had no obvious openings for the eyes or mouth, just a perfectly reflecting curve of mirror black steel. The other guard was adorned with the mirror opposite of this one, and as they approached the white masked guard nodded. He raised one armor-plated fist and knocked three times on the heavy oak. The sound resounded down the corridor with a hollow echo. In a moment that stretched relentlessly, the doors were opened from within by two more guards much different.

Danube marvels at the sight before them, but takes one last, foreboding look to the mirror guards of black and white who have silently returned to their unmoving state. They are led into a room that was vast in comparison with the confines of the halls and chambers they had passed on their way in. The ceilings were massive domes covered with murals. The decor was not the first thing to catch Danube's attention, but rather *who* sat in the room.

Before them, across a long, decorative table accompanied by fine and leather chairs sat two men, one at the head, and the other to his right side. The King was at the head of the table, three guards stood behind him. The one directly behind him stood in front of a stained glass window casting a mosaic hue, bringing ease and enlightenment to the mood presented. On either side of the guard were two others standing in front of the window, though these were smaller and made of glass which was as clear as crystal. Three guards, three windows, two men studying the love and history of the land amidst the most complete collection of ancient books in all the regions. This room was the king's study, Danube finally guessed, at last as he allowed his eyes to trail from the immediate sight of the king and scan the entirety of the room which lay before them.

He couldn't count the number of books filling the shelves that lined the rooms, seperated only by a sconce set in the dividers of the book cases from one ending and another beginning. Beneath the sconces were tables of solid glass, and upon these tables were ornamental pots containing unique ferns and flowers Danube had seen before, because they simply did not exist anywhere in Selador. One of these flowers was the color of blood and opened with a pattern so intricate and beautiful Danube could not even guess as to how many petals created the design. Beneath this flower was a gold plaque bearing a single word, 'Rose.'

The mural above became clear to him as they were led even further into the room. It was a massed piece of seven paintings, forming a collaborated depiction of the forging and presenting of the seven weapons. In the center of these seven paintings which enriched the ceiling of the room was a stranger depiction. A white tower was in the center of the picture, behind it the sun, behind it…a door, and to the left a black bird, a raven, clutching a golden key within its talons, flying towards the tower. To the tower's right, was the key hole of the door that became part of a complex symbol Danube had never seen before. Surrounding these pictures and the tower, sun, and door, was a series of numeric code written in a language Danube had also never seen. Bordering this code and the entire painting was the picture of a snake eating its own tail. The snake had thirteen stripes, and instead of the eye being painted, it was encrusted with a dark red ruby which flickered with the sunlight.

The king was a fair looking man; his face was clean shaven and chiseled with the features of his father, the previous king. The late King's death was sudden and tragic throughout the land, but sadly Danube had no news of it until the King had long since been buried. At the time, he had been deep in the Forests of Trengar hunting a terrible creature that had been terrorizing the villages and caravans. Deep in the Sage with his greatest warriors he had hunted it for weeks, until they at last had cornered it in a hollow near the southern coast. There, as night fell they faced the creature, but it was a massacre. Only Danube and one other man, a man named Albright, made it out alive. Once they had healed their wounds it was they who sought the beast alone and standing back to back amidst torchlight of an ancient ruin they managed to slay the monster of the shadows. How he wished Albright was here with him now, '…you always knew just what to do…' he thought to himself.

The King looked at Danube with clear green eyes which seemed innocent and childlike. Though similar in color to his darling's eyes, they did not hold anything familiar in the way he looked at him. He realized in this moment that he never would see a pair of eyes with the same fierceness and power which has entranced him in what seemed to be so long ago and yet only a short time passed.

The king adjusted the magnificent jewel encrusted crown upon his golden hair as he stood to greet his new guests. To his right, the man in black remained seated. His large black hat pulled low, casting a dark shadow across his face. He seemed intent on some manuscript lying before him, with a cluster of many other tombs and parchments he studied with great interest. Even as they entered the room, never once did this man look up.

As the king came around the side of the table, his purple and white cloak flowed around his body with a delicacy and fluidity that made him seem majestic. Danube took Kaire's hand in his and whispered in her ear, "You must bow my love, for we are before his majesty." Kaire nodded and together they took a knee, heads bent low with ceremonial honor.

"High Lord Danube Drakendor of Trengar, I am pleased to welcome you to my kingdom. You knew my father well and he always spoke very highly of you. It has been a long while since you have graced us with your presence. I am, as you know, King Ryon Jerum III, the sixth generation of my blood to hold sovereign power over the land. I do not hold my title loosely, and therefore want you to understand that our private meeting here today is not taken without the constant disapproval from my advisors to handle so many face-to-face meetings where I choose to handle matters personally. What I want you to understand, Danube Drakendor, is that I offer you a chance this very meeting. Because I wish to honor you for your great efforts to thwart the attempts of our enemies to capture the legendary weapons and bring destruction to our Kingdom, and because you have single handedly safely delivered three of the seven weapons. I wish to honor you, Danube Drakendor, last of the Drakendor, because you may very well be the last of the true blooded heroes of all the land, the perfect knight." The king gestured for Danube to stand, and he did. There was a long silence before Danube spoke, "It wasn't all single handedly, your highness, Kaire Ra, she... but how do you know of what I've done?"

"All in due time, my friend, but first I have something very dire, very critical, very... important that we must attend to, but I must ask you something first and foremost. Do you trust the kingdom of Jerum and do you solemnly swear to uphold the will of the land and the decree set forth upon mankind to safeguard the legendary weapons for the eternity of your life?"

"Aye, your majesty, to all, 'tis aye."

"Then I must ask of you, guardian of Selador...one last thing, to ensure the safeguard of the weapons and to control the chaos which spreads through our home."

"What do you have in mind? A vault or weaponry can be stormed and taken, but in the hands of its master, its power can be used in the defense of the land."

"Very true, my brave High Lord, but there happens to be something already discovered as a solution to a permanent safeguard for the weapons, an emergency failsafe so to speak, constructed at a predated time right in the middle of the kingdom just going unnoticed over time because of lost information on many of the structures built by the ancients which have gone forever overlooked... but, who am I to talk? I mean, why describe it to you when I can just show you?"

"What exactly is it...and where?

"Well, it is a tower, and it just so happens to be in the courtyard of the thirteen towers, ironic isn't it?" The king seemed surprisingly excited by talking about the discovery of the supposed ultimate safeguard built by the ancients as a last resort defense for the legendary weapons. Danube began to feel uneasy as the king gestured his guards to follow them out of the room.

Danube led Kaire by her arm, the king leading Danube one step ahead, alarmingly close for royalty. Danube turned to peer back into the room and saw that the man in the black hat still sat reading his scrolls, seemingly unaware of Danube's gaze until he suddenly looked up slightly, pushed the brim of his hat up with a single index finger, exposing a pair of eyes burning with fiery blue flames where his pupils should have been. The 'mirrorguards' casually entered the room after them, closing the great twin oak doors behind them. Danube felt a chill run through his body as he was swept from this view by the steady pace they had begun with the king and his honor guards.

The king was rattling on about the new discoveries they had made in unlocking ancient codex and technologies long forgotten. Kaire squeezed Danube's hand, and he leaned in close to hear what she had to say. She spoke in a whisper, "Danube...do you love me?"

"Yes Kaire... I love you."

"Then will you trust me when the time comes?"

"Aye, but I don't understand, the time for what?"

"When I ask it, you will know, you just have to trust...me..."
Her voice seemed mechanical and her hand felt cold and clammy, she

trailed off with her last words and grew weak suddenly, almost collapsing as she walked, but Danube steadied her quickly.

"Kaire! Kaire are you alright?"

She seemed disoriented and confused, but managed to gain her bearings enough to stand. The king had stopped talking and had turned around to see.

"Is your woman going to be alright, shall I send her to the sickened ward? We have excellent care."

"No! I want to see the tower! I want to know the Scythe, Staff, and Axe are safe and taken from us to burden!" she seemed to suddenly burst with anger.

"Kaire you cannot see any…" Danube began.

"Shut up! I know that! I still want to be in its presence," Kaire raged, seeming like a totally different person.

"Aye, then to the tower we wish to go," Danube said.

"To the tower then…" the king spoke with little humor towards Kaire's sudden outburst, but instead looked upon her with a disdain.

As they walked, Danube was forced to interject the king's ramblings and told of the attack on Singe and the events that had taken place. He even told him of Raven Warlack and what the man Hilgon Minge had told him. The King listened, but with an amusement to his gaze that seemed to glimmer the impression that he already knew the things of which Danube spoke. Nevertheless, Danube did his duty of informing the king with his own words and accounts as they walked steadily onward through the castle.

The white tower stood seven stories above the cobblestone courtyard to the tip of its single spire which gleamed with the glow of the afternoon sun. The tower was a perfectly constructed assembly of seven pillars, six surrounding the seventh and largest. This massive pillar rose up in the center and provided access to the core of the tower where the seven pillars met.

At the base of each of the six pillars was an alter depicting a symbol of one of the seven weapons. Each alter had its own design of statue, carved to hold one of the weapons. Danube looked to it with awe, a sense of beginning, a sense of end, this was one of the few true testaments to the power the ancients had possessed. The tower was the epiphany of symmetrical perfection, and Danube marveled at its serene glow.

"This, my friends is the white tower of the seven, the last and greatest defense of the land."

"Impressive your majesty, but what exactly does it do?"

"It is a massive magick transformer so to speak. It hones the energy of the collective power within the legendary weapons and the very magical essence of Selador. It channels that energy into the alters and holds the weapons there, inaccessible until all of the seven are in place, or released by the Legendary Bow of Jerum, which I possess and safeguard to the honor and decrees in substance with the greater good of the land. By doing what I ask of you Danube, you will be made the greatest hero known in the land of Selador, and honored throughout the kingdom."

"Aye, your majesty, I will do as you decree…"

"Good, then I decree thee High Lord Danube Drakendor of Trengar, approach the white tower of the seven. Find the alter with the sequel of the staff you now hold, and place your staff upon it, surrendering it to the almighty will of God." The king pointed an outstretched arm, covered in tattoos and jewelry to the white tower looming ahead.

Without a word, Danube looked to the king, the tower, then back to the king again. The monarch nodded as if saying 'Yes, go on.' Danube bowed, turned and walked towards the tower.

As he approached he noticed many more details that the tower possessed, but one in particular stood out from the rest. The doors upon the seventh pillar, the largest and center pillar of the structure. Danube knew that the doorway no doubt led to a stairwell leading up to the core of the tower, and to whatever secrets lay within the massive ancient magical structure. He stood before the first of the pillars; it bore the sequel of the Great Sword of Lindell, and for a moment Danube hesitated in his resolve to follow the king's command. Considering in that moment the probability that Michael Cross would still have the legendary great Sword, despite the fact that he surrendered the Staff for the good of the land. Leaving him virtually defenseless to the power of the legendary weapon were Michael Cross to turn to oppose him.

Danube held fast at the pillar of the Great Sword. He looked across to the next pillar adjacent from where he stood, the pillar of the staff, some thirty feet away. The alter of the Great Sword and the alter of the Staff stood as the entrance to the main pillar, a stone path led to its doors. Danube moved toward the alter of the Staff and found walking to be rather difficult. His mind willed, but his body held his gaze for some strange reason drawing to Kaire and the king standing with his barrage of guards overlooking every move he made. Danube felt a tense feeling of doubt bleed into his mind from some thought in his deepest subconscious.

He removed the sling bag he carried across his back and undid the drawstring . From inside the bag, he pulled out the axe of Zwentor and gazed upon its strange blue Damascus steel. Instead of walking towards the pillar of the staff, he changed directions and walking underneath the tower, toward what he guessed the alter of the Axe of Zwentor.

When he rounded the side of the pillar to face the Sigel, he was not surprised to see that it was indeed the alter of the Axe. He studied the structure for a moment, and then placed the Axe, hilt first, into the hole scribed into the alter face. A loud clicking commenced and the Axe turned as though it were a key locking, or unlocking, a door. A flurry of blue lightning trailed from the Axe and into the alter.

When the lightning subsided, Danube reached out to try and remove the Axe and found that it would not budge no matter how much force he applied.

"Test it if you'd like, Danube Drakendor... I assure you even with the power of another legendary weapon you cannot remove it from the tower." The king shouted across the low cut field of grass which separated them.

Danube held his Staff high, collecting the power within it. He fired a concentrated blast of energy into the Axe and then the alter, but neither would allow the weapon to be pulled from the grasp of the tower.

The king approached Danube from behind. He did not hear the silent click of his golden bow as its carved crystal arrow pivoted into position by a mechanism in the center of the bow. He knocked the silver string over the arrow. Danube turned as he felt the sudden gathering of energy into the weapon the king held. Danube's skin ran to gooseflesh, and the hair on his arms and the back of his neck stood up. "Observe Danube

Drakendor!" the king shouted, which seemed to come from within the arrow itself. Suddenly a blast of light shot from the bow and appeared to take the shape of an arrow made of pure light and power.

The arrow shot past Danube's face and struck the sigil upon the alter. The Axe of Zwentor turned back into place and released from the alter. Danube reached down and pulled the Axe free effortlessly from the slot.

"You see, Danube, I can allow the weapons' removal at any time, and I assure you…if it comes down to a battle, we will no doubt use the weapons in our defense. If that time comes, I swear to you Danube. I will return to you your staff," the king said, with a sincerity Danube could not ignore.

With a silent gesture, he returned the Axe to the alter and watched as it turned and clicked back into place. Danube walked underneath the tower again, back to where the pillar of the staff was erected.

He stood before the alter, admiring the ancient symbol upon its face. He took one last glance to Kaire and the king. He ran his fingertips over the runes of the ancient wood of his Staff, and then lifted it high into the air one last time, and drove it hard into the slot upon the alter's face. Clicking noises and the sounds of gears drove from within the alter as the Staff turned and locked in place.

Danube extended a slow and sympathetic hand to the old wood. It was the last thing he had that reminded him of home. Now it too was gone from him, just out of reach, given away for its protection and greater good. His fingertips once again traced the runes carved along the Staff, and he remembered the journey he had taken to bring it safely to this moment in time.

Despite this loss, he felt a feeling of success for having accomplished this great task for the land of Selador. He thought perhaps that the king was right. That he was indeed a hero, a guardian of Selador.

He saw the king approaching from the shade beneath the tower. He looked up with a smile, a sense of pride surging through him. The king was smiling as well, but as he approached the smile drifted to a menacing grin. The bow was still in his hand, the arrow still nocked in place.

Before Danube could say a word the king leveled the Legendary Bow, and fired an arrow of pure energy directly at him. He rolled to the side using the alter and pillar for cover. He swiftly gathered himself and moved to dash around the side of the pillar, when suddenly one of the three royal guards appeared from around the other side of the pillar, and slammed a gauntleted arm into his face, breaking his nose and spraying blood into the air. He staggered back, blinded in pain.

Danube quickly wiped the blood and tears from his eyes just soon enough to see the fiery energy bolt of another arrow strike him in the chest. He felt the air rip from his lungs and his muscles spasm into a strange and vacant numbness that made him crash to the ground.

He struggled to move as he lay in the lush green grass in the field at the foot of the White Tower that loomed overhead. No matter how hard he tried he could not move an inch, he was completely paralyzed by the power of the legendary weapon. He watched as the clouds in the clear blue sky drifted across the sun overcasting its brilliance. He wondered if perhaps this was what dying felt like.

His thoughts of death were pushed from his mind as the king of Jerum appeared before him, eclipsing his vision of the sky overhead. The gallantly garbed king loomed over him, his bow secured and slung across his body once more.

———

"Do not worry Danube. You are not dead, nor are you going to die...just yet. The arrow I have shot you with has locked you in a state of paralysis that will remain as long as I will it." The king spoke with a chime of his own success and power.

"Why are you doing this?! Where is Kaire? What have you done with her?!!" Danube yelled with increasing frustration as he struggled against the king's powerful hold on him.
"Kaire!!! Kaire are you alright?! Kaire, you have to stop them!!!!" Danube continued to shout.

"She cannot help ya Danube, she never could, she never did..." A voice Danube did not recognize began to speak.

"Guards, get this man to his feet," the king ordered. Two guards, including the one who had broken his nose moments ago, approached the prone and defenseless Danube. Together, they hauled him up so that he was half-standing and fully able to see the face of the man that spoke.

Before him, the man in the black hat stood holding the hand of the blind and emotionless Kaire Ra, her face was vacant and cold, almost bereft of life.

"What have you done to her?!!!" Danube screamed.

"I'm sorry...I don't believe I've introduced myself. My name is Raven Warlack, we've never officially had our meetin' High Lord of Trengar, but I have heard much of you, and I must say thank ya for playing your part as nicely as ya have."

"You...Bastard!!! You're the one who's been causing all of this!!!?"

"Yeah, well don't give me all the credit. You definitely did your share of the work - I mean, come on. Thanks to you, I don't have to deal with Hilgon Minge and his outrageous demands. You helped me wipe out

---

344

an immense portion of the armies of the regions and have safely delivered me my lovely toy…Oh, and yeah, you've successfully played three of the legendary weapons into my hands…"

"You mean into *my* hands?" The king interjected suddenly.

"Yes my lordship, into your holy and powerful hands…" Raven replied with words that could only contain a layer of deceit. "…That reminds me…" Raven said as he turned to Kaire, "…you can give that to me now my love. I'll hold it for now," he said as he gestured to the Scythe. She quickly untied the leather strap holding it in place across her back, and handed it to Raven Warlack's outstretched hands, completing the ultimate betrayal.

"Marvelous, marvelous work…I really do appreciate everything you've done, but now I'm afraid your use is just about spent. I do however, believe you deserve an explanation in accordance with the woman you have come to wholeheartedly love… you see Danube, Kaire was at first seduced and tempted by my powers to the point where manipulation alone helped me gain the majority of control over her life and very will. I was hope, her only hope.'

"The only problem was that she still had this ability to feel her emotions, such as love…which is where you come in…I never intended for her to face Hilgon Minge alone. That was…unfortunate, and undoubtedly your own doing. It all relies on choice. Even still, when she was struck with the pure power of the Axe's lightning from the storm the clashing weapons created, it left a permanent scar on her mind.'

"You see, the Axe of Zwentor, and in theory all of the seven weapons, possess a special ability. In the instance of the Axe of Zwentor…we have the ability to control the thoughts of the mind to an extreme degree, and push a person far beyond their human limits. This ability, a secret to nearly all, was used to control the miners and workers of Zwentor in the ancient times, and even recently in terms of the followers of Hilgon Minge. The rulers forced their people by abusing this power to carve a city from stone using its citizens as slaves, driving thousands of people to work themselves to death."

"When Kaire was stricken by the power of the Axe, it forever made her susceptible to the powers of manipulation and control over the mind. This was ultimately a consequence of your choice, because of the decision to save your home you have sacrificed the only person that really mattered to you. This is why she cannot help you, Danube Drakendor. You have failed, and lost everything. Boohoo, shame on you…" Raven chuckled as he finished. Danube looked at him with the utmost hatred.

"King Jerum can't you see that he is a fiend!? He's manipulating everyone around him, including you! He's using all of us for some darkness he wishes to unleash upon the land, I know it! You have to stop him!" Danube pleaded with the king.

"Silence, Drakendor! You are hereby charged with treason and the attempted conspiracy against the kingdom of Jerum and of the land of Selador. You are sentenced to death without trial, execution by my own hand upon the morrow." The king spoke without conviction, unsure of his current position.

"Well we have to protect our phony baloney jobs, gentlemen…" Raven muttered to himself with a smile.

"What was that?" the king asked.

"Nothing your majesty, just reveling in the cleverness of using Mr. Drakendor as a scapegoat for our more shady endeavors, and how it will reinforce our position of security in the eyes of the people…"

"Hmph…once we have all the weapons the opinion of the people will no longer matter, and I will have the means to do what my father never could. With the ultimate power of the weapons together I will be able to unite our kingdom and cleanse it of the unworthy, diseased, and rotten filth of the people that have gone unchecked for far too long," the King proudly stated to his tiny audience.

Danube was broken in this moment, as his paralyzed mass was dragged away by the king's royal guards. He watched with a broken spirit, and broken mind, yet it was as Raven Warlack took the hands of Kaire Ra's in his, and kissed her passionately that his heart was broken.

Part 13:

The Desert

I

Michael returns to consciousness in a haze of blinding light resonating within his vision with a cascade of halos reaching towards the hot desert sun overhead. The Dark Wind still battles furiously against the invisible force keeping it at bay, suppressing its power from reaching any further into the desert.

After a moment Michael forces himself to sit up as he winces in pain from his slowly clotting wounds and his bruised back and shoulders. He struggles against the soreness to remove his coat and shirt. The shirt is tattered and torn beyond repair, and his wounds still bleed. He tears his shirt into strips and cleans the gritty sand from his cuts as best as he can. With the cleanest strips of cloth he can find, he bandages the still bleeding hole in his chest and the many small cuts upon his body. When he is finished he sees that he has one strip of the white shirt remaining. It is nearly clean of any blood, spare for a few specks here and there. He holds it before him and judges its length as he remembered from a dream some time ago. He can see that the length of the shirt is that of the blindfold he had used in his vision of the desert when he was still in Lindell. He carefully folds the cloth, taking care to keep it from getting any more debris on it. He places it in his inner vest pocket, which he pulls on once more over naked bandaged skin.

He climbed to his feet and shook his coat violently in the air. When he was satisfied with the amount of sand he shook loose, he quickly pulled it over one arm and then the other, wincing but ignoring the painful protest of his battered muscles.

Michael retrieved his sword that was now protruding from the side of the dune next to where he had lain. He strapped the sword over his back once again, because despite the pain it felt right. It was a good feeling, and it brought with it thoughts of relief for once rather than the sensation of being a burden.

Michael adjusted the woven cord securing the sheath in place and began looking for his bag, his belongings, and more importantly his waterskin, but to his dismay he could find no trace of his effects. Panic threatened to overwhelm him as he frantically dug through the many dunes of sand to find them, but Michael knew they were lost. Taken by the desert and swallowed up by its sands. He knew thirst would be the death of him before he ever found the hide covered liquid life that was so dear to his existence. In mental anguish, he looked out over the desert to the climactic force of the Dark Wind.

He knew that only one choice lay before him, that there was no turning back. Michael Cross could only go forward, farther into the unknown of the burning, blinding white desert sands stretching beyond as a monolith of infinity. Michael began to walk towards the horizon that stretched on to the point of nonexistence. He strode with a new resolve to push the sword as far from the hands of Raven Warlack as he possibly can.

He remembered what Warlack had said, about wishing that he could choose the desert over the path he has chosen in his life, and how he wished he could venture into the desert to try and find atonement for his sins. *Raven's going to have to make his trek sooner than he expected if he wants the sword, and if this is the end I was meant to meet, then I'm going to make sure*

———

he has to cover a lot of ground first. Michael thought to himself as he climbed another dune.

The winds of the desert began to blow harder and kicked up massed torrents of sand. Michael squinted his eyes as a whirlwind smashed against him; the sandstorm had begun.

Michael reached inside his vest and pulled out the folded strip of cloth and quickly wrapped it over his eyes and around his head. He tied it in the back, blindfolding himself.

He let his other senses guide him as he continued his trek up and down the many dunes. This blind trek went on for what felt like several hours, but it very well could have been days. Michael found himself lost in time and lost in mind, no consciousness of where he was going or where he was, but all in all he knew…just which way to go.

2

The texture beneath his feet changes and he knows that he has descended from the last dune and out of the reach of the storm.

He no longer feels the grainy blast of sand, but the dry heat of a waterless wasteland baking in the heat of the sun. Michael removes his blindfold.

Before him lies a sea of impossibly arid earth, cracked and lifeless, sucked dry of any moisture within. The heat beaming down upon this barren land rises and casts reflections upon the horizon like ghosts. It was a sea of fire, and Michael's mouth ran dry at the sight of it, but still he presses on. He continues his long walk for what feels like days, and yet the sun never seems to move from overhead, as though night would never fall.

Michael has grown weary, his organs and muscles now screaming for water and rest. His body was overheating, and his head was a living kiln, cooking his brain. His vision became a colorless haze of spots and light. He falls to his knees, and he hangs his head in weary defeat. Michael knelt alone amidst this desert sea, surrounded by its merciless expanse, consumed by his hopelessness.

His head hung impossibly low, his hands cupped over his face and head as if trying to hold all of the pieces together, he knelt in silence. Somewhere in the back of his mind he heard a familiar voice, *IT IS HOPE NOT DESPAIR, WHICH MAKES SUCCESSFUL CONCLUSIONS MICHAEL CROSS. PUSH ON A LITTLE FARTHER, LOOK THROUGH THE HAZE OF YOUR BLINDNESS, AND SEE, SEE JUST HOW FAR YOU HAVE COME...* Michael found his way to his feet and caught his bearings for a moment, hoping it would allow his vision to clear.

When the obstructions faded to a thick hazy cascade of the endless desert before him, something grabbed his attention in the distance. He struggled to find a pace towards it, in time breeching the distance.

As he came upon the forlorn object jutting from the dry desert floor, it begins to come into focus. He struggles to make out what it is, until it finally clears to him as the rays of sunlight reflect off its surface. It was a sword, driven blade first into the ground, lengthy strip of faded blue cloth is tied to its pommel. The meager excuse for a flag was all but tatters, ripping wildly with the wind. When Michael came upon it, he could see the sword was far from splendid, and was in fact tainted and rusted beyond repair. It appeared as though it were ancient and sand pitted pockmarks were littered deep along its face and hilt. Michael looked at the sword with a lost sincerity. He could find no meaning in its semblance, but knew somehow that it was a marker of something, or someone.

Michael felt frustrated and confused. *So this is how far I've come? To the rusty old sword in the middle of the desert? Yeah, that really gives me a great feeling of accomplishment…thanks,* Michael thought bitterly to himself.

As if in response, *COME MICHAEL…ONLY A LITTLE FURTHER…I HAVE SOMETHING FOR YOU…* Michael gripped the sides of his head at the sound of the voice within his mind. The voice he at least believed was in his mind, but could have just as easily have come from within the howling wind of the desert itself. Michael was driven, and so continued on.

The flat, cracked ancient seabed became dry hills. The dry hills of packed sand became dry hills of loose sand. Along the way Michael passed by several swords stuck blade first into the desert, a strip of cloth tied to the pommel like the first, but of a different color or sign. Each time he passed them by, guided by the voice until the desert once again flowed and rolled as infinite dunes. Many flaunted a sword as a marker upon their peaks.

He found his way over the many dunes, not stopping until he ascended the top of one of the enormous monstrosities of sand. At its peak, Michael could see out over the desert beyond, which once again transformed to the dried cracked earth. From that eternally parched and compressed sand stood thousands of weapons, all planted blade first into the sand bearing the 'flags' of many colors long since faded by the desert sun.

They looked like graves, markers of some long ago battle, but he could see they had all come from different eras by the designs. He stood in awe at the sight, letting his eyes wash over the scene, finding himself completely mesmerized by the sheer numbers until his eyes passed over one sword in particular. A white strip whipped in the air from its tightly knotted place upon its pommel. Wrapped over the hilt was his hide waterskin, held in place by a fine leather cord that was now familiar to him. He could see that it had been freshly filled and had swollen with the mass amount of liquid within. The sun glistened off its wet hide as excess droplets fell, sizzling to the desert floor, affirming the fact that it had indeed just been filled.

Michael didn't hesitate to question it. He rushed for the sword holding his measly chance for life. He carefully removed the water bag from its hilt, and removing the stop, lifted the bag and drank in several slow gulps. His cracked lips smacked with the fresh moisture as he cherished every drop. He drank a little more, replenishing his body and quenching his thirst. He returned the stop and slung the bag over his shoulder where it belonged.

"Thank you…" He muttered aloud, awkwardly, his voice sounding strange and out of place in the desolate desert. He had begun to wonder if he had truly lost his mind.

'YOU'RE WELCOME MICHAEL…' The voice was loud in his thoughts, and actually seemed, in a way, to come from behind him. Though *'behind him'* in his head was an impossibility, Michael turned around looking back up the dune he had just descended from a moment before only to find sand and sky.

Perplexed, Michael returned his gaze to the many markers of those voyagers of long ago, only to find the silhouette of a man upon the horizon. It was a man in white, a figure that walked slowly away towards the horizon. He walked steadily and silently amidst the swords, never once disturbing the path of the many strips of cloth tearing through the wind, and together they made a sound like the wings of a thousand angels.

The man shouted back at Michael, "You're almost there Michael, you

———

354

just have to keep going a bit further. You can follow me if you like…"

Michael couldn't help but wonder if he had indeed lost his mind and if the figure shouting to him from afar wasn't just an illusion of the desert, created by his mind and the mirages of the heat. *The water is real, very real, cool, refreshing, good. It must have been placed there by someone, why not this man, this seeming specter of my mind?* Michael wondered as he followed the man who may very well have been an apparition.

Michael tried to hasten his pace, but found that no matter how fast he walked, he made no ground on the man who was eternally beyond him. The man spoke, and though he was far ahead, he did not shout, and yet Michael heard every word with a clarity that resonated as if the man were standing at his side.

"You are Lord Michael Cross, are you not? Last of the Cross, wielder of the Great Sword of Lindell, disgraced by Raymark?" The last, burned with a fresh tear to an old wound.

Michael, after a moment, spoke in a distant tone, reflecting on old clippings of memory within his mind. "Aye…I am the one you speak of…"

"Why have you come to my desert Michael?"

"I had no choice, I…your desert? Just…who are you?"

"Why isn't it obvious Michael…I am death…." Horror ripped through Michael's face as the man said this, but then he quickly continued, "…Kidding Michael, only kidding…I am the Guardian of the Lost Plain, the desert of immortality, of lost souls, of…the end of the world. Please, make yourself at home. I have, but I've only had an eternity to devote myself to that purpose." Michael looked confused as the man spoke. Somehow the man registered his body language and spoke in a more serious tone. "As far as *who* I am…my real name you could not pronounce, but I have been called by many names and taken many forms. You may call me as you like, but many prefer Alan, Henry, and Cash…I was summoned to this world by the true God who created it, summoned many times to do his bidding amongst the worlds. This world Michael, this place we call Selador, was the last of his creations before the great silence. That is, of course, including the seven weapons this world was initially created to protect."

Ironically a great silence fell before Michael spoke, "What was the great silence?"

"What *is* Michael…the great silence is the time when God finally terminated his communion with his creatures of the worlds. He gave his last commands to his people, to me, and to many others of his many worlds, and has never spoken directly to anyone since…it is sad really, the lot in life we shall have to face, to never speak to our creator until perhaps the true death comes to take us."

"I know that the people of Selador were commanded to safeguard the weapons and hold peace amongst the regions, but what is *your* purpose, what was the last command the creator gave to you?" Michael asked aloud to the man in the distance who never turned to see his face.

"To safeguard the desert, and the point where the land turns to nothing, the place at the edge of this desert, and all around Selador for that matter, that becomes the open vacuum of time, space, and the raw matter our universe is compiled of. I was also put here in this desolate place…to wait for you, Michael Cross. To guide you from afar, and help lead you along the path of your destiny."

"You are the voice in my dreams, in my mind…" Michael shivered as he slipped into the tone that a certain woman named Eleanor had once spoken.

———

"Yes Michael, a person's subconscious mind is the easiest to speak through, and I must say…you have a very unique mind." Michael seemed to ignore what the man of many names had said.

"Why is it that I cannot walk at your side so that we may speak plainly, face to face?"

"Is that what you wish Michael?"

"It would ease my troubled mind." Michael replied.

"Very well then," the man upon the horizon said as he disappeared from sight. Michael stopped dead in his tracks, unsure of what had just happened before his eyes. As suddenly as he had vanished, he spoke from Michael's side. He turned to the sudden presence in his peripheral.

Alan stood eye level with Michael, his perfect equivalent in height. His face was that of an aged man, his skin worn to leather by the desert sun, yet bearing the traits of a once fair-skinned youth who had freckles with fine blonde hair once in his past. His hair was long and braided into two lengths on either side of his face and upon his forehead he wore an ancient red bandana, his hair and beard had both long since faded to strands of white and grey. The man's eyes were covered by a strange pair of spectacles. The black lenses formed perfect ovals over his eyes, and reflected Michael's own image back at him as he tried to hold the man's gaze.

The man wore a faded pair of denmen jeans similar to Michael's, and a plain white shirt beneath a long white overcoat stained with the dust and sand of the lost plains. He stood with his thumbs tucked neatly into his pockets, his shoulders slack, with lips slowly sliding into a grin.

"Pretty neat, huh?" The man asked.

"How did you…?"

"Nevermind that Michael, the real question that is at hand…is how far are you willing to go?" Alan interjected. Michael looked at him in puzzlement before he continued. "…to stop Raven Warlack?"

"Stop him? How could I even hope to stand against him? He is far beyond me…I can never hope to face that power again. Besides, what do you know about Rav…?"

"I did not ask you *how*; only how far you are willing to go in order to do so? What sacrifices are you willing to make in order to see in finished?"

"How can I possibly determine that, considering I don't even know what he is really trying to attain?"

"Does it matter Michael? When you get right down to it…to you, personally, does it matter what he's trying to gain? Considering what all he has done to you?"

Michael reflected once again on the spotty memories of Lindell that still rose close to the surface of his mind. "I suppose…that at this point, I would devote my very existence entirely, if it meant ruining his aspirations, and even killing him …as he brought ruin and death into my life so shall I bring it unto his."

"Are those your true feelings Michael Cross, your true devotion, set in mind, set in heart? Do you vow to do everything possible?"

"Aye…it would seem that it is now my lot in life, to repay what has been given."

"Knowing this Michael, I can now tell you just what it is that Raven Warlack seeks…" Alan said as he motioned for Michael to walk with him further into the desert remaining as an abyss of the unknown, still nagging a fear deep in Michael's heart. Yet still he followed, and walked at the side of the man called Alan, but only one man left the mark of his passing in the wake of the sands of time. Only one trail of footprints was pressed neatly into the desert. It was the path *he* took, the man called Michael Cross.

3

As they walked and the old man spoke, Michael drank from the hide bag, satiating his thirst once more.

"This world...the seven legendary weapons and even the people of the land, all serve as a safeguard of the most precious thing in existence...balance. This world is a gateway sealing the paths between the other worlds, allowing no mortal life passage to cross over. Except of course in the rare instances of dreams of those whose minds have found the pathways within their own souls, and who have broken through the blocks of the universe which otherwise keep their perceptive minds from...exploring. Sadly, they may only witness the other worlds, a kind of look but don't touch, because Selador remains to retain the hold upon the physical transversal between those plains...*mmmMhuh* ah can I get a *witness!?*" Alan spoke in his peculiar depths as Michael took another draw of water from the hide.

The water was refreshing, but Michael was far beyond his limits. His body burned with pain, his muscles ached, and his wounds throbbed uncontrollably. He was exhausted, broken, and beaten as he had been so many times throughout his journey. The sun burned down on him, baking his already burned flesh, and though his vision was clearer with his now quenched thirst he still swayed with the hazy vertigo of his stride. Alan's words were difficult to understand, and register completely. He struggled to make sense of what the man was telling him, and forced himself to listen with an intent interest to the reasoning and answers to the things he had been long pondering.

Alan could see the wear in Michael, and the dazed, incoherent stare that seemed to resonate from within.

"You are very tired…and wounded. I know this is difficult my friend, but you need only persist a little longer I promise. We are almost there, but I must insist that you hear what I have to say. Hear it, and listen very well, for what I am to tell you…is going to be…difficult."

"I don't understand. Where are you taking me?"

"Someplace you may rest," Alan said as they approached the foot of an enormous dune, "but there are many things I must tell you before we get there. Will you hear me Michael, and listen truly?"

"Aye, I will listen as best as I can. Though I do not fully understand what you are trying to tell me. I mean, Selador, all of Selador, is just some kind of safeguard, some protection for the *universe*? Like…"

"…a locked door? Yes Michael, but what does every lock have?" Alan probed

"…a key?" Michael asked uncertainly, for the strain of his journey had not yet cleared his mind..

"Yes, every lock has a key, but some doors have more than one lock, more than one key. These doors are of significant importance, practically speaking, if Selador was a door to the rest of the universe, a protection to all that serves balance throughout existence…how many keys do you suppose it would have?" Alan never broke his stride as he spoke, but Michael, perplexed by the question laid before him, halted a moment in his pace. Alan, noticing Michael trailing behind, stopped and turned to face him.

"Give up?" Alan queried.

———

"I have no idea…so, yeah, I yield…" Michael spoke with a bewildered gaze as he struggled to grasp the ideas Alan spoke of.

"…Seven…seven keys to unlock the doorway…I don't suppose you want to take a guess as to what the keys might be?"

"I'd rather not," Michael said as he resumed his pace up the dune, still struggling with exhaustion.

"Awww…come on Michael, don't be a poor sport. I'll even give you a clue…you've had one with you throughout your entire journey," he hinted with a mischievous smile.

Michael's eyes widened as he was bombarded with an alarming reality. "Seven keys…seven weapons…the legendary weapons are the keys to unlocking the doorway! No wonder Warlack wants them."

"BINGO!" Alan shouted.

"Bingo?" The expression was lost to Michael.

"Never mind Bingo Michael, you'll get it one day, but what I was trying to say was you guessed correctly. The seven weapons are indeed the keys to unlocking the gateway…You may very well be the only mortal in the land besides Warlack who knows this, because of this, you are the only one who can stop him, but you must be wary Michael. *He* is no fool, and knows that something lies within this desert, and *he* may also know that you will be coming to face him again…"

Michael and the man called Alan reached the top of the massive dune. In the distance, Michael could see an outcropping of rocks that formed a ridge that rose up from the desert to form a single, immense peak. It stood as a dark monolith upon the horizon of the barren landscape, stretching like a scar upon the bleak and absent land.

"There…" Alan gestured towards the ridge, "…do you see those rocks? We are not far," he said to reassure the downtrodden Michael.

Michael nodded in response with eyes that still held their glassy glare. The hide bag was opened once more and he drank, preparing himself for the trek ahead of him.

Michael and the man continued down the rolling sands of the dune, and into the cracked mosaic of the flat-pressed earth. They journeyed in an absolute silence for a time. While struggling to hold out for the rest of the short distance remaining, his thoughts eagerly toyed with the new knowledge which echoed in his mind. How the seven weapons were quite simply the keys to the balance of the entire universe, and Selador itself was the centripetal glue holding together all that stood as the very fabric of space and time for all realities. Michael wanted to ask Alan many questions, but each time he tried to speak he found himself unable to form the words.

He could only stagger forward through the burning desert, reaching to the rocks in the distance he subconsciously feared was nothing more than a mirage like the 'man' who accompanied him along this trek.

Alan began to speak, but Michael never heard his words. Michael was consumed with the thoughts forming in his mind, rendering him unable to speak. His head was suddenly filled with pain as a splitting anguish ripped through him. His vision instantly wavered as he collapsed to his knees. His hands shot to the bandages of his wounds where fresh blood now freely poured from the once clotted gashes and punctures. Dehydration had done its damage, and his mouth went hot, causing him to taste metal, and the baking of his brain within his skull at last succumbed to stroke from the unbearable heat. He may have surpassed the limits of his body far beyond that of most men, but he would now pay the price.

Memories of his life flashed before his eyes, the good, the bad, and the ugly. His only love and a single clear image was his last as his face hit the dry, compressed sand of the desert floor. Long ago, a day at the beach, when his love was young, her golden hair blowing with the wind as the sun's rays warmed her silky skin. She smiled at him as she drew in the sand with her fingertips.

The wind picked up across the desert, the light dust rolled over the landscape, small clouds kicking up around Michael's nearly unconscious body. Alan kneeled over him, gripping him by his shoulders and shaking him, trying to rouse him from his delirium. "Michael! Wake up Michael!" Alan commanded over the increasing sound of the winds.

Michael's hand struggled to trace something in the sand of the desert floor, but just as the lines were made they vanished with the wind.

"Michael…come here, Michael…" Michael could hear the voice of his lost love. He could see her smile, see her laugh, and could see what she had traced in the sand.

I

$\heartsuit$

U

…Was etched in the sand by the gentle touch of her slender fingers…this was the last of what he saw until all faded into darkness.

He felt himself being lifted, carried to some faraway place, carried to peace that he longed to have. Beckoning, like the peace only death could bring, but something far greater than death itself would not allow him to

---

pass beyond the clearing. Some might have said it was the will of the one true god, but it may have been for a single man, a 'man' called Alan.

4

Echoes drifted softly through his mind as he awoke from what seemed a dream. He found himself lying in what appeared to be a tiled rectangular pool, each corner lit with the serenading light of a candle. *Where am I? How long have I been here?* His body was submerged except for his face. The water was warm and held a strong aroma of herbs and spice. The bottom of the shallow pool was coated in white sand so fine it almost felt like mud. His entire body was relaxed and calm.

He traced his fingers over his previous wounds and found that the skin had healed to the slick scar tissue that would forever be a reminder of his encounter. He lifted himself to a sitting position, the sweet smelling water dripped from his upper body in steady streams. He examined the scars more closely, finding them to be genuinely healed, but still rather tender to the touch. His vision came slowly into focus in the dim candlelight of the room. To his right the sword rested against the tile steps that wrapped around the outside of the tub.

On the steps were several neatly folded towels next to Michael's now clean and mended jeans and undergarments. His boots, vest, and coat were nowhere in sight, but on the floor next to the step were a pair of hide shoes similar to ones he had heard called moccasins. The room was unadorned except for a vast array of candles, mirrors, and a single wooden door at the farthest end of the room. Michael grabbed one of the folded towels and stood up in the tub, his feet sinking into the soft sand. He could feel the muck squishing between his toes as he moved.

He dried himself of the scented water and then sat on the edge of the tiled tub expecting to clean the sand thoroughly from his feet, but to his surprise, when he lifted his foot from the milky surface of the water, none of the sandlike residue remained on his foot or between his outstretched toes. Perplexed, Michael finished drying his toned and muscled shape.

He donned the clean and mended jeans. After examining the hand crafted soft-hide moccasins, Michael placed them on his feet one at a time. They proved rather comfortable, almost as much as the familiar weight of his sword across his back, the braided cord of its strap rubbing gently against his naked skin with a raw sense of security.

Once he was clothed, Michael turned to the door only to second guess himself, and glance back at the candles at each corner of the tub. *Should I blow them out?* he wondered to himself, only to notice in that moment that the flames rising above each candle did not reside upon a wick, but rather they simply hovered gently above the wax. They were in fact faux candles, which must be a form of magick, meant to remain lit. Reassured, Michael went to the door before him and opened it, unsure of who or what to expect on the other side.

5

Before Michael, just outside the magnificently crafted door was a grand staircase made from the most exquisitely carved marble he had ever laid eyes on. The walls, stairs, and ornate railings were all made from the same stone, crafted superbly with perfect symmetry. Michael cautiously descended the stairs, unsure of where he was or what mysteries lay further beyond. *How did I get to this place? Am I still in the desert? Am I...dead?* The questions rolled through his mind.

'YOU ARE NOT DEAD MICHAEL CROSS...' a familiar voice spoke within his mind. '...WELCOME TO MY HOME. PLEASE FEEL FREE TO EXPLORE...'

"Alan, where are you?!" he asked aloud.

'I AM HERE MICHAEL...ALWAYS HERE AND WITH YOU MY FRIEND...TELL ME, ARE YOU HUNGRY? DO YOU THIRST, OR ARE YOU IN NEED OF FURTHER REST?'

Michael pondered this a moment. He knew it had more than likely been days since he had eaten, but he was not certain of the passing of time. He tried to remember when the last time food had touched his lips and concluded it had been just before making port in the bay of Laotia. He had eaten an ample helping of freshly caught fish and several bowlfuls of sweet steaming rice that the crew had prepared. There was no doubt in his mind that he should be hungry, starving in fact, and yet he did not hunger. Everything about him felt content beyond anything he had ever known. He needed nothing.

"No, I feel...fine. I need nothing at the moment." He said at last as he descended the last of the marble steps.

'VERY WELL THEN...STRAIGHT TO THE TRIAL AT HAND...GOOD LUCK MICHAEL...I'M ROOTING FOR YOU...'

"Huh? What do you mean?" Michael questioned, perplexed. He cocked one eyebrow higher than the other; it had become an increasingly normal expression for him.

'EVERYTHING BEGINS SOMEWHERE MICHAEL...DEFEAT THE BEAST OF FEAR, AND YOU'LL HAVE THE STRENGTH TO SLAY THE

"Wait what?! Alan? What the hell is that supposed to mean?!" Michael shouted from the bottom of the staircase, frantically looking around him for the man who had accompanied him through the desert, but Alan wasn't there.

Before him lay a vast encircling hallway of carved pillars and archways encompassing the surrounding mountain walls, he looked just beyond these archways and giant pillars, and gazed into the massive cavern-like chamber beyond. These pieces were engraved in perfect harmony from the very rock of the inside of the mountain, and Michael at last wondered if perhaps he were inside the rock ridge he had seen before his stroke in the desert.

Within this colossal open space were many fountains and pools overflowing with waterfalls and bubbling springs, sculptures of heroes long since gone from the world, and half submerged ruins from the time of the ancients. The fountains were all beautifully carved artistic renderings of history and legend, each one its own impressive work of art. These many breathtaking pools, sculptures, and fountains were easy to catch the eye but not as easy as what lay just beyond, in the middle of the chamber lying motionless in the largest of pools.

In all of its time of existence, the world of Selador had only seldom seen the presence of beast or monster, and the creatures formed of magick from the abyss of pure darkness and light. Yet even these had trailed into accounts of mere legends. Certainly the land had its own share of ordinary life such as bird, bear, hare, and fish, and the many game creatures of the land. The horses had become a permanent partnership to humanity and their need for one another, but never, had the greatest creature of legend walked the land of Selador…except for one.

The beast which lay before him was like that of a large lizard, curled in the center of the pool like a cat dozing on its rug. Lying in the pool, its back arched at a peak of twenty feet, bearing a ridge of spike-like plates running from its head along its spine, all the way down its lengthy tail. The creature's scaly neck supported a huge armored head that was covered in bone plates and horns, and slept with its head partially submerged, leaving its eyes and nostrils above the waterline like a crocodile. The monolithic body of muscle and armor shifted heavily with its steady breathing.

On either side of its body, tucked neatly in, shrouding the true details of the creature were leathery wing-like appendages, tipped at the ends with intimidating talons. The last thing Michael noted was its long serrated tail emphasized by its blade-like tip which reminded him of a certain scythe a woman carried through a field of flowers not so long ago.

At the mere sight of this creature Michael quickly ducked behind one of the large pillars in hopes that he had not disturbed its slumber. A fear unlike any other ripped through Michael. This creature was the ultimate unknown, a beast which was vaguely mentioned even in the legends and lore of the ancients. Its description was thought to be a mere metaphor of man and the beast which he may become, but this, this creature, this rarest and most powerful of all creations lay before Michael in the flesh. It was as the ancients had deemed, and what Michael struggled to recall, the guardian, the greatest creature of the God of gods, the dragon.

Michael held himself fast, his back pressed hard against the pillar. He struggled to regain his steady breathing and free himself from the raw, primal fear that had gripped him from the overbearing power of the dragon beyond. The beast slept soundly, the deep rumble of its belly lurching forth from its nostrils in long shallow breaths, fornicating with the constant sounds of the flowing water within the chamber.

With each heavy breath Michael could feel the power surging from the dragon's heart in waves, thickening the very air of its presence. Thoughts of flight crept blindly to mind. *Escape from trial, escape from fear, escape from the sure possibility of death, but escape to where? The desert beyond these rock walls, back to Laotia? As if I could survive another trek through that hell-like desert…what kind of man would I be then? To always run? What kind of man flees from his destiny? If this is a test, then I shall do my best Alan, but if I have been played a fool, and this dragon is the face of my demise, the face of my true destiny, then I shall play my part to the bitter end…* Michael decided and with that, shook the fear holding him captive. He placed his hand upon the hilt of his legendary sword and thought once again that it would be the last time he would do so. Silently, he removed the blade from its sheath upon his back and moved from his hiding place behind the pillar, ready to face the dragon, to face his destiny.

His resolve was instantly shaken as he rounded the side of the pillar. The fountains still trickling their song, the pools still shimmering with brilliance, but no dragon lay before him. Soft ripples echoed where the beast had lain, but it was apparent their roles had switched. The hunter had become the hunted.

He held his sword at his side, and stepped softly into the chamber along the tiled path residing between the pools. He was ready, alert, and focused. He tried to reach out to the sword in his hands, to call upon its strength as he done so many times before, but the tarnished ancient blade felt cold. He knew the power was closed to him for a reason, and instead forced himself to reach within, to draw from his own power…from the

———

cross.

With each step he took into the chamber he felt a surging force well up within him. He struggled to clear his mind to channel this force throughout him. He scanned the walls and ceilings with his eyes, looking, searching for the beast. He reached the edge of the pool where the dragon had slumbered. Even still, there remained a faint ripple, evidence that something, whether the creature itself was an illusion or not, something had indeed been in the pool now struggling to still its waters.

As Michael stared into the moving water something flashed outside his peripheral vision. In a fraction of a second the hairs on the back of his neck stood and his muscles instinctively tightened his grip upon the hilt of his sword. He turned in a flash, but even still, he was far too late.

A roar like a hurricane accompanies the spiky blur that smashes into the tiles at Michael's feet, narrowly missing him. The tiled walkway explodes in a shower of broken stone as the force of the blow sends Michael blasting backwards and into the clear pool of water. As he fell, several shards slice his chest, arms, and left cheek. Droplets of blood were just beginning to seep from the fresh wounds as his body hits the surface of the pool.

He hit hard, his world became a dull aquatic roar, and the sound of this predestined battle was muffled by the rushing of the water. His fresh cuts stung at first, but were quickly soothed by the cool liquid. He drifted motionlessly to the dark depths… an unfathomable level that was far deeper than he had anticipated. As he sank, the water seemed to be changing around him, growing darker, a greenish hue seeping into the light from the surface above. Michael seemed to be sinking forever, though he knew the pool had been fairly shallow.

———

At last, with a muffled thud, he hit the bottom. The jolt seemed to wake his body from its stupor, and he quickly sheathed his sword and kicked off the bottom of the pool's floor, launching himself towards the surface in a desperate maneuver for oxygen. In scrambling haste, he didn't take note that the pool floor felt more like mud than the tile he had seen from above the pool's watery surface.

Michael was always a good swimmer, but with the heavy weight of the sword, swimming was not the easiest of tasks, and his lungs already burned with a desire for air. He pumped his arms heavily through the murky water, each stroke starving the little oxygen remaining in his straining muscles.

A brilliant light beckoned from above, and with a final thrust of strength, he broke the surface in a flash of reborn resolve. He gasped, breathing in the warm humid air as if it were his first breath. Michael shook the water from his face and blinked away the fog over his eyes as he swam for the edge of the pool. It was too bright, far brighter than the torch and glowmoss lit marble of the cavern pools, this was the light of the sun.

Michael cleared his eyes to find himself no longer in the cavern of pools but rather in the middle of a forest. The sky overhead was a crystal blue, almost cloudless, and a heavy yellow sun hung overhead flashing brilliantly. He tread water against the light current of the stream, making his way to the nearest bank. As he neared its edge the water grew shallower and Michael waded the remainder of the distance in. He climbed onto the gritty bank of sand, mud, and root.

Still catching his breath, Michael sat on the remnants of a fallen tree and poured the water from his moccasins one by one. He suddenly heard the sharp cry of his opponent echo from overhead, resonating amidst the hugetreetops of the alien forest.

He quickly fetched his moccasins with one hand and went for the hilt of his sword with the other. He heard the heavy beating of wings overhead as he took cover behind a cluster of trees. He watched silently as the magnificent creature flew past. Its dark silhouette bathed the earth beneath it in darkness. Its wings were far larger than the sails of any ship Michael had ever seen, and pointed to razor sharpness at each fold.

He remained silent, perfectly still, until the creature passed him by. His keen eyes were tracing the dragon's armored hide for any point of weakness, but he saw none. The winged marvel's flight took him to a great rock face which led up cliffs and shrub covered plateaus some seven hundred feet or more into the sky. Upon the flat top of this little mountain, near its only visible tree, rose a little hill of a single angled rock, it was this rock, this perch, which the dragon chose to roost. The creature flexed its wings in the air, extending to their full wingspan, and nearly blocked out the sun all together. It was this eclipse that bathed the strange forest into darkness.

A cold chill ran up Michael's spine as its eyes gleamed crimson like two torches in the night. The sky grew darker as black clouds rolled forth from the nothingness of the air, and thunder bellowed as they formed. Michael returned the damp moccasins to his feet and slowly moved from his cover. *Can he see me?* was his only concern as he moved quickly into the forest. He moved steadily, squelching the fear he felt to look from his path, and he frantically glanced to the mountain peak through the many trees.

What he saw made his heart leap. The dragon's red eyes gleamed as the beast turned its head in his direction. The clouds overcame the sun and the world was submerged in darkness. Michael returned attention to the pitch black forest in which he ran. He could no longer see it, but he had to make it to the foot of the mountain in the distance without being spotted by the beast again. Doubt crept to the fearful conclusion that it did not matterHe fearfully doubted his actions though, because the dragon already knew exactly where he was. Distress held the thought that those red eyes were upon him now, and as if in affirmation to his paranoia, he felt the sudden draw of air as the heavy beating of wings echoed from above. There was the sound of a hollowed inhale of the beast's lungs peaking with a tone like the whistle of a boiled kettle.

He felt the heat before it came, and sprinted blindly and frantically as the forest around him was bathed in flames. Trees exploded, red hot embers shot in every direction, catching brush and leaves alike. The light of the fire behind him helped light the way, but the heat at his back was unbearable and the smoke stung at his eyes. Over the roar of the flames Michael could hear the wings beating once more as it came around for a second pass. Michael dove over a cluster of stones just as he heard the roar of the stream of fire that shot from the mouth of the beast. The blaze ripped through trees and blasted stone to pieces from sheer temperature. Michael had barely found cover in time and was certain that most of his body hair had been singed off.

He knew he was not far from the rocky cliffs, but he feared as he climbed that he would simply be burned on the rock like an insect, but as if in response to this fear, the dragon returned to its perch upon the mountain. Its eyes gleamed down at him, inviting him, challenging him. Michael rose to his feet, bathed in sweat from the heat of the fires around him. The firelight danced across his skin and tender scars. It had taken an intense journey to forge this spirited champion, still standing as he was, still standing as a mere man, as the last of the Cross.

Michael looked up the rock wall, tracing the cliffs and edges, up and up until he met the gaze of his challenger. "Ready or not...here I come..." he said beneath his breath. Flames trickled from the nostrils of the dragon so high upon his perch, a single plume of smoke rising into the sky as if scoffing at Michael's bravery.

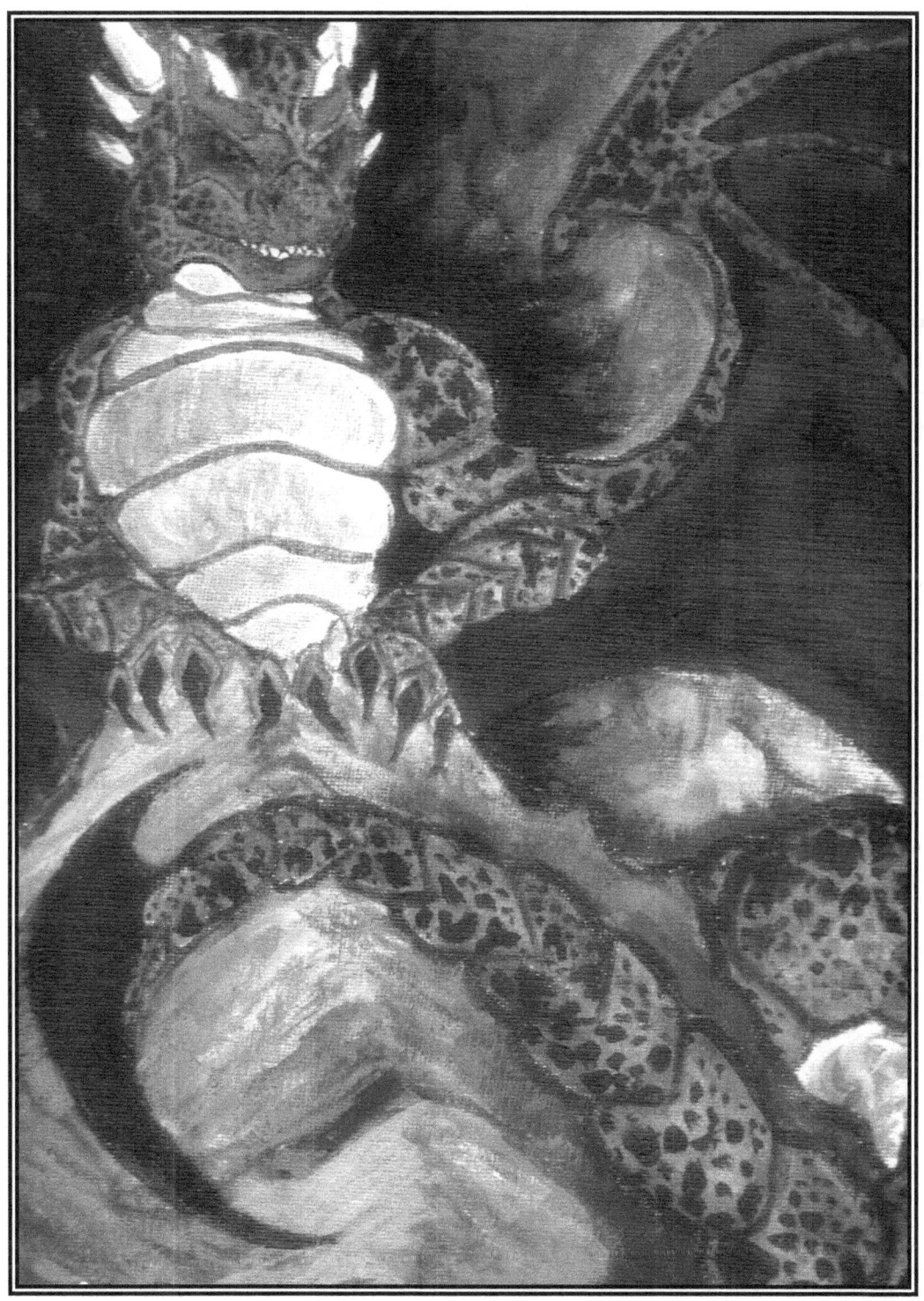

6

Michael's body burned with fatigue as he climbed up the wall of rock. He barely stopped to catch his breath upon the cliffs and ledges he came across, merely stretching his arms and legs and climbing on. Lightning clashed with the world, lighting his next footing or grasp for brief moments at a time.

He continued on until he came to an outcropping of rock jutting forth from the cliff face at an obscene angle. Judging the distance purely by the flashes the lighting revealed, Michael lunged from his hold on the rock, momentarily freefalling, and miraculously reached and grasped the ledge with one outstretched hand. He pulled himself up and onto the ledge and noted that he was now nearly halfway up the mountain.

For a moment he lay there, panting heavily, struggling to catch his breath. The distance remaining was far less than he really wished it to be, for at the top of this wall of rock his adversary stood perched and ready, no doubt picking his teeth awaiting the oncoming meal. Michael rolled onto his stomach so as he could look back down the way he had come, the way back. It would be the first time he had looked down since he had begun his mighty climb.

As he turned, small rocks and pebbles brushed by Michael's hand rolled over the edge, and time seemed to slow to a crawl as he beset the sight before him.

The forest, so far below him now, was burning. The monstrous beast had only made two passes with the molten fire. The image from this was etched into the land itself; a *cross*, burned into the forest below in the same way it had been carved into the face of Lord Raymark.

Michael clambered to his feet, he could smell the disintegrating

---

wood and feel the pain of the life being ripped from the trees, poured out of them like the sap from their bark. Their lives were taken as his had been stolen from him. The memories of that night, the night the *cross* had fueled him for the first time. He could almost hear the cries of ecstasy his wife had moaned beneath the hulk of Raymark's body echoing in the wind with his memories. His blood grew hot like the air rising from the burning depths below, and he found his resolve. Tightening the strap of his sword he turned, and climbed on.

7

Michael peered over the edge of the mountaintop trying not to be seen, but yearning to see the prize of the top, the way a hunter sees its prey. His eyes probed the sight before him, observing all that could be seen in a single glance.

The top of the mountain was like a plateau, perfectly flat, all except peak that served as the dragon's perch, overlooking the throat of the world itself. All is covered in a lush green grass swaying with the wind, distorting the shadows cast by the flashes of lightening, adding an almost lifelike quality to the dark shapes. A single tree sat gnarled and twisted in its middle, grotesquely misshapen by time. Upon its nearly dead branches is a single brightly colored fruit, appearing perfect in skin and color. Michael's eyes glance to where the dragon waits. His first thought is to quickly duck from the creature's sight, but he instead holds the monstrous gaze that has already met with his own.

The creature's wings have folded partway, giving it a shrouded and terrifying quality. Its scales reflect the darkness of the sky with a shimmering black glimmering with the faint hues of bloody red. Lightning flashes across the sky and Michael can see its reflection cast upon the creature's armored flesh. What starts as a deep rumble echoes from the depths of the beast, and slowly forms spoken words.

"COME MORTAL...COME FORTH AND MAKE YOURSELF KNOWN!"

The very mountain seemed to shake from the dragon's words. Michael climbed over the last rocks separating him from the dragon. Now all that stood between them was a misshapen tree and a tiny green hill.

He took in slow controlled breaths. Each step was placed with an uncertain caution upon the soft green grass, but he continued onward. Not a word was spoken until he reached the blackened gnarled tree with its single fruit of perfection dangling just within Michael's grasp from the tree's lowest branch.

"EAT MICHAEL CROSS...FOR IT IS THE FRUIT OF LIFE..."

"Is it poison?" Michael asked the Dragon with confusion. The dragon's reply was a roar of laughter, causing a blast of flame to erupt into the air.

"WHY WOULD I BOTHER WITH SUCH? I SEEK THE CHALLENGE YOU BRING, NOT THE SAVORY TASTE OF POISONED FLESH. THE MEAT OF THIS FRUIT WILL REPLENISH THE STRENGTH OF YOUR BODY AND HELP TO AWAKEN YOU TO THE TRUE POTENTIAL OF YOUR POWER...IF I AM TO BATTLE YOU MORTAL, I WISH TO DO SO WITH YOU AT THE PEAK OF YOUR GOD GIVEN POWER..."

Michael looked into the fiery red eyes of the dragon and knew that

---

there was honor in the creature's words. He pulled the fruit free with a snap of its stem and dusted its perfect skin. After giving it a quick sniff, he sank his teeth into the shapely fruit. Juices exploded on his taste buds at first so bitter that his mouth went numb with the worst cottonmouth he had ever known, but just as quickly the juice turned sweet and savory. He quickly went to work devouring it entirely. He then wiped his lips, and dropped the core of the fruit upon removing the last seed of a dying tree. He savored the remnants of flavor as he placed the seed securely in his pocket.

"EXCELLENT...NOW, ARE YOU READY TO FACE ME MICHAEL CROSS? ARE YOU READY TO FACE THE POWER WHICH IS YOUR DESTINY?"

"Aye, dragon..." Michael bellowed with confidence. He could already feel the effects of the fruit taking over. He was no longer tired, but alert and focused mind and body. He felt the strength wash over him, an aura of numbingly sensational power. He could feel the sword upon his back, could at last feel it calling to him, beckoning to be drawn forth into the world. He slowly reached for the hilt of his sword as he cautiously walked towards the foot of the grassy hill where the dragon perched.

"VERY WELL, MORTAL!" the dragon roared as it unfolded its wings, sending a torrent of air blasting toward the oncoming Michael Cross, who was un-phased by the oncoming wake of the gust. He simply continued forward, never breaking stride, hair blowing wildly as the muscles of his naked chest and arms flexed in the light of the storm as he gripped the hilt of his sword. The dragon's eyes flashed like flames as the mighty blade was drawn. Thunder rolled as the steel of his blade bled forth from the leather sheath upon his back. As the rumbling thunder faded to silence, the last few inches of the blade was drawn with a hiss. The steel harmonized with the resonance of the thunder, together creating the melody of a legendary weapon of the gods.

Michael readied the sword in his hand as the dragon began to beat his wings ferociously. Destructive torrents of wind crashed against the mountaintop as the dragon lifted heavily from the peak with a roaring screech as it took flight. Michael took a step as if preparing to rush the beast, but held fast at the sight of the dragon's lurching belly. Liquid fire erupted from the dragon's maw, firing straight at the place where Michael stood. In a flash of speed he rolled to the side, narrowly missing the inferno of death threatening to sear his flesh black.

Regaining his bearings, Michael stood as the dragon encircled the mountain and prepared to make another pass with its liquid fire. Michael stands at the ready, preparing for the dragon's assault and for his defiant stand against his archenemy. The dragon's eye's meet with his as he flies towards him bearing down upon him as an inferno once again begins to spill from the creature's lips.

The flames shot forth, and Michael once again rolls to the side just in time, but deftly regains his footing and jumps high into the air, pushing against the earth with his power as the monster passes overhead. His blade reflects in the light of yet another flash of lightning as the edge hits its mark. The dragon's majestic leathery wing is sliced deep into its main folds, and the wing splits as the dragon howls in pain. The current of air rushing through the dragon's wing proves its flight is broken, and it tumbles through the air. The beast's falling form just barely misses the scrambling Michael as it smashes into the mountaintop and tumbles over the edge of the cliff, screeching loudly as it goes.

The impact shakes the entire mountain as the shockwave sends fractures through the rock formations as the hill and nearly half the mountaintop cracks and splits away from the base of the mountain. Michael struggles for his footing and runs up what remains of the shallow hill as the world shifts beneath his feet. He reaches the peak as the rock shifts, slides, and begins to fall. He sees the dragon tumbling below, uncontrollably, and he jumps from the edge as the remaining hill crumbles into large chunks of rock and stone.

He free-falls, angling himself so that the wind runs smoothly over him, he begins to pick up speed as he falls, closing the gap between himself and the Dragon. He plummets the remaining distance, his sword held high as he descends upon the beast, striking down upon the monster's armored, spike covered back. The steel rings out against the dragon's hide, doing no damage as Michael slams against it. His body rolls across the creature's neck and just out of reach of its snapping jaws and rows of razor edged teeth. As he tumbles away from his entanglement with the creature, he swings wildly at the dragon's face, in a last, desperate attempt.

The blade hits home, slashing, dragging a gushing wound across the dragon's face just as it prepared to spew forth its fire once more. The creature cries out again in agonizing pain as blood shoots from the slash. Michael slips from the dragon's reach as the creature beats its wings wildly, struggling to regain flight, but Michael knows that he has no such hope. For because he is but a man, and cannot fly, he closes his eyes as he prepares to die.

He had hoped that, in death, he would at least have slain the dragon, but he has simply injured the beast. Half the Cross born upon the monsters face, an eternal reminder of the day he faced the mortal man known only as

Michael Cross. This in itself, Michael supposed, was worthy enough to die in peace, and so he waited. It was not falling that he feared, but the sudden stop at the bottom which scared him.

8

To his surprise, he came to a rather soft landing into a large pile of powdery white snow. His body sank more than thirty feet into the mound, and it took much effort to climb from the crater his freezing form had left. When he emerged from the hole, he found himself in the middle of a snow-covered blizzard wasteland. He turns in all directions, surveying all that his surroundings, taking in the soft white of the snow. He returns to his original sight, and there, where there had been nothing before, the dragon looms.

"ENJOYING THE VIEW?" the dragon queries as flames erupt from its jaws.

Michael has no time to move aside and instead holds his sword up in defiance, calling upon the power within him as he shouts, "ENOUGH!" The flames cease their descent upon him and wane out of existence as they approach the powerful aura encasing him. A trench of melted snow leads from the dragon to Michael, it halts and the snow in a circle around him is perfectly untouched by the flames, protected, as he is, by his aura.

"VERY GOOD, MICHAEL CROSS!!!" The Dragon roared in admiration.

A dark expression formed on Michael's face, making him seem half mad. "Give me your best shot dragon!" Michael taunted with a crooked grin. The beast roared with laughter that which shook the mounds of snow around them, causing much of it to shift and fall.

With a groan, the breastplates and scales shifted upon the dragon's chest as it took a mighty breath. Michael, determined, charged forward through the thick snow, ignoring the freezing cold stinging at the naked skin of his body.

Time seemed to slow to a crawl as man charged upon beast as the dragon's ultimate hellfire was summoned forth from the very depths of its belly. Michael, driving towards the monster, closed the gap between them. Already the roar of flames poured from the dragon's throat with the sound of it echoing painfully in his ears. He held his sword steady with both his hands, sweat pouring down his back as the cold air burns in his lungs. With each step of his tremendous stride, the snow crunches beneath his feet. He is close, but not close enough for a sword, not close enough to land a killing blow.

The dragon's eyes gleam down at him, locked solely on the approaching mortal man. The first licks of flame trickle from the gaping razors of its mouth. Michael searches his soul with the will of his heart, and calls upon the power of the *cross* once more. In the same moment that the emanating fire erupted from the jaws of the dragon, Michael leapt forward. His strength carried him a distance farther than a normal man, but his power, the power of the Cross locked inside him since his birth, carries him into the air a height and distance worthy of a mortal god. In the flash of an instant, the charging Michael, poised in midair, bearing down his final blow against the fearsome beast, is consumed from sight by the flames from the dragon's greatest inferno.

Yet out of the flames of the explosion emerges a flash of brilliant white light that pierces the very stream of fire bursting forth from the dragon. The light flashes with a sound like that of steel cutting steel. The sounds of the flames are drowned out by the roar of pain which erupts the scene in an even greater consumption of fire. A detonation ripples within the Dragon's firestorm and bursts forth in a single concentrated ball of energy from the domelike explosion.

9

The flames seem to burn away the shroud of illusion enveloping the very landscape. Snow melted away to sand, white hills became dunes, and the snowcapped wasteland once again became the desert Michael knew all too well. The dragon stood amidst a ring of fire, the flames slowly dying out around him. The creature shifted heavily as it breathed, nearly shuddering.

Michael stirred in the crater of broken glass formed by melted sand. His skin was blackened by the smoke, his hair was singed, holes were burned throughout his jeans and moccasins, but nowhere was he burned by flames, though he felt as if he had just been thrown into the side of a mountain. He rose from the smoldering crater, his eyes once again locked with the dragon's from about a hundred feet away. The legendary Sword of Lindell lay between them, steam hissing from its ancient steel, blade first into the desert sand.

Looking into the creature's eyes as he walked towards his blade, he could see that his aim had indeed been true. Upon the creatures face, just under its left eye, was a second slash. The first had been luck as he had fallen from the mountain above, a desperate attempt to inflict damage, but the second was meant to convey a stronger point. It was these two cuts in the dragon's face forming a cross that bled a deep irony into the scene. The mark of the Cross upon this being's face as its cold blood dripped with a hiss onto the hot sands. The dragon placed a taloned hand to the bleeding wound upon his face, and smiled with a growling chuckle.

Michael took a firm grip upon the hilt of his sword and pulled it free from the clutches of the desert sand. "CONGRATULATIONS MICHAEL CROSS, YOU HAVE OVERCOME YOUR FEAR OF THE CROSS, AND HAVE LEARNED TO UNLEASH THE TRUE POWER WITHIN…" The sands of the desert swirled around the beast in a whirlwind of massive proportions, fire and sand became one, concealing the dragon among the desert. All at once the flames ceased, the sands stilled in midair and fell to the desert floor just as if they had never been disturbed. Where the Dragon had reined in its imposing form now stood the familiar figure of Alan in his ancient white duster. His faded beard and hair tossed in the wind, his black-lensed spectacles glinted in the desert sun, and a blood red cross was cut perfectly into his ancient face beneath his left eye. Alan smiled broadly as he approached, Michael sheathed his legendary blade.

"You…are the dragon?!"

"Yes Michael, the dragon and I are one. Forged from the very nectar of the God hand to know the powers of illusion, to know of your coming, and prepare your test. Because ya see, all of this was your test. To see if you had the will and strength to overcome any obstacle placed in your opposition in order to achieve your ultimate goal."

"So did I pass?"

"With flying colors…"

"So the forest, the mountain, snow, none of it was real?" Michael asked.

"Illusions, all simply abstractions of the truth. You did swim, climb mountains of rock, and plummet off a seven foot cliff in a ballsy attempt to land a killing stroke to a dragon…"

"Ballsy?"

"…Brave attempt. Honestly Michael, I've never seen such a degree of resolve enacted by a mortal in my great many years. Your courage, your ability to drive through your fear, whether it be sure stupidity or a deeper will within your heart, it is what will make the difference between every victory and defeat."

"What about the fruit?"

"Fruit?" Alan raised an eyebrow above the rim of his glasses in question.

"Yeah, the fruit I ate on top of the mountain. Was it an illusion as well?" Michael asked.

"Ah yes, forgive my senility. That was *not* an illusion. It was indeed the fruit of life, and will continue to display its effects upon you from this day forward…"

"Effects?" Michael asked with a concerned glare.

"Yes, well, it has already unlocked your ability to tap into your power much easier, and may prove to have a lasting effect to your health as well."

"Uhh…Good or bad?"

"Let me just say that you are the first human in *this* world to ever eat such a fruit. It may extend your life, it may not. It may save you from death, but leave your flesh to rot until your tasks amidst the worlds are done…I honestly have no idea Michael. I only know that more likely than not, it will be a positive."

"How can you not know? Why would you tell me to eat it when you don't even know what it's going to do to me?" Michael asked angrily, with clenched fists.

"It was one of my directives…it is the will of fate…"

"The will of fate huh? Shouldn't *I* be the one in control of my destiny?"

"Aye Michael, every being should have the right to make the choice over the path of their destiny, but I'm afraid *you* do not have that luxury at this time. Duty has been thrust upon you by fate itself, a responsibility not only to the land, not just Selador, but all of existence. It is the words of before, the prophecy of the ancients; it has come true time and time again along the path of your journey. It is time for you to either fold or stand Michael Cross. The reason I gave you the fruit was because it was the will of the one true God. If I did not believe you to be what you are then I would not have given it to you."

"What do you mean, what I am? What exactly are you talking about? Who do you believe me to be?" Michael probed with a flustered confusion.

"That's for you to discover for yourself. I have tried to show you and teach you much in so little time, but I'm afraid our stint has grown to its end."

"What do you mean?"

"It is time Michael. Raven Warlack now has six of the weapons in his possession. You hold the last key and the only thing which can stand a chance against him. You must kill Raven Warlack before he propels the balance of the entire universe into chaos."

"That's a score I've been itching to settle, but until now I feared his power… wouldn't I be delivering the final weapon to him? I mean…if it were to fall into his hands…?"

"The burden rests on you, I'm afraid. See to it that doesn't happen. End him, end his evil purge upon this world, and change the fate of destiny's end. Take my hand Michael, there is something I wish to show you."

Michael looked cautiously to the dust covered ancient hand outstretched toward him, and felt that by shaking this man's hand he might as well be selling his soul, but Michael knew this man to be a dragon, not a devil. He could only be the willing volunteer to fate's bidding. *...but what the hell? After everything else I've been through, it can't be that bad.* Michael reasoned as he took the man's firm grasp in his. The handshake seemed to say 'trust me...I will never steer you wrong', the way a father's handshake must feel.

IO

The desert stretched infinitely in all directions. In the middle of this sepia colored scene, amidst the rolling white dunes of the landscape, rose a single patch of rocks, a tiny mountain with a single fruitless tree decorating its summit. Nearby, two figures stand silhouetted against the horizon. A man bearing a sword upon his naked back takes the hand of the white clothed stranger.

A flash of light far more brilliant than the sun itself reams through space and time. Splitting the existence of spectrum from the world until all is white...just before it all fades to black.

II

A cool fragrance of pine is in the air, teasing the senses, shallow and deep, drawing in the oxygen greedily from the thin air. The atmosphere of a snowcapped, pine-covered mountain was higher than any living human had ever climbed. Michael lay on his back upon a smooth slab of rock, overgrown by the moss-like grass of the altitude. Above him was a clear night sky; tonight the three moons of Selador occupied different regions of the hemisphere, each in differing phases surrounded by the infinite number of twinkling gems scattered across the heavens.

Slowly, Michael sat up, only to quickly lay back down as his head began to swoon with a dizziness he had never felt in his life. "Ughh..." Michael groaned clutching his head in agony.

"Here, drink this. It will make you feel better," a voice said from beside him. He thought it to be Alan's voice, but it sounded strange and distorted to his ears. He took the steaming cup the voice offered him and managed to sit up well enough to drink. The liquid fizzed and bubbled all the way down, but was surprisingly settling. His vision immediately cleared and as his symptoms vanished, he was unable to sit up unhindered by vertigo. He found himself upon yet another mountaintop. "Is this..."

"An illusion? No, this is the real thing..."

"Where are we?" Michael asked as he got to his feet.

"This is the mountain of Zion, which overlooks all of the kingdom of Jerum. Look there..." Alan pointed to many twinkling lights in the distance. "...you can see the lights of the towers marking the outer wall of the capital." Michael looked as Alan spoke, focusing to the point where he could just make out the outline of the towers' spires in the distance and the castle city beyond.

"He's there...isn't he?"

"Aye and he awaits you Michael, but do not fear him. He may be powerful but you hold the potential to become far greater than he could possibly imagine. Besides, we've got the element of surprise, and you've got a dragon backing your play. What do you have to worry about?" Alan joked with a toothy grin. Michael chuckled in response.

"First things first…I have a surprise for you. Come, follow me." Alan said as he turned and walked to a clearing free from trees and mossy stones. It was simply a patch of settled dirt, seemingly insignificant in every way. Alan raised a timeless hand and muttered inaudible speech as if greeting the very earth they approached.

Zion began to shake beneath their feet, and the clearing seemed to split into pieces. *Not again…* Michael moaned internally as he prepared to jump to safety, but before he could a great temple of granite that was guarded on all sides with perfectly formed pillars rose up from the vacated depths within the mountaintop. Once Zion had stilled itself once more, and the dust had blown away briskly into the chilled night air, the structure was completely revealed.

Michael could see that it was similar in design to that of many artifacts of the ancients that he had seen in his past, but he doubted anyone knew of this particular relic's existence. "What is this…a temple?"

"A tomb…" Alan said in a cold, dismissive tone. His expression grew grave, a far cry from his previous disposition, as if he was momentarily reliving an event somewhere in his memory.

"Whose tomb?" Michael choked, as he took in the sight before them with a fresh comprehension as to its purpose.

"Saint Illean Cross."

"Saint?" Michael asked, unfamiliar with the title.

"It is written in books long since lost to time, that Illean Cross was the first mortal of the Cross line, son of…a different creation of God. He was titled Saint, because of the great abilities of healing that he possessed, and for the deeds of justice and honor he held, but more importantly for the recognition of the power which you carry on to this day, the power within the blood of the Cross."

"So this guy, is like my great great-grandfather or something?"

"Probably something like that, but many more generations removed than I'm sure you'd try to care and grasp."

"So you say he was the first mortal descendant of…what exactly?"

"There's nothing in this world I can try to compare it to in order to make you truly comprehend Michael…"

"You're just not trying."

"No, I honestly cannot find it in myself to have the words you would understand. You see Michael, our world is based upon a mere fraction of the knowledge our people once possessed. Much of the lands history has lost or distorted to legend and fantasy over time. The only religion Selador's people collectively follow is the single directive placed upon them. However, it would seem that the people have communally failed as a whole in keeping that single purpose."

"Keeping the legendary weapons safe…"

"Precisely, and though I know much more history of this world than any mere mortal, I do not know how to explain to you the true origin of the Cross at this time, and for that I am sorry. If I could Michael, I would describe it to you, but it would take a lifetime of sharing the philosophies of other worlds in order for you to see it true, and we sadly do not have the luxury of time."

"I see," Michael said, accepting at last.

———

"I hope you find the truth before the end of your path Michael Cross, but before that time, there is much to prepare." Alan said as he started for the tomb, with Michael trailing behind.

The tomb was like the inside of a great hall. Tapestries long faded hung upon the massive walls. There were stained glass skylights in the ceiling above, a few broken and cracked, casting a mosaic of colored moonlight into the room. In its center lay the granite sarcophagus, the alter of a Saint since passed. A thick beam of moonlight shines down through a broken skylight above, casting a glowing ray upon its lid where a mass of dried and decayed flowers rest, untouched for millennia. The tomb is shrouded by the dim glow of color cast in the dark corners of the room.

Never breaking stride, Alan waved his hand before him and a strong gust of icy wind swept through the tomb. The flowers upon Saint's coffin instantly turned to dust and faded into the cold air like a ghost. Michael shivered from the cold and the position he held in such a sacred place. The air was thick in a way, macabre, drowning in the essence of that which had *passed*.

Alan reached the alter first and lay a steady hand upon its lid, running it along the full length as he moved to its crown, taking his time and admiring its craftsmanship. Michael stood at the foot of this stone resting place, searching Alan's face for some reassurance to their right to be in this forgotten hallowed place. Alan's unseeing stare simply reflected Michael's concerning expression in the dark lenses of his spectacles. Alan spoke slow and solemn, "What lies within this alter is something that has waited millennia for you, the Michael Cross, last of the Cross. It is a treasured relic of a time since passed…are you ready to receive what lies within this tomb?"

"Aye, if I'm going to stop Raven, I'm going to need all the help I can get."

"Very well then…" Alan said raising his hands over the sarcophagus. "…Armoure Baratus Necter Cros," Alan spoke sternly. The temple shook in a trembling frenzy that shattered the remaining skylights above, and in a sudden cracking explosion the lid of the stone coffin burst into three large chunks and flew to the floor.

When the dust had cleared, Alan still stood across the alter from Michael, only now he held a wide grin upon his face. "Neat…huh?"

Michael just shook his head and allowed himself to smile. Lying in the exposed coffin upon a well preserved suede lining was a perfectly displayed chest plate of shimmering polished steel, and upon its crest was the symbol of the Cross, etched in red steel inlaid upon the silver plating. Next to the chest piece, on either side, were fine steel forearm and shin bracers etched with ancient symbols. "They are…magnificent," was all that he could reply as he traced the insignia upon the armor with his fingertips.

Alan walked to a different part of the tomb where the moonlight shone freely in the room from the holes in the ceiling above. A statue stood erected at the far wall where Alan approached.

"Hey Alan, if this tomb has been keeping this armor safe for all these years…then where is Saint Illean Cross?"

"I do not know Michael…I do not know…" Alan said as he stared up at the bold and dignified face carved in the stone of the statue before him. He then reached down to the feet of the statue and picked up a leather bag. He bowed deeply to the ancient stone and returned to Michael. "Here, these may be of some use to ya, I reckon." Alan stated as he tossed the heavy bag to Michael.

———

Inside, Michael found a new shirt, black as night. Once donned he found that its sleeves were snug and cut short just past the elbow, leaving the forearm and wrists to move freely with the light padding of the vambraces once they too were clasped tightly onto his arms. He then pulled on the chest plate as well with little difficulty. The last thing in the bag was his tall black boots with fresh stockings tucked neatly inside. Michael removed his moccasins and pulled on the warm stockings, offering the hide shoes to Alan, who simply shook his head. "Hold onto'em, they may come in handy someday," he said with a smile.

Michael nodded and tucked them neatly into the leather bag before pulling on his familiar black boots once more. *So many miles…* He thought to himself *…only a few left to travel.* He clasped the bracers to the familiar black leather of his boots and admired how they conformed together as one.

Michael stood before the man-dragon, dignified and suited as the most honorable of heroes. His new armor shone in the faint light of the moon.

"One more thing…" Alan said as he suddenly removed his old white overcoat and held it out to Michael.

"Your coat?" Michael was bewildered as he took the hefty duster with honor.

"Ah, it'll look better on you anyway. I would be privileged if you were to wear it into battle." Alan smiled.

"Thank you…"

"Now then, are you ready, Lord Michael Cross?"

"As ready as I'll ever be."

"Then follow me," Alan said as he exited the dark chamber of the tomb and entered out into the open cold air of the mountaintop, Michael following close behind. The man, the dragon, the one called Alan stood at the edge of this great mountain of Zion peering through the flurry of sleet and snow to the growing hue of light in the distance.

"Is that…" Michael began.

"…Dawn. It will soon be morning, and time for the day's execution."

"Execution?"

"The man you know as Danube Drakendor, but there is no time to explain. Only know that other than me, he is the only ally you have in this world. That is, *if* you can save him, but there is one more order of business first, one last gift to give…" Alan waved his hand before him as he spoke. The reflection of a million snowflakes danced in the black lenses that covered his eyes. "…reach within the coat I gave you," He urged.

Michael, unaware of its weight until this moment, felt a heavy object within. What he thought was the inside pocket of the coat, but could now feel it pressing firmly against his side. He reached into this pocket, this 'holster' as it were, and slowly he drew. *The lost that is sometimes found, the things forgotten that sometimes return…the gun of Gell.* Michael marveled as he pulled the strange weapon from within the coat.

"Should you fail at keeping him from activating the tower…just make sure your shot counts, you've only got one." Alan warned as Michael admired the craftsmanship of the gun once again. He traced the fingers of his left hand over the runes in the blackened steel.

"So…I don't suppose you have a plan?" Michael asked at last.

Alan's smile grew wide beneath the dark spectacles he perpetually wore. "Aye Michael…I have a plan."

Part 14:

The Beginning

I

Danube Drakendor sat upon the cold damp floor of his cell. His legs were crossed, his eyes closed, an expression of deep concentration upon his face as he meditated on the death that lie before him. The morning light slowly crept through the bars of his only window, its view looked out to the courtyard, the white tower, and the gallows waiting to end his path. Many were already assembled for the morning's event. Danube had the ability to listen to the murmured voices had he wanted, but he had no desire for such. He needed not to care about what awaited, rather he dwelled on the pain within his heart.

"Kaire" he whispered to himself in his transient state of mind. He said her name with the same tenderness he always had, the same love, the same desire, but he knew that she was forever gone. Lost in mind to the darkness of the greatest enemy the land had ever known, and he was powerless to stop him. He strived to contrive a plan of escape, a way to save Kaire. To free her from Warlack's control, but each plan failed as he played it out within his mind.

Shackled hand and foot he wearily admitted defeat and continued to meditate on the peace that would come once he had reached the end of his path, but like a throbbing wound the thoughts of freedom continued to surface in his thoughts, only to be dispelled by mere fact. Fact, the shackles

---

which bound him were fed together by several chains conjoining in the middle by a single steel hunk of a lock, and it was this lock that destroyed his hopes of liberty. The lock bore a series of runes, a spell disabling the magick that could aid him. He was helpless to break these chains that bound him, and so he waited.

He heard the faint jingling of keys just beyond the ancient thick wooden door to his cell. He heard the teeth of the rusty old key finding its way into the gears of the lock, the clicks of the mechanism as the key turned, and the snap of the door's latch just before it groaned open.

Beyond this neat picture frame the doorway created stood thirteen men in the corridor just outside the cell, suited in full ceremonial armor and garb, no doubt for the occasion. The helmets and layers of steel plates glowed in the torchlight of the underground corridor lurking beyond the confines of his little room.

Danube rose to his feet with little difficulty and no help from the soldiers who had come to escort him to his date with destiny. He walked slowly from his cell. The soldiers parted, six on each side, one at the end of the little walkway the men created with flesh and steel. This man held before him an oversized shield in one hand and a short, fine edged sword in the other. He stood at the ready, his shield seeming outrageously large for the confines of the tight underground corridor. His eyes glared at Danube through the angular slits in his shining helm.

The six on Danube's left carried crossbows, each nocked tightly, ready to fire with the slightest touch. The other six bore a strange metal tube, the end the soldier held was made of wood bolted to the steel itself displaying a sort of mechanism. Either way, every man held their sight upon him, ready to fire at any moment. Danube approached the man at the end of the corridor calm and readied, for whatever came.

Like the throbbing pain that still shot into his previously broken nose, he again reveled once more with the thoughts of escape. *Better to die fighting than be executed as a traitor. As a free man I can hope to put a stop to Warlack and his plan, and have a chance at saving Kaire, but dead I can do nothing,* he concluded without any further thought. He slowly walked the distance to the man holding the outrageously large shield. "I am ready."

"Very well, you are to walk three paces in front of me. A line of my men shall accompany you on either side. You are to remain three paces from them at all times, or we will kill you. Do you understand this?" the shielded man demanded.

"Aye, but what I don't understand...is why there are only thirteen of you? Don't you know that's an unlucky number?" Danube queried with an out of place grin then sent a cold chill up the spine of the man before him. The man made to move in response, to order his men to show force for his insolence, but Danube moved faster.

As he grabbed the top lip of the man's shield the twelve turned taking only a moment to aim as Danube hauled himself up and over the shield, flipping over the man before him. Shots rang out, blasting like cannons in the narrow corridor, dephening the scene. The guns bellowed smoke as they fired, compromising visibility for the others, but still they fired. Unloading shots and arrows blindly into the abyss of the smoke filled corridor where four comrades and the attempted escapee had vanished. The screams of men rang over the shots as hot lead ripped through flesh and steel, and arrows pierced neck and joint. Three bodies struck the floor, killed by the friendly fire; the forth corpse still stood among the hazy mist of the waning smoke, held in place as a shield by Danube Drakendor, who,

---

399

unwilling to give up his chance at escape, ripped the short gleaming sword from the dead hand of the shielded man he held before him. He thrust the limp, lifeless form forward into the scrambling arms of one of the remaining five. The man dropped his crossbow as the weight of the corpse hit him, dropping to the floor in a collapsing heap upon the stone floor, causing the remaining four to frantically struggle to reload their guns and bows.

Despite his shackled feet and hands, he quickly felled two of the reloading men, and then finished off the man struggling to remove the hulk of his dead friend. He pierced through them, skewering them together in death, his blade sticking in their combined mass. Two men left…one just finishing reloading the strange musket style gun, and the other struggling to crank his bolt into place upon his bow.

Danube lunged for the man with the gun, entangling himself with him, driving the sight at the end of the hollowed blackened tube into the faceplate of the bowman's helmet just as he had finished reloading. With Danube's hands wrapped over his, he squeezed, forcing the man to take the shot. A roar of flame shot out from the barrel and out the other side of the man's skull as his helmet covered head was graced with a gaping hole by the lead round.

The crossbow fell from the guard's hand, and before it could hit the stone floor, Danube danced from his entanglement, ducked under the steaming barrel of the freshly fired musket, around the collapsing hulk of man and steel, and swept it neatly from the air with a flash of his hand. Just as quickly he turned, leveled its tiny sight, and fired. The arrow shot smoothly into the right eye slit of the musketeer's helmet. He screamed as he fell back in a spray of blood, dead before he hit the floor.

Danube, swept up in the adrenaline of the scuffle, dropped the spent crossbow to the floor, and wrenched free the bloody sword he had used to skewer two men. Frantically, he searched the bodies of the men he'd slain, looking desperately for the key that would unbind his shackles and free his will to the potential of his true power, but no key would fit his lock. Frustrated, he made his way for the only exit in sight; a single door at the top of a flight of stone steps which he shuffled to as quickly as he could.

Reaching them at last, he leap-hopped the steps two, three at a time until he came to the tiny landing at its peak. The door stood ominously before him, his fight had only just begun. With shackled hands he turned the iron ring latch of the old wooden door, and swung it open. The room beyond flashed with a brilliance he had not expected. Blinded by the light to the point where he did not see the man who slammed a heavy fist into his face, rebreaking his nose. Danube staggered back, teetering on the edge of the top step. Through tear filled eyes and a spray of blood he struggled to make out the figure of the man before him, the same man who had broken his nose before.

"Right place, right time. Score…me two, you zero…night night, friendo," the man gloated as he took a single step forward and slammed a heavy booted foot into his chest. Danube tumbled back down the staircase in a series of bone crunching slams upon the stone steps. He cried out as he fell, but his voice quickly silenced as he reached the bottom in a final crashing hulk. He was quickly consumed by darkness brought on by the immeasurable volley of pain that ripped through him. As the darkness fell over him he could hear a familiar maniacal laughing through the waning shroud of his subconscious delirium, the laughter of Raven Warlack.

2

Thuthump...Thump

They had hauled him to his feet and carried him up the staircases, down the corridors, through the doors, and out into the gleaming morning sun overlooking the large assembly within the courtyard of the seven.

Thuthump...Thump

Somewhere, Danube could hear the procession of drums rattling out their steady beat. *Thuthump...Thump* Deep and loud the sound echoed with each shuffled step the beaten and bloodied Danube took.

Thuthump...Thump The sound resonated, only not as a sound of the world around him, not the melody of some distant percussion rolling out the song of his untimely execution, but of the depths of his own heart.

Thuthump...Thump The noise continued as he was led through the crowd of soldiers, servants, and people alike. The mob was quiet, only shuffled murmurs filled the air as Danube was taken to the alter in the center of the courtyard, a giant circular slab of black marbled stone. It was a sharp contrast to the soft green grass of the courtyard it resided upon.

In the center of this circular alter rose two ivory pillars, a space separated them perfectly sized for a person of any proportion to stand between them, arms outstretched. Danube stood between these pillars, and as soon as he was in position facing south to the assembly of his captors, chains materialized from the magick lock bound to his shackles. The chains shot into the pillars on either side, melding into the very stone, chaining Danube helplessly in place.

The chains seemed to writhe almost in a lifelike manner, tightening and pulling Danube's arms taught to the point where the muscles in his arms nearly tore, causing him to grit his teeth with the pain.

Thuthump...thump, continued to echo in his sweat soaked head.

Before him, across the dewy green grass glistening in the morning sun, standing before the royal council, was a collection of his primary prosecutors, those men who had manipulated and deceived their way to attaining power.

High Lord Nieon Sulton of the Island of Laotia stood dignified and silent, admiring the ceremonial processions. To his left stood the cross scarred High Lord Raymark Lafey of the cities of Lindell, the same man who ordered the fires upon Danube's home. *How he desired to taste the cowards blood.* These two men stood to the left of the mastermind, the conjuror of manipulation, the spawn of darkness, Raven Warlack. He stood with the brim of his hat bent low, shielding his eyes from the morning sun and the perception of others. Kaire was at his side, the puppet of his right hand, his instrument to play as he chose. Her tattered clothes and bloodied white bandage over her eyes had been replaced with a series of mismatched black and red armor. The bandage over her eyes was now a fine black strip of silk. The Scythe was holstered across her back.

The great ruler of all of Selador, King Ryon Jerum, traitor by his own lust for power, stood before them addressing the entire assembly. "My fellow countrymen, my people, my honored guests, you have been summoned forth upon this day, set in the vast atrium of time itself to bear witness to the hand of justice in its most literal and physical form. Before you good people, is a man charged not only with treason, not only with widespread murder of the armies of the land, not only consorting conspiracy against the royal court, but of defiling the very things we hold most sacred of all, the seven legendary weapons which have been passed down to us by the ancients. The gifts from above bestowed upon us, mere mortals, offered unto our protection. No amount of suffering can atone for the deeds of the man you see before you, this former High Lord…Danube Drakendor, and yet we offer him this death to show the extent of our kingdom's mercy, the depths of our civilized nature. This death, this execution, will be quick, giving him to the hands of fate to decree judgment as seen fit by the will of God." The crowd hung on every word the king articulated.

Danube hung his head in shame at the false accusations tied to his name. *Dishonor…this must be in part what Michael spoke of. To be labeled as something one is not, to be labeled a fiend when one's heart is pure. Is there no true justice in the hands of fate?* Danube wondered bitterly as the king continued.

"Danube Drakendor! As High King. I sentence you. Do you have any confessions you wish to add, last words, last requests, any plea you wish to cry out to the court you see before you?" the king asked in mock magnanimity.

Danube lifted his head from its sorrowful droop. His eyes lingered across the collection of faces before him, but only one held the apple of his eye, his love, Kaire Ra. "My pleas will fall upon deaf ears my king, for you have manipulated this court with the aid of your sorcerer, and have sought to attain the weapons for yourself. I am simply your scapegoat prepared for the slaughter. I will give you no satisfaction of weakness within my heart. I will not plea, I will not beg, I will not give you the martyr you wish. My final words are for one and one alone. The only woman I have ever loved, the only one I can never have. Goodbye Kaire Ra, my sweet, soft devil of Reum, my true love. I know this is not your fault; you are helpless to resist, and for that I forgive you. May we meet again if fate allows…" Danube's eyes never left the stern, cold face of the woman clad in black, her dark hair fluttering with the breeze as it always did.

"Well spoken, last of the Drakendor. May you find peace at the end of your path. Are you prepared to receive your fate?"

"Aye …"

"Very well then, I hereby execute you Danube Drakendor, with the sacred power of the legendary Bow of Jerum," The king grandstanded with a dignified theatrical tone. He slung the weapon from across his back. The king unlocked the mechanism holding the crystal arrow in place following the length of the curved golden bow. He rotated the carved arrow on its pivoting mechanism to the ready position where it once again locked in place along the track of the bows notch and sight. The king pulled the fine silver string back and onto the notch in the very back of the crystal arrow.

With his hands firmly upon the bow and notched arrow, he raised the readied weapon of the gods, pulling back the arrow as he leveled it with his close range target. As he pulled back, a light appeared within the crystal of the arrowhead, and the more he pulled the brighter it became until the light was blinding. Danube closed his eyes and awaited his certain demise.

The king released his hold, and in a flash of hot white light an arrow of pure energy leapt forth from the bow like lightning. The blast ripped across the courtyard, burning the green grass black as it went. Over the sound of the crackling stream of energy roaring forth from the legendary Bow there was a whisper of steel as the arrow closed in upon its mark and suddenly burst into an explosion of white light that ripped through the kingdom in a sudden glorious flash.

3

The light subsided to the dull glow of the morning sun. Dust settled in the air. Danube Drakendor still hung, chained to the pillars of

---

retribution, unscathed. Before him, standing with the Great Sword at his side was Michael Cross. The retreating trails of the power he had unleashed withered from the sword and his body like steam.

Michael pivoted the sword in his hand, and changing his grip, thrust the sword into the ground reverse hand. The legendary Great Sword sang into the moist earth with a sizzling of the cooling hot steel of its blade. Upon the hilt, tied at its end like a flag, was a strip of the white cloth he had worn as a bandage. It whipped furiously with the wind, stained red in places with Michael's blood, sacred blood, blood of the Cross. This was his flag, his banner, like those in the desert, a marker of just how far he had come. He stands as a lean silhouette, his eyes sharp as a hawk, locking with the eyes of the man in black, the man called Raven Warlack.

"So...he lives," Raymark observes.

"Sooner than expected..." Warlack hisses. He grabs the slave girl Kaire Ra by her arm and pulls her close. Leaning in, he whispers something to her that is inaudible to the world. "Good bye, my sweet soft..." Finished with words he places a slender hand upon her cheek, pulling her in as he bends to kiss her, his large brimmed black hat blocking the embrace from the world as well.

Like an approaching storm came the distant sound of something in the wind, the indistinctive sound of leathery wings beating through the air, and a distant scream rising up from the depths, and howled through the air from the unknown. Over the walls it came, the Dragon of the Lost Plains. The mouth of the beast erupted with a fire that raged upon the kingdom. The flames set fire to the courtyard and houses, anything that could burn. People ran screaming in every direction, some frantically trying to subdue the flames, some simply running. The guards took to their tasks of the flames, and the soldiers went for the walls to defend against the Dragon's assault.

Only a score remained; Raven with Kaire on his arm, smiling at the chaos upon them as though greeting an old friend. Raymark looked frantically around, and then to Raven for order, and Nieon Sulton never moved or even blinked an eye. The king's men, those who remained, thirty three in all, looked to their king, who, stricken with disbelief and fear, looked to Raven Warlack.

"Why are you both looking at me? So what? It's a dragon, little change of plans." Warlack commanded.

4

With a shaking hand, Michael lifts the hide skin to his lips, and drinks heavily. The fizzing liquid works its wonders once again, and the dizzying effects of the teleportation vanish once more. He replaces the stopper and puts the half empty bag into the pocket of his coat as he wipes his lips dry.

"Michael?" Danube managed to utter.

"Wondering what took me so long?" Michael joked as he turned to face the other champion of fate.

"How the hell did you? This can't be, I should be dead…"

"Well, you're welcome, I guess? Here let me take care of that for you," Michael offered as he leaned forward and grabbed the lock in the center of Danube's chains.

"…Meckolum…" He whispered as he gripped the lock firmly in one hand and ripped it free. With the magick gone, the chains surrounding the lock shattered like glass into tiny metal shards that melted into the air before they hit the ground. Michael placed this too into one of the many pockets of his coat before helping the barely standing Danube to his feet.

"Michael, how did you know…?"

"Like an old friend once said…there's no time to explain." Michael said as he pointed up just as the dragon made another napalm spreading pass overhead.

"You're too late Michael. They've taken the Staff, we are but two and are powerless to stop them. Kaire, he's…corrupted her. We can't hope to face them all."

"That's awful weak coming from you. Are you telling me you need your Staff in order to fight?"

"I tried…I am powerless without it."

"There are many things in this world that hold power, but it is not these things which give a man his will to fight. The weapons are nothing more than keys, more pieces in this game, just like us. It is not the power of the weapons that is going to make the difference in this battle Danube Drakendor, but the will of good men. The will of two of a kind, the last of Drakendor and the last of Cross. Forgive my blood, and the sins it has caused, and let us make our stand! Are you with me son of Ishlie?"

"Aye, I am with you, but I sure as hell hope you're stronger than the last time we met," Danube said rising to his feet. He unwove the remaining chains from his shackles, and with a length of the chain in each hand as a weapon he joined Michael's side.

"Oh, I suppose I've had some practice," Michael said with a grin.

The two men walked towards those gathered together as their enemies. Michael, never breaking stride, pulled the Great Sword from the ground and rested it upon his shoulder.

———

They neared the thirty three that moved to intercept their approach to the king. The soldiers moved like a tide in unison, collective of one. They stood in full mail, their round shields before them, spears held at the ready, swords hot at their sides. Their helmets were the color of bronze in the morning sun and sharpened to a point at their crown, with eye slits narrow and oblique, crafted masterfully in pursuit of symmetry with the others, each exactly the same. With a grunt of a yell the men fell into formation, facing the approaching two, shields high, all at ready.

"Looks like a lot of em'." Michael said.

"Humph…"

"Maybe we should ask them if they'd want to talk things out," Michael jested with a grin. A fiery explosion erupted somewhere behind them as they turned and looked at each other. Danube simply glared and shook his head as Michael chuckled at his own humor.

The sea of men parted all at once, a single step to one side and the other. Nieon Sulton stood at the back, and stepped slowly, silently, forward. A great energy seemed to gather around him as time seemed to crawl upon his approach.

"He's mine…" Michael said as Nieon Sulton reached the front line and the men that had parted returned to place in another single step, and the parted masses became one again. Nieon readied the legendary Spear, its steel humming with the resonance of his movement as the air grew cold. Dark clouds had already begun to form as the tension between weapons grew.

Michael, unwilling to let any stand in his way charged forward, darting with his weight forward, the sword still high on his shoulder, with Danube a mere footstep behind. Upon seeing the daring charge, Nieon

Sulton took to foot as well, stepping with his silent gait, meeting the oncoming assault head on. The soldiers at his back followed his lead, marching towards the two charging men like the mass of a tidal wave rising up to smash down upon two ships adrift within the sea.

Seven paces apart, Nieon Sulton leapt towards Michael, cleaving the Spear through the air in a tremendous arch. As he charged forward, three of the king's men charged with him, all focused on the liberated Danube Drakendor. The other thirty halted their march, and waited with shields up for command.

Michael thrust the resting blade off his shoulder and high into the air, then driving down, swung the massive sword down upon the spear in midswing. Any normal man would have been felled by the heavy stroke of the legendary Great Sword with any attempt to block, but it proved that Nieon Sulton was no ordinary man.

With sea blue eyes, the dark skinned man locked his gaze with Michael's. The blades of the swords scraped against the ancient Spear in a sparking, hissing scream of steel as neither yielded. Michael's counterattack had become a block, which became a test of strength as each man pushed against the other. The power within their weapons surged into the air, summoning the dark clouds to brew into a raging storm. Lightning flashes overhead as Michael grits his teeth and calls upon the power of the Cross within him. Feeling it creep its way through his blood he lets a smile slip.

Nieon saw this and his brow furrowed, dark shadows creeping onto his face as he struggled to drive into Michael. Michael was unimpressed, unleashed his own strength upon the man, pushing him back, and then stepping forward and to the side. Michael moved the sword to follow through across the man's unguarded midsection to sever it, but as the edge of his blade came within a hairsbreadth of him, Nieon somersaulted forward and over the blade.

Time slowed to a crawl as in those very same moments, Danube, last of the Drakendor, dispatched two of his three attackers by swinging the chains he held around their necks, and in a series of steps and alternating jerks snapped their necks as his chains released. He stood, chains in hand at his side, and approached the third man like a predator stalking its prey. The man thrust with his spear as he held his shield high against the blow of one of Danube's chains. Danube sidestepped the thrust of the spear and wrapped his second chain around the pole armed weapon so gracefully that it appeared as a dance. With a twist and jerk of his arm, he wrenched the spear from the man's hand as he kicked forward, slamming his foot into the face of the shield. The man staggered back, stunned. Danube swung his chain out far in a tremendous arch as he stepped forward, and in a flash of lightning the end of the broken chain slashed across the man's neck.

Blood sprayed from the neck of the soldier to Michael's left as he spun around to receive the oncoming thrust of Nieon Sulton's spear. When he blocked it changed direction ever so swiftly, and what had been a single thrust became four, then five until suddenly, in the most unorthodox manner, Nieon Sulton pivoted his body and blade, masking his attack, and then swung an oddly angled uppercut that nearly cut Michael's face, but instead swiped a lock of hair. Before the auburn strands hit the ground, Nieon had again changed his attack to another hard thrust.

Michael rolled left, the tip of the spear dragging across his armor with a metallic hiss. His roll took him across the thrusting body of Nieon Sulton and to his exposed backside, where Michael drove the hilt of his sword down onto the man's back in a bone crunching smash, making him fall to the ground.

For an instant, Michael surveyed the surroundings. Fires burned everywhere, the dragon roared overhead, people screamed all over the kingdom. Before him, thirty soldiers still stood in lines of ten. Beyond them stood his enemy, and beyond Warlack was the white tower of the seven, looming over them all as if bearing witness. The first line of ten broke formation and charged towards them. Danube and Michael had only a moment to cast a smirking glance and then they too charged, Michael leaping over the fallen Nieon Sulton.

Michael drew back his heavy blade, and in a frenzy unleashed a roaring battle cry as he swung upon the first three. As he drove the blade through steel and flesh he could feel the power of the Cross surging into his veins. The drum like beating of his heart filled his ears as he was consumed by the raw, unnatural strength of his power. He drove forward, flashing his sword wildly left and right, cleaving and maiming, splitting and severing, he killed. Danube watched as he battled his own foes, breaking necks with the chain, and then taking a spear to several more with a volley of quick stabbing thrusts and bone breaking strikes, but his kills were quickly surpassed by the sheer numbers Michael felled under his heavy sword. The second line of ten charges forward to their brethren's aid, but they too are quickly ruined by the sword and spear and chain. It is a massacre, Michael stands with his sword drenched in blood held to his side, Danube with spear in one hand, chain in the other, the little grassy hill they stand atop is soaked in blood, littered with the fallen, mutilated dead and dying, but one figure emerges, rising from the deceased.

Nieon Sulton finds his way to his feet, snapping several vertebrae in his spine back into place. Holding the Spear before him, he scraped the extremely long fingernail of his little finger along its steel, and the sound reverberated through the air. Michael turned to see the man as he stood with a menacingly twisted grin. The expression looked alien upon the usually emotionless face. A trickle of blood flowed from one corner of his mouth giving him the look of the insane. Michael leveled his blade, and walked back to where the man stood.

Danube faced the ten as they took the opportunity to charge, but just as suddenly, they were halted by the low sound of a command, and so they waited as Michael finished his fight with their leader. Danube watched as Michael closed in on him, his enemy's fingernail still scraping annoyingly down the spear ever so slowly.

Michael raised his sword, but as he did Nieon lunged forward, kicking Michael in the chest. Michael staggered back, but then caught his bearings in time to see the razor edge of the spearhead screaming towards his throat. Time seemed to move to a crawl for Michael, and he could hear each beat of his heart as the seconds passed. He shifted his weight and stepped aside, one. The spear changes directions and the strike is blocked by Michael's Great Sword, two. Michael pivots his blade over the spear's darkened steelhead, and slides the blade along it as a guide, and smashes it into the throat of Nieon Sulton, severing his head in a single, clean cut, three. In three moves Michael Cross killed the mysterious Lord of Laotia.

The Spear is flung back in the direction of the remaining line of ten where they march forward in unison, advancing over the legendary weapon. The line of ten then splits as they had done before, when they were still thirty three, allowing the entrance of someone else to the front of battle.

The cross scarred Lord Raymark Lafey stood side by side with the dark haired beauty Kaire Ra, her scythe held readied at her side, its primeval tarnished blade radiant in the flashes of lightning overhead. They came like ghosts, seemingly stepping on the scene from the deepest memories of both Michael and Danube. Raymark pulled the spear from the blood-moistened ground and admired it a moment before walking the remaining distance to Michael.

"Aghmm…" Raymark cleared his throat. Kaire stood silently at his side. "…*He* wanted me to tell you, that it's not too late to take his offer, and believe me Michael, though I would rather have you killed and fed to the dogs, I can honestly tell you that it is a good offer to take. And you," Raymark pointed a black gloved hand to Danube, "You were underestimated in your potential. We see this now, and *he* wishes to grant you pardon, take Kaire here and leave, to live your life however you may choose, or join us and reap all of the glorious benefits of the things *he* can bestow. There is no reason anyone else has to die here today." Raymark sold a good line, but despite his flashy red cape and fiery red hair and nice clothes, the man was still hated in the deepest intensity by both men.

"Oh there's plenty of *reason!*" Michael said through clenched teeth.

"Past aside, accept the offer, or sadly we will be forced to kill you." As Raymark said this, the ten armored men converged behind them into a line once more. They all raised spears at once, ready to throw and kill the two men at the instant Raymark commanded.

There was a screech from the heavens above, the strong torrent of wind as the dragon made his descent. In an explosion, the dragon set fire to all ten men in a blast of flame from a single pass. The men screamed and fell to the ground in a burning hulk. The dragon roared in approval overhead for hitting his mark.

Raymark could feel the heat of the flames at his back, and turning felt the chilled horror of reality. He returned his gaze to Michael with a contorted snarl.

"You were saying?" Michael questioned the snarling beast that was Raymark Lafey.

5

Raven Warlack led the king towards the tower. At times he had to grab him by his robes and lead him through the chaos, but closer and closer they came to fate and farther away from the battle that could mean death.

"Wait! Wait…stop Raven, I must protect my kingdom!" the king pleaded.

"Your kingdom is nothing in the grand scheme!" Raven hissed as he pulled him along.

"But the dragon, at least let me shoot that infernal dragon!" the king was to the point of wailing, but as he said this Raven stopped, turned, and smiled.

"Yeah, sure…go ahead. This should be…interesting."

The king grabbed his bow, locked his arrow, and nocked the fine silver string. Taking aim, he caught sight of the dragon just over the white tower. He pulled the bow back and light collected in its crystal tip. Holding his mark in his sights, he judged the shot and released just as the dragon opened its mouth to set fire to yet another wall.

The stream of light nailed the dragon in its bony armored chest plate, blasting a hole into it, cracking much of his armored exoskeleton. The beam of light worked through his body and shot out his backside piercing a magnified beam of light up into the heavens amidst the black clouds and lightning. The dragon roared in agony as its body was ripped apart by the light, and then in an explosion of pure white, the dragon, the one called Alan, was gone from the world of Selador forever.

"Nice shot…" Raven muttered to the king. Both held a bewildered gaze.

"Ya think?" the king said in a dumbfounded tone.

Michael felt pain in his heart for his lost guide, but the loss only brought resolve. He could take no offers, his purpose, his destiny was at hand, and he had to stop Raven Warlack from unlocking the tower.

Raymark grinned at the sight of the dragon's destruction. "Lose your pet?" he jabbed.

"It's all right, I'm about to relieve Warlack of his," Michael said to Raymark with a cold killer gaze.

"Is that so?" Raymark said as he leveled the Spear. Kaire in turn leveled her Scythe at the ready to strike down Danube in an instant.

"I'm going to carve a cross into your heart!" Michael yelled as he charged towards the man who had taken his wife, taken his life, and tainted his honor. The blade of the Great Sword sliced through the air, down to the unprepared Raymark. Amidst the clashing of legendary weapon colliding with legendary weapon there was a louder clap of thunder from the heavens above as the black clouds finally broke rain. But it was not the spear blocking the legendary Great Sword, but the Scythe of Vengeance. Blindfolded in the pouring rain, Kaire stood with her back to Michael, the blade of his Sword snagged in the nook of her Scythe. Raymark took the opportunity to attack Danube, who was bewildered by the speed at which his love had moved.

The Spear sang as it cut the air between it and Danube, but at the last moment he lifted his own spear, and though breaking it, took most of the momentum out of the attack to move aside. Using the chain, Danube whipped at Raymark's hands and face, keeping him at bay temporarily.

Michael tries to move into position to return to fighting Raymark, but each move he makes Kaire steps in the way and attacks. He is forced into a dance of blocking and dodging all the while trying to get to Raymark instead of fighting her. He is blinded by his anger, his lust for revenge. The power of the Cross pumps through him at an increasing rate, doubling as his frustration grows. Finally, he turns to her and prepares to unleash his power upon her.

The rain pours down as the energy surges from Michael and Kaire like fire. "Get out of my way Kaire!" He yells, but she holds.

"Fine, have it your way!" Michael says as he charges forward, and drives all of his fury into his strike.

Danube sees this, and desperate to reach Kaire he makes a stray step towards Raymark, taking a deep slash in his side in the process, and smashes his forehead into his face, head butting the *cross* scared lord, breaking his nose. Raymark drops the Spear to the ground as he clutches what remains of the cartilage in his blood gushing nose. Tears run down his face as he curses Danube in inaudible gargles.

"Hurts don't it?! Try having it done twice in the span of one day!" Danube says as he swiftly kicks Raymark squarely in the face, undoubtedly breaking his nose even more, and with enough pain to have an idea of just what it would be like.

Raymark fell back, unconscious, blood streaming down his mangled face. As Danube turned, expecting to see Michael poised and ready to kill his only love, he was shocked with morbid terror as Kaire pivoted the Great Sword from Michael's grasp and flung it into the air. It landed twenty feet away, blade first into the ground. Danube sprinted forward, lunging towards the defenseless Michael Cross as Kaire pulled back her Scythe, readying to pierce his gut with the sharpened curved blade.

"Kaire! NOOO!" he yelled as he pushed Michael aside from the death stroke. Danube could see the steely malice in the face of the woman who once loved him with the fiercest intensity. He watched as her teeth clenched in satisfaction as her Scythe's blade pierced flesh. The blade sunk into his stomach, blood sprayed with the blade as it leapt from out of his back.

"Aaggghh…Kaire…" he struggled to cry as his mouth filled with blood. With one hand he grabbed the hilt of the Scythe, the other he grabbed his love by the throat, choking her. His grip was fast and firm, and in seconds she began to strain, clawing at his hold with her free hand. Unable to breath, she released her grasp upon the Scythe and clawed at his hand with both of hers. Danube pulled the weapon out of his body in another spray of blood, and threw it aside.

Kaire gasped and clawed, but could get no air, until at last, when Danube was sure that she too was near death, he felt her body shudder beneath the pressure of his grip, and knew that the evil holding possession over her was vanquished. He released his grasp on her throat as they both collapsed to their knees. The rain halted its shower from the clouds above and the morning sun ripped through the dark clouds for a glorious moment. Kaire gasped for air as she felt for Danube's hands. "DaN…uBe…" she sobbed in broken speech. He took her hands in his and placed them to his face.

"I am here my love," he struggled to say.

"Oh DaNube…I'm…sorry…" She struggled to form the words, struggled to draw in air into her lungs.

"Ssshh…It's ok now love, it'll all be ok now…" Danube whispered to the dark haired beauty he held in his dying arms.

Michael turned from the sight of the lovers' last embrace, a twinge of

---

guilt in his heart, and walked to the Sword standing solemnly waiting…his flag blew impatiently in the wind.

A noise came from behind, near Danube and Kaire. Michael turned in time to see the bloody faced coward Lord Raymark fetching the Scythe. He held the scimitar in one hand, the Scythe in the other as he sprinted away towards the white tower in the near distance.

"Aww, hell!" Michael exclaimed as he pulled the legendary Great Sword from the ground once more. He sheathed the sword and sprinted for the small hill Raymark crested on his approach to the white tower.

7

Michael reached the base of the huge white tower of the seven. Raymark had long since disappeared from sight,Warlack and the king were also nowhere in sight. Michael unsheathed his sword, and cautiously moved from alter to alter. The Scythe, the Spear, Axe, and Staff were all in place within their alters. When he reached the alter of the Staff he saw that adjacent to it was the alter for the sword he held, the keyhole to the key. Unwilling to let the day be lost, Michael grabbed the Staff with his free hand and strained to pull it from the stone, but under no strain of pressure would the Staff move.

"It will not release…" A voice said from behind the other side of the alter. Michael whirled about, his sword held at the ready. "Please! Don't kill me! I have been deceived by Warlack! He has taken my bow and left me to die!" pleaded the king as he emerged from his place of hiding.

"You, it was your greed and lust for power that allowed this to get this far! You damn fool, I should kill you just to repay justice to the land! Tell me where Raven Warlack is hiding!" Michael demanded.

"Right behind you…" Raven whispered into his ear as he had done before. The black blade of the Katana of Gell slid through a crevasse in the back of Michael's coat covered armor. The steel shot through his body in the same agonizing place it had been pierced once before, simply one inch higher, and as the blood covered black tip of the blade pierced through the front of his body, Michael was transported to the same painful moment.

Michael collapsed as Raven pulled the Katana of Gell free from him. Blood flowed from the wounds twice as fast as before, and because of a single inch difference Raven had severed his aura's flow through his body. It was a critical wound that this time made him drop his sword. Michael's head swooned and his vision blurred as he fell to the soft grass at his feet.

"You…" was all that escaped his lips as consciousness slipped from his mind and darkness took him.

Raven Warlack and the king stood over him as he lay there dying. The blood of the Cross spilling from his body, soaking the ground beneath him in crimson. Raven sheathed his sword and bent low to the ground near Michael's head. "Snooze you lose…" he whispered in Michael's ear as he picked up the Great Sword that had fallen beside him.

"That's it! We've done it! We've actually done it!" the king exclaimed, overjoyed with the moment.

"Not quite yet my overeager king, where is the Bow?" Raven demanded.

The king moved behind the pillar and pulled the Bow from its propped position, and held it up for Raven to see.

"Good," Raven said as he approached the alter of the Great Sword and thrust the it in place. The mechanisms within clicked and locked, uniting it with the alter as part of the tower forever. The flag that was Michael's bandage, stained red with his blood, whipped wildly in the wind.

422

"At last, all that remains is for you to place the legendary Katana of Gell into its alter and I shall have all of the power of the seven weapons at my command harnessed within my mighty Bow! Soon I will be unstoppable, and…" the king was interrupted by the manic voice of Lord Raymark, "…and all the people of all the regions shall bow unto you, blah blah blah, we've heard it all before," the red haired man frowned at the king.

"Yes, as I have heard you say a thousand times, you ill begotten greedy fool!" Raven Warlack hissed. The king looks fearfully back and forth between Warlack and Raymark. Raymark grins a toothy smile and whispers "You've been played!" as Raven unsheathes his katana one last time, decapitating the king in a swift silent stroke, the cut is so clean that the king remains motionless for a split second, remaining as a complete form, and then as the moment passes, his hand releases his grip upon the Bow, his neck sprays blood, and his head rolls gingerly to the ground with his body close behind. Raymark retrieves the Bow out from underneath the corpse of the king.

Briskly the two men walk side by side to the alter of the Katana, Raymark's red cape flashed behind him as they walked, whilst Warlack's black coat whipped into the wind with its own rhythm. When they reached the carved stone alter, Warlack admired the ancient steel of his sword one last time before placing it into its slot. As the blade was locked into place electricity filled the air. The ground beneath them began to shake as a torrent-rumbling sound came from deep within the tower. Blue electricity shot forth from each of the six weapons in place upon their alters. The bolts of energy snaked its way along them, up the six massive pillars, and into the base of the tower where the energy met, and shot up its spire and into the sky.

The dark clouds which had resided amidst the morning sun all but transformed into a mass of swirling grey, converging over the axis of the tower's spire and the energy shooting forth into the heavens above. The temperature of the air all over the world of Selador shifted in that moment, growing cold, beyond the point of freezing. The very grass beneath their feet began to crystallize with frost, crunching as Warlack and Raymark walked to the very center pillar where the stone door to the tower slid aside with a grating of rock and a hiss of compressed air. Lord Raymark followed Warlack to the door.

8

Darkness…a never ending well of despair, the impending hand of death crawling up the spine like the cold surrounding him, penetrating every inch of his bare skin. *Is this what its like to die?* Michael wondered within his darkened unconscious mind. *How could I have let this happen? I was so close!*

MICHAEL… a familiar voice reverberated within the recesses of his mind. *WAKE UP MICHAEL!!!* the voice commanded from the unknown.

Alan? Michael thought.

YES MICHAEL, IT IS I, OR WHAT REMAINS… the voice echoed within his thoughts. *YOU ARE DYING MICHAEL, BUT ALL HOPE IS NOT LOST,* Alan's voice continued.

CALL UPON THE CROSS MICHAEL, CALL UPON THE STRENGTH INSIDE YOU. GET UP MICHAEL, GET UP AND FIGHT BEFORE ALL HOPE IS LOST.

———

Michael did not know if it was by the command of the voice or by the will of something from the depths of his heart, but Michael felt a new source of power surging within him. He found the strength to open his eyes. He struggled to look beyond the frozen blades of grass obscuring his vision to Raymark and Warlack walking towards the center of the tower, the base pillar now revealed an open doorway with a spiraling staircase beyond. Michael lifted his bloodied form to his knees, and from there watched as Raven Warlack entered into the white tower. The man in black looked back at him his cold blue eyes locked with Michael's grey ones. He tipped his large brimmed hat as he always did, and disappeared within the tower. Michael rose to his feet, expecting to feel the open wound gush blood and cry out its protest, but yet as he stood he felt nothing, no pain, no discomfort at all. In fact, the wound itself had disappeared.

'THIS IS THE LAST TIME I CAN INTERVENE MICHAEL CROSS. GOOD LUCK, AND MICHAEL… MAKE YOUR SHOT COUNT.' Alan's voice echoed within his thoughts one last time. Upon hearing the words, Michael checks the gun at his side beneath his coat. He swings the barrel and cylinder open, and loads its single enormous shell into the hollow chamber, then jerks it back, locking the barrel in place, loaded, and hot, ready to fire.

He holsters the weapon inside the coat and runs for the doorway to the tower as it begins to slide shut. Sprinting full boar, Michael makes it inside just as the stone slab slides into place and seals shut forever. Before him is the spiraling staircase which leads to the top of the tower. He hears muffled indistinguishable voices from above. He cannot hear what they are saying but he knows from whom they are spoken.

Up the many stairs he climbs, and only when the voices are clear does he slow his pace, creeping, stalking his way up into the heart of the tower as he listens. "Place the bow in the cerebellum upon the alter..." He hears Warlack instruct. "Now then, upon my words nock the arrow and pull back as hard as you can, hold, and when you here the last of my words, release. Get it?"

"Yeah, got it," Raymark chimes.

"Good," Raven Warlack says just before his voice slips into an ancient tongue, "...Seladorae, CosTensuat, al el Maladorae..." Upon hearing the incantation being summoned by Warlack, Michael no longer wastes any time, and begins to sprint up the few flights of stairs remaining. "...Operenla DerGaurdia." In the instant he heard the words stop flowing from Warlack's lips did Michael hear the twang of the bowstring as its energy was released.

The entire tower shook from the blast as if it were being torn apart from the inside. Michael was slammed against the wall and nearly plummeted down the shaft of the tower before gaining his footing. He ran hard up the stairs, and rounding the last of them he came to a simple wooden door. Behind the door he could hear what sounded like a vacuum of air ripping the room apart and the hiss and crackle of immense amounts of electricity surging violently within the room.

"What the hell is it?!" Raymark yelled over the torrent of sounds.

"A gateway," Warlack calmly spoke.

"To...to what?" Raymark nervously questioned, his voice wavering with fear.

"Our destiny!" Warlack cried out with a bitter satisfaction.

Michael, determined not to let the opportunity pass, kicked in the plain wooden door separating him from his mortal enemy. As the door swings open Michael watches as Raven Warlack grabs Raymark by his flashy red cloak and hurls him into the swirling vortex of light dominating the center of the circular room. Raymark disappears into the spinning electric field of energy as Raven Warlack turns to face Michael, hands outstretched, legs crossed in the pose of a messiah.

"You're too late Michael! It…is finished," Warlack chuckles as he pivots, crouching as he turns, preparing to lunge into the portal. Michael's hand flies to his side with blinding speed as he draws the gun from its holster, aims his shot carefully, realizing in this moment it is the first time he has ever used this kind of weapon, and fires just as Raven Warlack jumps forward. His body vanishes through the gateway just as the bullet rips into his left arm. There is a spray of blood and the waning gargle of Warlack's cries of pain as he disperses into the vortex of the gateway.

Michael looks to the smoking gun in his hand and watches as the remnants of the shot he'd taken slip through the air like the vanishing smoke of Albright's old pipe, and realizes what has befallen, realizes that Raven Warlack has slipped from his grasp. That he has failed in stopping the man of nightmares. He does the only thing he knows to do, Michael Cross follows.

Through the eyes of the Dreamer,

Kol Sterlin Meckley

Epilogue:

The Hand of Raven Warlack

I

See this, desperate pursuit, this resolute decision to brave the unknown. To know that all is lost, all has been failed, and only justice can bring any semblance of balance back. The last of a line crosses from one world to the next as he follows the pure representation of darkness through the rift.

His body is torn apart molecule by molecule, his essence held in place only by his spirit as he is atomized through the rift of space and time encompassing the multiverse. He is pulled forward until he can feel with agonizing, unworldly pain his form retaking physical shape. The blocks of his being shifting and building back together by some unknown, incomprehensible power. He screams to infinity, but there is no sound.

He can feel the vacuum of air as he is thrown from the rift and his body, mind, and soul at last become one again. He flies from the portal of cascading light and color as his white duster and bag flares about his complete form as he slams into a white drift of snow next to a fallen tree.

The sound of the portal is drowned out by the tremendous wind of a blizzard which assaults the scene. Michael climbs from his hole in the snow. Shielding his eyes from the storm, he looks up and catches a final glimpse of the portal as it closes and disappears.

He felt a twinge of pain and a grave weight of remorse wash over him. The way back to Selador, the way back home was gone. So much left behind, so many lost, because he wasn't strong enough to stop it. *Albright,*

Willum, Jayce, Danube, Kaire, and countless others all died because of their treachery…I will make them pay…but where are they now? Michael thought to himself.

He stood, dusted the loose snow off and checked his bag and body to ensure all was still intact. *Ten fingers…ten toes..? I'll check the rest later…* Everything was in its place, even the gun from Gell, still warm from the shot he'd taken at Raven Warlack only seconds before following him through the portal. He knew he had hit him, maimed him perhaps, but he had not killed that elusive man. Either way, Michael knew that if he had indeed landed in the same world as his enemies there would be signs of their passing, some inkling as to their previous presence in this place. Michael glanced about the snow-covered, blizzard beaten forest around him he found what he was looking for.

'*There…*' lying some thirty feet away was what was left of Raven Warlack's left arm. It was lying in a pool of blood, but bleeding no more. To the right of the hand, a distance into the forest was a trail of the same slippery liquid. Michael walked steadily to the spot, and upon reaching it, he knelt down for a closer inspection. Raven's hand was perfectly intact, with his signet ring still upon his thumb and on his ring finger, *No…it can't be…* was Michael's gold and emerald wedding band. *…but I gave that to the beggar prophet in Reum…unless…?* Michael clenched his fist in anger for not realizing it before. Not only had Warlack been in the tavern that night in Lindell, but he had been in Reum upon his arrival disguised as the beggar. *It would seem you've been there nearly every step of the way…more than I had ever imagined…* He rolled the thoughts within as he reached for the hand.

As his fingertips closed in, the hand began to twitch. He instinctively pulled back with a frightened jerk as the hand slowly began to clench and

---

430

unclench its fingers. He watched cautiously as the hand continued to move ever so slightly. He noticed the veins and arteries of the wrist continued to expand and contract as though they still beat with the pulse of Raven Warlack's icy heart.

The longer he watched, the slower the pulse became until the veins stilled and grew black. Michael could still feel the strange resonance of Warlack lingering within the now lifeless hand. From within his bag he pulled a red kerchief, and with it picked up the ghastly appendage. It was colder than ice even through the wrapped layers of cloth. It felt strangely slippery and yet solid as a rock, frozen in place. He removed his ring from the hand and put it safely in one of the many pockets of his bag.

Just as he was about to toss the hand into the woods, he felt the familiar guiding twinge in the back of his mind. He gently held the hand in the direction of the blood trail, and for a moment he thought he felt a slight pulse. Getting to his feet, with hand in hand he walked steadily towards the trail of blood leading off into the forest. As he reached the trail, no doubt moving closer to Raven and Raymark, he could feel a strange warmth begin to return to the appendage. He continued into the forest and it began to regain its pulse, faint, ever so faint, but in the hands of the tentative Cross it was easily distinguished. Testing it more, he strayed from the path of blood and felt the pulse weaken and the hand grew colder the longer he waited. They were no doubt still on the move.

As he continued on, the hand again began to slowly regain its life, so with this new found 'compass' Michael Cross began his hunt. He did what he could to keep warm but the wind tore through his coat and even through the steel of his armor and clothing underneath. Shivering madly, he battled onward through the whiteout, one hand stretched out before him wielding

---

431

his unseemly tracking device, the other holding his coat tightly shut around his body. For long passes of time the blood trail and prints had been blown away by the drifts of snow, but the hand seemed to guide him true nonetheless, and he continued along his endless trek.

The span of finding clues to their direction continued to become even more difficult to find in the increasing plight of the storm. If not for the accursed hand he surely would have lost track of them hours ago, but he had not. He continued his arduous trek of seven miles crossing dense forest, frozen riverbeds, and rocky, ice covered outcroppings with danger lurking around every corner threatening to take eye, limb, or life in one fatal slip.

But through all, he has triumphed and stands at a clearing at the end of the path from the dense forest he has trudged through. In the center of this circular clearing resides a simple stone well. Michael scans the outlining ring of trees for any sign of life, but neither sees nor senses any. He cautiously steps into the clearing and approaches the well.

2

The stones are ancient, the crank worn to a rickety, barely working husk, and the rope creaks and groans with the weight of the water that fills the old bucket at its end. Miraculously, it makes the climb to the top and Michael drinks from it, replenishing himself a bit from his hefty trek. *Surely they must have stopped by now? After such a distance, and Raven's loss of blood, they must be exhausted...they must be close...* Michael thought to himself as he drinks. The water is clean, cold, and refreshing, but it does nothing for the hunger creeping into his gut or for the fatigue building in his muscles. He had long since wrapped the hand in the kerchief using the ever-strengthening pulse to guide him along the path, but with a moment to spare, to rest, and collect his thoughts, Michael took the opportunity to better inspect the hand for any change.

The winds had died down to a faint whisper and the snow fell in large fat flakes that floated eerily to the ground. This clearing was somewhat protected from the storm, but it had a hinky feeling about it. As Michael pulled back the cloth, unveiling the hand, he was bombarded by the horrible stench of rotting meat and death. Michael turned away and gagged at the horrible smell. He quickly forced himself to look, and to his surprise the hand looked perfectly normal except for it being severed from its rightful owner. It was still pale and colorless, but its pulse was now prominent and steady. As he inspects it closer it suddenly moves, contorting from his grasp, up, and onto his face gripping him tightly with inhuman strength. Michael screams as he rips the hand from his face, and hurls it at the well. It smacks against the stones with a thud and falls to the ground, twitching for a moment and then growing cold and still. *He is close,* Michael thought, *they were here not long ago.*

He reaches for the hand once more to guide him to his enemy and he is again assaulted by the smell of rotting flesh days into its horrendous decay, but the hand still looks normal with no sign of the rot the stench implies. Perplexed by this phantom smell, he rewraps the hand as he scoops it up and turns to retrace the path he follows. As he looks up from the tightly wrapped and tied appendage he comes face to face with a wolf like humanoid creature.

This strangely beautiful canine holds his gaze from a few lingering

---

steps away, its enchanting cerulean eyes penetrating into Michael's deepest cords of fear. Before he can react, their stare down is broken as the wolf lunges towards him with white teeth snapping wildly. Michael struggles as it takes him off balance and knocks him to the ground. He fights to keep the canine's jaws from his flesh. Michael tries to fend it off with his steel bracers, one against its throat, the other arm bashing wildly at the creatures face.

He desperately tries to draw upon the strength of the Cross from within, but where the furious hurricane of his power once dwelled now resides a mere lingering sensation of something that only used to be. Despite the absence of power he had possessed in the world of Selador, he still holds true to his timeless resolve, and remains unyielding to the hungry wolf. He fights with all his heart even as its fangs sink into the flesh of his left arm. Blood sprays as it bites down, and the clearing is filled with Michael's agonizing screams accompanied by the steady thudding sound of the bracer on his right arm, all the while smashing into the creature's skull.

The wolf clamps down again and again on his arm with a searing pain that echoes through his mind in a searing flash accompanied by the screeching sound of the wolf's claws scraping against his armor. At the peak of his pain, Michael cries out in a way that would have broken the hearts of his fallen friends, and deeply moved those of two who stood at the edge of the clearing.

From the corner of his eye there came a small blur of black fur, and he knew another of these wolves would do him in for sure. But as the smaller creature finished its mad dash it let out a battle cry of a howl and lunged at the werewolf. The little black dog tore and bit wildly at the creature, knocking it off of Michael. Given the opportunity, Michael rolled to the side and tried to get to his feet, all the while overcome by the sound of the fierce battle of the tiny creature that had come to his aid.

Though strong, he had already lost much blood from the fresh wounds, and as he tried to stand his legs gave out. He fell to the icy snow at his feet unable to fight or flee. He helplessly looked on as the combat continued.

The little black wolf was circling with the larger creature, locked in a dance of death Michael knew all too well. It was in this brief moment that Michael noticed the werewolf held a feminine form, her fur black and blue as the night sky above. She made a mad lunge for the tiny wolf, but the little dog was too fast, and in a flash was well out of harm's way. In an earth shattering blast, a shot rang out as a hot lead round grazed the upper part of the creature's arm. The werewolf howled in pain, turned, and made to fetch the hand of Raven Warlack that lay in the snow nearby. In another blindingly quick dash, the small black wolf darted forward and snatched the hand out from under her. Before the creature could retaliate another shot rang out, kicking up snow and dirt between them. The beast let out a final howl and fled into the woods. A final shot rang out in pursuit, narrowly missing its mark in a shower of tree bark. In seconds, the creature disappeared into the white sheen of the forest beyond.

The dog-wolf dropped the hand from its mouth with a distasteful groan, and barked a torrent of curses at the fleeing creature. He shook the snow from his body with a scoff, and quickly trotted its way to Michael with pride. Michael held his good arm up instinctively in defense, but the little wolf simply licked his hand and pawed at him with a concerned whine.

Michael's vision began to blur from the loss of blood. He turned in time to see his second savior, a slim figure clothed in white, lever action rifle in hand, steam still rising from the heat of its muzzle from the shots it had taken. A slender, gloved hand removed the long flowing scarf that concealed his savior's identity to reveal the face of a beautiful woman. The fur of her cloak seemed to radiate with an aura of light that soothed him.

As he slipped from consciousness, Michael caught her sparkling blue eyes as the wind let loose golden locks of hair from beneath her shroud and a single memory floated eerily in the depths of his mind. Despite his lingering memory of a woman of Singe, this was somehow different, but the look she gave him was the same, that of relief, of aid and succor. The light of this angel dimmed with the world around him as Michael slipped from the consciousness of this new world.

To Be Continued…

Author's Note This is a drawing I created when I first started writing this story. Though not what happened I still felt it necessary to include in the final version.

Artwork Contents

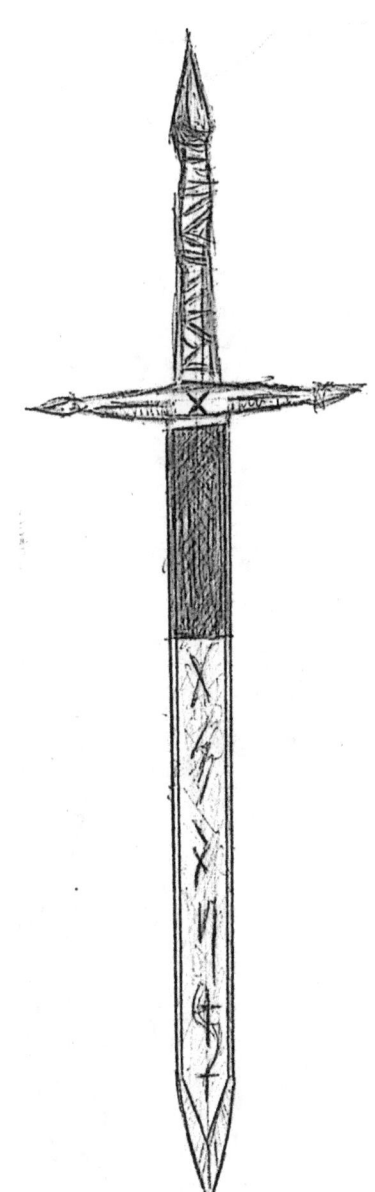

All concepts, names, characters, places, and other ideas associated with the world of Selador, The Last of the Cross, or the Destiny's End series are protected under the secured P.M. Copyright by Kol Sterlin Meckley on 10/27/2007

www.ingramcontent.com/pod-product-compliance
Lightning Source LLC
Chambersburg PA
CBHW080742250626
47162CB00010B/2988